KEEP
SAYING
THEIR
NAMES

KEEP SAYING THEIR NAMES

×　　×　　×　　×　　×

Simon Stranger

Translated from the Norwegian by Matt Bagguley

 ALFRED A. KNOPF　NEW YORK　2020

Library of Congress Cataloging-in-Publication Data
Names: Stranger, Simon, [date] author. |
    Bagguley, Matt, [date] translator.
Title: Keep saying their names / by Simon Stranger ;
    translated from the Norwegian by Matt Bagguley.
Other titles: Leksikon om iys og mørke. English
Description: First edition. | New York : Alfred A. Knopf, 2020. |
Identifiers: LCCN 2019033876 (print) | LCCN 2019033877 (ebook) |
    ISBN 9780525657361 (hardcover) | ISBN 9780525657378 (ebook)
Classification: LCC PT8952.29.T8 L4513 2020 (print) |
    LCC PT8952.29.T8 (ebook) | DDC 839.823/8—dc23
LC record available at https://lccn.loc.gov/2019033876
LC ebook record available at https://lccn.loc.gov/2019033877

Jacket photograph by Simon Stranger, taken in the
Falstad forest, by the monument that marks where
Hirsch Komissar was killed on October 7, 1942
Jacket design by Chip Kidd

Manufactured in Canada
First American Edition

For Rikke, like everything else

KEEP
SAYING
THEIR
NAMES

A

×　　×　　×

A for accusation.

A for arrest.

A for all that will disappear and slide into oblivion. All our memories and feelings. All our property and possessions. All that makes up the framework of a life. The chairs one used to sit in and the bed one used to sleep in will be carried out and placed in a new home. Our plates will be laid out on the table by new hands and the glasses raised to someone else's lips, who will sip the water or the wine, before resuming their conversation. Items once loaded with history will lose all their meaning and be transformed to mere shapes, like a piano might appear to a deer or a beetle.

One day it will happen. One day will be the last for all of us, none of us knowing when, or how.

×

According to Jewish tradition everyone dies twice. The first time is when the heart stops beating and the synapses in the brain shut down, like a city during a blackout.

The second time is when the name of the deceased is mentioned, read, or thought of for the last time, fifty, or a hundred, or four hundred years later. Only then is that person really gone, erased from this world. This second death was what made the German artist Gunter Demnig start casting cobblestones in brass, engraving them with the names of Jews murdered by the Nazis during the Second World War, and embedding them in the pavement outside the houses where they once lived. He calls them *Stolpersteine*. They are an attempt to postpone the second death, by documenting the names of the deceased, so that passersby will look down in decades to come and read them, and in doing so, keep them alive, while ensuring that the memory of one of the worst chapters in Europe's history is also kept alive—as visible scars on the face of the city. So far sixty-seven thousand *Stolpersteine* have been laid throughout Europe.

One of them is yours.

One of these stones has your name on it, and is planted in the pavement outside the apartment where you once lived, in the central Norwegian city of Trondheim. A few years ago my son knelt beside this *Stolperstein*, brushed away the pebbles and sand with his mitten, and read aloud.

"Here lived Hirsch Komissar."

My son turned ten that year, and is one of your great-great-grandchildren. As is my daughter, who was only six years old that spring. My wife, Rikke, stood beside me. Also in this circle of people, was my mother-in-law, Grete, and her husband, Steinar, all of us gathered as though for the burial of an urn.

"Yes. He was my grandfather," said Grete. "He lived right here, on the second floor," she went on, turning to the building behind us, to the windows where you once stood looking out, in another age, when people other than ourselves were alive. I knelt down, and my daughter hung her arms round my neck, while my son continued reading the bare facts etched into the cobblestone.

HERE LIVED

HIRSCH KOMISSAR

BORN 1887

ARRESTED 12.1.1942

FALSTAD

KILLED 7.10.42

Grete said something about the surprise invasion, recounting the story of how her father had seen the soldiers on the morning of April 9, 1940. Rikke stood up to join the conversation, and my daughter slid off my back and nestled up to her. Only my son and I continued looking down at the brass plate on the pavement. His finger stroked over the last line, then he looked up.

"Why was he killed, Dad?" he asked.

"Because he was Jewish," I replied.

"Yes, but why?"

From the corner of my eye I noticed Rikke looking at me, following both conversations simultaneously.

"Well . . . The Nazis wanted to kill anyone who was different."

My son became quiet.

"Are we Jewish too?" he asked. His brown eyes were clear and concentrated.

I blinked a few times, trying to recall what he knew about the family's history. What did my children know about being Jewish, and about our ancestry? We must have talked about how their great-great-grandparents on their mother's side had emigrated from various parts of Russia more than a hundred years ago. I knew we had talked about the war, about their great-grandfather

Gerson—whom they had both gotten to know before he died—and his escape to Sweden.

Rikke drew breath to say something, but then fell back into the conversation with Grete, and my eyes locked with my son's.

"You're Norwegian," I replied, but I felt there was an element of deceit in my answer, and noticed Rikke looking at me again. "And a part of you is Jewish, but we're not religious," I said as I stood up, hoping that Rikke or Grete would say something too, that they would have a better answer than me, but their conversation had already leapt ahead, following the logic of association, and was now somewhere else entirely.

We went on our way, but my son's question stuck with me. *Why was he killed, Dad?*

Shortly after, I started browsing through various archives, and before long some of the pieces became more visible. Soon I could picture the snow in the center of Trondheim, and the steam from people's breath as they passed the small, crooked wooden houses. And soon I was able to see how the end of your life began, on a day like any other.

It is Monday, January 12, 1942. You are standing behind the counter of the fashion boutique that you and your wife own in Trondheim, surrounded by hats on stands, and mannequins wearing coats and dresses. You have just welcomed your first customer of the day, and told her about this week's special offers, when you have to put down your cigarette and the order form to pick up the phone.

"Paris-Vienna, can I help you?" you say, automatically, as you have done thousands of times before.

"*Guten Morgen*," says a man on the other end of the line, who continues, in German: "Am I talking to Komissar?"

"Yes, that's correct," you reply, also in German, thinking momentarily that it might be one of your suppliers from Hamburg calling, perhaps because of a problem at customs again. Maybe it is the summer dresses you ordered, but in that case it must be a new employee, because this voice does not sound familiar.

"Hirsch Komissar, married to Marie Komissar?"

"Yes? Who am I speaking to?"

"I am calling from the Gestapo's security service."

"OK?"

You glance up from the order form, aware that your customer can sense there is something going on. You place your cigarette on the edge of the ashtray again and turn your face toward the wall, while your heart pounds in your chest. *The Gestapo?*

"There is a matter we would like to discuss with you," says the man in a low voice.

"Very well," you reply apprehensively, and are just about to open your mouth to ask what that is when you are interrupted.

"Please come in for questioning at the Mission Hotel. Today, at two p.m.," says the voice at the end of the line.

Mission Hotel? For questioning? Why on earth are you being called in for questioning, you think with your face still turned to the wall. Could it have something to do with Marie's brother David and his communist views? The spike from a headless nail pokes out from the door frame. You hold your thumb against the metal, pressing the point into your skin while closing your eyes.

"Hello?" says the voice at the other end, in an impatient tone. "Are you there?"

"Yes, I am here . . . ," you reply, lifting your thumb from the spike and looking at the white spot where the blood has been pressed away from the flesh.

"Some of my colleagues think I'm taking too much of a risk calling you like this . . . ," the man says. There is the sound of a cigarette lighter being lit right next to the mouthpiece.

". . . they think I should have sent a car and brought you in right away, so that you don't just take your sons and disappear. After all you are Jews . . . ," continues the voice, emphasizing the last word, then continuing in a more hushed tone, almost confidingly. "But I know that your wife, Marie, has been admitted to the hospital . . . A fall on the ice, wasn't it?"

"Yes, that's correct . . . she slipped and fell on the ice a few days ago, and fractured . . . a bone in her hip," you reply, unable to remember the German word for "femur," not quite sure if you've ever known it. You make your point anyway.

How could Marie be so stupid as to walk in high-heeled boots on those icy streets, you think. So foolhardy, always elegant, and with an unwavering need to decide everything herself. If you so much as hinted that she could do things differently, perhaps be a little more careful, or you suggested that writing newspaper columns, or organizing meetings at home where political issues are discussed, was reckless—and might very well be seen as political incitement—she would just sniff at you. A dark look would fall across her eyes before making it clear that she would keep doing things her way. Now she has done exactly that, and just look where it has led, you think, as you stand behind the counter, still clutching the telephone.

"A fractured femur, yes . . . ," says the faceless person at the other end, reminding you of the German designation, ". . . so I very much doubt you or your sons are likely to run away, right? If so, we would have to take care of her."

Take care of her. You nod quietly, even though no one can read your body language through the telephone, before replying that you will not be going anywhere.

"Good, Komissar. Then we will see you here at two p.m. You know where to find us, right?"

"The Mission Hotel? Yes, of course."

"Good. A good day to you."

There is a click as the person hangs up, and you stand there behind the counter, with your thoughts scattering like a flock of birds. What will you do now? You look up at the clock. It is several hours until two o'clock. There is plenty of time, enough to simply run away from it all, you think, and consider, momentarily, creeping into the stock room and exiting through the delivery door. Vanish in secret and just run, as far as you can, without stopping, ignoring the taste of blood in your mouth, the looks from strangers, or the tiredness in your legs from running uphill. You could have run all the way to the woods, gone into hiding among the pine trees, and just kept going, toward the Swedish border, where your daughter, Lillemor, is already living in safety. It could work, you think. But you understand right away what a false notion this is, because what about Marie? What about your two sons, Gerson and Jacob? If you just ran off, that would put them in danger, you think while folding up the order form with your available hand. Even if you were able to notify Jacob, through the man you know at his college, you wouldn't get hold of Gerson, because Gerson is out in the Norwegian countryside somewhere, with his college friends— and what would happen to him, when he arrives back in town from the cabin trip and finds German soldiers waiting outside his bedsit? And what about Marie?

Are they true, the rumors which have begun circulating in the shops, at dinners, and at the synagogue? About Jews being sent to special camps abroad. Or are they all just tall tales, exaggerations, like the monsters you imagined creeping around in the dark when you were a child?

You close up the shop, write a note saying CLOSED DUE TO ILL-NESS, and hang it on the inside of the door, before turning the key and walking up the hill toward the hospital.

What *matter* are they referring to? Perhaps it is nothing more than some vague accusation, nothing substantial enough to have you arrested, you think, on your way up the hill. You are careful to tread where it's been gritted, and cling onto the railings to avoid slipping on the steps, on the clumps of polished ice that resemble small, flattened jellyfish.

There's no reason to believe that it's about anything serious, you haven't done anything. It is probably a formality, perhaps a poll of the Jewish population, or in the worst case, that they want to interrogate you about Marie's brother, you think, as you round the corner to the hospital.

A few hours later you are being questioned at the Mission Hotel, accused of spreading news from the BBC. One of your relatives has been overheard, at Café Bondeheimen in Trondheim, speaking with a friend about events he would have no knowledge of unless he had access to an illegal news source, like a radio; and during questioning you are accused of having known about this illegal activity without reporting it to the authorities, and for sharing news from England yourself. Immediately afterward you are led to a prison cell in the basement, where you sleep on a thin mattress and are forced to go to the toilet in a concrete hole in the floor. You hear screams and cries from one of the interrogation rooms before the steady hum of voices and footsteps returns.

The next morning you still believe you are going to be released, that someone in the system will realize that you're no danger to the Third Reich, and that it would be cheaper and easier for them to let you continue about your business. But then, three soldiers enter your cell, greeting you politely before asking you to place your hands behind your back. The metal handcuffs feel cold against your skin.

"Where are we going?" you ask, in German.

"Move," one of them replies, leading you up the steps, and along a corridor, to a courtyard where the snow lies heavy. A black car waits with its motor running. You are pushed into the back seat. Then you are driven out of town. It takes a while before it dawns on you where you are going.

Falstad prison camp.

It is an hour's drive from Trondheim. A yellow-brick building constructed around a courtyard and surrounded by wooden barracks and barbed-wire fences, where the snow has formed a thin white layer on the twisted metal threads.

The gates open, and you are escorted through the entrance, past a bare birch tree, and into the building. You are taken up to the second floor, where there are rows and rows of cells. Wooden doors, with curved grills in front of the hatches. The face of another prisoner appears at one of them. Two guards stand outside the cell and watch while you get undressed, then you are locked in a rectangular room, with a window at one end and a bunk bed. The bolt slides shut behind you, and the anxiety increases as you realize that you cannot escape; that this is perhaps the end, and that everything has happened for the last time. You see the seriousness on the faces of some of the prisoners, and the apathy on others, who just sit, staring at the wall.

A for the alcohol you crave during those first weeks in the camp. How you long for a hit that might numb your thoughts and surroundings, to ease the confusion, the rage, and the terror, and lull you into a memoryless stupor.

A for the associations that strike you, suddenly and anytime, on your way to forced labor, eating in the cafeteria or out in the woods. Moments of sudden, unexpected recollection, as though everything that exists is a gateway to something else.

The ruts left by truck wheels in the earth outside the camp suddenly transport you to the small dirt roads where you grew up, in Russia's Jewish zone, at the time of the last tsar, with light brown hens clucking behind the fences and the ragged dog around which you always took a detour to avoid walking past.

The guard leaning back with his eyes closed in the summer sun reminds you of your student days in Germany, and the blissful moments of happiness you felt when you took a break from your books to recline on a bench in a park, in a country not yet occupied by Nazis.

The freshly washed shirt, drying on the line by one of the barracks—billowing in the wind like a ship's sail—takes you back to the fashion store you and Marie built from scratch; or back to the refugee housing in Sweden that you foolishly left, where clothes always hung outside on washing lines, while the children roamed around.

And always, when the camp falls silent and you are able to lie in your cell with your eyes closed, you picture their faces: Marie's dark hair, and the fire in her eyes when she talks about something she cares deeply about; the faces of Gerson and Jacob, your sons; and Esther, who everyone calls Lillemor, *"Little mum,"* perhaps because she is so petite, or perhaps because she has always been like a second mom to her baby brothers. She loved carrying them around when they were little, feeding them and imitating the sounds they made in order to make them laugh.

You picture the recalcitrant look on Gerson's face when he is put in his place, sad at the thought that you didn't support him more; Jacob's shyness and his embarrassed smile when he gets nervous or too agitated and starts to stutter; and the lightness in Lillemor's entire being, thank God she stayed in Sweden. You try to remember every detail of their faces, but find the images becoming grainier or more blurry, as if the camp was a machine that erases your memories gradually, week by week, month by month, until nothing is left but presence, sweat, labor.

A for all the stories hidden beneath this *Stolperstein*. A sudden and overwhelming number of stories that have emerged over the last few years, like the armies of insects that used to scurry from underneath the stones you lifted as a child.

Dear Hirsch. This is my attempt to postpone the second death and override oblivion. There is no way for me to tell the entire story of your life and what happened to you, but I can gather some of the pieces, put them together, and try to reimagine the things that are lost. I am not Jewish, but my children, your great-grandchildren, share your Jewish blood. Your history is their history. How can I, as a father, explain to them why someone hated you so much?

This small metal plate with your name engraved on it would soon lead me to the story of a villa on the outskirts of Trondheim. A story so monstrous and unlikely that at first I couldn't bring myself to believe it was true, because this house merges our shared family history with the story of Henry Oliver Rinnan, one of the most infamous criminals in Norwegian history.

A house with a peculiar nickname that begins with B in Norwegian: Bandeklosteret—"the Gang Monastery."

B

×　　　×　　　×

B for building. In the decades after the war, local people in Trondheim would cross to the other side of the street as they passed the villa that was called the Gang Monastery, as if the evil from the place might somehow leak into the air and infect them. It was within these four walls that the Norwegian Nazi Henry Oliver Rinnan and his gang made their plans during the war; where they interrogated prisoners, tortured, killed, drank, and partied. A journalist who inspected the house shortly after the Nazis had surrendered wrote this about his experiences:

> They have torn the whole house apart, seemingly driven by a rampant thirst for destruction. Every room appears to have been used for target practice—the walls and ceilings are riddled with bullet holes—and where they felt that the wallpaper was still a little too

intact, they have cut it into shreds. Even the bath and bathroom walls are full of holes from projectiles. One must assume that the shooting played a role in the mortal terror of the prisoners sitting in the pitch-darkness of the tiny cells in the basement.

This villa also turned out to conceal another story, which I first heard about in the kitchen of one of your grandchildren: my mother-in-law, Grete Komissar.

It was a Saturday or Sunday, a slow morning where nothing really needed to be done, when time itself stretched out. A jazz record played on the stereo in the living room, where the calm piano-playing merged with the sounds of the children trying to balance on a large gym ball: small bursts of laughter followed by short thuds as their bodies hit the carpet. I was in the kitchen with Grete, who had already begun preparing dinner, chopping up pears and putting the long slices into an oven-proof dish with some chicken legs and vegetables. We must have talked about something to do with childhood, because when her husband, Steinar, appeared in the doorway, he asked if I knew that Grete had grown up in Rinnan's headquarters. Although there was something familiar about the name, I was completely unable to place it, let alone say who it was. He tried jogging my memory by using the man's first name—Henry—adding that he was a Norwegian Nazi and double agent, and outlined the extent of the cruelty that had been inflicted inside the house. Torture. Murder. Grete wiped the hair off her forehead with her arm, still holding the kitchen knife in one hand, her other arm being too greasy from the chicken fat. The situation was strangely tense. It was obviously a subject she would rather avoid, but it would have been too awkward to start talking about something else entirely, so she was more or less trapped in the conversation, standing between the kitchen table and the counter.

There was the sound of a thud from the living room, and I heard my wife, Rikke, ask the kids if they could go play on the floor above us, before she appeared in the doorway and snuck past Steinar.

"And you grew up there?" I asked. I had known Grete for more than fifteen years, but this was something she had never mentioned.

"Yes, I lived there from the time I was born until I was seven," she replied.

"What's that?" asked Rikke, aware that she must have missed something.

"I just told him that I grew up in the Rinnan band's house," Grete repeated, and cut the last pear in half, as if this was nothing special whatsoever. From the look on Rikke's face I could tell that this was news to her as well. Grete put down her knife, turned on the tap, and wet her hands. Then it seemed as though she felt like talking about it after all.

"We actually put on these little theater performances in the cellar," she said, emphasizing the word *cellar*, while pumping soap from the dispenser. "In the very same room the Rinnan gang had used, just a few years earlier," she added. Together with her older sister Jannicke, Grete had dressed up in their parents' clothes— ladies' shoes, and hats, and necklaces, all far too big for them—and used clothes brushes as microphones. Children and adults from the neighborhood were invited, and Grete's role had been to stand at the top of the stairs and collect the handmade tickets, before sending the adults down the steps with their heads ducked and eyes flickering left and right.

This image of the little girl at the top of the stairs, and the children's songs being sung in the torture chamber presented a new set of questions: Why on earth did this Jewish family choose to go and live in a house that had become such a symbol of evil in Trondheim? Was it that cheap? Did they want to reclaim history? And did the house somehow affect those living in it?

Keen to learn more, I read everything I could find about the Rinnan gang, and looked at pictures of the house where Grete had grown up. And it was as if something had been stirred that morning, because in the weeks and months to come, Grete talked more about her early childhood.

When Grete and Steinar were selling the apartment they still owned back in Trondheim, we went to visit them one last time. We strolled down the street where the Paris-Vienna shop was once situated and paid another visit to the *Stolperstein* with your name on it. Then we got in the car and drove out of the city center to the Gang Monastery: a low house, with dark windows, and an old red car outside. It was as though time had stood still.

"Shall we ring the doorbell?" asked Grete. I nodded, and since no one else moved, I walked down the short gravel path and pressed the button. Waiting and waiting for the door to open, while trying to figure out what to say.

B for bullet. A copper-colored slug pulled from one of the walls, now standing on the shelf above my writing desk. The tip is dented, like a chef's hat, from its impact with the brickwork down in the cellar. A result, perhaps, of one of the games the gang members played to soften up prisoners, where they would tie a man to a chair and shoot at him, competing over how close they could get without actually hitting him.

B for babies and bulging cheeks. B for bare legs flailing in the air over the changing table, for small, chubby legs barely managing to stay upright while the arms are stretched out for better balance. B for beginnings—for the beginning of the story of the Gang Monastery is the story of a kindergarten, run by Else Tambs-Lyche, in the cellar, in the years leading up to the war.

B for boots and brothers, in a memory from early childhood. Most of us grow up oblivious to how the weight of innumerable events and feelings from our early years will collect like sediment on the seabed and sit deep within us, creating landscapes and mannerisms that may affect us for the rest of our lives. Just as this winter's day might have done for ten-year-old Henry Oliver Rinnan.

It is February 1925, an hour's drive north of Trondheim. Snow flurries swirl in the air outside the school in the small town of Levanger, collecting in little snowdrifts on the window ledge beside Henry Rinnan, who sits in deep concentration at his writing desk. His bangs hang over his eyes as he hunches over his work, and he is just reaching for his eraser to rub out the curve in a *g* he is unhappy with when he notices something. The teacher stops abruptly in the middle of a sentence, looks straight at Henry's little brother and asks how he is.

You look so pale . . . are you ill? she says while stepping from behind her desk. Henry notices how the others look up from their books to see what is happening. He sees them exchange glances, small sparks that ignite their expectations, because now the teacher is moving between the rows of desks. Soon she will see exactly what Henry's brother has been trying to hide all morning—that he is wearing ladies' boots. A pair of black ladies' boots that were never collected from his father's shoe-repair shop. Henry knew that this would be a problem; he had tried to prevent it, had tried to tell his mother that she could not send her son to school wearing ladies' shoes. But his mother had waved his little brother's winter boots in front of his face, pointing at the gaping hole between the sole and the leather, and, in a voice which left no room for rebuttal, made it clear that his little brother could not go to school in such tatty winter footwear, that his feet would be soaked through before he even reached the corner. There was nothing more to be said about it, and Henry was unable to stand up to her, so that was that. Luckily, the heels were not that high, but whenever his brother walked in them it was plain to see that there was something off; they were several sizes too big, his feet rattled around so much he had to curl his toes up to stop them from sliding, forcing him to take strange, unnatural steps. Henry had tried to act like nothing was wrong. They had walked right past the gang of boys at the school gates, who were busy with something else, so no one had actually noticed the shoes until they came into the classroom. Inside, Henry watched as some of them looked over at his little brother's feet and saw how two of the girls in the class nudged one another and sniggered. But at that moment the teacher walked in, which meant everyone had to behave themselves and stand by their desks and say: "Good morning!"

They returned to their seats, and he knuckled down to his schoolwork, concentrating on joining the letters, one by one, in neat loops. It was important to get everything perfect, otherwise the teacher might scold him, or write something in the margin that his parents would read, which he had to avoid. He couldn't bear to see the disappointment in his mother's face. So he grabbed his pencil, and wrote word after word, and had almost forgotten about it when he heard the teacher comment on how pale his little brother looked—and now she is heading toward his desk. Henry feels the heat welling up in his face as his little brother retracts his feet under the table and tries to wind them around the chair legs. But it doesn't help, because now the teacher has stopped, and is clearly so astonished that the words just spill out of her mouth, as though she has lost control of them.

"Why . . . What on earth are you wearing on your feet?" she asks, as the other pupils begin to giggle. Henry feels his heart racing, and the embarrassment burning his cheeks. Then he looks over at his brother, but his little brother says nothing, just sits there looking apprehensive, his eyes looking to the side, clearly unsure of what to say. Whatever he does, Henry thinks, he cannot tell the truth— that his father, a shoemaker, hasn't bothered to repair his own children's shoes. It would be better for him to come up with a white lie. He could say he just took the first pair of shoes he found, for example, or that he was fooling around to see if anyone noticed. But his brother doesn't say any of this, he doesn't utter a word. But he has to say something, Henry thinks, because the silence is making things worse, adding to the shame already hanging over him. So Henry lets out a little "ahem" as if to clear his throat, to draw the attention of the teacher and the other pupils toward him and away from his little brother. He feels them staring. The attention makes his heart beat even faster, makes him feel even more insecure and nervous, but he cannot show it, and now it's up to him to speak, smooth it all over somehow, he thinks, forcing himself to maintain eye contact with the teacher.

"Oh, he's just been messing about trying on shoes at the workshop back home," says Henry Oliver, smirking a little, in an attempt to make her believe that it's all just an amusing prank not worth worrying about. But he can tell by the look on the teacher's face that she doesn't believe him, because she doesn't smile back, she actually crouches down beside his little brother, places a hand on his shoulder, and points out how thin he has become. With real concern in her voice she asks, Are things difficult at home, and of course she understands that this might be humiliating for Henry and his little brother, so she says it as quietly as possible so the others cannot hear, but in doing so she makes matters even worse. Because it then becomes clear to everyone that it is something to be ashamed of; that it is something no one else should hear. And everyone can hear it, he is certain about that, because although she only whispers, her words reach every single ear in the room, transforming their staring faces into half-open mouths and smiling eyes.

Now his brother has to say something, Henry thinks, only he doesn't, he just seems totally confused, and looks up woefully, first at the teacher, and then at Henry, while his eyes glaze over with tears, blinking repeatedly. He sniffs, and raises his forearm to his nose. There is silence. Total silence.

"Things are fine at home, thanks," says Henry, in a clear and resolute voice. "He's just been a little unwell. Could you kindly continue with the lesson," he says, returning to the sentence he was in the middle of writing. He grabs the eraser and rubs out the loop in the *g*. Then he brushes away the crumbs from the eraser and grasps his pencil, demonstrating that there is nothing more to be discussed, and that he really must continue with his schoolwork, all the while listening intently, trying to read the mood in the classroom, as he moves the tip of his pencil across the page.

It is as though his senses are sharpened, because Henry notices how all the staring subsides, and he hears the sound of chairs scraping the floor as people sit up properly. The sound of pencils scratching on paper, and of the teacher who opens her mouth and finally resumes the lesson. But at the same time he notices that some of them are whispering, the pressure of laughter building in their chests, desperate to come out like the steam under a saucepan lid. Luckily the final school bell rings, so he puts his books into his satchel and gets hold of his little brother.

They have no choice but to walk through the schoolyard, past the ridiculing looks. A gang of slightly older boys start laughing loudly and pointing at his brother's boots.

"Well, look at her! See you later, Miss Rinnan!" says one of the bigger boys as Henry's little brother walks past, and the joke causes the boys nearby to erupt. It's a taunt beyond mere cheekiness, which they all try to hide, but Henry just cannot allow it. The anger boils up in him, a wave of darkness that takes over his body, and before he has time to think, he swings a clenched fist and smashes it right into the face of the pupil who ridiculed his little brother. He has no right to talk like that! No right to talk to his brother like that, thinks Rinnan, feeling the hardness of the boy's cheekbone against his own knuckles, and the anger seething within him, and he sees the boy bring his hands to his face while recoiling in pain. There is a brief moment of uncertainty among the group before the other boys throw themselves at Henry. Suddenly everything bursts into chaos—wild eyes and screaming mouths. Hands reach out at him, fingers grasp at his hair and his satchel, and in a flash he is lying on his back, with his arms and legs pinned down in the snow, angry and gasping for breath.

"You lot! Stop that right away!" shouts a teacher who leans out of a window with his pipe in his hand. And they release him reluctantly, one by one, allowing him to stand up, but not without whispering a threat into his ear. Just you wait, Henry Oliver. You're not fucking getting away with this!

He brushes the snow from his trousers, still trembling with anger, so much that it is difficult to draw breath, like he is winded, but now he grabs his little brother's hand and walks, double quick, just to get away from it all; from the school and the other kids before things get worse and impossible to put right again, he thinks; and he sees the laughter in the eyes of a girl from one of the other classes, how ridiculous she thinks he is, and it is of course understandable, he would have started laughing too, if this weren't actually happening to him, except it was. Now there is an air of humiliation clinging to him, a ridiculous story that the whole school will be talking about for weeks to come. Just the thought of it causes the desperation to well up in him, because they'll find an opportunity to get him again, without him knowing where or when. That's what he meant, this boy who whispered in Henry's ear: just you wait; it was a warning of course, a promise that they would continue beating him up later, that they were not quite finished with him, Henry thinks, while gnashing his teeth. He has always been so careful, ever since he began school, done as he should have, stayed away from conflict, mastered the art of smiling disarmingly. He has allowed the bigger boys to be the ones causing trouble, kept his distance while they charged about, having play fights and kicking soccer balls, because he knew he couldn't look after himself, that he did not have it in him. So it was best to attract as little attention as possible, live as inconspicuously as possible. That had been his strategy, and now it was ruined.

If only his brother not been so stupid and started crying, Henry thinks, gripping his brother's wrist even tighter, a little too tight perhaps, as well as increasing the pace along the gravel track. His brother whimpers a little, but he will just have to put up with it.

He needs to learn to behave differently, or he will always end up being a victim, the one the other pupils single out when they feel like picking on someone, and that will affect Henry too; he will be infected by it, like a bad smell, he thinks, and that is something he would sooner avoid, being so short already. The shortest in the class, and obviously the one from the poorest family of them all, he thinks, while striding ahead quickly, yanking his little brother behind him, seeing him grimace from the corner of his eye, hearing him begging to be let go, but Henry ignores him, he wants to punish his brother for the way he behaved. He could have grinned at the others instead, acted as though nothing they said affected him, but no; he had to start crying, had to break down like he did, even though he knew that it would come to no good, Henry thinks, dragging his brother around the corner of the school and down the road. His brother pulls on his arm, and snot runs from his nostrils, and the tears well up in his eyes again. You're hurting me, Henry Oliver, he sobs, and the sight of tears running down his brother's cheeks makes Henry let go immediately, stroking his fingers as gently as possible over the spot he had been gripping. He says sorry repeatedly, while adding that he didn't mean to hurt him. Perhaps for a moment he did, but not really.

"Are you OK?" Henry asks. His brother nods, while rubbing his wrist with his mitten. Then they continue home, and Henry knows he must make his brother smile again and wipe away any trace of tears before they get home, because if his mother sees that he has been crying she will start asking questions, and he will have to tell her everything, and then what? Then his mother will have even more to worry about, and she doesn't need that right now, with eight children and married to a shoemaker who barely has any work. She cannot do anything about his problems anyway. She can't change the fact that they are so hard up, or that Henry is so short, or that the others laugh at him. He asks his brother to remove his mittens and blow his nose on his hand, and then wipe it off in the snow. His brother does as he is told. His hands turn red from cold, but he gets rid of the snot. Henry takes his own gloves off, molds a handful of snow between his hands, and strokes his brother gently under his eyes with moist fingers.

Then he says: "We're not going to mention this at home, right?"

"No?"

"It'll only make Mom and Dad worried, and they have enough to think about. Right?"

"I guess so," his brother replies, before continuing down the road. Henry tries to come up with some games along the way. Walks his fingers along the sleeve of his brother's jacket and into his armpit, to trick him out of the somber mood; make him think about something else, so he wriggles his fingers into his brother's armpit, and he watches his face soften up again; watches how the fighting and the cold and the crying vanish, creating a space for them to talk about something else again, as they used to. They amble toward home, kicking a clump of solid ice.

Soon they are walking among Levanger's wooden houses, through the graveyard, with its little white church, and row upon row of colorfully painted terraces on the opposite side of the road. This is where they live. A two-story wooden house, painted green. His father's workshop on the ground floor, and their apartment above.

Henry sees his mother pass quickly by the kitchen window, probably on her way to peel potatoes, rinse clothes, or chop vegetables, and notices the happiness now draining from his little brother's face, and the events from their day at school coming back.

"It'll be OK," Henry says smiling, placing a hand on his brother's shoulder and stroking it downward. "Come on!"

The house smells of boiled potatoes, and the hallway is full of shoes.

"Hello?" Henry calls out, as he always does, making sure he uses the exact same tone of voice, to avoid rousing any suspicion. His mother comes out from the kitchen with beads of sweat on her forehead and spots of white flour on her apron. His youngest sister stands behind her, holding on to her skirt, a little unsteady, reaching upward, wanting to be picked up.

"So. How was school today? Wasn't it nice to have warm feet?" she asks, and the words must have made his father sit up suddenly in the living room, because Henry hears the springs creaking in the old armchair, and immediately after that his father appears in the kitchen doorway where he stands, smiling, and waving the little boy's winter shoes in the air to show him that they have now been fixed.

"There. Now you don't have to walk around in ladies' boots tomorrow at least," says his father, and Henry can see the humiliation in his face: how his facial muscles tighten, so that his smile, even if it's not genuine, is at least trying to be a smile, trying to hide what he and his mother are thinking, and what the others are thinking—that he should have repaired the shoes a long time ago. That is what a good father would do. Then again there are eight of them, and the hallway is a chaotic muddle of shoes, and their father cannot be expected to check every single shoe every day, Henry thinks, ignoring the fact that he has heard his mother ask his father to fix the shoes several times during the last two weeks.

"Thanks, Father," says his little brother, taking his shoes.

"Now . . . did anybody notice them?" his father asks jokingly, nodding toward the ladies' boots, and Henry is suddenly relieved when his little sister grabs the tablecloth, threatening to topple all the glasses and vases and drag it all over the edge, because it means his mother doesn't notice the strange tone in his little brother's voice, or the embarrassed look on his face when he replies, in a quiet, timid manner:

"No, Father."

B for the building at Falstad prison camp: a yellow two-story building, constructed in stone around a square yard, with an assortment of barracks around the outside. Small basic huts for the guards and the pigs and the cows, in addition to outhouses and carpentry sheds, before one reaches the barbed-wire fence around the perimeter.

B for the birch tree you pass in the yard, with its dirty white trunk, and with layers of snow on the naked branches, in shades of blue and white, like the color of the fabric samples sent to you from your shop in Trondheim.

B for the books, full of flowers and ferns, categorized with neatly handwritten labels and compiled by Jonsvannsveien 46's first owner, long before the house became Rinnan's headquarters. A professor with the peculiar name Ralph Tambs-Lyche, who collected plants, systematized them, and made one of the largest botanical collections in Norway. A Norwegian-American botanist who worked at the university before being arrested and sent to Falstad. His wife, Else, used the house's cellar as a kindergarten, which meant the hallway was always full of small boots when he came home from work.

B for the bags packed into the car, and the beech trees whose leaves are uncoiling from buds on a spring day in Oslo, 1948. The sun shines on the rooftops, causing yesterday's raindrops to sparkle as they drip from the gutter. Gerson reaches for the handle on the trunk of the car, moving about in an unnecessarily agitated way. It's not like they are trying to get anywhere on time, other than Trondheim before nightfall. Jannicke crouches down on the pavement, and is about to pick up a stone and put it in her mouth when Ellen lifts her up, forcing the stone from her little hand, even though Jannicke resists and tries to twist herself from her mother's grip. She begins crying *Mine! Mine! Mine!* while Ellen puts her in the back seat and Gerson sits down behind the wheel.

The remaining furniture was carried out earlier that day and sent in advance by truck. The decision to move had been made a few months before that. First in the form of tiny hints, because whenever Gerson chatted to his mother on the phone, she often mentioned, between the lines, that she needed help to run the business; that it was far too much for her to cope with alone. Then she had come to visit them, traveling the daylong trip to Oslo by train, and Gerson had stood on the platform and waited for her, watched her climb down in high-heeled boots, wearing a hat so wide that it brushed the door frame as she walked out. She had waved, and stood aside, because a stranger came along with her suitcase. His mother had always been like that. So well dressed and elegant that the very notion of carrying anything herself would be against her nature. Gerson just stood and watched how she kissed the man on the cheek as a reward, before waving him off. Then she turned to Gerson, without showing any sign of picking up her luggage herself, so Gerson had to go over and lift it for her. I would have done it anyway, of course, he thought; nevertheless it was the way she took it for granted that irritated him: this attitude of entitlement. But he just had to bite his tongue, just smiled and replied briefly to her retorts, as he was expected to, because even though she asked him how he was, she wasn't interested in hearing more than a succinct "good" for an answer. She did not want to hear about the problems of finding a job, how drastically life had changed with the birth of their daughter, or how the war had snatched his future away just as his life as an adult began. Marie had her own concerns, always did have, thought Gerson, remembering how Ellen had laughed when he told her about his summer holidays as a child. How he and Jacob had been booked into a hotel, all alone for several weeks, even though they were no more than 10–12 years old, because their parents were so busy working.

Marie was talking about how cramped it was in Ellen and Gerson's apartment before she had even walked through the door, and Gerson had seen how Ellen had slumped, how her smile froze, because she agreed of course. She too came from a prosperous family, the daughter of a factory owner.

"We will move, Mother. We've bought a plot here in Oslo, and once the house is built, we'll move in," said Gerson, while taking her coat.

"That's precisely what I want to talk to you about," said Marie, as she walked on into the dining room. "I have found a house for you, a house in Trondheim, right in the center. A house with a garden, and an indoor toilet, not in the alleyway like here. A detached house, Gerson, and a job in the clothing shop." His mother turned to Ellen, who sat with Jannicke on her lap, and told her about Paris-Vienna, about the dresses, the fabrics, the hats and coats which Ellen could borrow and take home if she wanted.

Marie said nothing about the house's background then. A few weeks later she called Gerson, and casually mentioned it toward the end of the conversation, just before hanging up, as if it were a random detail.

"Oh, and by the way. The house was used by the Rinnan gang for a couple of years during the war."

Gerson turned his back to the living room and screwed up his eyes.

"Hello?" said his mother. "Are you there?"

"But . . . Mother? Why didn't you mention this before?"

"Because I was afraid Ellen would blow it all out of proportion and make a big drama about it," said Marie, in Yiddish.

"But . . . don't you think we should . . . have knowed about it?" replied Gerson in Yiddish, as he heard Ellen babbling away to Jannicke in the background.

"Known about, or gotten to know about," his mother corrected. "But what does that have to do with it anyway, Gerson? The war is over, the Rinnan gang was out of the house years ago. It's a beautiful detached house in a nice area, with a garden. It's the only way you'll get yourselves something proper, and anyway I need you up there, Gerson."

Gerson fell silent, and Marie switched back to speaking Norwegian.

"Should I have just said no thanks? Should I have just said that my son won't take the house and cannot move to Trondheim, because he and his wife are afraid of ghosts?"

"No, Mother," replied Gerson, as he heard Ellen walk in from the living room, carrying Jannicke.

He said nothing. Each time Gerson felt ready to tell Ellen about the house's background, something got in the way. The decision had been made, and they were in the car. Gerson turned the key in the ignition, and off they drove, while two-year-old Jannicke slowly forgot what she was angry about. Soon the tension from the carrying and the organizing slipped away, and they began chatting. They watch the houses glide by outside the windows. A truck piled up with hay. Stripes of thin tree trunks flicker past, while Jannicke drags her tiny fingers over the glass and presses her tongue against it. Gerson smiles in the rearview mirror. Starts to imagine life in Trondheim, and work at Paris-Vienna. He inhales deeply and feels Ellen place her hand over his own, on the wheel. Then he quickly turns to her and smiles, changes gear, and places his hand on her thigh, just above her knee, feeling her warm skin just beneath her tights; he pictures them all as a contented family in the new house's garden. It has got to work out.

B for the baritone voice of the prisoner ordered to entertain them at Falstad. In the middle of work the soldiers would sometimes ask him to sing for them. The sawing would stop, as would the banging of hammers from the carpentry sheds and the constant shuffling of hands and feet. And then it was as if something was awakened in each one of them. With a clear and beautiful voice, the baritone would sing, with his head tilted back, like an elegy to the heavens, his phrasings softening their circumstances. Their aching muscles, and the constant stinging from small cuts and blisters would disappear for a few seconds. The guards' faces would loosen up, become relaxed, a little more human, before they would pull themselves together and slip back into their roles.

In moments like this you consider the possibility that some

of these young men could be the same ones you saw in German cities ten years earlier. When they were 10–12 years old, and ran through the streets on scrawny legs, with gangly arms, and eyes that glowed with curiosity and joy. Maybe you smiled at one of the guards when he was a little boy, or chatted briefly in a park with another. But now?

B for Bar Mitzvah or for the benches in the Trondheim synagogue which you helped to purchase.

B for the bedroom the Rinnan gang used, photographed at the end of the war with drawers, clothes, rubbish, and papers spread all over the floor and wallpaper torn to shreds. It's the afternoon, and I'm working at home in Oslo and searching through some online archives. The first photo shows the exterior of the villa. A house with an arched window on the second floor, and shutters that open and close in front of the windows. The barbed wire around the property has already been removed, along with the guards who used to stand outside.

The naked backside of a man's thigh with a swastika branded onto it pops up on the screen in front of me, in black and white. Then I hear footsteps approaching, I must have been so engrossed that I didn't hear anyone come in, and now my daughter is standing right behind me. I hastily close the browser window, only to reveal a photo of three whips.

"What's that, Dad?" my daughter asks, before I quit the browser entirely.

"I'm just reading about the war," I say, and press my cheek against hers. Lift her up, and carry her warm little body away from the computer.

B for bottles of liquor photographed that same day, stacked up in the cellar behind two large barrels which are bridged by a heavy iron bar, bent in the middle, presumably from the weight of those forced to crouch with their limbs tied—before being hung from it, whipped, beaten, and branded.

B for the blood on the floor in the basement of the Gang Monastery, dripping from the axe that one of the gang members is holding. It is the end of April 1945, and Rinnan walks into the washroom in the cellar. He sees the boxes standing in the middle of the room, as well as the large pools of blood slowly running into the drain. Rinnan gives a nod of acknowledgment to the man standing there, breathless, the axe hanging loosely by his thigh.

C

×   ×   ×

C for Cadillac.

C for cowboy.

C for *cremaster,* a muscle that develops in the testicles during puberty, when hormones secreted cause hair to grow on the legs and crotch. It deepens the voice and brings a harder, more angular look to the face, over which a tallowy layer spreads across the nose and cheeks, emphasizing the transformation, and the gradual departure from childhood.

Sometimes, when Henry is alone in the hallway, he'll scrutinize himself in front of the mirror, thinking that his shortness is a result of them being poor. Sometimes he'll overhear his mother talking to a friend or a shopkeeper, telling them he's just a late bloomer, that he'll catch up later on; and her words fill him with hope, but it never happens; he gets older, but his height never catches up with the others. He still finds himself outside the pack. He says that he doesn't want to play soccer anyway, that he doesn't like the game, but in reality he lies in bed dreaming he is on the soccer field, dribbling past player after player until it's between him and the goalie. He imagines lobbing the ball elegantly over the boy's head, who throws himself to the ground, and his teammates racing toward him, lifting him onto their shoulders, their faces full of triumph and joy. This never happens of course; he stays quiet instead. Polite. Cautious. As unobtrusive as possible, because if you're not seen, you can't be bullied.

When he is thirteen Henry borrows a magazine with a drawing of a cowboy on the cover from his uncle. And while the family sits drinking coffee—and his father goes on about how the communists should be cut down and destroyed before they take over the country—Henry sits there reading the story of the cowboy and discovers a portal to another world, transporting him far from the streets of Levanger, from the schoolyard, and from the boys who bully him on the way home.

When he is fourteen he wakes up one night with an unusual stickiness on his belly, and his hands on the breasts of someone's big sister, whose naked body melts away right before his eyes.

When he is fifteen, he goes through confirmation, and like many of the other children Henry's confirmation gift is to have his rotten teeth pulled out and replaced with dentures. New smooth teeth that he can stroke his tongue over, teeth that glow white in the mirror.

At sixteen, his body ceases to grow any more. So this will be him. As far as he will go. A laughable height of five feet three inches.

He is the shortest sixteen-year-old in Levanger, his head only reaching the shoulders of most of his classmates, and his body seems unusually small compared to his head, as if he belonged to a slightly different species. Another, uglier branch of humanity, smarter than most, he knows that, but shorter; and it doesn't help being polite, or that he behaves himself, or acts responsibly at school and does everything he is told either. The adults seem to like him—although only because he doesn't cause trouble and never tries to draw attention to himself—but the other pupils fail to notice him. The boys aren't interested and neither are the girls. He should have been taller. He prays to God, asking if he can keep on growing, but nothing happens.

Had his parents been equally short, he could have blamed them. But his mother and father and brothers are just like everyone else. Only he stands out. Why? Why him? There's no answer, and no solution. The best he can do is grow a long forelock, then, using pomade, comb the whole lick of hair back into a quiff, as high as possible from his crown, and hope that the extra inch makes it easier for him to blend in with the other boys. But it doesn't. He is still the odd one out, different, and visibly weaker, so of course the other boys are going to pick on him. Henry understands this; it is clearly the way nature is designed. He sees it everywhere he goes. The strongest take everything they want, they make their own rules, and make others obey. That's how it is. Of course the other boys will surround him, and push him around when the grown-ups aren't looking.

Henry grits his teeth, trying to let it all bounce off him, knowing that there is nothing he can do.

Often the harassment continues when he closes his eyes at night. He will picture the gleeful looks on the boys' faces while they push him back and forth, and the only thing on his mind will be that he mustn't crack, that he must never break.

C for cars. It is spring 1931, and sixteen-year-old Henry walks down the street next to the ocean when he notices a crowd of teenagers outside Hveding Sports, the shop where his uncle works. He has been there many times in the past, ever since he was a small child and had to stand on tiptoe to see over the counter, while his father bought things for his bike or the workshop. This time Henry has come into town to get a glimpse of the Ford his uncle has purchased. A real Ford, the first one in town, with shining black bodywork and dark-brown leather seats. Hveding Sports, after much discussion, has opened a car dealership and also the city's first gas station where future car owners can fill their tanks and buy accessories in the shop. To mark the occasion they have placed a real Ford automobile in the shop window facing the street, although right now Henry can barely see it because of all the people standing in the way. His uncle is bent over the hood showing something to the youngsters, but then stands up straight, a clear head height above the others, looks at his nephew, and shouts to him.

Henry feels the urge to turn and run, or just walk past pretending not to hear anything, but he can't do that, they already made eye contact, and his uncle will tell his mother if he starts behaving strangely.

"Henry Oliver!" his uncle shouts while waving. "Come here! I have something to show you!"

Henry looks at the others, and notices one of the boys he fought with after the incident with the ladies' boots—one of those boys the girls always look at. Henry crosses the sand-covered street, and around a pothole still full of water from last night's rain. He blinks, and tries to think of something clever to say, but what might that be?

"Hey, how nice to see you here!" says his uncle jovially, placing a hand on Henry's shoulder. The others step aside and make way for him. They don't dare not to, with his uncle standing there. "Take a look at this!" he says, resting his hand on the roof of the car. Henry leans over and peers through the windshield at the leather seats, and the steering wheel molded on the inside to fit one's fingers perfectly, and all the buttons and levers.

"Nice, isn't it?" his uncle asks.

Henry nods, while his uncle walks around the car and opens the driver's door.

"I thought I'd take her for a test drive. Fancy coming with me?"

his uncle asks, smiling playfully. The others look at him enviously; Henry can't hold back the smile now spreading across his face.

"Yes please!" he replies. "When?"

"Hmm . . . ," his uncle replies, dragging it out a little more, milking all the attention from the boys and a lady trundling by with a pram on the far side of the street. "How about now?"

"Now?" Henry replies.

"Yes! Now is the best possible time. Jump in!"

His uncle opens the door on his side, and Henry reaches for the handle, with his heart pounding in his chest. The gang of boys are close enough to hit him, push him. But would they do that now? With his uncle there? He opens the car door, forcing them all to take a few steps back, then sits down inside this gleaming marvel of metal, wood, glass, and leather, in which only he has permission to sit. He pulls the door shut carefully to avoid damaging it, with the pride swelling up within him, and looks out of the window at all the envious faces. Because this is all they got. No more than a look at the car, while he is sitting in it; he is getting to ride in it. Henry strokes his hand across the teak dashboard and its shiny polished steel trimmings.

His uncle turns to him.

"Are you ready?" he asks, and Henry nods nervously, but excitedly. Of course he is ready. Suddenly his uncle turns the key, rousing the motor from its sleep, pushing his foot down on the pedal, and revving the engine, which sends a roar of noise from under the hood in front of them. Then he places his hand on the gearshift, pulls it into a notch, and off they go, down the street by the sea, away from the boys. They take a left onto the main street and cruise through town as people turn and stare.

"Watch this," says his uncle, and he shows Henry how to change gear, how to steer, and how to accelerate. He demonstrates how a flick of a little switch makes the wipers sweep across the windshield. And outside, the people and houses glide by, as if they belonged to another world.

"Have you ever driven a car before, Henry Oliver?" his uncle asks, once they are a little further out of town.

Henry shakes his head, and his uncle takes his hand.

"Give it a try," he says, placing Henry's hand on the wheel. Henry recoils, and tries to pull his arm back, but his uncle just laughs, saying, "Come on, Henry, it's OK!" Henry realizes that he has no choice, and in any case he really wants to, so he leans across, places his other hand on the wheel, and he steers! For a brief moment he is the one driving the car, as the road hurtles toward them. For several minutes he is the one in control, as he swerves around a hole in the road and hugs the bends, all the way back to town. Then his uncle takes the wheel again, saying that Henry can let go, and they pull up in front of the shop. The boys are gone.

They fall silent in the car. Henry sits with his palms flat against his thighs, as he does at school. His uncle clears his throat, pulls out a cigarette, and taps it on his knee.

"Now then, Henry Oliver. That wasn't so bad was it?"

"No. It certainly wasn't," replies Henry, smiling. "Thank you!"

"You're welcome. Want one?" asks his uncle, handing him the cigarette box. A beautiful tin box with an Arabian palace on the lid, and the lettering of the word *Medina* snaking around one of the domes.

"Erm . . . I don't know," replies Henry, because although he has tried smoking before, with cigarettes stolen from his parents, he has never sat like this, being treated like an adult. He blinks a couple of times, and decides to take one. Lights it up and feels the burning in his chest as he inhales.

"So, Henry Oliver?" asks his uncle, blowing a cloud of smoke at the windshield, which spreads in all directions and evaporates. "How is my nephew doing?"

"I . . . I'm doing fine, thanks," Henry replies, taking a drag himself.

"Yes, I hear you're doing well at school . . . but aside from that? You don't do any sport or anything, do you?"

Henry shakes his head. He exhales and takes another drag,

straight after the previous one, immediately aware of how nervous it must make him look. He can't even hold the cigarette in a relaxed manner, unlike his uncle, who wears his cigarette as if it were an extension of his hand, like it quite naturally poked out between his index and middle finger.

"No, I'm not really interested in that sort of thing," replies Henry, glancing up at his uncle to see how he will react.

His uncle looks straight ahead. Nodding quite calmly, showing no sign of disappointment, as though he doesn't consider this to be a problem, as far as Henry is concerned.

"Very well. Then you must have a fair amount of time on your hands . . . even though I'm sure you spend some of it with your friends. Right?"

Henry nods once more and takes another drag, the ash starting to grow dangerously long. I mustn't let it fall off and make a mess in the car, he thinks. His uncle rolls down the window. There is a little handle on the door, which in itself is quite amazing. Henry winds it around on his side, watching how the glass slides down into a slit in the door and disappears. His uncle flicks his cigarette ash outside. Henry smiles and does the same.

"Our business," his uncle says, while pointing at the shop right beside them.

"Yes?"

"We could actually do with some help, Sverre and I. We've discussed it several times, that it would be great to have a part-time assistant. Would that be of interest to you?"

"Yes! Thank you, of course it would!" replies Henry, smiling nervously. Noticing how his facial muscles aren't quite keeping up, because this is huge. Imagine if he could start working there. Properly!

"Great, I'll talk to your mother about it. Would you be able to start tomorrow, and see how things go?"

"Tomorrow?" asks Henry.

"Yeah, why not? There's no reason to wait, is there?"

Henry nods quickly again; he can hardly believe that this is real, that he's actually sitting here, in this car, being offered a job! His uncle allows the smoke to snake upward, before flicking the stub out the open window.

Henry runs home to break the news to his father, who doesn't seem quite as enthusiastic. Most likely jealous that his wife's brother has done so well in life, thinks Henry. Then he realizes that his father probably knew about this already, and that his mother was probably the one making it happen.

The following morning Henry is ready. His father has polished his shoes for him, a form of apology perhaps, and he walks beside the churchyard and round the corner toward the shop and garage. He has been there a hundred times before and knows how it looks inside and where everything is.

Even with his eyes closed, Henry could describe the interior in detail: the wooden bench stretching the length of the room, and the brown cash register, with its buttons and levers and the black wooden crank on the side that has to be pulled down halfway to release the spring that fires the drawer toward him. He would be able to describe the bags hanging in the window, and not least, he would be able to describe every inch of the Ford on display in the window beside them. A wonder of black metal, gleaming chrome, and wooden details. What he would not be able to articulate is the feeling of lifting the white shopkeeper's coat from the hook, slipping his arms into it, and seeing himself in the mirror, transformed into someone else. He would be unable to describe how his nervousness vanishes when he pulls on this uniform; and how his associations with it change him, bringing him a strange new form of confidence. Suddenly it's easy making small talk with strangers, listening to their stories, helping them figure out what they need. After always being so quiet and timid, he notices that words and phrases now come easy to him, allowing him to see people in a different way. He draws back the veil from all he's been harboring and assumes the role of the world's best shop assistant: someone who knows where every item is placed; someone who knows which customers can be tempted to make an extra purchase, a pair of gloves or mittens for example, or some tools or chain oil for someone who needs to fix his bike anyway. He loosens the rope pulleys on the wall to lower the items hanging from the rafters. He makes the customers feel welcome. He returns home with money for his mother, quite amazed at how the confidence and competence that come with the uniform seem to vanish again the moment he removes it. Because then he returns to being just Henry Oliver again, sneaking back home as quickly as he can to avoid being spotted by any of the gangs.

He has never imagined how happy he could get by lifting the hose from the gas pump on the rare occasions a customer needs fuel. Or from the magic smell of gas fumes, that make the air seemingly vibrate and assume a more material form like a mirage before gushing into the car beside him to be transformed, converted into speed, sound, and pleasure.

A month passes. Henry's uncle heaps praise on him, as does the owner himself, and his mother is truly grateful for the money he brings home. He spends his afternoons in the garage in the backyard, learning what every engine part is called and what function it has; spending as much time as he can under the hood, with his hands covered in oil. There's just one snag among all the joy of his new daily life: the salary is too meager. Once the money for food and the repayments on his parents' loan have been deducted, there is nothing left for Henry to spend on himself. He considers asking his mother if he could keep some of it, just a tiny bit, but he doesn't dare to, because as soon as the thought strikes him, he pictures her in the kitchen, stern faced, shaking her head while listing all the things the family needs. He would have no argument, of course, he cannot win that discussion. She would never understand the importance of him joining his classmates at the temperance café and being able to buy himself a hot chocolate or a bun. He has to make up excuses instead, saying that he can't make it this time and that he has to go home.

He should have asked if he could keep some of the money, but doesn't have the nerve. So he exists as an outsider, secluded from the others and all they are able to do, because his mother knows exactly what he earns, and there's no way of skimming off a little for himself, for a quick trip to the café, or an extra treat. It's so unfair! he thinks on his way to the shop. Why should he always be the one left out, no matter how hard he works? It's not fair. Those who get things in life, get everything. Those who are born tall, good-looking, and confident; they get money as well. The other boys his age can all afford to visit the café on the high street, where anyone who is anyone meets. They have the money for cigarettes, chocolate, and cinema tickets. It's only he who has to remain separate from it all, like a fish trapped in an aquarium, watching what's happening on the other side of the glass, but never able to come out and join the conversation like everyone else. Never. Ever. No matter how much he works. Only he is never invited to birthday parties, never picked for the soccer team, never noticed by the girls. Only he walks around in oversized clothes handed down from his cousins; in trousers that have to be shortened, and coat sleeves so long his fingertips resemble animal noses poking out of a cave, checking if it's safe outside.

Maybe I should ask for a pay raise, thinks Henry. But he knows the owner will never raise his salary. Even though the business is so successful that its rich owner can strut about in a suit and waistcoat and drive around in his own car. Even though turnover has increased considerably since Henry began, because he is doing such a good job. It's just not fair, he thinks, stroking his finger along the side of the cash register, thinking about all the coins sitting in there, right there, on the other side of the cold metal. And he gets an idea, clear and simple, because there is one solution to put all of this straight, a simple way of raising his salary to the level it really should be at, ensuring that Henry gets what he deserves. It's just a question of not registering a few of the sales and keeping the money—as a kind of tip—since he is so efficient, and the person responsible for so much of the increased profit. Just trifling amounts, so small they will never be noticed. It won't make the slightest difference to the shop owner. But for him? For Henry it will mean he can go to the café like everyone else, which is crucial to whether he's on the inside or not. Besides, he's earned the money anyway, right?

Henry places his hands on either side of the cash register and glances over at the door to the back room. He sees the owner bent over some paperwork, with a cloud of cigarette smoke rising over the writing desk. His uncle has gone out, or is in the warehouse. Then a customer enters the shop. An elderly man. Someone perfect to practice on, Henry thinks, as his heart thumps in his chest, but he doesn't let his nervousness show. He stands attentively, smiles, and greets the man politely, just like he always does, making sure to keep both hands on the counter, standing up straight, and speaking in a loud and clear voice while scrutinizing the man. He notices how absent-minded and inattentive the white-haired customer seems, how he fumbles about in his coat pocket to find something to wipe away the glistening drop hanging from his nostril.

Then the money comes out, and the opportunity.

It's quite simple. All he has to do is keep his finger in the cash drawer when he closes it, and wait until the old codger has left the shop, before sneaking the money into his trouser pocket with a flat hand.

Seconds after—with the bell over the door still jangling loudly, his heart beating hard in his chest and his right hand gripping the coins—it's as though the sale never happened. But the money is definitely there, and after work he takes a walk near where he knows the other boys normally hang out. He meets someone from his class, a quiet boy who is not too popular either, and asks if he wants to go to the café. "It's on me," Henry says, and thankfully the boy accepts. So off they go, with Henry still gripping the coins tightly and with a huge smile on his face.

The café is run by the temperance movement, so there are no beers or spirits on the tables, but you can smoke there, and tell stories. He buys two cups of hot chocolate, noticing the looks from the others and hearing the clinking of coffee sets and the fantastic hum of voices and laughter. His schoolmate takes him to a slightly crowded table. Henry takes a seat, trying to hide how nervous he is, and just listens, while sipping his drink. One of the others is talking about a film, about a cowboy who saves an entire town. Everyone is listening to him. Then, during a quiet moment, Henry seizes the moment, and asks if they have heard a story that he has read about in one of the magazines. The others look up from their cups, without any hint of sarcasm, quite the opposite in fact, they listen, and say, No, which one was that?

It's almost as if the boys had been sitting there waiting for someone to walk in and entertain them, because they listen intently to every single word, totally engrossed, as Henry retells the story of a dusty little town in America, a bank robbery, and a suitcase full of money. They are captivated as he draws them in, talking so quietly they have to sit on the edge of their seats in order to hear what happens, to keep up with every detail. The story begins with characters from the magazine he's reading, but soon he becomes the main character, and no one at the table reacts to this sudden change in roles, no one flinches at Henry being part of the story now, because now he has their full attention, no one else.

Soon he has to go home for dinner, but as he stands up one of the other boys asks if he will be back tomorrow.

"Yes, of course," replies Henry casually, as if it was the most normal thing in the world. "Nice place, this," he says. And then he leaves, while the happiness and pride wells up inside him, and for the entire walk home he knows what he has to do the next day: pocket a little more cash. Enough to go back to the café. And while he ambles home, he is already planning what story he'll tell them all next time.

It goes on like that for the rest of the year. He is careful. Mindful to never take too much from the cash register; to never fall foul of temptation, even though there's no sign of him being discovered. No. Just small amounts. Just enough so that he can afford to drop by the café, or join the others at the cinema now and then: following the crowd of expectant youths into the movie theater, hearing the murmur of voices, and watching the red velvet curtain sweep aside, like a slow-moving eyelid, opening up onto another world.

Cinema is so realistic that the characters can now speak, and the guns, the doors, and the cars all make noise. It's almost like being pulled into the screen and becoming the main character. The music, images, and dialogue make him feel as though he is right there, at the center of all the drama, feeling the tension as if it were his own. But it costs a whole crown to get in, and that means he has to steal more money than before, smile politely to the customers, and make sure to keep them chatting about the weather or whatever it might be, while his finger casually holds the cash drawer open. Thank you so much, and See you again! A tinkling of bells over the door, and the coins can be slid back out of the drawer and into his pocket, where they lie, totally quiet, yet full of power, glowing with possibilities. But then.

One afternoon when he is alone in the shop, the door is suddenly thrown open, and two boys walk in. The same boys who used to torment him at school, just because they could. They must have been waiting for him to be alone; chosen a time they know that both his uncle and the owner would be out, and when most people in town are busy having lunch. Henry feels his heart pounding in his diaphragm.

"So! Is this where you're hiding?" asks one of them, while

approaching the counter. "How has a pygmy like you managed to climb so high in life?"

The other boy lets out a series of small giggles, before placing the flat of his hand on his mouth and pretending to be an American Indian.

Henry doesn't respond. He cannot let them see how much the words sting. The older of the two boys dives over the counter. Henry tries to struggle free, but the boy grabs his hands and pulls his arms back across the counter, leaving Henry with his face pressed down on the woodwork.

"What are you doing?!" Henry asks in dismay.

"We're just helping the pygmy move up a little higher in life," replies the boy standing behind him, straining on the last word, as he pulls hard on a hook suspended from a pulley hung from the roof. Then he feels something being pushed through his belt loops, and cold steel under his shirt, fumbling hands, and dry rope scratching against his skin.

The boy in front lets go of his arms, and for a moment Henry is free before they start pulling on the rope. His trousers tighten at the seams, and he is hoisted up, rotating several times, as the counter and cash register get smaller, until he's flailing around under the roof, several yards above them.

"So, how's the view from up there?" one of them asks. Henry doesn't answer. Refusing to give them the pleasure.

"Kick your legs, little jumping jack! Someone will come and change your diaper and comfort you soon!" the other boy shouts, his eyes flashing with laughter, as he secures the rope to the wall. Then they both walk out.

The bell jingles again, and the fair-haired boy sticks his head around the door again and shouts, "Thanks! Have a nice day!" before the door clicks shut, and their footsteps crunch on the gravel outside.

Henry dangles there, in total silence.

He wonders how long he'll be stuck like this before someone finds him. And how will he explain? How will he cope with all the gossiping this will lead to, from neighbor to neighbor, all over Levanger? Fuck those bastards! Fuck all this hassle and bullying! It never ends, he thinks while trying to twist himself around, but unfortunately he can't quite get his fingers on the rope, in fact his swinging around makes the rope graze his lower back and the desperation in him grows; the tears well up, but he refuses to cry. I'm not going to give them the fucking pleasure, he thinks, while clenching his teeth. He screws up his eyes and breathes deeply through his nose while forcing back the tears, because he will have his revenge for this. Just fucking wait, he thinks, and in his mind, what just happened begins to change. He imagines the two bullies walking in, just as obnoxious and revolting as they were in reality, but in his daydream what happened next is quite different: when they lean across the counter, Henry stops them by standing bolt upright and giving them a cold stare.

"What are you doing here?" he shouts, noticing how uneasy they look. "If you're not here to buy anything, then get the fuck out!" he says. "Don't waste my time! Do you hear me?"

Henry smiles to himself, as he pictures them glancing nervously at each other, totally unsure what to do next, now things aren't going to plan, because they hadn't expected this! One of them tries to grab his shirt collar, but Henry is too fast. He twists quickly out of reach, as though in a fast-motion film, before jerking his elbow back and smashing his fist into the other boy's nose. Hard and precise. Suddenly the tough guy isn't so tough any more, and instead stumbles backward in disbelief holding his hands to his face, with tears streaming from his eyes. Then the other one tries to throw a punch, but Henry ducks—no, actually, he doesn't duck!—he grabs hold of an ashtray sitting on the counter, a cut-glass ashtray, full of crumpled butts and ash, and smashes it into the other boy's cheek! So hard that there's a crunch of cheekbone and gristle and teeth, and cigarette ends flying everywhere! And what a pleasure it is! What a triumph to see those two bastards falling apart, and crawling away gasping, spitting blood and teeth from their mouths, because now they have both been neutralized.

After that Henry simply jumps over the shop counter. A gallant little leap, grabbing them by the backs of their coats and dragging them toward the door like insubordinate little brats.

Time and space cease to exist as these scenes play out in his mind, over and over, but with slight variations. His trousers chafe his groin on either side, and every time he tries to move, the rope burns the skin under his arms and along his sides. How long has he been hanging there? Finally the door opens, and Henry lifts his head to see an old man enter the shop. Luckily it's not one of the regular customers; not someone he'll see frequently, who'll remind him of this humiliation every time they meet.

"Dear God, what on earth happened?" asks the man, hurrying behind the counter to untie the knot.

"It was just a joke," replies Henry with a smirk, explaining to the stranger that it was just a prank between friends, and that the others are bound to come back at any moment. The man seems to believe him, and Henry manages to smile and laugh about it while he is lowered to the ground. He returns the rope to its rightful place and quickly goes to assist the customer with the items he needs, before anyone else comes in.

Then he takes money from the cash register, more than ever this time, because he has someone in mind, someone that might help him. A guy who sells things illegally, and can supposedly get hold of anything between heaven and earth, if you have the right money.

Soon Henry's uncle returns and asks if everything is going all right. Then he sits down in the back room to work on the new orders, read the newspaper, and smoke.

More customers enter the shop, looking for balls, pumps, and weights, and Henry helps himself to a little more cash, stuffing it into his trouser pocket. Finally, he hangs up his jacket and closes the shop, while shouting goodbye to his uncle.

A few hours later Henry buys his first gun.

×

C for the café Gerson stops at on his way to Trondheim in 1948, a roadside café deep in the pine forest. He's not really hungry, but they have driven quite far already, and when the sign appears he is suddenly unsure how many hours it might be until the next food stop. Ellen's head droops slowly forward as the car begins to brake, then she blinks her eyes and looks up at him. Jannicke still lies there with her head in her mother's lap, her eyes closed, her dark curls and pudgy white cheeks. To think that it ended up being them, him and Ellen, together. He would never have guessed it if someone had asked him before the war. But she is pretty, he thinks, and from a solid family background. Without question a good family, who owned a tobacco factory in Oslo and a villa with cars and chauffeurs and seamstresses. Most of that vanished during the war, but there's always hope of getting some of it back, he thinks. In any case neither of them had much choice, thinks Gerson, as the gravel crunches under the tires, because there hadn't been too many young people living in the refugee housing in Sweden and, other than the women there, who would consider him? Who would want to date a Jewish-Norwegian refugee? His mother had her part in it too, steering them toward each other by inviting Ellen's family round for coffee, and making sure that they did things together. Ellen's twin sister already had a boyfriend, but Ellen was available and so they ended up together.

Gerson's mother had been unable to hide her disappointment over the small amount of money returned to the family when the war ended and they were finally able to move back. For a moment he imagines a different life, picturing himself at the university, working on a new project. He pictures himself winning a prize in a mathematics competition, and then immediately blinks the images away again, because that was another life, one which cannot be his, he thinks. It is yet another thing destroyed by the war, but he cannot complain, he has no right to, he thinks, because he is after all still alive. He wasn't transported to a concentration camp on board the *Donau,* or imprisoned in Falstad, like so many others were. He is alive, unharmed, and this life, despite everything, isn't so bad.

"Where are we?" asks Ellen.

"I thought we could stop and eat," Gerson replies, still twisted round in his seat. Ellen places a hand on Jannicke's cheek and strokes the hair from her forehead.

"Good idea," she says, smiling warmly, looking so pretty just then, with her eyes glowing so openly that Gerson feels a pang of guilt, and for a split second considers telling her about the house they are moving into.

"Ellen?" he says.

"Hm?" replies Ellen dreamily, letting go of his hand again, and lifting the sleeping bundle from her lap.

"Were you going to say something?" she asks.

Gerson shakes his head, and looks at his beautiful daughter lying there, so innocent, so pure.

"Time to wake up, my little treasure," she says. And then his daughter draws several breaths in a succession of little jolts, as if her sleep were an abyss she had just poked her head up from, and with that, the opportunity to say something disappears.

D

× × ×

D for the doves in the sky above Falstad, that sometimes fly in formation over the meadows and fields, in an undulating dance with the sky.

D for the drinking of the prison-camp guards, when they are off duty and their voices lighten, their laughter often reaching the cell where you are lying. It brings back memories of your childhood, when you lay in bed listening to the sound of grown-ups at the parties your parents threw, when their voices changed, became louder, happier. That's how it is with the German soldiers. Sometimes you get the punch line of a joke and smile to yourself, almost involuntarily, before turning around and trying to disappear into sleep.

D for Dora, the name of the U-boat base Hitler planned to establish outside Trondheim. This concrete structure was never finished, but it was converted into the National Archives a few years after the war because of its massive walls. I read all about Dora and its history, parallel to researching Rinnan's childhood and my search for answers to this family mystery. Because why was it *you* who was picked out? Was it really just the allegation about you spreading news from the BBC, or was there more to it? How did your name come up in the first place?

D for the dance halls in the area where Henry grew up, where the boys would saunter nonchalantly up to the girls, and with an air of confidence start chatting to them, seemingly unaffected by whether they were rejected or not. *How do they do it?* thinks Henry, again and again, standing on the periphery of one of these events, observing everything. How do they manage to appear so indifferent, so worldly wise?

Henry doesn't have the nerve to approach any of the girls, but he goes anyway, as the driver, since none of them have a license, and they definitely don't have a car they can borrow and drive around looking for a party. So Henry does the driving, both to the dance hall and back home again in the evening, just as he does on this particular Saturday night. It is late, and it has been a successful night. The boys in the back seat talk wildly, each one louder than the other, about that night's escapades, but Henry isn't listening. He just has his foot pressed on the accelerator, reveling in the fantastic sensation he gets as the car speeds along the tiny road so fast that the gravel sprays into the air, and the trees fly past in a blur on either side. Just a light push with his shoe is all that's required for the power hidden under the black hood to be unleashed. A wild dance of pistons and exploding gas hammering down on the crankshaft, whipping the wheels forward, along a small gravel road in the dark, on their way home from the party.

Every Friday or Saturday they drive to a new place. Houses and people float by, while the boys sail—on a wave of happiness, expectation, and camaraderie—all the way up to the dance hall. And it might be a new place each time, but the atmosphere is always the same. The lighting and the music wafting from the entrance are the same everywhere. A hum of life and desire and adolescence. The way the men stagger around, drunkenly through the long grass, is the same in every town. As is the laughter of the girls grouped together, in light summer dresses, their hair tied up in buns, and their hips and breasts pressing against the fabric. The overt lechery and voraciousness of the men who slip their arms round these women and pull them toward them is the same wherever they go.

What he would have given to own that arm, where it now lies nonchalantly across that thin dress; to stroke his fingertips downward, over every inch of her body through the fabric? What he would have given to own those eyes, as she turns to the man leaning up against the wall over there; to own those lips as she leans back halfway and allows herself to be kissed?

It's no good. There's no point trying to enter the venue at all, because who would dance with a man so short that his face is pressed against her breasts? A guy so short that she would just stand there lit up like a beacon of embarrassment, a full head taller than her partner? His height keeps him away. So Henry just pulls the car up and parks outside the dance hall without getting out, and when the others ask if he wants to join them, he gives them a mischievous grin, telling them he already has a date with a woman nearby.

His friends disappear into the party, and Henry drives on.

Sometimes he parks near the roadside.

Other times he drives around, aimlessly.

In his imagination, things are different.

In his imagination, the gravel crunches under the wheels as Henry pulls into the drive of a nearby farmstead, and parks outside a white-painted house, beside a red-painted barn, next to a cluster of raspberry bushes. A lamp arches out from the wall, and insects buzz around in the golden light. Henry knocks on the door, and a few seconds pass while he pulls off his leather gloves with his teeth, and places them suavely in his coat pocket. Then the woman who lives there opens the door. She nearly always resembles Greta Garbo, only a bit shorter. Henry has seen the Swedish actress's films over and over again. He has stroked his finger over the face on the film poster, and when no one is looking, over her breasts, down to her stomach, and then down to her crotch, hidden under the picture of her tight-fitting dress. Greta Garbo came from a poor background too, from nothing, but look at what she has become! World famous, sophisticated and well dressed, always elegant and sensual, as she was in *Mata Hari,* where she played the role of a spy who seduces men with her dancing, then dupes them into giving away information, before ending up in front of the firing squad and being shot. The scene is both heartbreaking and gruesome, but luckily it's only the character that dies, not the actress, so Greta Garbo can appear later, in other films, as well as in Henry's fantasies and in the faces of the women he looks at. Sometimes she is present in the form of women resembling her, when he has driven the boys to a party somewhere.

The lonely woman in the secluded house smiles teasingly and reaches for his hand. She is warm and soft and willing. Sometimes they do it right there in the hallway, inside the door, wearing her high-heeled shoes and her dress pulled up to her belly. Other times she drags him into the bedroom and unbuttons her blouse, slowly revealing her bra, and he strokes his hands over her breasts. Watches her undress completely, right in front of him.

These daydreams are so realistic that sometimes he has to reach down into his trousers while sitting there, alone in the woods, and start touching himself, loosely at first, fumblingly, and then harder, faster, while yet another woman that resembles Greta Garbo lies down in front of him on the bed, her long blonde hair spread across the pillows, and there, at the edge of the woods, a short distance from the car, he comes inside her, into this warm wetness that he has never experienced in reality, but which sends waves of heat through his entire body, until his sperm shoots out into the dark and hangs in threads from the leaves and the twigs. Then he snaps out of his daydream again, suddenly back at the roadside, in the bushes, with his trousers around his knees. He wipes his hands on the grass. Looks for a stream or a puddle where he can wash away the sticky globs from his skin, holds his hand to his nose to make sure the smell has gone, scrubs his hands with some leaves, checks the time, and then carries on waiting.

The other boys stare open-mouthed and in disbelief when Henry tells them about his encounters with these older, more experienced women. These stories, which he shares in the car afterward, are so vivid and detailed it's as though these women really exist; and on this particular Saturday night, that's exactly how it feels, as they drive home in the dark from Namsos. Henry has just told the boys about his latest conquest and can see how wide-eyed they are just hearing about it, how jealous they are, after a night limited to dancing and kissing.

The long grass by the roadside flickers past in the car headlights. The boys in the back seat scream and laugh, overexcited by all they have done, exchanging small details, reveling in saying the names of some of the women, followed by a conclusion they all seem to agree on, a comment about breasts, followed by another burst of raucous laughter. It's all such amazing fun for them. But for Henry, the driver, it's not much fun to listen to at all. Quite the opposite! They sit there talking about things only they have experienced, leaving him out, when he is the reason they get to these dance halls in the first place. Only he has access to a car, yet still they sit there like a bunch of cockatoos cackling away, without a care, without involving him in the conversation, as though he were their private chauffeur!

Well, they'll see. If I'm only here to drive, then I'm at least going to have some fun, thinks Henry, licking his lips. He tightens his grip on the wheel, wearing the driving gloves he bought with his own money: leather gloves with holes in the knuckles, skin tight around his fingers, like a racing driver. Now he leans right over the steering wheel and hits the accelerator. Listening as the revs get higher, and the pistons struggle so hard to keep pace that he has to hit the clutch and change gears. Bushes fly past in the headlights, occasionally thrashing the side of the car. The laughing in the back stops. He sees the smiles vanish from the boys' faces. The dirt road is hard and bumpy, and the potholes, carved out by the rain, send shudders through the bodywork.

"Easy, Henry!" says one of his friends—the one who normally takes the lead and does most of the talking—clinging to the back of the driver's seat with both hands. "We're not in any hurry!"

Henry smiles at him in the mirror and sees the fear in his eyes.

"What's wrong? Are you scared?" asks Henry, pressing the accelerator even harder, feeling how the car vibrates on the bends, how the centrifugal force presses their bodies to one side.

Faster and faster.

His friend doesn't reply. None of them speak. They just sit there, pinned to their seats, clinging on tightly. The needle on the speedometer creeps upward as they approach a long straight section. Now we'll see how fast this car can really go, he thinks, changing gears again. Then something in the headlights grabs his attention. Two glowing eyes, right down on the road surface, a cat perhaps, but then he sees the rest of the animal—a rabbit, sitting in the middle of the road—a furry target, an unexpected prize, like a teddy bear at the fairground.

"Watch this, boys! It'll be rabbit pie for dinner tomorrow!" he shouts, pushing his foot to the floor as hard as he can.

"Henry!" shouts one of the others, the one sitting in the front passenger seat, who almost never says anything, but Henry doesn't answer, he just hunches over the wheel for the two seconds it lasts, this moment of joy, speed, and excitement, while the car roars toward the little furry creature sitting there stupefied.

But then.

The rabbit suddenly hops away, toward the bushes by the road-side, and it can't do that, it's not allowed to do that, thinks Henry, swerving after it, it's not going to outwit him and escape, no fucking way. Henry turns the wheel and takes aim, certain he's going to make it.

Then it all happens fast.

The rabbit vanishes from the headlights.

A friend in the back seat screams his name.

Then the car veers off the road and tips over. There's a crash, then a bang on the side, and suddenly he is lying with his face pressed against the door. The car leans at an angle against a stone. There are shards of glass in his lap, and a large crack snaking across the windshield. There is swearing, and groaning.

Henry opens and closes his eyes several times, feels the pain in his chest caused by the steering wheel. He's lying against the car door, on top of his arm, which aches, but he's alive. He's alive, and he can at least move his arms and legs, he thinks, so it cannot be too serious. Now it's just a question of saving face. It is not the time to think about what will happen when he shows the wrecked vehicle to his uncle, he cannot think about that now, because then everything will unravel; now he has to act like nothing happened. He turns his head, looks at the friend in the seat beside him, with shards of glass in his lap and the folds of his jacket. The boy holds his hands to his bleeding face.

"Now then. Any signs of life back there?" he asks, making sure his voice sounds totally unaffected, as tough as always. But he gets no reply other than a few wordless whimpers and groans.

"Well, I'll be damned. There'll be no rabbit pie after all," Henry mumbles, rolling down the window. Luckily the door isn't damaged, so he manages to open it all the way and crawl out. The boy sitting beside him follows him, his nose dripping blood onto the door.

Henry stands up and brushes the splinters of glass from his trousers. The two boys in the back seat clamber out too. One of them has his teeth clenched, and holds his forearm as though it's broken.

"That fucking rabbit!" says Henry. "Why did it jump out of the way? Just as I was about to hit it?"

The other boys give him a dubious look.

"Well, don't just stand there gawking!" Henry shouts. "Help me to get this cart back on the road!"

He walks over to the driver's side and grabs hold of the metal. The others wander groggily toward the trunk and stand there in single file. There is a servile look in their eyes, as though they are unable to do anything unless Henry asks them. They push when he tells them to push, they wait when he orders them to, and they push even harder when Henry shouts at them to roll the car up the embankment again, until they finally get back on the road.

Everyone gets in. It is quiet. The engine starts. Henry turns around, demanding their full attention, because if any of them tell the owner of the shop what led to the crash, he will lose his job, and that means he'll never be able to borrow the car again, and then he'll end up being left out again.

"Listen. I'm going to tell you what just happened," Henry says in a quiet voice, making sure everyone is listening closely. "There was no rabbit. There has NEVER BEEN a rabbit. Right?"

"What do you mean?" one of them asks, and Henry gives him a hard stare, like the heroes always do in the films he has seen—when they take control of the situation.

"Here's what happened," he says. "There was another car, and it came right at us. Way too fast. So fast that we saw nothing but dazzling lights. A maniac who forced us off the road and didn't stop, even though he must have seen that we ended up in a ditch. That is what you will say. Is that understood?" he asks.

They look up at him confused, as if it was difficult to grasp. "Is that understood, I said?" Henry repeats himself, louder this time, and everyone nods, replying, "Yes, Henry Oliver" in stammering voices.

No one dares to stand up to him. It's quite incredible, he thinks, all the bravado and manliness gone from their faces. Suddenly they are no more than terrified kids standing before their father.

D for the dew, clinging to the grass one morning outside the prison camp, making the ground sparkle in the sunlight.

D for the date January 12, 1942, and for the drama in Marie Komissar's voice when she calls Gerson on the phone. The trembling seriousness when she says the words that change everything: "They've taken your father!"

E

×   ×   ×

E for execution.

E for emblem.

E for the *Electricity Department* logo, embossed on the plastic phone that Gerson sits hunched over, in a cabin outside Trondheim, January 12, 1942.

    Gerson, wearing a wool sweater and knickerbockers, sits in the living room surrounded by friends. They are all students, all unattached, and the room is full of laughter, cigarette smoke hovering in the air above sweaty anoraks, and sexually charged looks on their faces. At least, the room was filled with all this before the telephone in the hall began ringing, and the friend that owned the cabin suddenly called out for Gerson because the call was for him. It was all absurd: that the family had even installed a telephone line there at the cabin; and that it had rung, cutting through the conversation, and worse still—that the phone call turned out to be for him. Why would anyone try to contact him here?

"They've taken your father!" his mother whispers into the mouth-piece. The words don't quite sink in, just confuse him, leaving him staring silently at the telephone. On the floor beside him stand dozens of boots, with black plastic ski bindings poking out from the toes, like the bills on a family of platypuses. Clumps of ice, still clinging to the bootlaces, starting to melt.

"Gerson, are you there?"

"Yes, I'm here . . . When was this?"

"This afternoon! They called him in for questioning at the Mission Hotel . . ."

"Why? What for?"

"I don't know . . . We should never have come back from Sweden!" his mother replies. He can hear that she's about to cry.

The door to the cabin opens and one of Gerson's friends comes in with a bucket of snow for them to melt, and a broad smile that vanishes when he notices the silence in the room.

"Can't he just run away?" Gerson asks quietly.

"No. He won't. Not while I'm in the hospital! And because of you children," she says. Gerson hears her welling up.

"Does Jacob know?"

"Yes, he's totally beside himself. Your father has spoken to him."

He hears his mother turn the phone away from her mouth to hide the sobbing.

"I'll come right away!" says Gerson. He hangs up, and sees the grave and questioning looks on everyone's faces.

"What's going on?" asks one of them.

Gerson stands up, with his hand still on the telephone. A wave of heat runs through him, prickling his cheeks.

"The Germans have taken my father."

"Why?" asks a blonde-haired girl.

"I don't know . . . I have to go home. I'm sorry."

Gerson stuffs his clothes hurriedly into his bag, and notices how the looks from his friends have changed: from joy and laughter, to pity, shame, and confusion. He gets the feeling they're looking forward to him leaving, because even though they feel sorry for him, there's something that makes them wish he was gone. Suddenly his whole presence has brought back the darkness and seriousness from which they've come here to escape.

I should have known, thinks Gerson as he stuffs the last sweater into his bag and ties up his boots. *They should have all known that this would happen sooner or later,* he thinks, before standing up, hugging the girls, and shaking hands with his friends while thanking them for the trip. His friend, the one who had borrowed the cabin, says he will drive him into town.

Gerson carries his bag and his skis out to the car and sits quietly as they drive into Trondheim, resting his forehead on the cold windowpane, thinking about their fateful decision to return to Norway, in 1940. The family had managed to escape to Sweden when Norway was invaded, had immediately packed their belongings, driven as fast as they could to the railway station, and abandoned their cars, crossing the border on the last train to leave before the checkpoints started. But time had passed, and after a while Gerson's family heard that it was safe to return; that it was possible to carry on as before, as long as you kept your head down. So they had returned to Trondheim, to their apartment, and to a normal life. Everyone except his sister, Lillemor. If only they had stayed there with her!

Gerson opens his eyes and looks out at the landscape, the fresh snowfall twinkling in the sunlight. A neat trail of rabbit tracks cuts across a snow-covered field, like a line of stitching across a gigantic sheet.

His friend drops him off on the curb outside his parents' shop and he sees German soldiers through the windows. His mother, who has been discharged from hospital, even though she cannot stand up without a walking aid, gives him a long hug. One of the uniformed men tells Gerson that his room has been searched and that they are bringing him in for questioning. As they bundle him into a car, his mother calls something out to him that he doesn't quite catch. Where are they taking him? He imagines a prison, or a prison camp, while the car makes its way through the city center and eventually stops in front of a building now used as the Gestapo offices. The Mission Hotel.

The soldiers shove him through the doors, into a maelstrom of soldiers, captive Norwegians, and makeshift beds.

From among all this a young man appears, dressed in boots and jodhpurs, a short guy who strides past all the functionaries and addresses himself directly to the commander. Gerson's attention is initially drawn to the man's diminutive height, the intense look on his face, and the fact that his head is too big for his body. But what he will later recall most vividly is his accent. The man's German is full of grammatical errors, and he speaks with a clear Trondheim accent. He is Norwegian.

E for the excitable gang of fresh-faced boys, walking about on the outskirts of Levanger, past neatly kept picket fences, warm yellow light in the windows, and gnarled old trees heaving with fruit. Henry leads the way.

"Here," whispers one of them, nodding toward a garden where a huge tree stands, laden with apples.

"Perfect, I'll keep a lookout," replies Henry, pulling a gun from his inside pocket and turning it from side to side. The others lean over to take a look.

"A gun?" whispers one of them. "Have you got a *gun*?" he asks. The other boys glance quickly at each other in an attempt to gauge the situation.

"What does it look like?" sniggers Henry. "Now get over the fence!" His friends do as they're told, scaling the fence clumsily, trying not to get snagged on their trousers, then vanish into the darkness of the trees. It is a totally silent, totally dark August night, with nobody about. The whole thing is like a scene from a film. What if they weren't just pilfering apples, thinks Henry, the excitement pulsing through his veins and around his body. What if this wasn't a boring little street in Levanger, but a city in America? Like New York, or Chicago? Then they wouldn't just be raiding someone's garden, they would be robbing a federal bank. They would have hidden their faces behind carnival masks or balaclavas, covering everything but their eyes; and in low voices told the staff behind the counter to hand over the money and to stay away from the alarm button.

Henry watches the silhouettes of his friends under the treetops: tugging on the apples that cling stubbornly to each twig, causing the branches to shudder. Then a window opens, and a man leans out.

"Hey! What do you think you're doing?" he shouts, at which point Henry raises his gun and instinctively fires two shots into the air. He feels it recoil through his arm like a snake biting his hand. Two loud cracks that echo through the streets. The other boys jump, so frightened that they drop the apples, which end up rolling down the road. Henry picks one up, as the adrenaline pounds through him, and runs, around corner after corner, until they reach safety. They all stop and pause for breath.

"Where did you get hold of that?" asks one of them nervously, nodding toward the weapon.

"What makes you think I'm going to tell you?" replies Henry, chomping on the apple, staring intensely at the boy, and grinding the flesh between his teeth. A second goes by. Then another, but the boy doesn't reply, clearly lacking the nerve. And when Henry sees the fear and uncertainty on the boy's face he feels a swell of pleasure, because there is a different look in his eyes now.

A look of admiration, or respect.

Henry's confidence grows over the following weeks; he behaves differently and appears more outgoing than before. Somehow it must show, radiate from him, and make him more attractive, because soon after this incident he meets Klara.

The woman who, for a short while, changes everything.

E for everyday life at the prison camp, when you are woken at five a.m. by the shouts from the guards. When you pull on your prison clothes as fast as you can, eat some bread and drink coffee substitute before walking single file with the others into the yard for the morning roll call and division into work groups. If you are lucky, you might be put to work in the carpentry shed where you'll stay indoors amid an atmosphere of friendly humming and the fresh smell of wood shavings and sawdust. If you are less lucky, you'll be sent to the quarry, or the forest, to smash rocks with a hammer, or dig up enormous tree roots and saw them up for no apparent reason.

E for the everyday taste of soup for dinner, with pieces of turnip or potato swimming about in the gray water.

E for the everyday screams from the yard outside, whenever someone is beaten or forced to crawl on all fours during punishment exercise, until they lie motionless, unable to take any more.

E for Ellen Komissar, as she and Gerson finally drive along Trondheim's narrow streets, with Jannicke sleeping again on her lap. The car always seems to act like a mechanical cradle, she thinks, the hum of the engine lulls the little two-year-old to sleep the moment it starts. Ellen turns to look out at the charming little wooden houses—crooked and strange, like theater scenery almost, or doll's houses—and begins to look forward to starting anew. They never managed to find themselves a proper life in Oslo, but they can start one here, and she's excited about seeing the shop again, and about trying on the clothes that Marie imports. Now she can be one of those self-assured people walking about in clothes from France and Germany and Italy. Her attention returns to the road, and she leans on the seat in front to see where they're going, Jannicke's head pressing against her tummy. She points at a side street.

"Isn't it just here?" she asks.

Gerson looks clearly uncomfortable, leaning forward rigidly and gripping the steering wheel far too tightly, his eyes darting left and right.

"Is it?" he asks, sounding flustered and almost driving right past. It's so typical of him, thinks Ellen. So typical to think she doesn't know anything; that she can't contribute to anything.

"Yes, look! Nordre Gate. It's down there!" she says. Gerson swears, she can see him sweating, he tries to change gear but moves far too quickly. Another car has come up behind them, and he grinds the gears between the cogs. The transmission screeches loudly, and wakes Jannicke who immediately starts whimpering as though reacting to the tense atmosphere.

Gerson snatches the gearshift again and jerks it far too hard, forcing the car into reverse. He turns to look past Ellen's head and starts backing up, way too fast, with the other car still behind them.

"Gerson!" Ellen shouts as they race toward the car. She sees a man staring bewilderedly at them before Gerson shifts gears again and pulls into the side street. They both fall silent. Ellen sees the look on Jannicke's face, takes hold of her hand, and tries to give her a reassuring smile.

Gerson parks right outside Paris-Vienna's large display windows, overlooking the street corner, while Ellen balances Jannicke on her lap and points.

"Look," she says, "there's Grandma's shop! Let's go in and look at the dresses." Jannicke looks up with large, sparkling eyes. Ellen feels her daughter's arms around her neck.

She opens the car door, while Gerson takes out his cigarette lighter, and together they walk over to the shop. Suddenly the door opens and out comes Marie, in a wide-brimmed hat with a silk band, a light blouse with lace trim tucked into her waistband, and a hip-hugging black skirt. She raises her hand and gives an elegant little wave. There's always this air of perfection and aristocracy about her, thinks Ellen, brushing the fluff from her blouse. "Welcome to Trondheim!" she says, giving Ellen a hug and then turning to Jannicke. "And look at you!" she says, but Jannicke simply turns her head away indifferently, enough for Marie to abandon her attempt to communicate with the child and look at Ellen instead.

"So, how was the trip?" she asks, while turning to the door and opening it without waiting for a reply. "It's so nice that you're here!"

Ellen looks at Gerson and gives him a little shake of the head, but he doesn't seem to understand what she means, so accustomed to his mother's quirks that he no longer notices. They enter the shop, and Ellen decides to put both the journey and her mother-in-law's lack of interest aside, because the shop is truly fantastic. She walks over to the clothes racks and runs her fingers across the fabrics. Silk, chiffon, wool—beautiful shiny buttons. It's like a treasure chamber. Finally Gerson has a job, with a regular income. It might just be worth the price of moving from Oslo, away from her parents and her twin sister. The two of them have always lived in the same place, done the same things, and shared everything; they have never been apart for more than a few hours. Now they will be in separate cities.

"Here," says Marie, grabbing a bottle of port and three small glasses from under the counter. "We must celebrate!" she says, handing them their drinks.

"Thank you, Mother," says Gerson, taking his glass and then looking at Ellen as if waiting for permission to drink. They clink glasses, and she too takes a sip. She feels the instant warmth running through her body and has to let go of Jannicke, who is prying herself from her mother's hips in an attempt to get down to the floor.

"Yes! Can you believe it, we're here!" says Ellen. "With our daughter, and a job, and soon a house!" she says, but notices something going on with Gerson, who is is blinking fast and biting his lips.

"Yes, we're very lucky," he says, his voice sounding a little too flat.

"You really are," says Marie, her little glass chiming as she places it on the counter. "Of course, it helped that so few others wanted to move into the house . . . considering its history."

Ellen looks confusedly at Gerson. *Considering its history?*

"But the good thing about it is that you're really getting your money's worth," she says.

"What do you mean?" Ellen asks.

Marie looks confusedly at Gerson for a moment.

"But . . . haven't you said anything?" she asks him.

"Said what?" asks Ellen.

"About the history of the house?"

Jannicke crawls across the floor straight toward a clothes rack loaded with dresses, so Ellen has to race after her and pick her up.

"What about the history of the house?" she asks Gerson, currently looking down at his glass of port while twirling the stem between his fingers.

"Yes, well, there was a reason that we got the place so cheap," he says.

"And what was that?" asks Ellen. "Is it in bad shape? Has something happened?"

"The house was used as Henry Rinnan's headquarters during the war," says Marie.

Ellen feels the hairs prick up on her arms. She also has to struggle with Jannicke, who is trying to clamber her way back down to the floor and continue her expedition.

"Henry Rinnan?" she asks. "Is that where they did their . . . ? Are we . . . are we going to live in the Rinnan Gang's house?"

"Yes. But, my dear Ellen," says Marie with a smile, "how else do you think you could have afforded a detached house with a garden in a neighborhood like Upper Singsaker?"

×

E for elastic bands, kitchen essentials, and household ephemera, stacked in boxes along the walls of the house during the first few days, as if acclimatizing themselves to their new home, before daring to sneak from their boxes and find their places.

E for the energy, squeezed out of you by the forced labor in the prison camp, little by little, until you feel the urge to give up, and just lie on the ground with your cheek up against the dust, the pine needles, and the smell of soil. Just lie there and finally relax every muscle, close your eyes, and not worry about the guard screaming at you. Not worry about the boots kicking you in the ribs, or your fellow prisoners trying to lift you up again. Just lie there wanting to sink into the earth and become one with it, accept that death is not something to run from, but rather something to welcome with open arms, since death is the fastest and the only sure way out of here.

F

× × ×

F for fellow.

F for follow.

F for felon.

F for fence.

F for forced labor and for fatigue.

F for the fear that still exists to this very day, and for fascism that continues to grow, like a tumor within society.

F for fate.

F for firing squad.

×

F for Falstad. It is a mild October afternoon, and I am being driven by taxi from the railway station an hour north of Trondheim. There are fields left and right, and the narrow country lane has dashed lines on either side as though a giant, brandishing a pair of scissors, might come and snip it from the landscape.

I see a brown road sign, bearing the international symbol for *place of interest:* a looped square with corners that turn back on themselves, just as history turns back on itself and repeats the same patterns and motifs. Love, joy, fear, hate. Desire, possession, sickness, birth.

Then it appears.

A two-story building, with yellow walls around a walled courtyard, an arched entrance with a clock tower above. A beautiful building originally designed as a school for the mentally impaired, far away from the nearest town.

I recognize the tree in the courtyard from online photos and documentary books. An old birch, with yellowing leaves now, many of which have already fallen to the ground. The very same tree that you walked by, that cold October morning when you were forced to walk through the gate and out to the road, toward the marshy forest nearby, the last morning of your life.

The birch tree stood in silence. The sun rose over the landscape, penetrating the golden leaves, causing the dewdrops to sparkle and the bark to go brittle. The shadow of the birch tree creeping slowly across the square like the hour hand on a clock, until darkness fell upon the landscape, swallowing everything it came across.

A few hours later a new group of prisoners was led through the gate. Some of them stared dead ahead to avoid provoking the guards; others looked around trying to figure out what sort of place they had been brought to. One of them was Julius Paltiel, a young man who would later marry into the Komissar family after Jacob and Vera Komissar were divorced. In one of the books he and Vera

Komissar wrote together, Julius Paltiel recalls an episode by this tree in the square. It was October 1942, just after you were killed, and Julius was out in the yard with several other inmates when one of the German soldiers ordered them to remove the leaves from the ground.

"Are there any rakes?" asked one of the inmates. And the German soldier just laughed at them, forced them onto their hands and knees, and told them to move the leaves with their mouths. Julius Paltiel had to crawl across the square, bury his face in the leaves, and feel the sickening taste of half-composted mulch on his tongue. All while maintaining a look of concentration. He turned his head. Spat out the leaves. Crawled back, and then buried his head in the earth again.

Julius Paltiel survived his detention at Falstad and was sent to Oslo, where he was put on a train heading south, bound for the concentration camps.

He survived the train journey through Europe.

He survived the three years in Auschwitz and the death march through Czechoslovakia to Buchenwald. He and a few others hid when the other Jews were shot; he felt the disappointment at not being released with the other prisoners in March 1945, and had to wait for the U.S. forces to rescue them in May.

I met him more than fifty years later at a dinner at Gerson's house, and what really struck me was the man's composure. One of the very few people to return alive, he was not a broken and bitter man who cursed life for all the suffering he had endured; quite the opposite: here was a person with a rare calmness in all that he said and did.

Julius Paltiel sat quietly, spoke quietly and friendly, with his sleeves rolled up so that the amateurish tattoo of his Auschwitz prisoner number was visible. It still seemed like the whole man was shining.

Standing on the second floor of Falstad, looking out of the window at the birch tree below, I picture his face once again. The friendliness of someone who has been hardened, over and over again, until only the most basic part of humanity is left. What makes some grow stronger from such adversity and evil, while others break down, demoralized, crippled, destroyed?

Does it depend on what you're already made of? Your early childhood experiences? Is it the sense of being loved, cemented at the core of your personality—versus a feeling of cold? What about Rinnan's siblings? Only two of them stood by him.

Rinnan did actually confess to one of his brothers while they were driving, telling him that the Germans had hired him as a spy, but when he offered his brother a job, working alongside him, his brother simply asked Henry to stop the car, and got out and walked all the way back to Levanger.

The man guiding me around Falstad comes out of his office holding his car keys and asks if I'm ready to see the monument, which was erected at the spot where the prisoners were shot. We set off, driving along a dirt track through the woods until we reach the graves: pyramid-shaped stones poking up from the heather. A large shell-shaped rock sits on the forest floor, inscribed with the names of those who were killed. Tiny leaves obscure some of the names but I find yours almost immediately. I run my finger over it, close my eyes, and try to picture the scene on that morning long ago. Picture you standing here, right here. My guide from Falstad points out the stone marking the spot where you were first buried. I take some photos. We barely speak to each other as we walk back to the car. I thank the man and go on my way.

My next appointment is with the current owner of "the Gang Monastery"—and this time I'll be going inside.

F for Flesch, pronounced *flesh*, and also the surname of the new security chief for central Norway. You saw this bureaucrat several times while you were imprisoned at Falstad, and you always noticed how the soldiers around Gerhard Flesch became both more nervous and tougher. Transformed into stricter and more brusque versions of themselves, afraid of what the officer would do to them if they showed any sign of weakness or compassion. The man had the general appearance of a functionary, thin hair and clear, friendly eyes quite at odds with his behavior, which included random kicks, punches—and summary executions, which had most recently taken place earlier that morning, one day before you too were killed.

F for fine weather. F for fruit trees in Jonsvannsveien. Wizened old trees that reach across the picket fence, with green leaves and white blossoms that Ellen knows will disappear in a few days.

"Look!" says Gerson eagerly. "All these apple and plum trees! Don't you think we'll love it here?" he says, addressing his daughter up on his shoulders, but Ellen realizes this rhetorical question is actually directed at *her*, and she nods. "I'm sure we will," she replies, and she means it too, because the garden really is beautiful. Large, and full of fruit trees and red currant bushes. It is very different from what they had in Oslo. The villa itself—perched so nicely on the hill, in such an upmarket neighborhood—will also be theirs. A relatively low structure built, bungalow-style, in an L shape around a conservatory where a long dining table sits decked with vases full of flowers. Poking out from the roof, sloping up from the ground floor, is the arched window Ellen recognizes from the photos Marie had sent. The very same window she remembers from Rinnan's trial. But she can't think about that now, she has to pull herself together, she thinks, while looking up at her daughter; at how content she is sitting up on her father's shoulders; how her whole face with her large cheeks lights up when she looks at the garden. She points with her sweet little hand and says: "Tree!"

Ellen glances at the cellar windows and instantly feels a whirl of thoughts fighting to get in. She turns to look at her daughter instead.

"Yep! We're going to be happy as clams here!" she says, while smiling at Gerson, and stroking her thumb and forefinger over Jannicke's soft little hand. They are so incredibly privileged. She has to keep that in mind. Nothing else.

She cannot dwell on the house's history, because Gerson is quite right: it has already been used as a kindergarten for two years, any unpleasantness will have been swept out, and the building reborn as a family home. So instead of picturing barbed wire around the house, and prisoners being dragged from cars and inside to be interrogated, she must focus on the *other* history. The one about the little children running in the garden and crawling up the stairs, one step at time, with chubby thighs and sweet little curls on their heads. It is *them* she must focus on, pull herself together and remember how lucky they are, because they really are lucky. She has met a wonderful man, she is moving into a detached house, and her entire family has survived the war losing nothing more than their wealth. For other Jewish families, empty apartments are all that remains. Entire families wiped out, reduced to names only mentioned at the synagogue or when you meet an old friend and ask about mutual acquaintances. How did it go with him or her? *How many of them made it?* you might ask, and watch the nervousness on the person's face, as they blink perhaps, or suddenly begin scratching their neck before replying that everyone is gone. And you must never ask about the little ones, as Ellen has learned, one must never ask about the children, about the two-year-olds and the four-year-olds and the seven-year-olds. Because they are gone too.

She is lucky. They are lucky. To get away, to escape being killed, like Gerson's father and Marie's brother. They are lucky, says Ellen to herself, again and again. But she just can't shake the feeling that something isn't right. A shiver runs through her as they enter the garden. *Did you know that they tortured hundreds of people in these rooms?*

F for Ford.

F for factory.

×

F for fanaticism.

F for family, for Marie and Jacob, who sometimes visit you in Falstad that spring, just as many of the other prisoners get visits from their loved ones. And even though you feel joy and relief at seeing them both alive and well, there is something else overshadowing the joy as you stand there, on opposite sides of the fence. It is the shame of wearing prison clothes, being unkempt, so exhausted and worn out. It is almost as if you don't want to hold their hands through the metal wire of the fence and touch the soft skin, because you don't recognize yourself, and from the looks you see in their eyes, neither do they.

F for the poverty-stricken farmlands of 1920s Norway. While some of Henry Rinnan's biographies highlight how poor his family was, as does Per Hansson's *Who Was Henry Rinnan,* there are others who raise doubts about this claim and say the opposite; that the 1920s and '30s were of course hard times, but that Rinnan's family were no worse off than most. They were poor, perhaps, and there were many children; but they lived in a house in the middle of town, and his father had his own business. Rinnan's uncle ran a hardware store where he also sold cars, and even opened his own gas station. Henry's grandparents owned a farm just outside of town, and as some have pointed out, this meant they must have been able to go there to get meat and vegetables if they got in a pinch at home. None of this suggests that Henry Oliver Rinnan suffered more than anyone else. And as for the incident with the ladies' shoes—as recalled by Rinnan's teacher in an interview—it's not hard to imagine how this may have resulted from a single decision, one chaotic morning, in a young family. How many parents have not found themselves in a similar bind, where yesterday's gloves lie wet in the child's ruck-sack, sealed in a plastic bag by the kindergarten staff, forcing you to find something else to keep their little fingers warm? Gloves that are far too big perhaps, or you might tell the child to pull its hands up into its coat sleeves.

F for filters and fenders and fan belts. Spanners and screws, bolts and tubes. Henry learns it all while bent over the hood of the Ford. Disappearing into the workshop to repair it whenever he can, fascinated at how all of its parts work together—and his pride swells with each smile from his uncle.

"Great job!" he would say as Henry emerged from under the hood, covered in oil and dirt, and he knew that it was true. That this was something he could master.

G

× × ×

G for Granada. The city in the mountains of Spain. In 1066 it would have been several days' march to reach it from the sea. It was here that one of the first known pogroms took place after the persecution of Jews by the Roman Empire. This year around four thousand Jews were abused, attacked, and killed by the Moors, heralding the start of a history of persecution.

G for your grip on the spade handle which gnaws at the hollow between your thumb and forefinger, while you lift the spade, again and again, clearing the soil from the tree roots in Falstad forest. The blue-pink blisters on your hands burst after a few days, leaving flaps of dead skin over raw stinging flesh.

G for the goodwill from some of the prison guards. Those who turn a blind eye to the smuggled letters and food, and look the other way when these violations are discovered. Just as a child gets a sense of which adults it can fool with and which ones are strict, you too develop a way of interpreting the tiny variations in the guards' mood and tone. You come to recognize which soldiers are there by their own will and conviction, and which are just doing their duty; just wearing a uniform that could easily have been a doctor's coat or a priest's robes. You hear a story of this goodwill from a fellow prisoner who, with a smile on his face, tells you about a gift from a nearby farm that slipped out of the garment it was hidden in, just as the prisoner walked through the gate after finishing work. A bottle of milk and some cured meat suddenly lying on the ground, in full view. The guard gave him a friendly smile before looking away for a few seconds, just long enough for the man to bend down and conceal the food.

G for Grete. "What do I remember? I remember the garden where there was a climbing frame to play on. Jannicke and I shared a room next to the kitchen, and I remember the room with the arched window upstairs. Mother would lie down up there whenever she had a migraine, and we would have to stay quiet and stay out. I remember that Jannicke and I had a secret society up in the loft, and that Jannicke found remnants from the war up there. But she can tell you about that. I remember that we had theater performances in the cellar, and that I stood at the top of the stairs handing out tickets. Otherwise I don't remember that much, but for me there is no doubt: Mother was broken by that house."

G for gravestones in the Jewish cemetery in Sofienberg, Oslo, near the house where Rikke lived when we first met. Much of the original cemetery was made into a park where the living now sit sunbathing, or push strollers, or balance on tightropes between the trees, presumably oblivious to the bones lying just beneath them. The only part remaining is the tiny Jewish cemetery on the corner.

I already knew that Jewish gravestones should never be removed, since their names must not be erased. Rikke had told me this when we visited the Jewish cemetery in Prague, which looked like an overgrown forest, full of gray and black stones covered in names. Some of those buried in Prague had died hundreds of years ago, but the gravestones in Oslo were considerably more recent and considerably smaller. Rikke once told me that seeing the Sofienberg cemetery was a reminder of her family history, since many of those lying there had names she had heard in conversations. The Dworskys were there, as were the Kleines. Names that had popped up occasionally at dinner with her grandfather Gerson or in books about Norwegian Jews. As we passed the cemetery that afternoon, almost twenty years ago, we noticed that many of the gravestones had been toppled, clearly on purpose. Rikke was so upset that she immediately wanted to straighten them up. I followed her in, conscious that I was doing something forbidden, and remember looking around nervously before trying to undo the vandalism. We gripped our fingers round the cold wet stone and attempted to lift it with all our strength, but it was far too heavy, and we were forced to move on, leaving the names lying facedown on the earth.

G for Gestapo, for genocide. All those who will be murdered must be dehumanized first. Differences in fashion tastes and style must be done away with: away with blue velvet blazers and favorite shirts with pinstripes and white buttons; away with wristwatches and leather shoes; away with floaty summer dresses and flowery blouses, pearl necklaces and sparkling rings.

Then the haircuts: away with bangs hanging just over the eyes, that can be swept aside by a subtle flick of the head; away with plaits and ponytails and curls, fastened at the back with bobby pins; away with bushy mustaches that poke out stiffly from the cheeks, and away with beards that rest softly on the chin, and which sometimes collect breadcrumbs, or a drop of sauce which a wife might lean forward and brush off with a handkerchief.

All traces of a personality must be taken away, to stop the executioner from seeing himself in his victims. It is the distance required. Otherwise the deed would be almost impossible, like attacking your own reflection.

When the transformation is complete, prisoners can be rounded up, weeded out, and killed. Without compassion and in a tidy, orderly manner, as one might go about exterminating rats that have multiplied in the city and are spreading disease, filth, and worry.

G for Gerson. The mood in 1930s Trondheim gradually dehumanizes him, and by the start of the war he finds himself excluded from a growing number of categories. He is no longer a Norwegian. No longer a student. No longer a Trondheimer, a drummer, a jazz enthusiast, student, mathematician, son, or brother. He is a Jew. And as a Jew he is suspicious. The same goes for his brother, Jacob, and his mother, Marie. When their apartment is raided, the soldiers find photos of Aryan girls on Gerson's desk, and summon him for questioning to confront him with the pictures. They tell him to stay well away from Norwegian girls if he wants to avoid ending up at Falstad with his father. Then they release him.

The family agrees that it is best if Gerson moves to Oslo and tries to rebuild his life there. Soon he is forced to give up his studies as the family savings have been confiscated by the authorities.

Gerson calls on a friend of his father and gets a job as an accountant. Several men, arrested on the same charges as his father, are executed. Marie's brother is one of them. Time goes by. The family apartment is also confiscated. Jacob has to move in with another Jewish family, and Marie moves to a boardinghouse. Soon Jacob hears rumors that they are under surveillance, and both his mother and his brother decide to move to the capital. Spring comes. Summer comes. It is 1942, and Gerson hears tiny snippets about what is happening to you: that you have been sent to northern Norway as an interpreter for Russian prisoners, who are building snow barriers by the road.

In a folder of typewritten papers, Gerson has written about his childhood and about the sudden change of conditions in Norway. The thing that turned everything on its head:

> In spring 1942, the situation was relatively calm. At that time, the total number of Jews arrested was negligible, but the synagogue in Trondheim had been seized by the Germans, misused and converted into an army dormitory. There were a number of incidents that suggested the German authorities in Trondheim were in the process of planning a more systematic campaign. [. . .]
>
> Then, on October 8th, came the shock.

On that day in 1942, the newspaper normally lying outside Gerson's bedroom isn't there. He gets dressed and hears his landlady crying in the kitchen. He knocks and opens the door, as she stands at the kitchen table with the newspaper between her hands and a grave look on her face.

The news article says that you were executed at Falstad, the day before, along with nine others. It says that you are one of ten men shot in retaliation for the campaign of sabotage by the resistance, which had recently bombed and destroyed railway lines, cutting the ore supply to the German weapons industry. The newspaper calls the ten men victims of "forced atonement."

Gerson's landlady puts her hand on his shoulder, and his eyes begin to sting, he feels a knot in his stomach and a strange numbness spreading through his body. He has to get out of the country again. His brother and his mother too. As quickly as possible. With his hands shaking, he packs his things and calls Jacob. He asks his brother to meet him, right away, unable to speak without sobbing, as though his voice needs more air to function. He gets a tearful hug from his landlady and then he sneaks out.

For several days Gerson and Jacob live at a safe house, but the atmosphere is tense as the Germans could arrive at the door at any moment. Eventually the man of the house tells them about a better place to hide: at the home of a widow in the city center. Gerson starts laughing when they are told the address and assumes that the man is joking, but it's no joke. They will be the closest neighbors to Victoria Terrasse: the Nazi headquarters in Oslo.

G for the greenhouse in Oslo, where Jewish families and resistance members would show up each day and hide among the foliage. Waiting, while their escape to Sweden was organized by members of a group called Carl Fredriksens Transport.

It began on October 7, 1942, when Rolf Syversen was walking around the huge greenhouse at his nursery near Carl Berners Plass. Strolling between the rows of potted plants and vases, until he noticed something moving behind one of the crates. What was it? An animal? Had someone broken in?

It turned out to be four brothers, four Jewish brothers, who ran a nearby shop, and who were now on the run after hearing that the police were under orders to arrest all the Jewish men in the city. The gardener recognized the men and contacted some friends, one of whom owned a trucking company, and between them they arranged for a truck to come and smuggle the men into Sweden. *But weren't there others trying to escape?*

The brothers quickly provided more names of others who needed help crossing the border, and the group began contacting them. No sooner was the first truckload on its way to the border than the four of them were busy planning the next transport.

The rest is history. Over the following six weeks these four Norwegians saved approximately one thousand men, women, and children from execution or deportation.

One of them was Ellen Komissar.

One of the others was your wife, Marie.

One thousand people, both Jews and resistance members and their families. How many descendants do they have today? All those who would never have existed had no one risked their lives for the refugees, all those who would never have existed had Sweden closed its borders and deported the families again. And how many people were never born because of the Holocaust? When the concentration camps were liberated seventy-five years ago, and the graves were exhumed, the surviving families were left with only crumbs of the lives they once lived. How many descendants would there now be in Europe had the six million Jews *not* been killed? Fifty million? More?

In January 2017 the four Norwegians who ran and led Carl Fredriksens Transport were commemorated with the Righteous Among the Nations award at a grand ceremony in Oslo's city hall. And since Rikke's family had been among the survivors, we received an official invitation in the mail. That night we passed the security guards and through one of the huge doors, into the main hall, where we sat with hundreds of others, many of them elderly, and many of the children wearing kippahs, something I would otherwise never see. I recognized some of the older people there, because prior to the award ceremony I had been on a reconstruction of the historic escape, along with some of those who had originally made the journey across the border, and some who were the children of those who reached safety before the transportation began.

It was a remarkably mild January; the sun shone gloriously upon the landscape, and I had managed to get a seat in a car with some members of the Mendelsohn family, whose parents had been transported to Sweden. The driver was a family friend, a history enthusiast, who had picked me up at Carl Berners Plass, where the evacuation had begun. We followed the original route, starting at the original location of the nursery, then driving east out of Oslo, through the green landscape of fields and across a wide river, where wooden posts stuck up from the water in the morning light, amplifying the silence; almost magical, manmade objects that no longer have any function other than to just stand there, silent and alone. We drove by the bridge that the trucks had to pass, where German soldiers had once stood, and entered the forest, onto a narrow road where the ice had grown thick in the shadow of the pine trees. Finally we parked our car and met two others who had also come to walk across the border. One of them was Freddie Malkowitz, a small seventy-eight-year-old man with gray hair and a friendly demeanor. The road was so slippery we had to walk down the middle, where spinning car tires hadn't polished the ice; and while we trudged onward, Freddie told us about his escape. He was four years old at the time, and remembers being loaded all the way into the back of the truck, just behind the driver's cab, with his mother beside him, packed in with people he didn't know. A tarpaulin formed a roof over their heads, stopping anyone from looking in from the side and preventing them from being discovered. He told us about the silence, about how they had been told to not say a single word, not even whisper, until they were in Sweden. "There was no sound at all under the tarpaulin," he said. "Nothing but the hum of the engine, the smell of the wood chips used as fuel instead of gasoline, and the straining of bodies as they squashed against each other on the bends."

Suddenly the truck stopped. Freddie could smell burning. Then the tarpaulin was pulled back, and he heard voices shouting in German and Norwegian. He had no idea what was happening at the time, but one of the bags of wood chips had caught fire, and Alf Pettersen was climbing hurriedly onto the roof to drag the burning sack off. He had then given a Nazi salute to the guards blocking the road and shouted at them; telling them to help extinguish the fire instead of standing there staring. "He must have looked very convincing, because the guards instantly grabbed the burning sack and began throwing armfuls of snow at it, so focused on their task that the truck was able to drive off," Freddie said, smiling.

We came to a clearing where a five-meter-wide strip had been cut through the forest. And beside the road an old sign that said "Swedish Border," written in black on a yellow background.

The five of us stood there looking around, and Freddie ended his story by saying that he had been startled by someone shouting with joy once they reached the Swedish side of the border.

"We'd been told to stay absolutely silent, you see," he said with a little smile on his lips. "And when you're a child, you take these things totally seriously, so I was really quite upset at first, when the Swedes on the other side called out: '*Welcome to Sweden.*'"

He chuckled a little as he recounted this part, just as he did during the interview shown on the large screen in Oslo's city hall later that evening at the award ceremony. The Norwegian prime minister had given a speech, and shortly afterward a hunched old lady was led onto the stage by her daughter. She walked over to the podium and gripped it with both hands. Then she leaned toward the microphone and looked out at the packed room.

"I am Gerd," said the old lady, in a loud and clear voice. Sitting in the first row was the prime minister, the Israeli ambassador, and those who had survived the war thanks to Carl Fredriksens Transport. At the back—just in front of the cameras and the security guards wearing black suits and earpieces strung up to electronic transmitters—I sat with my family. The children were silent, and my son held my hand.

"I am Gerd," she said once more. "And I was twelve years old when the police came to get me, on November 26, 1942. A Norwegian policeman and a German soldier. They told us we had to come with them, and when my mother asked *where to*, they just said that we had to hurry up, so my mother packed only one bag, and we went outside. We waited a long time for a taxi," she said, gazing steadily across the great hall. "But the taxi was delayed for some reason or other. We drove down to the harbor, where there was a ship, and I was just about to reach for the handle and open the door when a German soldier approached and said: *Zurück!* He said just this one word, *Zurück—Back!*—and when I looked out of the window, I saw that the gangway had been drawn in and the ship was about to set sail. And so, we were driven back to our apartment."

I sat in silence, watching my two children as they took the whole story in. The lady at the podium was the grandmother of a child in my son's class, and must have been roughly the same age as my children on the day she was talking about.

"I should have been on that ship," she continued. "Their plan was to send me off, and then put me on a goods train and transport me to Auschwitz, where they would have sent me straight to the gas chamber and burned my body to ashes. That was their plan. Except our taxi was delayed, and so we didn't go," she said while throwing her arm to the side. A simple arm gesture to indicate the total arbitrariness ruling the lives of every human being.

The assembly room was totally silent. Tears were rolling. I looked at Rikke, who smiled back at me misty-eyed. Had it not been for Carl Fredriksens Transport, she would never have been born.

Gerd quickly left the stage, still alive, but only two hundred yards from the harbor where she should have boarded the *Donau*. She had finally escaped to Sweden, thanks to the four people at Carl Fredriksens Transport who worked day and night that autumn. New lists, new drivers, and new transports of silent people in overcrowded trucks.

But when Carl Fredriksens Transport stopped helping people across the border, it wasn't because of exhaustion or because they were afraid. It was because someone had infiltrated them. A Norwegian, claiming to be a refugee, who had sat through the whole journey before sneaking back over the border into Norway to report on them. Presumably a man with connections to the network of spies run by Henry Oliver Rinnan.

Today the nursery at Carl Berners Plass is gone, replaced by high-rises and row houses, but on a small hill overlooking the road, there is a memorial park—with the wonderfully simple name

"This is a nice place"—created by the Jewish artist Victor Lind, who survived the war thanks to the transports.

If you follow the path up from the road, you end up at a polished memorial stone, shaped like the Star of David, which bears an inscription in memory of those who died. My daughter attends ballet classes nearby, so I am close to this memorial several times a week, and not long ago I suddenly ran into the artist, at one of the most unlikely places: the bottom of an outdoor swimming pool in Oslo's Frognerpark.

It was a cold and clear night, on October 7, 2017—seventy-five years since you were killed, and I was standing at the bottom of the diving pool along with Rikke and our children.

The sixteen-foot-deep pool had been drained for the winter and was now converted to an open-air theater stage. Gone was the warmth from the sun. Gone was the hum of voices and the slapping of small feet on the concrete steps and the dark patches of water on the tiles. Gone were the hands waving from the seven-meter diving board and all the children and youths peering down nervously from the top.

The season was over, and there we were, looking up from the bottom with floodlights pointing up from the sides that made the concrete structure of the diving tower shine bone-white against the dark October sky. The piece being performed was called *The New Human*, and we stood with our heads tilted back, staring up at the four actors, each standing on their own diving platform, each wearing a striking colored bathrobe. Next to us there was an elderly man, seated on his own fold-up chair, and Rikke leant over to me and whispered that he was Victor Lind, the artist behind the memorial at Carl Berners Plass, and that it was his daughter who had written the theater piece.

When the performance at the diving pool ended, I went over to Victor Lind and asked him about his work on the memorial and his reasons for making it.

"They didn't have to do it, you know. It was just a gardener, the owner of a freight company, and a policeman and his wife. They didn't have to do any of it. And one of them even wound up being shot."

I smiled at him. The lights went out. I didn't ask him about his own escape. There was a light drizzle in the air, and we were among the last people left at the bottom of the pool. Behind the ten-meter board—where I had stood many times in my youth but never dared jump from—a star twinkled in the sky.

"They didn't have to do it."

G for the gravel outside the Gang Monastery, and for going into the house for the first time.

If a house is like a body, then the entrance hall is not its face, even though it's the first room one has to walk through. The entrance hall is more like the welcoming handshake, or a first glance, something quite superficial, that still gives an impression of the person, in the same way as the hall of a house gives an impression of who is living there, through the choice of floor tiles and wallpaper, or the smell of curry or meatballs.

The first to walk in the hall of this house were the workers who built it in the 1920s. Wearing boots and tool belts, and blowing smoke from their cigarettes, tiny clouds that evaporated into the air and the walls and the ceilings.

Then come the first owners: the professor and botanist Ralph Tambs-Lyche and his wife, Else Tambs-Lyche. They arrive in the entrance, full of expectation, and peer into the living room before he grasps her hand and shows her the other rooms. This is where they will live. This is where she will run a kindergarten in the cellar while Ralph teaches at the college.

After that, little feet. Little boots, sized 20, 21. Tiny little mittens and coats. Crying babies and laughter. Conversations about the war. About the invasion.

Then, a couple of years later, there is a knock on the door.

Ralph opens the door to find soldiers standing there, with hardened faces and gleaming buttons on their uniforms.

"Are you Ralph Tambs-Lyche?" asks the soldier closest to him in German, taking it for granted that he can reply.

"Ehhh . . . *Ja?*" answers Ralph, who can hear the sound of children laughing in the cellar beneath him and his wife calling to one of them, her voice full of life.

"You have to come with us."

"Why?"

"You are under arrest because of your subversive political views, and your work at the college."

"Oh . . . Can I just let my wife know about this?"

The soldier nods.

"But don't try anything stupid," says the uniformed man, and with a simple arm gesture he sends the rest of the troops around the house. The soldier stands and waits on the porch.

Ralph is driven to Falstad prison camp. His house is confiscated, and Else Tambs-Lyche carries her possessions out through the front door. The key turns and clicks, and the hallway falls silent.

Several months pass. The dust settles on the wooden floor, like sediment descending on the seabed. The little room lights up and falls dark in a pulse, following the rhythm of the sun. Then, one day in 1943, there is the sound of a car engine, there are footsteps on the gravel outside, and the door opens once again. In walks Henry Oliver Rinnan. He rubs his hands together and strides into the living room.

Crates of wine are carried over the threshold. Weapons. Ham. Bread. A bullet from a revolver screams through the hall and hits the wall, splintering the wood. Gang members walk in and out. Prisoners are brought in, dragged through the room with their hands tied behind their backs.

Time passes. Corpses are carried out in wooden boxes, blood drips onto the carpet and seeps into the fibers.

Several years later, in walks Gerson, with his arm round Ellen's waist.

Ellen holds Jannicke in her arms, pauses for a moment.

The beautiful little girl looks up, trying to interpret the hesitation in her mother's eyes. Gerson looks at them both, then reaches out his hand and lifts her up.

"Look, my darling!" says Gerson, smiling. "Look in here!" he says pointing into the living room.

This is where they are going to live.

H

× × ×

H for Hirsch.

H for hope.

H for Henry and his storytelling at the temperance café, and for the hope that the other boys will listen to him this time as well; that they will gather round, sit wide-eyed on the edge of their seats, and soak up everything he says. Henry leaves on his own afterward—lacking the nerve to go to the park with them to meet the girls, he always invents excuses to go home. These girls never pay any attention to him anyway. They simply look troubled and turn away if he approaches them, pretending to pick up the threads of another conversation or suddenly become engaged in something else, anything at all, as long as it gives them the chance to avoid him. That's how girls are, every single one of them. However, one weekend something happens, something quite new and unexpected. Henry has driven the boys to a dance hall just outside Levanger.

It is June, and the air is full of laughter.

He sees her the moment he steps out of the car, because she turns and gives him a lingering stare. Who is she? Has she heard some of the ridiculous stories circulating about him? No, it doesn't seem like it, there's no sign of pity in her eyes, he thinks. He shuts the car door and runs his hands self-consciously through his hair, allowing himself one last glance at her to see if she's still looking at him. A smile spreads across her face. Henry smiles too. He has to find out where this might lead. Luckily she is standing with one of his friends, one of the boys he is supposed to be picking up, so he has an excuse to approach them. The girl steps aside slightly, so that Henry can slip in between them, and smiles. She is short, shorter than him.

"Are we leaving?" his friend asks. Henry shakes his head, aware that the girl beside him is waiting for a response, and says:

"No, we're not in any hurry . . ."

And so this is how happiness enters Henry's life: like an unexpected wave of affection. In the form of a woman, standing suddenly before him, eighteen years old, with long wavy hair that curls round her ears. She is shorter than Henry, not much, but just short enough. The biggest surprise, though, is how there's no sign of her wanting to leave. No glancing round the room for her friends, she just stays there and chats with him. Insecure perhaps, or shy, but she stays. It's almost too much, almost too unbelievable. After years of being an outsider looking in at the world, as though staring into an aquarium. Now she is standing there, for real; a real, warm, living, breathing body, with lips drawn out into a smile and two eyes carefully searching for his.

Henry reaches out and carefully touches her arm, just a little. He strokes his forefinger over her pale skin, and the freckles and fine blonde hairs. He feels a spark, an electric shock running from his fingertips and up his arm and down to his groin; and it appears to be the same for her, because she doesn't pull her arm away. On the contrary, she moves her arm closer to his hand while her cheeks start to blush, and her eyes turn more serious, darker, and then she puts her arm round him.

They talk. He learns her name, Klara, and tells her his, and where he is from. A few days later they meet again, at her house, alone.

What joy.

To watch her unbutton her blouse, right in front of him. Not in his imagination, but in real life. To feel her soft, soft skin. To finally feel a woman's body against his, for the very first time, and feel how every inch of her can be brought to life, made to glow and tremble.

The morning after, he wakes up beside her and gazes into her sparkling eyes before she curls up closer to him and rests her head on his chest. An enormous sense of calm, a feeling of victory, surges through his body. She is his. Only his.

They get married.

Henry's grandfather makes a suit specially tailored for his height. Now they will see. Everyone who said he'd never meet anyone, that he would never come to anything. Now they will see him leading his wife down the aisle and through the church door. Now they'll see him bringing furniture into their rented apartment. New, stylish tables and chairs—which the bank has allowed them to buy on the installment plan, thanks to his steady job at the hardware store—and a double bed, made of dark wood. Soft, white bedsheets in finely woven cotton will hang in the sun on the clothesline, giving passersby a hint of the lust-filled nights they spend coiled around each other.

It's a wonderful and unique joy, to be able to kiss her on her cheek and then walk out the door to work.

To twirl her wedding ring around her finger with his thumb, a few years later, and feel the hard metal against his skin.

To see the look in her eyes when she tells him that they are going to have a child, and to hold her from behind while nuzzling up against her neck.

All this joy brings an unexpected feeling of peace. As though he has gone his whole life looking over his shoulder, watching out for everyone he passes and for every single sound. Now it seems like he can finally drop his guard, breathe out, and just enjoy being alive. At last he can savor all the wonders of this world; those things that were always there, that he was never allowed to see.

The only sore point in all this joy and happiness is money. They are not exactly poor, but Klara drops so many hints about things she wants, and there's so much he would like to give her. But it's no good. He should be earning more at the shop. It's only fair, he thinks, since *he* is the one working the longest shifts behind the counter, selling items until his feet are sore and his back aches. *He* is always the one helping the customers with a smile, telling jokes and remembering their children's names or some other detail about their farm, something that bonds them, so that the customer buys something extra, something they didn't even know they needed. Even then, he still doesn't earn enough; not enough to afford everything that Klara and his son deserve, he thinks, while tidying up the stock, and carrying boxes, and dusting the shelves. If they need new clothes, that's what they should get. If Klara wants to go to the café, OK, then they should be able to go to the café and treat themselves to a hot chocolate or a coffee or a piece of cake, like everybody else does. Why shouldn't they?

Why shouldn't he, who is working so hard, be able to live like everybody else? The shop makes a profit and is always full of customers, and who is responsible for that? *He* is. Yet *he* is the one continually short of money!

It's not fair, he thinks. He has to find a way out of this, find some way of earning more, but how? It's no good just putting a little bit aside each week. It's simply not enough, he thinks, in between serving customers and restocking the shelves. He broods over it at bedtime when dropping his false teeth into a glass of water; and he thinks about it while playing football with his little boy on the grass outside the house.

Then, in a sudden moment of clarity he sees a way out. A brilliant solution to this whole problem.

H for herbarium. It is March 10, 1942, and in the canteen at Falstad you recognize one of the prisoners who was brought in the night before. A rather tall man, with clear eyes, dressed in the same uniform as everyone else. He looks at you and raises his hand to say hello. It is Ralph Tambs-Lyche. You have met both him and Else many times in the past. Sometimes in the street, when he was usually on his way to the forest to find new plants for his herbarium; and also at the Student Union building, where he delivered fiery lectures about workers' rights and the unfair distribution of the world's resources. You once visited him and his wife at their villa in Jonsvannsveien, and went up to see his herbarium, in an upstairs room, with an arched window facing the garden.

H for home. For the rooms in which one sleeps and awakens. Where one can escape the stares from the outside world and just be oneself. It's July 1950—the middle of the year, and the middle of the century. Ellen watches the nanny playing with Jannicke in the living room and attempts to smile, but she can't quite do it; her face will not cooperate. It's as if the walls are closing in on her, and the floors are whispering to her. It was different at first. She too was excited at the prospect of having a detached house and starting a new life, in a new city, with a husband and children and a garden and a housekeeper. Of course she was. At first she liked going to Paris-Vienna to look at the new hats Marie had made, and try the dresses and order jackets they would adjust for her in the back room. She and Gerson would then walk, arm in arm, through town with Jannicke in her pram, or accompanied by the nanny, and she would see how people looked admiringly at them. They were a beautiful couple.

And the shop, which Gerson helped run, made it possible for her to keep up with European fashion trends. It was everything she had dreamt of while living as a refugee in Sweden—in limbo, with no idea of what the future held. Now she had it all, but her daily life smothered her enthusiasm. She took the shop for granted, and as Gerson had pointed out, how many dresses does one actually need? Over the last year her smile had frozen. It became increasingly clear that everybody else had a role, a responsibility—except her—she was somewhat in the way, superfluous. She didn't work. She didn't look after her child. Didn't make food, because she couldn't. So her job was simply to pass the time; to visit the café, to look around the shops. But now, her belly is so large that it is difficult to go out, and it is pointless trying on new clothes. There's a child in there, tickling her stomach from the inside. People smile when they see her, and strangers suddenly feel at liberty to place their hands on her tummy and tell her how wonderful it is to have children, but she doesn't think that it's wonderful. She's ashamed at the thought, but she sees nothing wonderful about getting this baby, her second child, due just after New Year's. The cold weather and snow is on its way too, so it will be impossible for her to go out. She'll be trapped indoors, in Rinnan's house; and although she's previously managed to chase off these visions of the past—like a bird that has flown in through a window—it's become more difficult. She keeps hearing new stories about the crimes that took place within their walls. More and more details, slowly breaking her down.

She passes the door to the cellar, and cannot stop thinking of the people who were dragged down its steps, with their hands tied behind them. She thinks about how they were hung there—from an iron bar supported by two wooden barrels—it is as if she can hear the screams; the screams of pain, and the sound of bodies being struck by clubs and chains. Just as her neighbors and friends had told her. Tortured by cigarette burns. Whipping. Nail extraction. Why does everyone feel obliged to give her so much information? It's like they can't control themselves, as if they're compelled to recount every single morbid detail, as though saying it out loud will make the evil easier to take in. Don't they realize that she is haunted by all this, that they are like ghosts, waiting until she is alone so they can catch her unawares?

They should never have moved, she thinks, moving away from the cellar door and up the stairs, toward the room furthest away. A room on the second floor, with an arched window and a built-in bed. They should never have moved, because now it's not only the scars of the war she has to carry around, as everyone has to. It's not just the despair she must deal with, or the migraines, which force her to lie in bed, in the dark and the silence, with a pounding head. Now she must also deal with the history of the house.

One day she takes Gerson on a tour of the building, letting him know exactly what she thinks, recounting the things she has been told or read. She points at the fireplace and says: "That's where they burned their documents as they fled." She points into the living room and says: "That's where Rinnan held his kangaroo court and sentenced several of his own gang to death." She points into the bedrooms and says: "That's where they slept, and had sex." Then she walks over to the cellar and stops at the door.

"And down there, Gerson!" she says, with an anger she didn't even know she possessed boiling up inside her.

"Do you know what they did down there?"

"Yes, I know," replies Gerson calmly, but she sees his irritation growing.

"Yes. And does it not bother you?" asks Ellen.

"It's almost ten years ago, Ellen."

"Yes?"

"Yes . . . Do you have any idea how many gruesome things have happened throughout history, in places all over town? Since the first Stone Age settlers? Something every five yards I expect, but no one's too bothered about that, are they?"

"This is quite different! You know it! Yesterday Jannicke came up from the cellar with a bullet that she'd found. She didn't know what it was of course, but I did! What should I say to her? What should I tell her it is?"

"I don't know . . . Can't you just say that you don't know?"

Ellen bows her head and screws up her eyes. "But Gerson," she says, her voice now thin and frail, "don't you see that this house is going to destroy us?"

Gerson places his hand on her shoulder.

"I'll go down and remove every trace of the war that I can find, Ellen. I'll paint the walls. Will that make it better?" he asks. But it doesn't help. Ellen pulls away from his hand and says that she's going upstairs for a nap. She doesn't want to be comforted, not like that. Treated like a stupid little child who imagines creepy shadows in the night. She wants his understanding; something he is obviously unable to give.

H for hands. Hands tying a shoelace. Hands lifting a child up to the apple blossom. Hands sweeping up crumbs in a vigorous manner. Hands hammering nails into the sole of a shoe. Hands gripped round a whip. Hands that become fists smashing into someone's jaw. Hands that are bound together with rope. Hands that are holding a glass. Hands stroking cheeks. Hands sliding into gloves. Hands upon a fine woolen tweed. Children's hands against a windowpane, on a door handle. A girl's finger on her lips. It is Jannicke Komissar. Her face glowing in the light from the candle in her hand. With its flame flickering gently from her breath, she turns to her sister and whispers: "Come, Grete. There's a secret passage up here!"

H for hustling. Henry tells his customers about how they can now pay for things in installments, but the agreement has to go directly through him. He gets on well with these people, they've known him for years, and several of them take him up on the offer. It's so easy. So easy to say the right words at the right time to reassure them about the purchase, smoothing away their doubts like an iron over a creased sheet. They give him the money, and Henry runs a little business within the business. He takes the profits home and spends it on expensive food, better clothes, and new furniture. It's still difficult to pay all of the bank repayments when he is continually buying new things, but he refuses to give up. He will never, *never* tell Klara that they cannot afford a Sunday roast, or a new dress, or a new pot for the kitchen. Never. So, he must find a new way to supplement his income.

Soon Henry begins driving out to local farms offering various items he knows they need. *They're so gullible,* he thinks, so easy to persuade that he could have sold them anything. Just a few short rides in the afternoon or on the weekend, and he has all the extra money he needs; it's simple, and ingenious. The embezzling increases. Klara seems happy, even though her smile drops occasionally when she sees him come home with a new toy or a bicycle. Can they *really* afford it all, she'll ask hesitantly; is he *really* earning this much? He'll then simply give her a hug and say "Of course," and she will smile contentedly.

Then, it all comes undone.

It is midday, and Henry is lost in a daydream so real that he almost doesn't notice the bell ring when the door to the shop opens. But then he sees his uncle walk in, in an overly brisk and stern manner, with a bitter look of anger and indignation on his face; his taut lips no more than a thin line. He strides up to Henry and places his trembling hands on the counter.

"Do you know what I heard today, Henry?"

"No . . . what was that?" asks Henry, although everything about the situation indicates what this is about. His uncle opens his mouth and is about to explain what has angered him so much, but just then the door opens and an old man walks in with a bicycle inner tube under his arm. Henry's uncle turns abruptly, walks into a side room, and waits, while Henry helps the man decide whether he should buy yet another repair kit for the tire, or if the microscopic hole next to the valve will be so difficult to repair that he's better off buying a new inner tube. Throughout all this his uncle stands with his back to them, just inside the door to the side room, demonstratively tidying the shelves that hold the items Henry has been helping himself to.

As soon as the customer is gone, his uncle turns round and storms back up to the counter.

"Now, Henry Oliver. You know full well what this is about, don't you?" he asks.

Henry just blinks. He thinks he knows—that it's all over—but tries his best to empty his mind and says nothing.

"OK, fine, then we'll do this the hard way. You know that guy, Kristoffersen?"

"Yes . . . ?"

"He came up to me today, all happy and excited, telling me there was a guy driving round the area selling goods for me . . . He had purchased some gloves, from this shop, at a very good price . . . Does any of this sound familiar?"

Henry says nothing. Just lowers his head as he feels his energy draining away, because now he can no longer hope that this concerns anything else. It's over. He has been caught.

"He even shook my hand vigorously while telling me all this. Beaming with joy, while I stood there like an idiot with no idea what he was talking about. Because I didn't see it. Because I've been such an unsuspecting fool for so long. Do you know what I'm talking about *now*, Henry Oliver?" his uncle asks, raising his voice at the end.

Henry doesn't reply.

He makes no attempt to escape, and no attempt to excuse himself, because he can't, and anyway why should he? He would do it again. He had no choice. It was the only way he could earn enough to live a proper life, and neither his uncle nor his business partner ever noticed any of the missing stock. His uncle had done extremely well from it all. He'd thrown extravagant three-course-dinner parties, where guests were collected and driven to the door in the Ford; the car Henry himself had repaired. And who drove them? Why, Henry of course, who dropped them off, held out his hand and helped bejeweled old ladies down the steps. His uncle has profited more than enough, and never noticed anything missing because business had gone so well. While for Henry these extra funds had enabled them to get by and live a little too, not just struggle their way through life.

It was only fair. *But how can I explain that now?* he thinks. It seems better for Henry to keep his mouth shut, hang his overall over the counter, and walk out without saying a word. With the shame and anger and fear running through him, because what in the world will he say when he gets home? How will Klara react? And his parents? Everything will fall apart, he thinks, as it all churns over in his head. His family's whole existence depends on his income, and now it will be taken from him, taken from them. Will society never allow him to participate? Will he always be denied even the tiniest shred of joy and well-being?

Henry rushes down the road with his head down. Kristoffersen! That idiot has ruined everything! Why on earth did he blabber? People in the street pass him by as normal, with their children and shopping bags, plans and conversations, while he gets trampled into the dirt yet again by this petty little shit hole. This goddamned fucking shit hole!

What is he supposed to do now?

What the fuck is he supposed to do?

Run away? He can't do that. He has to stay with Klara and his son, and he can't just lie about it either, because she will find out the moment the bank comes knocking to reclaim the money they have borrowed. He stops by the bank, and the poorhouse. They explain what will happen: he will lose everything, absolutely everything. The house, its contents, everything. He feels like crying, like smashing something, but bites his teeth and walks out the door again, he has to get away from there. *Fuck! Fuck! Fuck!* he thinks, while his legs lead him down to the seafront, and along the water's edge where the seaweed lies exposed on the rocks, and up through the town center again, past the churchyard. There's no way out. He has no choice other than to tell her.

Klara just nods silently. She doesn't get angry or start crying, and that is perhaps the worst reaction of all, because it means that he has nobody to comfort, nowhere to put his hands or his cheeks or his insecurity. Klara just stands there, perfectly straight with her chubby arms by her side, nodding carefully, as though he had just told her something about a neighbor or the weather.

"So what will we be allowed to keep, Henry?" she asks. Henry takes a deep breath and sits there feeling dejected.

"I don't know," he replies.

"The house. Will we get to keep the house?"

Henry shakes his head and hears Klara whisper *Oh my god* to herself before burying her face in her hands and beginning to cry. Henry places a hand on her shoulder while she pulls away from him, sniffling. Then she looks up.

"The furniture?"

"No, Klara. They're going to take everything apart from the bed. But they're going to find a place for us to live . . ."

"They? Who are *they*? The poorhouse?" she asks, using the common word for the government's Social Security Office.

Henry nods, as she sniffles again, and the grief drains the energy and confidence from him. It's like he is falling apart, becoming weak again, like he was before. And that is something he cannot allow. He will not. Because it's not his fault! He would never have stolen from the till if they had just paid him better! It would never have occurred to him. It's actually his *uncle's* fault, everything is, but how can he explain that to Klara? She wouldn't understand any of it. Nor would she understand that it was actually all for her benefit. For her and their son's benefit. All this driving around from town to town, farm to farm, working dawn till dusk, it was all for them! Doesn't she realize that?

Klara takes a handkerchief from her dress pocket. Her eyes are wet, and tears stream down her cheeks. Then she looks at him, coldly and calmly.

"So, Henry. When are they coming to collect everything?"

"Tomorrow."

"Oh well," she says while running her finger along the edge of the table, as though saying goodbye to it. "Oh well."

The creditors arrive the next day and remove the chairs and the table around which they ate Sunday dinner. They take away the casseroles that Klara would use to make sauces and stews. Henry stands in one of the side rooms, forced to watch everything being carried out while a crowd gathers outside, whispering and gossiping and taking in the moment with greedy looks on their faces. It is plain to see that they're taking pleasure in it all, wallowing in the scandal, with an insatiable urge to gloat. An urge to elevate themselves by trampling on him and his family. Dammit! They know nothing. They're just a bunch of privileged, petit bourgeois pigs, who will never, *never* miss a chance to crush someone less fortunate than them! Spoiled bastards, born with silver spoons in their mouths and the world at their fingertips. Fuck them all!

When everything has been taken away, a man in a suit comes out and asks Henry to sign some papers confirming the repossession of the house. He also asks them to accompany him to the office at the poorhouse. Henry tries to take Klara's arm but she moves away. It's just a subtle movement, but he feels the rejection. At first he thinks that it is understandable, and that she'll get over it, but her rejection continues even after the local authorities give them an apartment.

She seems to pull away just slightly whenever he tries to touch her, and there's now a tough look in her eyes, a distance, accusing, as though *she* hadn't benefited from the money he brought home. Like *she* hadn't enjoyed the lamb steaks, the trips to the café, and the new skirts and blouses. *Fucking hypocrite,* he thinks. She can't reject him like that! She has no right! Everything he has done has been done for *her,* for *them.* She can't turn him down *now,* he thinks. That night, he grabs her, pulls up her skirt, and without giving a damn if she wants to or not, places his hand on her crotch. With his other hand holding her still he pushes his finger between her thighs, even though she's not wet, and then pushes her onto the bed and unbuttons her blouse. He doesn't say a word, but his breathing quickens, and he feels the anger raging through him. *Ungrateful bitch! Like you didn't go along with all this and do well from it? Eh? You, who always complained when we were short of money and never once asked where the extra cash came from! Never!*

He lies on top of her and forces himself on her, vaguely aware of her lying there, motionless, with her face turned to one side.

Time drags now that there's nothing for him to do. The days have no purpose, no work, no acknowledgment, no money. Henry can't bear sitting at home, with Klara's relentless moaning, a constant reminder of his mistakes, just by virtue of him being alive. Every time she opens her mouth, every time she looks at him, and every time she rejects him he is reminded of the fiasco. So he goes out instead, wandering about on his own, wishing he could get away from Levanger, from the humiliating looks from everyone he meets. It's not hard to imagine them reveling in his misfortune round the tables at the temperance café. How they lean over to each other and lower their voices before recounting what happened to Henry Oliver Rinnan. He who had always been so full of bravado.

Henry pictures their smirking faces, the vile self-satisfied looks they give each other in the living rooms, on the farms. So fucking ordinary, all of them! So limited by what everyone else says and thinks. They'll soon fucking see what he's made of! He doesn't need anyone. Not friends, nor neighbors, nor family. Not if it has to be on these terms. He's stood out in the woods crying far too often, but now the tears are gone; hardened like drips from the ceiling of an isolated cave. *I'll get back on my feet again,* Henry thinks, while gritting his teeth, inhaling sharply through his nostrils, and walking aimlessly out of town, *one way or another, I'll get back on my feet, and they'll fucking see!* He passes two local men who stop talking and watch him hawkishly, and he feels his cheeks burning from the gloating and looks of schadenfreude. Like he cares about what's going on in their tiny heads anyway.

Idiots. Why would he ever need to talk to them? Who cares if they don't invite him and Klara to their dinner parties and coffee mornings when he doesn't want to be there anyway? It makes no difference to him, no difference at all, because he couldn't give a damn about their absolutely stupid parties. He doesn't care about sitting in their parochial sitting rooms, competing over who has the newest sofa or bureau or dinner service which they have randomly pointed at, and then talked about, only to then dismiss it with false modesty saying *We only inherited it* or *We're paying for it in installments.*

Fuck them! Fuck all those stupid assholes, thinks Henry, as he trudges through the streets.

H for Gerson's and Jacob's hair—as they hide in a downtown loft perilously close to the Nazi headquarters. Dark, almost black hair. A clear giveaway to everyone that they are not Aryan.

"You'll have to dye it," Mrs. Eriksen says as she places a brown bottle from the pharmacy on the table in front of Gerson and Jacob. She had been the boys' nanny, in another life. Before the war and the separations, she had lived in a nearby house with her parents in Trondheim; and her job was to look after the two boys, to make food for them and wash them. To scrub their scrawny bodies and comfort them when the soap stung their eyes. She would wrap them in towels and sit them on her lap, and say *Hush, hush, little one, is everything OK?* Now they are adults. Jacob rotates the bottle and peers at the label. *Liquid Peroxide.*

"*Aha? Liquid . . . per . . . ox . . . ide,*" stutters Jacob in a halting tone, as he sometimes does, smiling apologetically at Gerson, who takes the bottle to look at it himself.

Gerson had heard about this stuff before; that there is something women once used to lighten their hair, before the war.

The former nanny carries a bowl of water to the table and fetches a couple of towels, which she lays across the boys' shoulders. Then she asks Gerson to lean forward and pours some of the liquid peroxide onto his hair, rubbing it in with her fingers; massaging his scalp and giving him goosebumps. His hair becomes totally saturated, and the peroxide runs down his cheeks. Then she puts her hand under Gerson's chin, lifts his head, and looks him closely in the eye. For a moment he is paralyzed with fear that she's about to kiss him; that she might lean forward and press her lips against his, something he had often fantasized about in his youth; but she just rubs her finger around the mouth of the bottle and brushes it over Gerson's eyebrows. First one, then the other.

"There. Now you just need to lean forward and allow the peroxide to work," she says while going over to Jacob. Gerson looks down at the table, listening while she repeats the process on his brother, and he starts thinking about his mother again; about how she would sometimes bring them into the kitchen, just like this, along with their father. Then she would cut their hair one by one, and their dark locks would cover the floor like black brushstrokes.

Finally Mrs. Eriksen returns with the bowl, and starts to ladle ice-cold water over his head. It runs over his scalp, down his neck, and into his ears, but he says nothing. He lets her rinse it all away and dry his hair.

When he eventually lifts his head, he looks straight at Jacob's face and explodes with laughter, laughter he tries to stop with his hands, because not only has his brother's hair gone lighter, it is as orange as a carrot. A completely unnatural hair color, unlike anything he's ever seen on any human being.

The former nanny vainly attempts to restrain her laughter too, because they cannot draw attention to them being in the loft, but she just can't help it, and Jacob starts laughing as well.

Gerson goes over to a mirror leaning against the wall and

chuckles at his own reflection. What else can he do? He has been transformed. Not into a blond-haired Norwegian, but into a luminous carrot or a pantomime character.

"Now it's *this* we have to hide," he says, tugging at his orange hair.

They try rinsing it away, over and over, but it's too late. The bleach has soaked all the way in, stripping the pigment from every single hair. Now they just have to get away from there. Away from Oslo, from the Nazis, and from the war.

They wait in the loft for several weeks, with nothing to do. Mrs. Eriksen comes up to them on several occasions, saying that they'll soon be collected and transported, only for the plans to be abandoned at the last minute when someone gets arrested or someone from the resistance is exposed and captured.

She says she'll try harder to find them an escape channel. It's too risky for them to contact their mother; they cannot show any sign that they are alive. Not now.

All they can do is sit and think about those they have lost. The news of their father's death looms over every conversation. A constant and persistent murmur that grows in intensity until it sometimes drowns everything out. The grief doesn't come in waves, regular and predictable. Instead it feels like a cold, heavy container in Gerson's chest, filled to the brim, that must be carried carefully so that it doesn't spill over. Sometimes the tears burst out while he is washing his face and sees his orange hair in the mirror. He might smirk a little, but the smile will immediately freeze, because he will picture his father, running a comb through his hair or stroking his mother's back as he passes her in the living room. He will suddenly hear his father humming to himself or talking to his mother or a friend from the congregation. And then the container spills over, and the tears pour down his cheeks.

October turns into November. Living in the apartment opposite there's a woman who works as a secretary for the Gestapo. She is often visited by soldiers, who laugh and shout as they walk through the building. On one occasion someone pounds on their door, wanting to come in, and Gerson and Jacob stand silently up against the wall in the attic, expecting to hear footsteps on the stairs. But the soldiers are not looking for *them*, they just want to complain to the landlady about the strips of light escaping from between her blackout curtains.

November 15 comes. They wait in silence, terrified and bored. November 20 comes, and they continue to wait.

Then, finally, on November 25, they are told to be ready, because a taxi will come and collect them the following morning, November 26. The brothers are oblivious to the ship that lies in Oslo's harbor, waiting to transport the city's Jews across the sea and to the concentration camps.

They pack their bags, thank the landlady for letting them stay there so long, and try to go to bed early, but Gerson lies awake until well after midnight. While hundreds of the city's taxi drivers prepare for their assignments, drawn from a list of all those being collected and transported to the harbor, Gerson sits quietly in the dark, trying to picture it all. This is it. First thing tomorrow, they will be off.

So little a life can seem when stripped to the bone. When an apartment and its furniture is gone. When plates and cutlery, paintings and carpets, books, shoes, watches, and jewelry are gone, and only the body and the few clothes one is wearing remains. Gerson sits on a little bed along with Jacob, waiting for the taxi to come. His rucksack, containing food, drink, and a change of clothing, is packed. This is all that remains of a lifetime's work and the huge journey you have undertaken, Hirsch, from one social class to another. From a small Russian village to the life of a European socialite. Now it is all gone.

They wait. And wait. Then a car approaches and stops outside. Is it soldiers?

Footsteps come up the stairs. The key turns in the lock, and the door opens. It is Mrs. Eriksen.

"Come on. It's here," she whispers. Gerson stands up, then Jacob. They say farewell to the attic and step out onto the staircase. Mrs. Eriksen goes down first, to make sure there are no soldiers on their way up, before she tells them to come out. They creak, step by step, all the way down to the door.

"I've told them where you're going, you just have to get in," she says, giving them both a hug.

Gerson walks out to the waiting cab, climbs into the back seat, and looks at the driver's face in the mirror. Jacob gets in on the other side, and straightens the hat which is hiding his luminous hair. Gerson looks up at the night sky, and at Venus, which for hundreds of years was called the Morning Star.

"To the station," says Gerson, making sure. The driver nods and starts the engine. Twenty yards away a patrolling German soldier turns upon hearing the noise from the engine but then continues on his way. And they drive. It is long before sunrise, and the streets are dark and empty except for a few birds picking at some garbage they dragged from a dustbin. They drive along the waterside, past the massive ships docked in the harbor, and on to the Eastern Rail Terminal, where the driver parks the car and tells them that their landlady has already paid. Then they walk over to the station platform, keeping their heads down, trying their best to remain in the shadows.

The platform has lamps running its length and they suddenly find themselves illuminated, with their orange hair poking from under their hats, and with fifteen minutes to wait before the train arrives. Jacob immediately walks over to the nearest lamp, takes a quick look around while stretching out his gloved hand, and twists the lightbulb halfway until the light goes out.

He stands there smiling mischievously at Gerson, who quickly joins his brother in the dim light and pats him on the shoulder. Then they wait, closely watching every movement of the others arriving on the platform. Finally the train comes. They climb aboard, sit down in an empty carriage, and the train rolls out of town. When it stops in a small town closer to the Swedish border, they get off and continue by bus as instructed, sitting permanently slouched in an effort to flatten themselves; make themselves invisible, no more than two knit caps poking up from their seats.

So while hundreds of taxis shuttle Jewish families to the ship waiting in the harbor in Oslo, the two brothers ride a bus in the other direction, hiding their faces whenever a truck passes. Eventually they come to a stop, deep in the forest, where they get off and stand there waiting among the spruce trees. Waiting and waiting and waiting.

Finally they hear the sound of an engine in the dark.

Maybe we should hide among the trees, just in case? Gerson thinks. Jacob appears to be thinking the same thing, but neither of them is able to make a decision, because what if it's not a soldier but a truck that's been sent to pick them up? Isn't there a risk that the truck will just drive past, and they'll be left standing there, holding nothing but a rucksack in late November, in the Norwegian winter?

He's unable to give it any more thought before two headlights sweep round the bend, lighting up the tree trunks and blinding him. The vehicle slows down, pulls onto the roadside, and the engine stops. Gerson lowers his hand and sees a friendly face, a man who asks if they are Gerson and Jacob. There is laughter and relief. They drive.

The forest flashes by. Wispy-looking pines with dry, orange flakes peeling from the trunks.

They smile at each other, but don't dare celebrate, not yet.

The driver turns off into a narrow lane with straw lying beside it. A fence round a cow pen stands barren and desolate. Gerson catches a glimpse of the driver's face in the rearview mirror. A young man, about the same age as him. Why would a stranger take such a risk? To organize this escape across the border, on foot, by car, by boat. What makes these people risk their own lives helping refugees like Gerson?

Soon a farm comes into view. A white farmhouse and a red barn. There's a blue tractor, and a rusty pitchfork stuck into the roadside, with curved finger-like prongs, and there are the remains of other tools and machinery, some of it going rusty and in the process of returning to the earth.

A sturdy-looking man, with a beard and a stained work shirt, stands in the farmyard and waves the driver into the barn where their next means of transport awaits: a flatbed truck, standing beside a gigantic heap of straw. Three men and a woman in their twenties are there too. They are all Jewish. One of them is a pianist called Robert Levin.

"Where are we going to hide?" asks Jacob.

"There," says the man with a wry smile, pointing at the cargo bed.

"Under a load of straw?" asks Gerson. The farmer nods.

"Make sure you've eaten and gone to the toilet first. Your next chance will be in Sweden."

One hour later Gerson, Jacob, and Robert climb onto the cargo bed and sit beside each other. Gerson places his hands on his chest like a pharaoh—so he can reach the itches on his face more easily, or remove any straw that's tickling his nose or mouth. And then they are showered with grass. Stiff, dry straw, although some is wet and slimy, where the fibers have composted from having sat around for too long.

Gerson closes his eyes and holds his breath. He feels the straw scratching his chin, and his lips, his fingers, and it also slides under his shirt and trousers. A straw burial. Not in a coffin, lowered into the darkness of the earth, but on the back of a truck bound for the Swedish border, all the while hoping that the Germans don't stop and inspect the vehicle en route. Only to reach the border, they must first use a car ferry, and the Germans control both the ferry and the ferry port.

The straw scratches at his cheeks, his neck, and his hands, while his body is transported along roads he cannot see. All he's aware of are the bumps in the road, jolting his head and his shoulders. And all he can hear is the sound of the diesel engine below.

His sense of the terrain is nothing more than vague weight shifts as they go uphill and downhill, and the centrifugal force that squeezes him to the side on the bends.

Gerson keeps his eyes shut, and lies there constantly worried that the German soldiers will appear. He imagines various scenarios in which they lift up the straw; two or three brusque German soldiers, who force him to stand up on the cargo bed, in broad daylight, with dry grass hanging from his coat and trousers, or sticking up from his hair like a scarecrow. He pictures the Jewish girl he had started seeing in Oslo. Where is she now?

He tries to focus on something else, like the business he would like to start, but it only lasts a short while. Just a little bump in the road, a junction where the vehicle has to stop, or the whistle of a train, is enough to force him to imagine the scene of the Nazis forcing him out of the truck. Again, and again.

Sometimes he's executed on the spot, just dragged out, shot in the head with a revolver, and thrown in a ditch. Sometimes he is driven away in a car and sent to prison or for interrogation. From there the daydream becomes more vague, less tangible, because he lacks the material to spin the imagery from. He has heard stories and rumors about the transportation of Jews, but knows too little about the surroundings to be able to imagine anything more than sheds, barbed wire, soldiers, and mud.

How long have they been driving? Fifteen minutes? An hour? He needs to pee but has no choice but to hold it in. After what seems like forever the truck suddenly brakes and slows down. Are they there? His pulse thunders in his ears and pounds in his stomach, a ceaseless rhythm, passed from mother to child, again and again, through centuries and millennia.

Then the tone of the engine sinks as the truck stops completely, and he hears someone shouting outside, a man, but it's not the driver, and he's not speaking Swedish either. *Is it German?*

Yes.

A car door slams shut. The straw scratches against his cheeks, pokes his eyes, and tickles his nostrils. There are voices right next to the cargo bed. First the soldier wants to know where the driver is heading. Then he demands: *"Steuern die Last."*

Gerson hears hands raking through the straw and instinctively screws up his eyes, believing that it's all over, that the hands will soon find him. Then someone speaks in German, something Gerson cannot make out. Have they found Jacob?

He listens, but now it's gone suddenly quiet. The soldiers have stopped talking. He hears the crunch of gravel nearby. Then he hears the *swish* of something being poked into the dry grass. Is it a pitchfork? The tip of a rifle? There's another *swish* as the object passes through the straw and is then pulled out.

Why on earth would anyone be transporting straw across the border? thinks Gerson as the metal object is again thrust into the straw. He regrets not asking earlier, because isn't this a totally incomprehensible cover story? Does anyone actually believe that Swedish farmers don't have piles of their own grass?

Swish. German voices. A slight movement in the straw around him.

He lies as motionless as he can. Squeezing his eyes shut, not daring to breathe. He could be struck at any moment. Will he manage to stay quiet then, if the prong from a pitchfork skewers his thigh, or his chest, or his cheek?

Swish, swish, swish.

Something hard hits Gerson just above his knee, and he feels the grass moving by his kneecap. Something jabs the bottom of the cargo bed, right next to his ear, giving off a loud metallic clang. A third pokes him in the arm. Not enough to penetrate his skin but hard enough to hurt. Can the soldier tell he's struck something from his end? That his outstretched arm has come up against some resistance?

A second goes by, and another. Something hard is twisted round, so that the point catches his skin. Then the object is pulled out again, and Gerson hears a voice say that everything is all right; they can drive aboard the ferry.

Gerson feels a vibration in his back as the engine starts up again, and they continue toward the ferry. He wants to scream with joy, cry with relief, but does neither. He just lies there with his eyes shut, his bladder fit to burst, and in pain from the cut on his arm where the metal scratched his skin.

As they drive on board, the ferry rocks left and right, and the drone of the boat's engine rumbles through his body. Then there is a louder noise, probably from the boat being put in reverse, followed by a gentle thud as it reaches the other side. An eternity seems to pass. There are shouting voices. The metal door opens, and they drive off, and Gerson feels his pulse now pounding in his neck. *Shouldn't they be there by now? What's going on?* he thinks, noticing every single movement in the truck's bodywork, and every bump in the road where his body momentarily falls through the air. Then the truck comes to a complete stop, and the engine is switched off again. Gerson lies totally silent, almost without breathing, not sure if they've arrived at another checkpoint. Suddenly he is told to come out. Gerson stands up, brushes the straw from his face, and then recoils when he sees a pistol in the truck driver's hand. Is he going to rob them? Is this all just a trap, and the driver is really one of the double agents Gerson's heard rumors about?

"Just come out!" says the driver, turning around. Gerson now feels brave enough to stand fully upright, and looks around to check if it really is safe. There are no other trucks nearby. No German troops waiting for them, ready to whisk them off to a concentration camp or simply execute them right there, in the forest.

They find themselves on a bridle path, surrounded by pine trees and spruces. He spots Jacob, with his hat in his hands, still looking totally ridiculous with his yellowy-orange hair, full of straw. Gerson starts to laugh; the pianist does the same.

He climbs down from the truck, brushes more straw from his trousers, and finds that both his legs have gone numb after lying down for so long.

"If you walk two hundred yards down there," says the driver, pointing, "you'll come to a crossing with a signpost. Then you'll be in Sweden."

The pianist and the three others reach out to shake the driver's hand, and Gerson and Jacob thank him over and over again. Then they start walking. Gerson feels the urge to start running but forces himself to walk in a normal manner.

After a few yards he turns to look back and sees the driver climbing into the truck. They go round a bend and come to a scar in the forest, where the trees have been chopped down in either direction. A yellow signpost stands there, saying RIKSGRÄNS SVERIGE, Swedish Border.

Jacob puts one foot across the invisible border and smiles craftily. Gerson steps across too, making sure that he is definitely over the line, that he really has crossed the border, that there is no doubt about it. And then his brother throws his arms around his neck, and Gerson feels suddenly overwhelmed with relief, and it just makes him laugh. He laughs and laughs, while the tears roll down his cheeks.

They made it. They are safe!

I

×   ×   ×

I for the ice that sometimes tangles in the prisoners' beards during winter—strands of frozen mucus and spit, clinging to every whisker, from nostril to neck—their weather-beaten faces taking the shape of something wild and unkempt, like in nature.

I for the impunity of the prison guards, forcing you to do push-ups while they beat you with clubs.

I for the indignation growing within you, from the shoving, the food deprivation, and the browbeating. How can you possibly maintain any dignity, any humanity, when the whole system you've been placed in is designed with one objective—to take it all away?

I for Ivar Grande, who became the Rinnan gang's second-in-command after joining in May 1942. He was a tall and athletic man whose marriage came to an end when he met fellow gang member Kitty Lorange. The two subsequently married, and Kitty Lorange became Kitty Grande. Ivar Grande had no trouble getting people to like him, and was described as an effective infiltrator. He was handsome and confident. A man that turned heads, someone that people automatically listened to. Rinnan noticed how the others turned to Grande for his opinion, even though *Rinnan* was their leader. This was a problem, until Rinnan had him moved to a post in a city at the coast, where, soon after, Ivar Grande was shot and killed. Kitty Grande, now a widow, withdrew from the gang shortly after.

I for the interview with the Norwegian News Agency in 1946, in which one of the three medical experts at Rinnan's trial said the following:

> There is no doubt that Rinnan has quite a peculiar hold over his fellow humans. I have had several conversations with him, and am not ashamed to say that I too have felt his suggestive power. Not only that, but he is impressive to talk to in many ways, and possesses a high level of intelligence. When he nevertheless ended up as a major criminal, it may have been primarily due to the severe abnormalities in his emotional life. But I do not think there is anything abnormal in his power over fellow human beings.

J

× × ×

J for justice.

J for jackboot.

J for Jew. Jewish culture has its own language and a wealth of stories, handed down from one generation to the next. The Jewish people—my children's ancestors on their mother's side—left the Jerusalem area thousands of years ago, gradually moving northward and eastward and then, around AD 700, into Russia, where, by the Middle Ages, they had become what was probably the largest Jewish population in the world. Then, in the late 1700s, it was decreed that all Jews had to assemble in their own territory, and at some point, around 1880, the persecution began—the pogroms—which over the course of a few decades led to the exile of two million Jews, who fled

Russia and ended up in places like the U.S. or Scandinavia. One of them is you. One of the descendants is Rikke.

J for June, and for the summer months you spend working in northern Norway as an interpreter for the Russian prisoners of war. You show them how to construct snow barriers, and you negotiate work hours and food rations on their behalf. Living and working under a sky that never darkens, with the midnight sun shining across the sparse landscape of boulder fields and grassland. You see them assembling the snow barriers by the roadside, a look of fear in their eyes reflected by your own, fear of what the German soldiers will do when they have no use for you any more. You swat at the mosquitos buzzing around your ears, and eat watery soup, and every night wonder how your family is coping back home. Autumn comes, and suddenly you are told that you are being taken back to Falstad. You hear rumors that martial law has been imposed, and of an attack on the Norwegian resistance. And you watch the north Norwegian landscape pass by, through the windows of various cars and trains: first the endless plains full of grass and heather, then the scattered dwarf birches, then the spruce trees begin to appear again, first small, then more concentrated, taller and denser as you approach Trøndelag and the prison camp.

J for January 1950. Ellen Komissar is climbing the stairs to Marie's new apartment on her way to a late Hanukkah party with the family. Gerson and Jannicke are in front, skipping up the stairs hand in hand. Ellen, however, is more than eight months pregnant and could give birth at any moment; she feels heavy, her thighs keep colliding with her belly, and the nylon tights she got from Paris-Vienna are slipping down with each step. She maneuvers her hand under her winter coat, grabs hold of the tights through her dress, and yanks them back up over her hips while gripping the handrail.

Then she's suddenly overwhelmed by a wave of heat, and sweat begins to trickle down her back.

She pauses to catch her breath and opens her coat up to allow some cold air in. *I can't arrive at a party dripping with sweat,* she thinks, but her worrying only makes things worse because she doesn't feel at home in her own body. She doesn't feel beautiful and feminine, just inflated, her arms and legs so bloated with fluid they look like tree trunks. *What's so beautiful about this?* she thinks, while staggering up the last few stairs. Gerson picks up his daughter and supports her on his hip, before turning to his wife.

"Are you OK, Ellen?" he asks, and Ellen nods, glancing up at him briefly. He looks so handsome in his tailcoat, his scarf wrapped round his neck; whereas she'll soon be bedridden, struggling with the delirium of sleep deprivation, breast-feeding, and wearing a blouse spattered with baby-sick. Soon she'll be lying there, ugly and ruined, while Gerson is out meeting the most beautiful women from Trondheim's best families. Those who can afford to shop at Paris-Vienna and order clothes from the continent or bespoke hats with personally selected details. He's bound to grow tired of me, she says to herself, thinking of her father, who recently became involved with his secretary and divorced her mother, who in turn spent several weeks in a psychiatric hospital near Oslo. I should have been there, thinks Ellen, I should have gone to visit her, but it's not possible, not when I could give birth any minute. For a moment Ellen feels like all her defenses are about to crumble, and she just wants to sit on the stairs and cry. But she can't. She has to smile back at Gerson and tell him that she's fine. I have to be strong and remember how lucky I am: lucky, lucky, lucky, she says to herself. She smiles at Jannicke, peering down at her between the railings on the floor above; such a beautiful little girl, with sparkling eyes and beautiful dark hair. They continue upward, to the door of the apartment. Gerson puts his hand on her shoulder, but although she knows he means well, her back feels far too sweaty and she moves away from him. She gives him a sheepish smile and reaches for his arm, to show him that she hadn't meant to be so dismissive, but he is no longer interested. He takes Jannicke's hand instead, as if Ellen doesn't exist.

They ring the doorbell, and Marie lets them in. Marie seems a little overwrought, smiling far too broadly, as though she is over-stretching her charm, talking far too loudly and laughing too suddenly, as they remove their coats and enter the party. They are the last guests to arrive. Ellen sits down with Jannicke beside her and they begin to eat. She allows herself to vanish into the conversation, and tries not to think about her twin sister, who she finds herself missing several times a day. Her twin sister would have understood right away. She would have seen how unhappy Ellen is instantly. Not only that, but her twin sister would never have judged her because of the doubts she's feeling or the thoughts she's having or over how she's never managed to feel any real appreciation for having survived the war and being given the opportunity to live in their house. She reaches for her wineglass, noticing Gerson looking disapprovingly at her, but she must be allowed *one* glass. Marie passes Ellen the potatoes and once again asks how she is, and Ellen smiles back as graciously as she can.

"I'm fine, thank you! Everything's fine. Just look at how lucky I am," she says while smiling at Gerson, and for a moment she almost believes it herself.

J for jubilation, and for the job that lifts Rinnan out of poverty and saves him from financial ruin. He starts working as a truck driver, hired by a man called Ernst Parow to make deliveries around the local environs, to every single inhabited place and farm near Levanger. Having a job makes a normal life conceivable again, but the prospect of an ordinary existence is no longer enough, he wants something else, something greater. So although Henry continues going to the temperance café, it's not so that he can sit there telling stories; no, he's not bothered with that any more. Instead, he reads magazine and newspaper articles beforehand, then goes to the café and hurls random questions at the other guests. Just to put them in their place.

"What's the capital of Bolivia? Do you know? No, of course not," or "Is there anyone here that can tell me what the word *discrepancy* means? No? I thought not."

He just loves exposing their insecurity and shame; enjoys watching them mumbling and scratching their heads, squirming while desperately trying to come up with an answer. Then, after confirming just how much smarter he is than everyone else, he leaves.

Maybe he sometimes wished he could just sit there, like he had done in the past. But why would he do that? Now Rinnan drives from farm to farm on his delivery rounds, talking to the farm owners and learning their names so he can provide them with the best possible service; and while doing all this, he learns all about them and their political views. Secrets he doesn't yet know the value of.

Then the Winter War breaks out. Henry imagines the Finnish soldiers, camouflaged in white against the snow, fighting the Russian Communists among the boulders and pine trees. He sees it all so vividly when he shuts his eyes at night. The silence of the Russian winter landscape, the rabbit tracks in the fresh snow, and the dark flakes of bark scattered under the fir trees; torn off by the wind or by the hands of tiny squirrels climbing above. Complete silence. Then Henry rises from the snow, invisible to everyone, and fires a shot.

Many are keen to take part in the war. And in Levanger, an office opens where men can sign up. Henry waits in the queue and tells them he wants to enlist, to defeat the Communist threat from the East, and that he isn't remotely scared. In fact, he is *raring* to go.

All those enlisting must be weighed and measured. Henry too, even though he tells them it's unnecessary, but there's no way around it. And there's a *woman* doing the measuring of course, a sweet young girl in a white coat, with slender arms, and long bangs falling down into her sparkling eyes. She asks him to remove his shoes and stand against the wall, beneath a height indicator poking out from a yellow measuring rod. He hears the indicator being slid down from where the previous man had stood, someone a good eight inches taller than him, before it finally stops, resting on top of his hair which has been combed back into a bouffant to add more volume. But of course the nurse has to flatten his hair with the height indicator, and she presses it down onto the top of his head. Henry stands there quietly, gnashing his teeth. The nurse makes a note of his height and, without showing any reaction at all, mumbles *five feet three inches, yes* . . . to herself as though it's totally normal. But he can tell how ridiculous she finds it, and the fact that she is now trying to hide it from him just adds to the humiliation. As if she thinks he can't cope with her saying it out loud. As if he isn't already constantly reminded of how small he is, every single moment, of every single day?

Henry walks home, already impatient to receive his enlistment letter. Now he finally has an opportunity to escape all this. A chance to get away from Levanger and all its small-town mediocrity, and go where the real battles are being fought, where real heroes are being born. Some other locals have enlisted too, but not many, and Henry sees the respect he gets from people when he tells them he has signed up. It's only a matter of time before he'll be heading north. But the waiting drags on.

A week passes.

Two.

Finally the verdict arrives in the mail. Rinnan tears at the envelope with his fingers, as though tearing through the layers of boredom and powerlessness, looking for the entrance to another world, another life. He reads what it says. It is a rejection: *Not fit for service.*

He is totally stunned, and reads the words over and over again to be certain of what it says. *Not fit for service.* No explanation.

Fuck!

Is it because of his height?

Is the Winter War a height competition now? Do you have to be two meters tall to wrap your finger round a trigger? No! Do you have to be six feet tall to handle a car? Storm a building? Or shoot at the enemy?

Of course not! The anger boils up within him, but nothing prepares him for the humiliation he encounters on the street a few days later, when he passes a group of men—out strolling with some women they're trying to impress, of course—and one of them whispers, quietly but loud enough for Henry to hear: *I heard that Rinnan won't be going off to war until they've made tanks small enough for him.*

What the fuck!

How he could wring the necks of these assholes! How he could knock the smiles off their ugly fucking faces, all of them; everyone on the street, everyone working for the state, and the government, and local councils. All these handsome fucking idiots who've done NOTHING MORE than be born tall enough!

They'll get what's coming to them, thinks Henry as he keeps walking with his eyes fixed on the pavement. They'll fucking see! One fine day, when he has outgrown this town, and become something great, *then* they will come begging on their knees. Even if it's just for a chat!

"Just you wait!" he growls into his own chest.

"Just you wait!"

J for Jannicke, and for a conversation we had at her seventieth birthday. It was at the end of summer, the garden was filled with laughter and loud conversations. Desperate wasps were swarming around the guests, eager to eat the floating strawberries in the glasses of prosecco. Jannicke and I were standing a little outside of the party, and she was sharing some of her childhood memories. "Grete and I had a club, which we had called the Candle Club because there was a secret corridor up in the loft, and it was so dark we needed candles to see anything," she told me. "It was quite stupid, of course, because we could have set the house on fire, but at the end of the corridor there was a room that Rinnan had seemingly kept hidden. It was there that we found the . . . the little bag I just told you about."

The conversation paused for a moment, while I shuddered at the thought of this bag and what it contained. Jannicke had just mentioned it quite briefly, as an example of the horror of the house where she grew up, but then an uncle or cousin came by to say hello, and the tone in her story shifted.

"I'd always felt that my childhood in that house had been of no consequence, but then something happened. It was a while after we had moved back to Oslo, and by then I was old enough to work in a kiosk at the Majorstua subway station. And there was a drunk who would often come in, a slightly rough and disheveled man, but he was a regular customer, so we'd talk whenever I saw him. One day he told me that he'd been a member of the Rinnan gang. He never said who he was, but he must have been one of those who escaped the death penalty and had served his prison sentence. He talked and talked about what they had done in the house, about the torture, and it made me feel quite sick. My colleague said that I went totally pale, and I had to sit down in the back room afterward," Jannicke told me, laughing, and said that we could meet for coffee to continue the conversation, before she took a sip from the glass and walked over to someone else in the family. All the time, the wasps were flying around us, buzzing, impossible to chase away, like the picture of these two girls in the attic, and the discovery that they made.

K

× × ×

K for kiss.

K for knobbly knees, pale after a month without sunlight.

K for *kalott,* or *kippah.* Two words which I first heard said out loud at a swimming pool just outside of Oslo, on a winter's day at the end of the millennium. I stood there in my bathing shorts, lily white, someone who would never voluntarily wear shorts, because I had a complex about my legs back then and thought exposing them made me look even scrawnier than I already was. Anyway there I was, at the pool in the middle of the winter, taking part in a CPR and first aid course because I was preparing for a summer job at an activity club for children on a nearby island. As soon as I walked in, I noticed a young woman sitting on the floor, a short distance from the edge of the pool. She was the only fully clothed person there, and it didn't take much more than a glance for me to realize that there was something between us, even though she looked quite different from the sort of girl I thought I was looking for. She had short hair, black trousers, a blue-black tie-dye top, and clear brown eyes. We looked at each other, a little longer than one might normally do, before she turned back to her friend. She was talking about how she was doing fine, how she had a new boyfriend, and I remember how my heart sank. How typical, I thought, I would just have to forget her. A few minutes later I was standing by the poolside talking to someone I knew, I can't remember what about exactly, perhaps a detail from a film or a book, but suddenly I found myself fumbling for the word for the garment Jewish men wear on their heads. And that was when the girl from earlier turned her attention toward me and said, "Kippah or kalott."

She turned out to be the leader of the summer club, and her plan was to spend just the upcoming summer in Norway before returning to Spain to study in the fall. She had an unusual name, Komissar, and by the time summer was over, the relationship she had been in was over, so we got together, and she decided to stay in Norway. I moved into her apartment, we traveled, studied, and got married. Soon we had a child, and then another, and suddenly twenty years went by, while our lives became more and more entangled.

K for kindred spirit.

K for Kristallnacht.

K for the killing, as the war spread across Europe consuming everything in its path. A dark spot, smoldering at the heart of Germany, that quickly became an inferno, engulfing city after city, country after country.

For Rinnan, the war comes in the form of a shout from the street below his bedroom window. He opens his eyes and sits up to see Klara standing naked at the window, partly hidden behind the curtain, and he rushes over to see for himself, with a semi-erect penis that he often has when he's just woken up. He hears what's being shouted more clearly, that Norway is under attack: the war has arrived.

Finally! thinks Henry, throwing on his clothes and rushing out without wasting his time on eating breakfast. Finally! And this time it won't matter whether he is short or tall. Now they'll just accept him, and if they ask any questions he'll tell them all about his driving skills. Who else in town can drive as fast, and as safely, as him? Who else in this part of Norway has the same knowledge of every bump and bend that Henry Oliver Rinnan has amassed, from driving his friends to the dance halls, and then from all the deliveries he has made all over the place?

Nobody!

Nobody! Nobody! Nobody!

Rinnan is the man for that job, and they all know it—and this time no one is going to take it from him.

Henry collects his uniform. They have been told to use the old uniforms, but there's no way he is doing that, not when there are piles of brand-new ones right in front of him. It's no problem, he thinks, there's plenty of them, and after finding one his size he starts getting changed, well aware of the transformation the outfit will bring him, because clothes really do make the man. Henry puts on the trousers in front of the mirror, fastens the jacket with its gilded buttons, laces up the boots, and one can see right away that this is a man prepared for anything, ready to brave whatever comes. He joins a division of Norwegian soldiers; a secret group hiding out on a farm, driving to the airport and loading deliveries of ammunition into the truck before jumping behind the wheel again, gripping the hard white plastic in the palms of his driving gloves, slightly nervous about all the explosives stacked behind him, waiting to be detonated, blasted through the bodies of German soldiers.

What a life! Lying in the dorm with his fellow soldiers at night, sleeping among equals. Telling stories, listening to the radio, discussing the latest news from the frontline.

A week passes. Two weeks.

Then he hears that Norway has capitulated, that the cowards in the south have dropped their weapons. It's all over. And now they are being asked to surrender.

No, they are *ordered* to do it. Henry tries to persuade the others to continue fighting, by forming a secret unit, but it's impossible because suddenly the Germans are right there, in their blue-gray overcoats and with a vehement look in their blue eyes.

The surrender destroys everyone's morale, they become hopeless and demoralized. The whole division is shut down, from one day to the next, and all the soldiers are transported to a German prison camp outside the small town of Snåsa.

At the camp, Henry waits in the mud and the fog, his fingers and forehead pressed against the cold metal of the prison fence. And as the days and nights of endless boredom drag on, his imagination comes to life, distorting reality once again.

He imagines himself and a friend overpowering one of the guards by smashing a rock over his head. They crawl under the fence and slip into the darkness of the forest where they stumble across a column of German trucks transporting weapons. It's perfect. No one seems to notice as they climb aboard one of the trucks, where they help themselves to machine guns and crouch there with their chins against their knees, trembling with excitement. The driver, however, has seen them in his side-view mirror and races to the back of the truck with a revolver in his hand, but Henry aims his gun and shoots at the German, who throws himself to the ground, before racing off into the trees.

"You, there!"

Henry snaps out of his daydream, the fantasy melting away at the sound of the man's voice. Now he's suddenly back at the camp again with mud under his feet.

"Get away from the fence!" shouts the soldier in German. Henry walks back to the other prisoners, and refines the story about his escape until every detail is right.

Two weeks pass. Two long weeks of boredom and waiting, fearing what might happen next, before Henry finally receives orders to pack his bags and line up outside the dorm beside the waiting trucks, with their massive tires and green tarpaulins. Henry jumps in the back along with the others and is driven back into town.

This could have been the end of the war for Henry.

He returns to his old job, carrying on where he left off, and although Klara isn't especially pleased to see him, his boss at the trucking company is as grateful as a man rescued from a shipwreck. After all, who else was going to help him? For the rest of the spring Henry drives round the whole area making deliveries. He already knows many of the families on the farms, but now the war is the main topic of every conversation, and he quickly becomes aware of who sympathizes with the Germans, and who doesn't, before driving to the next place, the next sale. The praise and the money roll in. In fact, his boss is so happy that he invites Henry to a dinner party one day. A real party, attended by businessmen and German officers.

Him!

Invited to sit at the officers' table!

Henry cleans himself up, combs his hair, and tries on various shirts, repeatedly changing his mind about what to wear. To his irritation, Klara cannot understand what all the fuss is about, so he has to restrain himself when she asks why he cares so much about this dinner invitation. "Don't say a word," he says. "Not *one* word."

Henry buttons up his shirt, gently tugs the white sleeves out of the cuffs of his dinner jacket, which his grandfather made, and kicks the door open with his shoe. His baby daughter screams from the kitchen, a brief outburst of frustration from not getting what she wants, but that's Klara's problem, not his. He just walks out the door and heads to the party. He sees the looks of acknowledgment from some of the people he meets on the way, and also notices those who do not look at him. *If only they knew,* he thinks.

Soon after ringing the doorbell, however, this happiness and pride turns to humiliation at the hands of the German officers, because they completely ignore him. Henry manages no more than a *hello* before they continue their conversations, in German, a language he barely understands. Even so, they carry on regardless, laughing and sniggering in their shiny uniforms, while Henry sits there silent and unsure of himself.

But the third man he meets, Gerhard Stübs, seems a tiny bit curious. Lucky for him, Stübs has learned to speak Norwegian and asks, out of courtesy, what Henry does for a living. Henry gives the officer a slightly forced smile and tells him about all the driving he does, about how he delivers goods to all the farms in the area, and that he has done so for quite some time.

"You must know the locals quite well then?" asks the man, suddenly appearing to be far more interested, because even though one of the other officers asks him about something, he ignores him. All his attention is focused on Henry.

"Oh yes!" Henry replies. "I know everyone . . . Nobody knows the area, and the people in it, as well as I do," he says, before taking a sip from his glass. The officer looks down at his plate for a moment, dries his mouth with a white napkin, and then looks up.

"So you must know who sympathizes with us, and who doesn't?"

"Oh yes," says Henry nodding. "Of course. I've driven to every single village and farm over the last ten years. And after the last few months I have a pretty good idea about who is for and against the occupation. I know who's hiding weapons, and on which farms, and those who have radios hidden in the attic, if you are interested . . ."

Now the other officers start looking at him too, and the lightheartedness vanishes from their faces. The officer now leans across the table. He offers Henry an open cigarette case and asks one of the others to give him a light. Now it's suddenly all about Henry, the whole party, all the attention—just like it was back at the temperance café, only far better, weightier, more important—because he has got something they really want. The man opposite him mumbles something quickly in German to the two other men, presumably a summary of what they had just discussed, before turning back to Henry.

"Listen, Rinnan," says the German. "We're fighting a war, a war we intend to win, for the sake of our children, our grandchildren, and our entire common future."

Henry takes a drag on his cigarette while the officers stare at him. The room is silent, and he feels the nervous excitement in his stomach but tries not to let it show. He blows smoke from the corner of his mouth and nods, to show them he is listening.

"And in this war, information is very important. Especially information of the sort you possess. Can you tell us more?"

Gerhard Stübs wants to know about every farm and every village. Henry is able to tell him, with the same detail and accuracy as he would describing the house he grew up in. They eat and drink, and Henry describes the hidden arms depots and the resistance members. He tells them about the people with radios hidden in their lofts, and about the people smugglers, and as the evening draws to an end Stübs thanks Henry for the chat and says that he would like to stay in touch with him. That he could be a valuable resource for them.

There's nothing in any way pitying about how the officer looks at him; no sign of disdain or contempt, just a look of acceptance, which brings a smile to Henry's face.

A few days later, a courier arrives at the house. Henry hears the knock on the door, and Klara walks in with an envelope in her hand. A small cream-colored envelope with "Henry Oliver Rinnan" written neatly on the front in black ink. Henry stands up, knowing immediately who it is from, and with his heart pounding he opens it up. It reads:

Reich Commissioner Gerhard Stübs wishes to thank Henry Rinnan for the pleasure of his recent company and asks if he will come to Hotel Phoenix, Trondheim, tomorrow, in room 320, to discuss a possible collaboration.

"A possible collaboration!" With him!
Henry reads the letter several times, stroking his fingers over the words.

A possible collaboration ... room 320 ... extremely pleasant meeting ... tomorrow, in room 320 ... kind regards, Gerhard Stübs.

The following day is June 27, 1940. Henry has once again driven the fifty miles from his home in Levanger. This time he walks nervously across the square in front of the Hotel Phoenix in Trondheim, on his way to meet Gerhard Stübs. He looks at his watch again. It's the second time he has walked round the square, because he arrived a little too early, but now there are just ten minutes left, which is fine. They will see that he's punctual, and that he takes their meeting seriously, he thinks. At the hotel entrance there's a large sculpture—which seems to have no other purpose than getting in the way—of an imposing bronze bird, which he passes before entering the foyer, where his steps echo so loudly that he becomes even more nervous.

The man at the reception desk looks up from his newspaper and asks how he can help.

"Ehh ... I ... erm ... have a meeting with Gerhard Stübs," Henry says. "In room 320?"

"The elevator is over there," says the receptionist, pointing disinterestedly toward the far wall.

He approaches the elevator, a gleaming cube of mirrors and polished brass, with a backlit button displaying the number 3. The doors slide open onto a corridor, and suddenly he is there. He knocks on the door, and a man shows him in; one of the men from the previous night, only this time he's wearing a German uniform. He shakes Henry's hand.

Two other men are sitting there as well, two officers. Henry greets them and tries to appear relaxed, but he is far too excited, far too conscious of his own facial expression, too concerned with how he talks and how he walks across the room before taking a seat. How do they do it? he thinks, pushing his chair up to the table, and wondering where he should put his hands. How do they stay so composed, as if they're not even thinking about how to behave or what they say and do. They just *are,* and just *do.* Should their head or neck itch, they would just scratch it without any further thought and continue talking undisturbed, which is exactly what the Reich commissioner does right now, scratching his cheek while asking Henry to repeat some of the things he said about the resistance and the hidden weapons.

Luckily, Henry is able to put his nerves aside, and encouraged by the look on the commissioner's face, he eventually manages to relax and focus on the story—just as he used to do at the temperance café—feeding them morsels of the truth, watching how they lap it all up, follow his breadcrumb trail, bit by bit, until the main point snaps down on them.

They are amazed. He can see it in their faces, and Gerhard Stübs almost glowing with fatherly pride. So when Henry is finished they make him an offer, something far greater than he could have dreamed up.

The SS officers want to hire him.

They want Henry to note down anything suspicious, anyone who seems to be doing something they shouldn't. Anyone with an illegal radio, or supporting the wrong side, for example. They want him to be their eyes and ears, as Gerhard Stübs puts it, and report everything back to them.

"Like a spy?" Henry asks.

"Like a spy," Stübs replies, nodding and smiling. In addition, they would like him to infiltrate the Norwegian resistance movement, reveal where they are located, learn where they hide their weapons, and report everything to Gerhard Stübs.

His code name is "Lola."

They offer him a good salary, more than he ever earned at the hardware store, plus extras like free cigarettes, rationed food, and liquor.

Stübs's cigarette curls under his thumb as he grinds it into the ashtray.

"So, Rinnan. Perhaps you need a few days to think about my offer?" he says. Henry just shakes his head, saying that he needs no time at all to think about it. They shake hands and run through the formalities. Then Henry is led out into the corridor and shown to the elevator.

He wants to scream with joy as the elevator doors close behind him, and admires himself triumphantly in the mirror while the whir of machinery lowers him to the ground floor. He doesn't even bother looking at the man at the front desk, because who is that guy anyway? A student, an unemployed worker, an alcoholic? The concierge says something to him, but Henry just strides right past, feeling like a veil has been torn from his eyes, revealing his future to him. He steps out the door, and the warm summer evening smells of lilac and grass and perfume and cigarettes; and for the first time he realizes what the sculpture depicts. *Well, if it isn't a fucking phoenix!* he thinks, pleased with himself, and he pats it gently on the head.

Henry says nothing about the actual details to Klara, she wouldn't understand anyway, but he tells her that he has landed himself a meaningful job as the assistant and local guide for the German regional commander. He tells her to keep it secret for now. Then he tells her how much he will soon be earning and watches all the worry slip away and a smile return to her face. The family is saved. Klara will have to join the National Union Party, but that's no problem, she says, because the truth is, everyone will have to if they're going to continue living under the new regime.

Klara cuddles up to Henry, the heat radiating from her body, and as he closes his eyes, a huge sense of relief descends upon him.

When he opens his eyes again the following morning he already has a plan. After breakfast he goes out and buys an outfit for the evening: a dark brown suit, similar to Gerhard Stübs's uniform. Then he jumps in the car and drives out of town, along the winding roads, and up to the farm where they'd been arrested by the Germans only a few months earlier. He feels like all this is part of a bigger plan. As though everything that has happened has led him here.

What luck to have been caught by the Germans! What luck to have been here already, driving the ammunition truck, to have seen the Norwegian operations before the net closed. And isn't all this information of tremendous value to this secret agent now!

Henry parks his car in the yard between the barn and the farmhouse and notices a little girl inside, tapping a wooden spoon on the window frame, before her mother appears and pulls her away. Moments later the front door opens and a man, wearing rubber boots, steps out with a coat slung over his tatty overalls. It takes a few seconds for him to recognize Henry.

"Well I never . . . Did they let you go?" asks the farmer. Henry gives him an earnest nod of the head.

"Yes. Luckily we were released from the prison camp after two weeks," Henry replies, shaking the farmer's hand enthusiastically.

"If only they knew what we knew," he continues, quieter now, with a wry smile. An air of seriousness hangs between them.

"Are the weapons still safe?"

The farmer nods, with a twinkle in his eye.

"Can you show me where they are?"

The farmer takes him around the barn to an overgrown thicket of nettles and raspberry bushes. Only somebody looking very closely would see that the nettles, with their tiny stinging hairs, had been pushed aside, revealing the lighter green underside of the leaves.

"Two yards into the bushes," he says.

"Great! Safe and sound," Henry replies, while patting the man on his shoulder. "It's crucial for the resistance that these weapons stay here. Is that all right?"

"Yes."

"I really must thank you for your bravery."

"Oh, it's nothing," the farmer replies, quietly, but Henry can see how proud the man is, even though he's resisting the urge to smile.

"Oh, but it *is* something, it's the bravery of people like you that will help beat the Germans and get them out of this country!"

The farmer replies with a nod. Henry pats him on the shoulder again, like a good friend might do, and then starts walking back to his car.

"One final thing," says Henry quietly, as he opens the car door.

"Yes?"

"You might get some National Union people coming here and snooping around. It could even be Norwegians who've changed sides . . . So it's vitally important that you tell no one about these weapons. Understand?"

"I understand!" says the farmer. "I won't mention it to a living soul!"

Rinnan gets back in the car and puts on his driving gloves. Then he turns the ignition switch and pictures the reaction of his German boss, the head of the Gestapo at his desk nodding and smiling while Henry reports all the secret weapons to him. On his very first day of duty! He's going to uncover everything. Soon his little notebook will start filling up with observations, large and small, about everything he finds suspicious. He begins to think about the shops and cafés he should visit; the places where communists and resistance members usually meet. Now he'll show them. Now he'll show them all that he is the best agent they could ever have wished for.

K for the kiosk in Trondheim, where you would sometimes buy a newspaper on your way to the harbor, with its enormous box-like warehouses, the blue-black sea lapping gently at the concrete and tractor tires hung round the quayside. I picture you walking here one morning. The sun hangs low in the sky while the massive cranes, arched with their gigantic metal beaks, cast long shadows over the city. It's a day filled with the whining and screeching of machinery. Random shouts here and there. A man whistles. I picture you walking along the docks, chatting with some of the boat captains, and I imagine your anticipation as the ship glides in from the fjord. There is something almost hypnotic about it, like staring at a bonfire, because although the fjord doesn't change and the ship approaches ever so slowly, it is just enough to keep you transfixed. The orange hull plowing through the water. Seagulls circling overhead, before the birds realize that it is just a freighter, unlikely to provide them with food. I imagine the tiny shapes of people moving on board or just watching from the deck. All in all it's enough to keep you there, watching everything until the ship comes into dock and screeches against the rubber of the gigantic tractor tires. Then the vessel is secured, with ropes so thick they could have come from a colony of giants, so heavy they have to be pulled across by smaller ropes, before the enormous loop can be lifted over the bollard on the quayside.

I imagine you taking the opportunity to practice your languages on these trips to the docks—German with the German workers, French with a wholesaler, and Russian with a ship's captain—before you return to your shop with a box full of buttons and feathers and silk ribbons. I learn that it was these trips to the harbor that led to speculation that your life was merely a cover—that the shop, and the family even, were all a decoy—that you were a spy for the Russians, for the British, or both.

K for the knowledge of what took place in Rinnan's headquarters, the Gang Monastery, as the taxi pulls in and parks by the roadside. It is October, and I am finally back at the place where all these stories converge, this time by appointment arranged via email several months in advance. I check the time on my phone while the taxi driver prints a receipt. It is 5:55, so I'm just a few minutes early. It's a secluded street, not somewhere you would normally go otherwise, and with the colder weather now keeping the children indoors, away from their scooters and trampolines, the neighborhood is almost completely silent. The only sound comes from a moped changing gears a few blocks away.

"Good luck!" says the driver. He's quite familiar with the story of the house and often went there when he was a child, just to look at it. Just to be near it. I thank him while shutting the car door and turn to survey the building. Then I walk down the narrow gravel path and ring the doorbell.

The door is opened by a tall, slim man, whom I recognize from the various news articles he's appeared in. We shake hands, and after a few short questions about my journey, he welcomes me in.

The rooms that reveal themselves before me appear surprisingly normal, as if I had expected it to be like a museum. Several doors lead from a corridor which I recognize from the floor plans I've seen, and from the sketches Grete has made for me.

"Is that where the children's bedroom was?" I ask, and the owner opens the door to a room now used as a library for comic books, all in neat chronological order, and including complete editions of Donald Duck that go back decades. Like Ralph Tambs-Lyche before him, the current owner is a collector. There are also quite a few boxes of LPs. I look toward the corner where Grete has told me the beds—that she and Jannicke slept in—used to be.

It was also the room where the eight-year-old daughter of one of the gang members slept. A little girl who presumably lay there at night listening to the noises from the cellar and fell asleep to the constant hum of voices.

The owner of the house then shows me the living room, with the adjacent kitchen. On the fireplace there's a row of small bullets, strangely soft and with flattened tips after colliding with the stone walls; bullets which the owner found when he tore down some wall panels. He shows me the kitchen and the door leading out to the garden before we go upstairs. On the floor above there is a door which leads to a kind of closet full of old bric-a-brac, and I see the tiny opening in the ceiling through which Jannicke and Grete once crawled with lit candles and found their secret room. Next to us is the door to the bedroom with the arched window, the room Rinnan used as his communications center, with a direct line and telegraph to the Mission Hotel. The owner clears some papers from the desk, and I turn to see a bed that is built into the wall. It was here that Ellen rested when she got her migraines, it was here she lay, I think, but I say nothing to the man living there. I just ask if it's OK to take a few photos on my phone. Then we go back downstairs.

"So I expect you want to take a look at the cellar?" the man says, opening the dark wooden door toward him, releasing a smell of musty cellar air. I nod, smile, and follow him down a staircase with crumbling stone walls either side. The door at the bottom is already slightly open. Perhaps he went down there and opened it before I arrived.

This door was once covered by a large sheet of paper on which one of the gang members had taken a marker pen and drawn a medieval door with diagonal slats and iron hinges. The real door handle was poked crudely through the paper, and at the top, above the door's arch, it said THE GANG MONASTERY, along with a sentence about drinking that I've never been able to decipher: "If you're tired and weary, a shot is the [...]."

On entering the room, I turn around, half expecting to see the other drawing, one that I knew once hung on the other side of the door; a drawing of a skeleton holding a scythe with the words WELCOME TO THE PARTY! written above it.

The ceiling is low, and I try to imagine the various items I know were once here. On the left there was a bar, which several years later became the stage used by Grete and Jannicke. I'd already seen the two barrels, and many of the other things that used to be in the cellar, at Trondheim's Museum of Justice earlier that day.

The owner of the house shows me more of the bullets he found while refurbishing the house. Then he shows me where the prison cells once were. Two small dungeons, evident from the dusty old screw holes and light patches on the wall where the wooden struts had been.

K for Komissar, the family name inherited from your father, Israel Komissar. A name confusingly similar to the titles of many of the men involved in your arrest, processing, and treatment. Perhaps because the words have the same origin, *Reichskommissar* (Reich commissioner). As far as I know, the name was given to your father because he worked as a forester for the Russian tsar—Komissarov: he who serves the tsar.

The name has been passed down to Gerson, and then to Ellen Komissar, who is alone at home, as usual, when this happens. It's an ordinary day, in the middle of the week: Ellen opens the door to the basement. A cold draft of stone and dust blows from the cellar, stopping Ellen in her tracks. She knows that she has to go down, because the maid is out with Grete, and the blouse that she wants to wear is hanging up to dry down there. Gerson is at work, and Jannicke is at school. For a moment she considers wearing something else—or dropping going out and going upstairs for a nap instead, but wouldn't that be a shame?

Sometimes Ellen wishes she could just disappear, or even better, that she could just run away from everything, abandon it all—like Nora did to Helmer in *A Doll's House*—and just leave, start playing the piano again, perform concerts. She sees herself facing a packed concert hall, receiving a standing ovation. She imagines packing her suitcases and just leaving, driving away from her foundering marriage, away from the horrifying images that suddenly pop into her head, away from the sense of failing at everything. But where would she go? How would she get money? It wouldn't work. She cannot do anything. She's just the grandchild of a Jewish tobacco magnate named Moritz Glott and his Norwegian wife, Rosa Olivia; she grew up in a stately villa, with chefs, seamstresses, and maids—an existence supported by a fortune the war had since robbed the family of. And even though her grandfather tried to protect all this wealth—by transferring his shares to his children and to his Norwegian wife—the authorities confiscated his property anyway. The tobacco factory in Oslo was seized, as was her grandfather's villa in Oslo and the country house in Konglungen. Her father Heggeli's villa was also taken by the Nazis, who turned it into a casino. After that they had no choice but to escape.

Nor did it help that her mother was from northern Norway, because by then any strain of Jewish blood was sufficient. The family hadn't understood the gravity of the situation until German soldiers knocked on the door of their villa. They had orders to arrest her grandfather Moritz because he was a Jew. Just as they were discussing why he should go with them, and what he had done wrong, her grandfather had suffered a heart attack, which ironically saved them all, because the soldiers' initial determination to arrest him was suddenly gone. Instead they asked Moritz to report to them if he survived, and as he lay on the floor with stabbing pains in his chest and while the family waited for an ambulance, the soldiers left. Moritz eventually made it to the hospital, which gave his family enough time to plan their escape. He and Rosa fled to a cabin in Gubrandsdalen, while Ellen and the rest of the family fled to Sweden with the help of Carl Fredriksens Transport. They had driven up to the greenhouse and hidden under the tarpaulin beside complete strangers: Ellen, her twin sister, and their parents, all huddled together in the dark, terrified that they would be stopped.

They made it to the border alive, and to a shelter, but the feeling of security never returned. Nor did Ellen's ambition to play concerts or become an artist. While she lived in Sweden, and the years went by, she met Gerson, and the war came to an end. But it never really ended; Ellen was haunted by the past whether she liked it or not, just like that morning when she stood at the door to the cellar.

The door looms before her. She stands there quietly, then shakes her head to herself and grips the handle. The door creaks as it slides open, which it always does, there is no reason to be so scared, she thinks, poking her head into the doorway, as the musty air rises up, cold and dusty. Then she goes down the steps, holding on to the railing, thinking for a moment that Rinnan's hand must have slid down the same length of wood, and she quickly lets go as if it had burned her. Her breathing gets heavier, but she forces herself to keep going down, step by step. She stoops down at the bottom and peers into the room.

"Hello?" she says to the empty room, making sure that no one is there. No one answers. Ellen walks further in, stepping on the floorboards. She's been down here before, of course, there's no reason for all this anxiety, she thinks, but she's never been down here alone, and when you're alone your imagination can transform what you see in a room and fill it with images and memories, just as the cellar does now. As she walks past the bar, where the Rinnan gang once poured drinks for themselves during interrogations, she briefly imagines them beating the prisoners, bound to the chairs, with whips and chains. She hears the screams and recalls the scraps of information people have divulged, while smiling ghoulishly at her, so insensitively, so unable to understand how much harm their words actually do.

Ellen blinks the images away and hurries through the cellar. She sees the bullet holes in the wall but keeps going, round the corner and into the laundry room where her silk blouse hangs from the clothesline, beside a tablecloth, some underwear, and a bedsheet. It's ridiculous to think that someone is in here, she thinks, there are no ghosts down here. But her hands still tremble while she unpins the clothes, so hastily that her white blouse falls to the floor, and she's forced to push the bedsheet aside and bend down. She grabs the garment, lifting it from the floor, and shrieks suddenly when she sees what lies under it—it's only a circular drain for the water to run down, but for a split second Ellen sees blood running into it, and hears the words from her friend: *Did you hear about that? They chopped up three people down there.*

K for kidnap.

K for knife.

K for Karl Dolmen. Nineteen years old and blond-haired, who reported for duty in May 1942 and quickly climbed the ranks to become Rinnan's closest confidant.

It was Karl who stood down in the cellar on that day in late April 1945, with a tormented look on his face. Out of breath, and with a blood-smeared axe in his hands.

L

× × ×

L for the Lisbon massacre in 1506, when a Christian mob—after a long period of drought and bad harvests—took out their despair and anger on the town's Jewish population, who were persecuted, imprisoned, killed, and burned. Almost all of Lisbon's five hundred Jews died over the course of a few bloody days in April.

L for the light in the garden at Jonsvannsveien, as Ellen remembers it falling through the trees during their first summer. She remembers peering up and seeing Gerson holding Jannicke's arms, helping her to jump up the stairs while the little girl beamed with joy. Ellen is lying down upstairs, in the room with the arched window, and in small flashes she remembers her life in exile in Sweden. The light in Gerson's eyes as he turned toward her. She remembers how easygoing he was, and how he stood up one night while several musicians were playing and was allowed to sit behind the drum kit; and she remembers the way his trousers tightened around his buttocks, and the way he smiled at her, only at her, as he sat down on the little drum stool, grabbed the brushes, and set the rhythm for a jazz song that was already under way; and she remembers the happiness she felt when they woke up together and she would stroke his thigh with her hand.

L for lips, for lust, and for the long mornings in bed, just the two of them, listening to the sounds of passersby just outside, so they had to be quiet during sex.

Now, as Ellen lies alone in the loft with a pounding headache, all that happiness seems like a thing of the past, and the light trying to break through the curtains only makes everything worse.

L for Landstadvei 1, the address of Rinnan's family villa in Trondheim, and for the little boy leaning against the upstairs window one afternoon near the end of the war. It is Henry's son, Roar, peering out with his forehead pressed upon the cold glass, looking at the landscape transformed by the golden light of the sun which shines down on the trees and the road. He watches a bird outside, while the sound of his mother banging about with the crockery echoes from the kitchen, and then he finally sees his father walking hurriedly up the road. The boy raises his hand to wave, but his father doesn't see him, just stares dead ahead, stops by a tree. He lights a cigarette. What is he waiting for? thinks the boy. Then he sees another man approaching, also walking quickly and nervously. The boy watches as his father hides behind the tree, and as the other man gets closer, sees him leap out suddenly, grabbing the man by his collar as he recoils in terror. He watches his father gesticulating with his free hand, which is also holding a weapon, and can just about hear his father's voice, shouting angrily. What has the other man done? Roar wonders, immediately thinking that his mother mustn't see what's happening. No one should see this, his father wrestling a stranger to the ground right in front of him, on the grassy slope where they normally go sledding in the winter, kicking the man so that he falls backward and starts rolling down the hill. He watches his father slide the gun back under his jacket, run his fingers through his hair, and straighten his forelock, before turning and continuing up the hill. Roar feels his heart pounding in his chest, his thoughts in a muddle. Suddenly his father looks up at the house, and the boy jumps down from the window, not wanting his father to know that he has seen everything.

L for Last Train, the Oslo bar which for many years was Rikke's favorite haunt. A small and cramped music venue, decked out like a train wagon, with black leather booths. At the end of the '90s the bar was still a place where cigarette smoke rose from the tables, and people would have to shout to hear each other over the music blasting from the speakers. One night she found herself chatting to a guy at the bar, wearing army boots and black jeans. He had a friendly face, and they liked each other and ended up talking for a little while before somehow it slipped out that he was not part of the antiracist community, as Rikke had assumed, but the opposite: he was a neo-Nazi.

"In that case there's nothing more for us to talk about," Rikke had said to him, "since I am from a Jewish family."

He appeared surprised and sad, as though something impossible had occurred to him. Then he asked Rikke what her surname was.

"Komissar," she replied, and the young man nodded a few times, letting the name sink in, before saying: "Komissar, yeah. Then you're on our list."

"What list?" asked Rikke.

"Our death list. Komissar is on it," he repeated and then stopped, as if he was withholding something.

Rikke gave him a hard stare and shook her head. Then without saying another word she returned to her table of friends, while the fear and discomfort started spreading through her body.

×

L for the leaden atmosphere, in the cells at Falstad, stale and musty from body odor.

L for the laughter that occasionally broke out among the prisoners when someone told a joke. You were surprised at how often this happened. As though humor wasn't the first victim of war after all, but among the last, as it helped the prisoners escape the barbed hooks of mistrust, bringing life back to their eyes and a more relaxed look to their faces—for a few seconds at least—in a moment vaguely reminiscent of mercy.

L for Lillemor, or Esther Meyer Komissar, as she was really called. The only one who remained in Sweden after the first time the Komissars fled to Sweden at the outbreak of war in 1940. Lillemor may be the only one of us who'll survive this, you sometimes think, when your circumstances allow you enough peace and energy to reflect; like while you are working in the quarry and the German guards are chatting among themselves. You never got to see it, but Lillemor outlived the war; she outlived everyone, and was almost ninety-nine years old when Rikke and I visited her in Stockholm in 2016.

It was a Sunday in early September, and we had arranged to meet at her home in a functionalist-style apartment block just outside the city. I had met her a couple of times before, the last time at Gerson's funeral, and I remembered her as an energetic and colorful lady who wore large sunglasses and red trousers and who had a passion for art, but that was already a few years back, and I had no idea what shape she was in now. Time can quickly slip away with the elderly, as it can with small children, where only a few years can separate a crawling baby and a preschooler with a satchel and ponytail.

With someone older, five to six years can make the difference between someone who's up and about and someone with dementia, but that was not the case with your daughter. Lillemor received us with a smile and a walker, upon which she balanced a breakfast tray and a cup of coffee. She wore a bright red cardigan and white trousers, matching earrings, and gray hair in a pageboy cut. We took off our shoes, presented her with the bottle of port and basket of strawberries we had brought, and made our way through the first few seconds of social fumbling, helped along by comments about how nice it was to see each other. Immediately afterward, when I stood in her kitchen helping with the food, she tapped her almost-ninety-nine-year-old finger on a mint-green plate I had in my hands and said: "We had that plate when I was a little girl. My mother and father bought it in America."

For a moment I imagine her five- or six-year-old hand, tiny little fingers and soft skin, merged with the sight of her wrinkled fingers and nearly blue nails. The little plate had once possessed an aura of greatness and wonder.

And then what?

A conversation in her living room, which was full of paintings and old furniture from your apartment. The little red loveseat that Lillemor said Marie used to sit in, for example, decorated with carvings and brocade, it survived too. We drank coffee, and she spoke, in Swedish, about her childhood, a monologue that repeatedly looped back to the same point, to something she had said only minutes earlier, but each time including new details, new descriptions, on several occasions wisely and surprisingly worded—such as when Rikke asked her how Gerson and Ellen had been able to buy Rinnan's house after the war.

Lillemor looked down at her hands for a moment and rubbed her fingers together before grasping a layer of imaginary garments and removing them: "One casts off one's feelings," she said, in Swedish. "One has to."

One must cast off one's feelings.

I leaned forward slightly on the couch, thinking about what I had heard about Ellen; how she had become increasingly sick during the time she had lived in the house, while Gerson seemed to be unaffected. "But . . . I get the impression that the house affected Gerson and Ellen quite differently," I said.

Her old hand reached out and placed the coffee cup on the breakfast tray, which was still balanced on top of the walker.

"Yes, there was something about Gerson," she said. "He never allowed anyone to get too close to him, so you never really knew what he felt. It was quite different with Ellen. She was totally . . . totally open," Lillemor said, waving her hand away from her chest and stomach, "completely unguarded, sort of."

The words hung in the air for a few seconds, and then the conversation leapt ahead, like a dog running around a park: sniffing a bench and a tree in one place, then racing off somewhere else, before returning to its owner, and repeating, in ever-increasing circles. Similarly, our talk that day ran away in various directions, but always returned to one of the core elements in any human life: childhood. Without either of us asking, the almost hundred-year-old lady told us that she had danced ballet at the theater in Trondheim since she was four years old.

"It's why I've managed to stay so healthy all these years," she said, stretching her arms out gracefully and straightening herself up in her chair. It was a *grand plié*, while seated.

When Lillemor did this movement, I pictured her as a little girl, dressed in a light-pink ballet costume, with ballet shoes laced around her ankles, like my daughter has, before the conversation took off again in another direction. Her story leaped through the occupation, stepped quickly through the escape to Sweden, before pirouetting to the final story about how she chose to stay in Sweden when the war ended and the others returned to Trondheim.

This mention of her hometown brought the conversation back to the start again, to the theater in Trondheim, and how she had danced ballet there when she was little.

"It's no doubt why I've stayed healthy all these years," she repeated, once again stretching her arms out in an elegant and weightless movement, but this time the back of her hand collided with the coffee cup on the walker, causing the light-brown liquid to spill all over her white trousers and onto the parquet. At once, her age was again reflected in her movements, and the spell was broken.

I took some napkins from the kitchen and allowed the paper to absorb all the spilled coffee from under her chair and round the wheels of her walker. She told us about the nanny you hired to look after the children, and she spoke warmly, and at length, about her mother, Marie, about how sharp she was, and how good she was at making speeches and writing articles; that she sang beautifully, and played the piano, and that she was the first woman to work at the law school—before she got pregnant with Lillemor.

She told us about the shop in Trondheim, about Paris-Vienna, and about how her mother had asked Gerson to move back to Trondheim to help her with the business, and how she tried to find a house for them.

"Time heals all wounds," she said, and then she paused before almost changing her mind, saying: "No, not all of them, but it heals."

L for lassitude. Ellen lies in the upstairs bedroom with her eyes closed, longing for another life, because even though several years have passed since she gave birth, she is still crippled by apathy and fatigue. She can't bear to be with the others, or be the mother she always wanted to be, because her life is so different from what she had dreamt it would be. She who had a whole family around her. Golden opportunities. She had played the piano since she was little, hoping to perform solo concerts in the university's main hall. She was young, and in love. And then the war came along and destroyed it all: the concerts, the boyfriend, the houses in Heggeli and Nordstrand, the seamstresses, the servant's lodge, the driver, and the factory. And now? Now she spends her days and nights in a torture chamber and shares a bed with a man who is almost never home. Now she lives at the end of her wits, through a life that compels her to leave the house as often as possible, to get away from her children as often as possible, even if she doesn't want to, even though it conflicts with how she sees herself, she just can't stop herself. She hears laughter coming from the floor below.

What kind of person am I? she thinks, while turning her face to the wall. She listens to how their Danish maid plays lovingly with the children, how she manages all the things that Ellen cannot deal with herself. The maid can look the children in the eye and laugh wholeheartedly and full of verve. Why is Ellen unable to do the same? Why is she only interested when she sees it all from a distance? When the children are out, or when Jannicke is playing with her little sister, or at school, *then* Ellen has no problem imagining what she will do with them. She will teach them to sew, perhaps, or take them to the theater or into town. She imagines them all walking together, just the three of them, and pictures the two girls looking up to her smiling and laughing, while the conversation bounces along lightly and they chat about everything between heaven and earth. But she never quite manages to make this daydream a reality. Every time the real girls walk through the door, with all their questions and their noise and demands, it's as though all these dreams evaporate, replaced by a dark mist that just engulfs her, forcing her to withdraw from it all, to lie down and listen to life being played out downstairs, without her.

Maybe I'm sick? she thinks, and closes her eyes again. Or worse: perhaps there's something wrong with me, some sort of genetic defect. Are other people like this? Neighbors, family, friends of Gerson? How do they cope with it all? How can they smile so much, laugh so much, talk so freely?

Are they stupid? Don't they know what happened, or are they just insensitive? Why is it only me who's unable to shut these thoughts out? she asks herself while she walks down the corridor to the living room. She passes the maid, who is humming to herself. So young. Such slender lines and dresses that accentuate her hips and breasts, just because of their cut, without a neckline, without the dresses being improper or too short, because they're not, there's *nothing* in the way she dresses that can be criticized, but nevertheless! Nevertheless there's something provocative about her, and it's not like she hasn't seen Gerson having a sneaky look. Peeping up accidentally from his newspaper when she walks by, just to get a glimpse of her bottom as she scurries out of the room holding a stack of plates or towels.

Dear God! Pull yourself together, Ellen! she thinks, trying to shake off her fears, but the paranoia comes back all the same. She had only recently walked in on Gerson and the maid while they were alone in the kitchen. They were chatting, several feet apart, it wasn't like she walked in on them in the bedroom, tightly embraced with the maid's dress pulled up past her thighs; but there was something about the atmosphere in the room, or more precisely, about how the mood changed when Ellen walked in. How the laughter subsided, and the warmth between them cooled, like a sudden change in the weather brought on by a late summer depression. She had attempted a smile, and in a light, enthusiastic tone tried to ask what they were talking about; but they were perhaps too surprised by her enthusiasm, and if they weren't already ashamed, then her presence must have reminded them of the betrayal about to happen? Or is she overreacting? Was she imagining it all? The Danish maid is certainly nice, charming, and shouldn't Gerson be allowed to talk to her?

My God, Ellen thinks, listening with her eyes closed to the sounds of life drifting up from the floor below. Would anyone blame him for looking at other women when I am in *this state?* she thinks, but it doesn't help. Her thoughts have led her into a deep quagmire, and there's no way she can extract herself. The more she struggles, the deeper she sinks.

She hears Gerson come in downstairs, hears them laughing and chatting, like a couple, and decides to take action. She has to do something. Something drastic.

L for Levanger.

L for limbo, and loneliness, and luck.

L for Little London, as the coastal city of Ålesund was nicknamed, where the boats carrying weapons sent from England reached land, and from where the little boats full of refugees set sail.

L for life, the toughness and solidity some children have, withstanding anything, like a dandelion growing through the solid street. Grete uses this description of herself when referring to the years after her parents were divorced and they moved back to Oslo to separate apartments. Gerson with a new girlfriend, Ellen to an apartment downtown which Gerson paid for. Grete told us about how her mother started going to art school, that she had barely any income but survived on Gerson's contributions. We heard about how Jannicke had to make dinner using whatever meager ingredients she could find in the fridge. Grete also told us how she would get free apples from the people running the store across the road. She told us how the years went by, and how her father eventually moved abroad with his new wife.

L for Lex Rinnan, "Rinnan's Law," which was a contract that the surviving agents of the Rinnan gang said they were required to sign. It made it forbidden to oppose Rinnan on anything. Nobody could question his decisions, and last but not least, it was forbidden to leave the gang. Rinnan's Law outlined what the penalties were for breaking these rules—and opposing the leader was punishable by death.

M

× × ×

M for mistrust, mistreatment, and monotony. For mud, and morale, and mortality.

M for misery, and the horror of Falstad's "dark cell," a place you did everything you could to avoid, because the dark cell was no more than a windowless closet where the guards would pour cold water on the floor to prevent the prisoner from lying down. One gray March morning you saw a man being shoved through the door of the dark cell. You saw him look down at his wet feet, without saying a word, before the door was closed and locked behind him. Later you heard him being dragged out and beaten, before he was thrown back into the cell again. You never found out what he had done, and whenever you heard the prisoner screaming in pain, your only immediate thought was of relief that it wasn't you. And whenever the guards looked up, aware that you'd seen what they were doing, you were mindful to keep walking and not give them an excuse to seize you too.

M for music, and how Marie would spend the afternoons at the piano in your apartment, playing sonatas by Chopin or pieces by Mozart. Melodies written hundreds of years earlier that would fill the apartment and create some continuity throughout the day, interrupted now and then by the children, who would charge over to the piano and hammer on the low keys with tiny, flat hands, so wide-eyed and innocent that it was difficult to reprimand them, even though one really should. The children got older, and the interruptions ceased, but her playing became more infrequent nevertheless. She would sit down to play the occasional étude but would often stand up again suddenly, with a wistful look on her face.

M for the monster that lies ready, waiting within all of us.

M for mankind, and that morning when Lillemor made a particular statement that I'll never forget. She said: "Humans are the most extreme of all animals. Humans can be so terrible . . . and so good." Then she gave a quick turn of her wizened hand. This "both" was the outside of a hand—that can curl into a fist and punch; and the inside of a hand—that can gently stroke a cheek, offer comfort, cradle a newborn baby's head, or carefully shape a mound of clay rotating on a potter's wheel.

M for more, M for mole, M for members. The face of Gerhard Stübs breaks into a smile when Henry enters the door to the Nazi headquarters again, at the Mission Hotel. He praises Rinnan for his first assignment and how he managed to reveal the hidden weapons on that farm. Henry tries not to smile too much and replies that it was nothing.

"We think you are ready for something bigger now. You probably know already how members of different resistance groups make our job more difficult?"

"Yes."

"Your job is to infiltrate the Norwegian resistance, reveal the members to us . . . ," says Gerhard Stübs.

"Like a mole?" Henry asks.

"Yes, like a mole. You must always be on the lookout, wherever you are. Take notes and report everything you find suspicious to me. Is that understood?" he asks. Rinnan once again offers his gratitude for Stübs's belief in him and then leaves. He walks through the mass of soldiers and functionaries, past the stacks of papers and boxes, and realizes that this time he really has to prove himself.

He puts his feelers out, having been told that nothing is too small or insignificant, and crams his notebook with information, keen to make an impression, so they'll know that hiring him was a smart choice and give him more work. He drives to the farms he previously visited and makes notes about where the weapons are hidden and of who sympathizes with whom. He perfects his routine, his lines, his techniques, and slowly begins to expand his territory. In autumn 1940, he travels to Romsdal, where he finds a talkative man working in a shop. They discuss the hopeless situation the occupation has brought, and the shopkeeper tells Rinnan how shocked he was when two women came in one day and said that they supported the Nazis.

"Isn't that despicable?" he says, removing a bit of tobacco from his teeth. Rinnan smiles and leans over the counter.

"Can I tell you something?"

"What?"

"Those two women. They were sent here by me . . ."

"What do you mean?" asks the bewildered man, taking a step back and looking nervously at the door as if momentarily considering escaping through it.

"I wanted to test you, to see how you reacted," replies Rinnan quietly, almost whispering. He taps his cigarette on the shop counter. "You can never be too sure these days. Some Norwegians have even defected to the Germans. So like I said, I wanted to test you by sending the two women ahead of me. Now we know for sure that you're on the right side," he concludes.

"But . . . but why?" the shopkeeper asks, still confused.

"I'm scouting the area to find anyone who wants to take up arms . . . form groups and help the resistance. Do you know of anyone I should talk to?"

The shopkeeper smiles with relief and provides Rinnan with an address, a new door he can knock on, new people who will let him in, new names that can be logged in his notebook that night, before driving home to report his findings to Stübs. He continues scouting the area on his own, by train, by bus, and by car, and at night he returns home to sleep, although his stopovers get shorter each time. He hugs the children, brings them food and presents, and watches how their faces light up with joy. That's what it's like to have *him* as a father. He provides them with sugar and fresh bread, new coats and thick sweaters. There are meat casseroles and desserts, spirits and cigarettes. And the other families? They live on restricted goods. Rations. Crumbs. All because they're not pragmatic or smart enough to grasp the mistake they're making. They need only look around, or glance at a newspaper, to see where things are heading, there are stories everywhere about how the Germans are winning, on ever-new fronts. It should be obvious who is going to win this war, thinks Rinnan. They are taking over, country after country.

Soon news arrives that Hitler wants to invest heavily in Trøndelag, and that he is planning an Aryan city. There is also word that an underground U-boat base is to be established in Trondheim, to halt the flow of weapons and enemy soldiers from Britain. The constant flow of boats carrying supplies for the resistance, who time and again manage to organize and attack—shooting soldiers, destroying train lines and bridges vital to the Germans—is a huge problem. Rinnan understands the gravity of the situation and realizes that he now has an opportunity to do something big. What if he could infiltrate the resistance around the coast! What if he could find out where the boats are coming ashore and who is responsible for meeting them! Imagine what that would mean! It could really earn him a reputation, not only in Trøndelag and elsewhere in little Norway, but in Britain too, and Germany. With Adolf Hitler even.

Henry walks through the doors of the Mission Hotel and nods to the soldiers, then he walks briskly down the hallway, past the secretary, who looks up and smiles.

Many know his name, and most of the soldiers know who he is.

Rinnan has become Stübs's main man, and Stübs now refers to him only by his surname. His forename is now just a skin that he peels off and leaves behind, like the dry, yellowy viper skins you sometimes find on the forest floor; the only visible sign that a snake has grown. "Henry Oliver" is no more. Gone is the bullying, the harassment and ridicule. Gone are the wanderings on the outskirts of Levanger with his head hung low to avoid the looks from strangers. Now he is "Rinnan," or "Lola." Now he is based in Trondheim, where he has been asked to move with Klara and the kids into a beautiful, two-story villa, where a politician of some sort has been kicked out. Henry is transformed. A secret agent, with a salary, responsibility, and access to all the free cigarettes and alcohol he wants. He walks through the streets in his dark-brown suit, with its wide breeches. This is how things are going to be from now on, he thinks. He presents Stübs with his plan to dismantle the resistance and is told to get to work.

It's so simple, almost *too* simple, thinks Rinnan. He knows Trondheim and its social strata very well and knows exactly where to begin. That's why they hired *him* and no one else, thinks Rinnan smugly while crossing the cobbled street with steady footsteps, heading to his destination; because he knows all too well where the communists and resistance members in Trondheim tend to meet: at the Union Building café.

He turns the corner and arrives at a large functionalist brick building which, despite it being the middle of the day, is packed with people reading newspapers, smoking, and chatting. Rinnan feels himself being watched as he walks up the steps and over to the bar. He orders himself a drink and, while the bartender fills his cup with steaming black coffee, scans the room quickly, pretending to search for an empty table. In reality he is trying to figure out who is worth closer attention and who isn't; who is only there to pass the time, and who has come here for a secret meeting or to recruit new men and women to the resistance.

A man with short dark hair glances up from his newspaper and gives Rinnan a quizzical look. Even though it lasts only a split second, Rinnan knows that his unfamiliar face has been registered.

The café is at its busiest, and Rinnan stands at the bar, surrounded by the loud hum of conversation, cradling his coffee cup and peering around at the other customers. Then someone stands up, leaving an empty seat right next to the man that Rinnan would like to talk to. He goes over and stops beside the chair.

"Excuse me, is anyone sitting here?" he asks, nodding casually toward the table. The man, who Rinnan has in fact selected, nods and says: "No, take it."

"Thank you," Rinnan replies, as he sits down. He takes a sip of his coffee and pulls out his cigarette case, which he gives a little shake and hears a solitary cigarette rattling inside. He opens the case and sighs deeply at the sight, pretends to hesitate, as if considering whether to save the cigarette until later, it being his last one, before changing his mind and placing the cigarette between his lips. Then he pats the sides of his jacket, looking for his lighter or the box of matches. He thrusts his hands in his trouser pockets but pulls them out empty and sighs once again before turning to the man beside him, who is clearly aware of what's going on because he is already waiting with a lighter in his hand.

"Do you need a light?" asks the stranger. He has a Trondheim accent.

"Thanks," says Rinnan, lighting his cigarette and blowing smoke from the corner of his mouth before placing the lighter back on the table in front of the man. In his hometown, Levanger, he would have been recognized at once, but not here. Not in Trondheim.

"Very kind of you," he says. "I'd forgotten that I was out of gas. And out of *these too*," he adds, shaking his cigarette case again and smiling sardonically. "Thanks to the Germans it'll soon be impossible to get hold of anything . . . ," he mumbles, almost under his breath, then takes another drag and waits to see if the man takes the bait.

"Quite right," replies the man, lighting himself a cigarette. *Here's my chance*, thinks Rinnan, turning to the man and looking him in the eye.

"I was a busy man before all this . . . ," he says, leaning forward and lowering his voice furtively, to create a private space between them, a little conclave, ". . . until this damned invasion!"

"Is that right?" replies the other man. Still leaning back in his chair, his body language underlining the distance between them. "And what was it you did?" Henry grips the cigarette firmly between his lips and extends his right hand toward the man, one eye squinting from the cigarette smoke. "My name's Ole Fiskvik. Crewman," Henry says, retracting his hand again. "Well, I *was* a crewman until the occupation . . . And you?"

Rinnan notices how the words sink in, and how they affect the man, like tiny sparks igniting his imagination and making his eyes come to life.

"Fiskvik? Are you by any chance related to that fabulous local politician, Arne-Johan Fiskvik?" the other man asks quietly while leaning toward the table.

Rinnan leans back a little, smiles, and says:

"Related and related . . . he's my brother."

"Is that so? A man who's done so much for this country?" exclaims the man while looking around the room, clearly having to restrain himself, because now he blinks in astonishment and leans even further back in his chair, *but that's fine,* thinks Rinnan, now he's on the hook. He's swallowed the bait, and now it's just a question of reeling him in.

"Yes, my brother's done a lot for communism," says Rinnan, taking another drag from his cigarette and blowing the smoke downward.

"He's actually been able to *contribute* something, instead of just coming here and hanging around, with absolutely nothing to do . . . ," he sighs and flicks the ash from his cigarette. "I *have* managed to save up a bit of money, but what do I need money for when it's impossible to buy anything? Everything's rationed!"

Rinnan looks up and sees that the man is thinking; the surge of activity in his brain as he weighs up the risks and possibilities.

"Well, there might be something you can do," says the man quietly.

"Oh, really," Rinnan replies. First to himself, mostly, as it takes a moment for him to register that the man is handing him a coded invitation. He looks the man straight in the eye and asks what he means.

"If you want, I might know someone you can contact," the man says.

"Of course I do. When?"

"It depends on how busy you are."

"I stopped being busy on April the 9th, 1940, unfortunately. So I'm free any time," Rinnan replies, waiting while the other man leans in to allow a stranger to pass, so close that it lifts the back of his chair.

"Really. What about right now then?" asks the man, his teeth becoming visible.

"Now? Well that is the best of all possible times," Rinnan replies.

They look at each other for a second or two, and the resistance man bursts out laughing.

"In that case, just finish your coffee and follow me," he says, rising to his feet. "You can call me Knut, by the way. Come!"

Rinnan takes a last sip of his coffee, and stands up. They walk out into the sun.

"There. Not so many ears listening out here," says Knut, wrapping his jacket tightly around him.

"You can't be too careful nowadays," says Rinnan, with a serious look on his face.

"Unfortunately not," replies Knut as he walks across the road with Rinnan following behind. "And still, we need all the help we can get."

"Then it was a stroke of luck that I ran into you today," says Rinnan. "I'm very happy to contribute," he says, making sure these last words come out with a degree of restrained enthusiasm.

"Do you have access to a car, Fiskvik?"

"Yes. The one I used before the war, it's in the garage."

"I'm involved with making a newspaper, you see . . . We need help distributing what we write."

"You mean . . . about the resistance?" Rinnan whispers.

They pass a woman with a pram, and Knut pauses for a moment, until they are a few yards apart, before answering.

"Yes, if that's not too daunting for you?"

"Not at all," replies Rinnan, shaking his head. "On the contrary."

"OK, Ole. I'll be honest with you," says Knut, stopping on the path just beside the river. Down by the shore a seagull pecks at another dead bird, burying its beak into its guts, then popping its head up to look around with its piercing black eyes.

"What we're doing is very risky. And no one gets paid for their work either. You understand?"

"I understand. Thanks. I really should think about it . . . Let's see . . . OK! I've thought about it. Shall we move on?" asks Rinnan, smiling at Knut, who starts laughing.

"Great, I hoped you'd say something like that. Come this way, Fiskvik."

"Where are we going?" Rinnan asks quietly.

"To our headquarters," Knut replies.

×

They hurry off double-quick down the road, then into an alley and through the door of a small bedsit. There is barely any furniture in the room and the windows are covered in blackout curtains. What was once a student residence is now an underground print shop, full of type cases, print cylinders, and paper rolls—an effective yet small-scale and amateurish operation. Two men look up at him and nod, and Rinnan introduces himself as Ole Fiskvik. He starts flicking through one of the newspapers, and a rush of excitement hits him. Just imagine what Gerhard Stübs will say when he reads this! Articles calling for people to resist, urging them to stand firm, a list of the successful operations carried out by the resistance, news of the Allies' victories from the front line.

"The equipment is old, unfortunately. But it's all we have," says the man.

"Oh, but this is great!" says Rinnan. "These newspapers will attract even more people to our side. That's how this war will be won. If you need anyone, I'd be happy to help distributing it!"

"We need help . . . ," says the man, but now with a more resigned look on his face. Rinnan sees him glance at the other two, as if gauging what they think, whether they think it is safe enough; and when none of them seem to be against the idea, but simply raise their shoulders, the man turns back to Rinnan and asks when he can start.

"I can start tomorrow," says Rinnan. "The sooner the better."

"Thank you, Fiskvik," the man says. He smiles warmly and suggests a time for them to meet again the next day.

Rinnan thanks the men for all their work. Then he peeks outside to check that the exit is clear before hurrying out the door and through the alleyways, while memorizing the route. After a long detour, to make sure he is not being followed, he finally slips through the doors of the Mission Hotel. There is so much to report that he is almost tempted to run through the corridors and up to Stübs's office. The Germans have spent months trying to roll up this network, without a single lead, and now, just like the case with the farmer and the weapons, he has uncovered everything in one morning!

The men greet each other, and Henry quickly unrolls the newspapers he took from the resistance, spreading them out on the desk before Stübs. The officer leans over the propaganda material while mumbling to himself. Then he looks up at Rinnan, asking where he got them from, and Rinnan recounts the whole story; about how he'd been able to single out the right man in a café downtown and win his trust by pretending to be the brother of a well-known local communist. He tells Stübs about their little bedsit, about the printing press and the network of people distributing the newspaper in all the surrounding towns. He talks about how their equipment is outdated and makeshift, but that they can still cause a lot of damage. Stübs puts his glasses down on the desk. Then he pats Rinnan on the shoulder and congratulates him on his work, saying that what he has done is *quite incredible,* that Rinnan has made an *outstanding effort,* and that he knew it was a good idea to hire him. Henry stands there, with a barely restrained smile on his face, as they shower him with praise. Stübs asks for the address, and Henry gives him the directions he memorized earlier.

The room then falls silent, and Stübs looks deep in thought. Then he gently strokes the palm of his hand on the desk and asks Rinnan to wait for a moment, saying that there is someone he would like him to meet.

Henry nods, wondering who it could be.

Stübs returns with two men. One of them in uniform, slightly balding and with clear blue eyes.

"Rinnan. This is our commander-in-chief, Gerhard Flesch," says Stübs. The new officer extends his hand, and Rinnan shakes it. Then Stübs addresses the man, in German, explaining who Henry is.

"And the third man here is your interpreter. Flesch doesn't speak Norwegian, but he's been working in Bergen since the invasion so he understands a fair bit."

Flesch nods. Then he says something in German to Rinnan that the interpreter translates, and for a moment there is a strange and embarrassing silence where they both have to wait for the meaning of the words to reach them.

"I hear that you have discovered the hiding place of some of our worst enemies?" says the interpreter.

Rinnan nods. He tells the officer about the print works and the underground newspaper, and about how this propaganda is being spread throughout the region. The interpreter translates, and Flesch nods approvingly.

"*And you have the address?*" Flesch asks the interpreter, but Henry understands enough German to nod affirmatively before the question is translated.

"Yes . . . they're probably still there," Rinnan continues eagerly. "You ought to send some men to get them . . . quickly," he says, but Flesch says he has a better idea.

"*These men. They think you are on their side,*" continues Flesch, with a knowing smile. "*And in addition, they're planning to distribute resistance material all over the county. Is that correct?*"

Rinnan waits for the translation.

"Eh . . . Yes?"

"*Then we must help them, Rinnan. Help them with their distribution. Perhaps you could get a stack of newspapers, and offer to drive around delivering them?*"

Henry picks up some of what's being said along the way, words like *helfen* and *verteilen*, but he waits for the translation, and even then it's unclear. *Help* them?

"But . . . why?" Henry asks.

"This will provide us with an overview of the entire network, and then we'll simply tear it down," says Stübs in Norwegian, swiping at the air between them as if tearing down an imaginary cobweb.

"So I'd be a double agent?" Rinnan asks. Flesch nods.

"We call it *playing in the negative sector*. Infiltrating and surveilling

the enemy, making them work for us while they think they're working for themselves. This way we can find out who the ringleaders
are . . . and eliminate the whole Trøndelag network. It may even lead
us to the leaders in the other cities too, like Oslo and Bergen . . ."

Rinnan smiles, because this is like something from one of the
spy thrillers he once read. It could be a movie, except now it's *him,*
Henry Oliver Rinnan, stepping into the screen to play the lead role.

*"Which is why, Rinnan, you mustn't say a word to anyone about this
group,"* continues Flesch. *"You mentioned something about them having
outdated equipment?"*

Rinnan nods while waiting for the translation.

*"It's better for us if they print lots of newspapers. The more they print and
distribute, the more enemies we can reveal. And I've got an idea for how we can
help make their work more effective,"* says Flesch. Then, looking pleased
with himself, he leans across the table and explains his plan.

That evening Henry is back at home with his family, balancing his
son on his lap, pretending his knees are the seat of a truck, driving
faster and faster along a bumpy road. The boy sits there screaming with laughter, waiting for the moment they are both anticipat-
ing, where the truck swerves off the road. Henry parts his knees,
and his son falls between his legs, holding on tight to stop himself
from crashing to the floor. He then twists himself round and cuddles up to his father while trying to catch his breath. Klara smiles
at them from the kitchen doorway, with their daughter suckling
at her breast. There is something mournful about her smile, but
that's just how it has to be, Henry thinks. Her problem. Once the
children are asleep he finds a bottle of liquor, and quickly pours
himself one glass after another, thinking about their elaborate plan
for the morning. This could be big. This could be very, very big, he
thinks contentedly while emptying his glass. Then he goes to bed,
without waiting for Klara.

Evening turns to night.

Night turns to morning. The light shines through the curtains and onto Klara, lying with her back to him. Is she awake? Maybe. Henry gets out of bed, gets dressed, and eats breakfast with his son, and then goes straight to the resistance headquarters. It's the safest thing to do in case one of them is following him, then they'll see him leaving his house and going straight to them. Flesch is organizing everything else.

He knocks on the door, and they let him in. Once inside he tells them he has got hold of a printing press from an old friend at a print house that has closed. He tells them what brand of machine it is and how many flyers it prints per hour.

"When can we get it?" asks one of the others, a man who hasn't said a word until now.

"It's waiting at the railway station. They delivered it this morning. All we have to do is drive there and pick it up, and make sure that no one is following us."

"OK, but what about the meeting later?" asks the man. The men exchange glances with each other. What meeting are they talking about?

"We'll be back before long," says Rinnan.

"Let's go!"

They drive out to the station and walk in pairs, pretending not to know each other. And while someone keeps watch in the parking lot the other two go in and bring the crate outside. They load it into the car, and drive off feeling relieved.

Back at their hideout they park nearby, making sure there are no Germans about before sneaking round the corner and into the bedsit.

They open the crate and lift out the printer. One man laughs out loud, while the others move closer for a better look at the new machine—a modern press, made of steel and glass, with rows of buttons and little round lights.

Henry explains how fast it can print, how many sheets pass through it per minute, and how it both prints and staples the sheets in the correct order.

"My God, Fiskvik? Are they really giving us this?"

"Not to keep, but you can borrow it until the war is over. The owner can't use it until the Germans are gone, and I told him that might happen a bit faster if we were able to borrow it. That was all he needed to hear."

"It's incredible," says one of the other men, shaking his head.

"How can we ever thank you?"

"By getting the Germans out of Norway!" Henry replies. "And if I can, I'd like to help!"

"You can! Like I said yesterday, we need someone to drive round the area delivering the newspapers . . . It's not without risk, but if you . . ."

"I'd be happy to. It will be an honor!" Rinnan answers, with a measured, humble smile, delighted at just how gullible the men are, but noticing the weariness in their smiles. It's a tiny glimpse of the mental stress they are living with, risking their lives, while perhaps having families at home. So grateful to have someone else to share the burden with that they don't ask any questions.

They give Henry a handwritten list of places to stop at, including the names of the contacts who will take delivery of the newspapers and distribute them. He packs some of the previous editions into a briefcase and thanks everyone again. But just as he is about to leave—eager to tell Flesch everything—two strangers walk in, and the whole mood in the room changes.

"*There* you are!" says Knut. "I want you to meet our newest recruit," he continues, walking over to Henry and bringing him forward. "This is Ole Fiskvik, the brother of . . . yep, that's right!" he says, beginning to laugh. The two men's faces remain serious. "Fiskvik here has got hold of a new printing press for us and is going to help with distribution. Fiskvik, these are two of our most important men. The leader of the Oslo group . . . and the leader of the Bergen group."

Henry greets them in a polite, almost servile manner, feigning respect, telling them what an honor it is, and taking care to give them both a firm handshake, because that's what these people tend to like, he thinks. The leader of the Oslo group informs them about a general strike that's being planned, one that will paralyze the whole of occupied Norway, and Rinnan hangs on to his every word. The other man talks about how they plan to sabotage German cargo ships at one of the ports. Henry tries to keep up with it all, but gets so nervous he has to find something to do with his hands, so he thrusts them into his pockets and pulls out his cigarette case, lights a cigarette, and continues listening intensely. He then slides the case back into his coat pocket but realizes that he might get better acquainted with the men if he offered them a cigarette too. So he rummages through his coat pocket again, past his keys and his gloves, and pulls out the case but realizes too late that it's another, quite different, box. The other men stop talking.

"Wow! Have you got two different brands on you? I'm impressed . . . ," says the leader of the Oslo group sarcastically. Luckily, the other man hasn't noticed and remains hunched over the plans spread out on the table.

"Yeah, can you believe it?" replies Rinnan, smiling diffidently. "I've been out of cigarettes for weeks and then suddenly got the chance to buy some, so I made the most of it. Now I don't dare leave them anywhere. Would you like one?" he asks, offering his cigarette case to the man, but suddenly the leader of the Bergen group turns around and picks up their conversation again.

"OK, everyone. We've got a lot of details to cover," he says, looking up at the clock. They're short on time, which is a stroke of luck, thinks Henry, because soon everyone is more focused on the task before them and not so much on him. So he stays where he is, in the background, repeating all the details to himself. Eventually, the leader of the Oslo group leaves, shortly followed by the leader of the Bergen group, a few minutes' gap between them for safety reasons. But the others remain where they are, and their attention quickly returns to Henry.

"Phenomenal," says Rinnan. "Just the sort of courageous men we need to see off the Germans."

"Indeed. But we all contribute what we can, Fiskvik," says one of the other men, patting the side of the printing press. The others nod, and one of them slides a pile of newspapers toward him. Henry takes a deep breath and picks them up, then, with a sober, appreciative smile, places them all in his briefcase. Now he has the names of even more contacts, at even more locations.

"And these are all good people?" Henry asks. "They're people you know well, right?"

He gets a pat on the back and a thank-you for being so vigilant, then he too slips out the door, feeling as though he could dance across the cobblestones. But it's too risky to do that. And he knows that he ought to go straight home to his family in case he is followed, but he just cannot wait to tell Flesch what he's heard. It has to be reported right away. So he walks a couple of blocks in the wrong direction, then turns a corner and waits a few seconds, with his heart pounding, before turning to look back down the road, but no one is following him. Then he continues through the town center toward the Mission Hotel while constantly repeating the names and dates the two leaders had discussed, until he finally slips through the doors of the hotel. Only then does he feel safe enough to pull out the little notebook from his inside pocket and write down every detail he can remember: the names of the two leaders, the dates of the attacks, and the addresses of the various hideouts. This is almost *too* good, he thinks, snapping shut the notebook, which rings with a satisfyingly loud clap. Then he rushes off to the office of Gerhard Flesch.

Flesch sits at his desk, leaning over a document and a half-eaten mille-feuille, cream oozing between the pastry layers, and he detects something is up the moment Rinnan walks in, with a pile of resistance newspapers under his arm. He tells them about the distribution network, shows them the list of names and places, and as if that wasn't enough, as a bonus, he can tell them that he met the leaders of two other resistance cells and heard all about their plans to sabotage the railway line. All this is translated to Flesch, who immediately shakes his head, and not in a negative way, no, no, no, he does it to show Henry that he has done something quite remarkable. *"An extraordinary achievement,"* he says, thanking him for his efforts before saying something that Henry will always remember: *"I knew we could rely on you!"*

Henry quickly finds himself involved in the further planning; consulted about what should be done and the most effective way to do it. And as they sit there discussing strategies, he realizes that everything has changed because of his spying. Because of the headway *he* has made.

The Nazis put their plan into action. Fifty-three people are arrested. Several of them are killed. Henry doesn't take part in the operation, but he hears about its success from the others. The strike and the sabotage are thwarted.

Once the operations are completed, Flesch invites Henry to his office to celebrate. They drink expensive brandy from cut-crystal glasses. They drink for victory, and Henry is told that he will be promoted, that his wages will increase, and that he will soon be given new and even more important assignments.

"Für Agent Lola," says Flesch, raising his glass for a toast. And the others smile and raise their glasses too.

Several days later, Flesch asks Henry if he has been trained in *Abfragetechnik*. The office secretary sitting nearby translates for him:

"Interrogation methods," she says.

Henry shakes his head. *"Nein,"* he says.

Flesch asks him to follow him downstairs to the Mission Hotel's basement, and although Rinnan has heard about the prison cells on the floors beneath the offices, he still hasn't seen them with his own eyes. Flesch summons the interpreter, and off they go, down the stairs until they reach the cells, where the air smells of iron and tobacco and sweat and fear, and where there is always someone screaming. Flesch stops at a cell and talks briefly about the prisoner inside, who they suspect knows something about the smuggling of the resistance members. He says that men like him are a danger to the entire Third Reich.

"That's how you have to view them. First and foremost as a danger."

The interpreter translates.

"Furthermore, you must tell yourself that they have a key, a solution—and their will is standing in the way of this. But we can unlock this will with another tool: pain."

Flesch nods at the soldier behind them, signaling to open the cell door. As easy as that. His will. All it takes is a subtle nod for doors to open, and food and drinks to be served. One sign from him can have people arrested, shot, or released.

Inside the cell, a seated man leans forward with his arms tied behind his back. On a table beside him there are various tools. A whip. A bradawl. A knife.

The prisoner looks up at him. His hair is lank and greasy, and his eyes flash with a mixture of fear and anger.

"You see?" says Flesch in German, while taking out a pair of yellow leather gloves. *"They need to be tamed . . . like wild animals who need to be taught who their master is . . . They need to be broken, and then they'll tell us . . . and help us to end this war, so we can all get out of this mess."*

He pulls the gloves onto his hands and turns to face the prisoner.

"Isn't that right?"

The punch catches Henry off guard. Flesch's clenched fist, wrapped tightly in a yellow glove, flies toward the prisoner, striking him above his cheek. There's a groan, and a string of bloody saliva hangs from the corner of the prisoner's mouth.

"A single blow from a fist is a great way to start. To warm up."

The interpreter translates, although clearly uncomfortable with the situation. Flesch punches the prisoner again. Henry feels his heart beating rapidly as the aggression in the room intensifies. The interpreter asks Flesch something in German, presumably if it's necessary for him to be down there, or if he can be permitted to leave.

Flesch punches the man again, with his left hand, and then shakes his head. Imagine having that sort of power? Rinnan thinks. He smirks to himself, remembering the time he gutted a fish in front of Klara, and how she turned away when he sliced open its belly and pulled out the contents, squeezing the fish's intestines, stomach, and liver, as they dangled from his fingers in a slimy cluster of purple and yellow. The prisoner sitting in front of them screws up his eyes while mucus and blood pour from his nose. Flesch removes his yellow gloves again, folds them carefully, and puts them in his coat pocket, before turning to Henry to say something for the interpreter to translate:

"Now it's your turn."

Not a question, an assertion. Henry nods and looks at the prisoner, conscious that Flesch and the translator are watching him. *It's a test*, he thinks, while clenching his fist so hard that his fingernails dig into the palm of his hand. *It's a test, and now I have to show them that I can do it*, he thinks. Then he punches the prisoner, his knuckles striking something unexpectedly hard. A nose bone, or a cheekbone perhaps. The punch is so hard that the prisoner's chair tips backward, balancing on two legs for a moment, before sending the man crashing to the ground.

Flesch starts laughing. *"What a punch,"* he says, in German, leaning over the man lying on the stone floor.

"Are you ready to talk to us now? Who is helping you? Who are your contacts?"

The interpreter translates. But the man keeps his mouth tightly shut, refusing to say anything. So Flesch stands up again, pretending to be disappointed.

"Oh well. Sometimes you just have to change tools to break into where

you want to go," he says, placing his boot on the man's face while the interpreter translates. The prisoner's cheek folds up against his mouth, reminding Henry of how he would stand grimacing in front of the mirror when he was a child. A gurgling noise comes from the prisoner's throat as Flesch twists his boot, placing all his weight on it before stepping on the man, like he was a tree stump poking up from a forest trail. Then he walks over to the table, where a selection of tools lie waiting: a metal vice, large enough to hold an ankle or an arm, a whip full of nails, several clubs, and some batons. Neatly laid out in a row.

"It's a matter of finding the right spot," he says, taking the bradawl from the table. Then he grabs one of the man's feet and pulls off his shoe.

"The sole of the foot is a good place."

Flesch pulls off the man's sock and strokes the underside of his foot from ankle to toe. *"Especially here,"* he says, tapping his finger on the area between the ball of the foot and the heel, where the foot never touches the ground, and the skin is at its thinnest.

"Could you just hold on to the other foot please?"

Rinnan goes over and grabs hold of the prisoner's other ankle. The man tries kicking himself free, but soon lies motionless again. All that can be heard is the sound of his breathing. There's a piercing shriek as Flesch sticks the bradawl into the man's foot, pushing it slowly into the muscle.

"Are you ready to talk now?"

"Yeeees!"

A scream. Blood, spit, and tears pour out of him. Flesch looks over at Rinnan and pulls out the bradawl. Blood oozes from the hole in the man's pale skin; trickling down his heel and dripping onto the floor.

"I . . . will . . . talk . . ."

"What did I tell you?" says Flesch, satisfied, placing the bradawl back on the table, lining it up carefully with the whip handle. Then he bends forward, pulls out a notebook, and asks the prisoner to start talking. After a few minutes of crying, and in a voice hoarse from screaming, all the names are entered in Flesch's book, and Flesch rises to his feet.

"Any will can be broken. It's only a matter of time. So . . . I'm dependent on my men being able to carry out orders like this when asked," he says. "And my guess is that you won't complain if I ask you to perform interrogations. Is that correct?"

"No, of course not," replies Rinnan.

"Very good. This was your first lesson, Rinnan. There will be more."

M for "morning gymnastics," a word mainly synonymous with punishment exercise: endless running, jumping, and push-ups that last until you're so tired you collapse on the ground, gasping for breath with a raw throat and a taste of blood in your mouth. So exhausted that the idea of death feels like salvation.

M for migraine.

M for the months passing by, and the constant flow of new assignments. It is summer 1941, and during the meetings at the Mission Hotel, Henry realizes how increasingly dependent they are on him and his reports. December comes, and he continues to make notes of everything, large and small—working alone, day and night.

M for monitoring, and the mystery informant. Who actually was it that overheard the conversation at Kaffistova and then heard you sharing that same information? It must have been someone with a good understanding of Norwegian at least. Someone who didn't stand out too much, who could go there without arousing suspicion, I thought. And it suddenly dawned on me that there was of course one man who fit that description; a man who, to my knowledge, went from place to place in Trondheim during the autumn-winter of 1941–42, making notes of everything that appeared suspicious.

Henry Rinnan.

It is quite possible, even probable, I think. I can easily imagine Rinnan driving through Trondheim in January 1942, pulling up outside Kaffistova, turning off the engine, and biting the tips of his driving gloves before pulling them off. He grips a newspaper under his arm and draws a cigarette from the cigarette case. Then he walks past the Jewish watch shop and up the stairs to the café, where he orders a black coffee from the waitress and sits down at one of the free tables. He notices a group of men with dark hair and brown eyes, presumably Jewish, he thinks, while pretending to be interested in the newspaper spread out before him. In reality, he is paying close attention to the conversation these four men are having. He hears right away that they are discussing news from the BBC about the Eastern Front, quite openly, as if unaware of its being forbidden to listen to the news. *What a nerve!* Henry thinks, to sit there and blatantly spread propaganda that might weaken the German government. The conversation goes on, even when others might overhear it, even when the waitress comes to their table to offer them more coffee. They've gotten by too easily, they feel too safe, he thinks. Henry flicks through the newspaper to the crossword and begins to fill the squares with the men's names as each one is mentioned. He writes down all the information he can and is just about to leave when one of the men stands up, the thinnest of them, a man called David. Obviously Jewish when you think about it, and with clear communist leanings, a sentiment which leaked out of the conversation on several occasions. Henry smiles at the waitress and finishes his coffee before getting up to follow this David. Nightfall comes early at this time of year, so he decides to leave the car and just follow on foot, at a safe distance, but never so far that he might risk losing sight of the man. He watches how David pats the sides of his coat, tapping out the rhythm of some song or other, and whistling a strange, Jewish melody.

Now we'll see where you're off to, my little communist friend, thinks Henry, as he stalks from corner to corner. He watches David enter a clothes shop, called Paris-Vienna, and talk to a slightly older man wearing round glasses. But Henry decides that he'll come back and follow this man later because soon David comes out again. Henry walks over to a building on the far side of the road, which David then enters. He waits, while making a note of the name on the mailbox: David Wolfsohn. He also writes down the name of the shop, Paris-Vienna, making a mental note that he must find out the name of the shop's owner. Then he returns to Kaffistova, where he uses his charm on the waitress, telling her how he recognized some of David's friends but couldn't for the life of him remember their names.

"Isn't it terribly irritating when that happens?" he asks, and the waitress gives him the names.

Perhaps that is how things transpired.

The answer most likely sits behind the thick concrete walls of the Norwegian National Archives. Should this turn out to be true, it will mean that the stories about our families are even more closely entwined than I first thought. It will also make these stories even darker and more painful.

I mentioned all this to Rikke.

"Is there any way you can find out?" she asked. I told her about the national archives in Trondheim, about Rinnan's notebook, which I had read excerpts from in various biographies, and told her there might be something there, written in Henry's own hand, in a notebook buried deep within the concrete vaults.

The following day, I booked my flight.

M for the Majavatn operation. On May 5, 1942, the railway line used for transporting copper ore—extracted from the mines at Løkken and destined for weapons production—was sabotaged by the resistance. Then, on September 20, the resistance blew up a power plant at Glomford. And on October 5 they carried out another attack on a mine. Around the same time, two German soldiers were killed by a refugee-smuggler. These attacks exhausted the patience of the German occupiers. Now someone else would pay the penalty.

On October 6, 1942, Josef Terboven stands in the square in Trondheim and declares martial law, making it forbidden to be outside between eight p.m. and five a.m. The sale of tobacco is prohibited, as a blanket punishment. The cinemas are closed completely, and all other businesses have to close by seven p.m. In addition, the Norwegian police have to merge with the German forces, which results in over a thousand armed men patrolling the streets, ransacking houses, interrogating families, and arresting suspects.

On top of all this: Ten men are sentenced to death—to atone for the crimes of the nameless resistance members behind the attacks. One of them is you.

M for Marie Komissar, moving elegantly around her apartment as she and the maid prepare for a party, carrying large plates of food from the kitchen to the dining table. M for memories, and the melancholia that can throw Marie into a spiral of despair. A sadness she manages to avoid by filling her time with plans and distractions—such as this postponed Hanukkah party, which she had invited the family to before Christmas 1950.

She looks up at the clock and realizes that there is barely an hour to go before the guests arrive, so she quickly lights the hanukkiah: the eight candles symbolizing the eight days where God kept the almost-empty oil lamps alight in the Temple in Jerusalem after the Jews had finally won it back. She has often thought about what a strange story this is, not least because the miracle was so small.

It's soon crowded around the table. Yet she knows how conspicuous those who are absent will be. David will not be there. And your seat, beside Marie, where you always sat when you celebrated Hanukkah, will be taken by Gerson instead, with Ellen beside him, heavily pregnant. Then Jacob and Vera, and beside them an empty chair, where Marie's brother would have sat. Marie stares across the table, neatly decorated with crystal glasses, gold-rimmed serving plates, and white napkins. But all she wants to do is collapse, to raise a bottle to her lips, and surrender to her memories.

M for the members of the Rinnan gang. There are many photos of these young men and women, taken during their trial after the war, where they sit in the courtroom, row upon row, smiling and chatting with each other. Or to be more precise: photos of those who survived. There were about seventy members of Special Division Lola over the years, but the group never consisted of more than thirty people at any one time. Some were killed, others quit, as the group became increasingly effective.

The Rinnan gang itself begins with a trip to Steinkjer in January 1942, shortly after the liquidation of the resistance group in Trondheim. Gerhard Flesch now wants Rinnan to try and recruit some associates who can help him dismantle the resistance further south in the Møre and Romsdal region. The plan is to put an end to the smuggling between Britain and Norway, continually supplying the enemy with weapons, technology, and people.

Rinnan packs his bags and says farewell to his family, telling them that he'll be gone for a while. He lifts his son and gives him a hug, then does the same with his little girl, who has started running round the house. Klara gets a quick kiss on the cheek, but it's mainly for the benefit of his son, and he notices how she just allows herself to be held, devoid of affection, showing no sign of wanting her lips to meet with his as she did in the beginning. Now she just allows him to kiss her on the cheek before immediately twisting herself out of his arms. Is he really so unattractive? Isn't she proud of all the responsibility he has been entrusted with? Proud of everything they now have, thanks to his job? And all the money he earns for the family? *If not, then fuck her!* he thinks, as he grabs the suitcase, realizing that he's perhaps holding the strap a bit too tightly, and that he is also straining his facial muscles too hard. But he cannot let it go. Then he sees his daughter sitting on the floor, playing with an empty cardboard box, without looking up at him once. He goes to say something, to win her attention one last time, since he will be gone for so long, but what's the point?

"Well. Bye-bye, then," he says, partly because he means it, partly so that Klara cannot say that he just left, accuse him of being taciturn and cold, because he damn well isn't, he just has a lot on his mind—a huge responsibility—so they can forgive him for having a short fuse. When he comes home, he should be allowed to feel a little bit wanted, in both the living room and the bedroom; but there's no sign of *that* being the case. There's been no fucking sign of it since their daughter was born, he thinks, looking at Klara again, who smiles reluctantly at him and tells him to drive carefully. As if she cared! *It would suit her fine if I just crashed into a ditch,* he thinks as he sits alone behind the wheel, repeating her departing words to himself in a twisted and disdainful voice. *Drive carefully, won't you!*

How ridiculous! Is she trying to suggest that he's a bad driver? He's probably one of the best in the whole county, no one knows these roads like him. And besides, there was no genuine concern in her words, he thinks, while starting the ignition and stepping on the gas. What she said was actually quite insincere. It would be very convenient for her if he swerved off the road, collided with a tree, and was flung out of the car to his death. She would be able to live off his pension for the rest of the war, for the rest of her life if the Germans actually won, he thinks, and turns on the windshield wipers.

It is February, and the road ahead is a dizzying mass of snowflakes, like driving through a never-ending curtain of tiny white beads. But there are virtually no other cars on the road, and he slowly relaxes and starts enjoying the ride, even though it is slippery and the conditions are treacherous, because essentially it's all just an extra challenge, an obstacle he needs to overcome, and after a few hours he arrives at his hotel in Steinkjer.

Henry lifts his suitcase out of the trunk and enters the warmth of the hotel lobby, where he is met by the receptionist's dutiful manner and welcoming smile. He marvels at how everything is there to make him feel at home, to make his stay as comfortable as possible. Who else can afford to be a guest at a place like this? Only those in important positions, of course, high-ranking business people who travel from abroad, or Nazi officers. *And in any case, none of the guests hold such a unique position as* me, thinks Rinnan, smiling as he collects his room key.

He orders a glass of port to warm up. Then he eats and rests, preparing for a new chapter in his life as an agent; finding more members and expanding. He imagines the possibilities that might come from having more eyes and ears to keep watch; more hands to take notes about everything and report it back to him? It will allow him to do anything. He'll be able to *really* show Flesch how good he is, thinks Rinnan, ordering another glass of port. He smiles at the young waitress serving him, and when she asks if he likes the food, he replies: "Oh yes. Right now I couldn't feel any better . . ." and while she continues smiling warmly at him he adds, "Well, there is *something* I'd rather be doing," giving her a wink, because wasn't she unusually friendly to him? As though she was trying to flirt with him, or was at least unintentionally attracted to him. The waitress blushes, suddenly conscious of how tightly her white blouse fits her body when she reaches over for his plate, and how her black skirt clings to her hips. And he can see that she likes it, he makes a special note of it and is careful to smile and give her a generous tip, but there's still something reserved about the way she smiles back. She's probably just shy, he thinks, perhaps not used to being addressed so directly. What he really wants is for her to lean forward and ask which room he is staying in, then whisper that she'll come up as soon as her shift is over. But she does no such thing, just takes his money and thanks him politely, with a puzzled look on her face. Perhaps she has a boyfriend waiting for her, maybe someone working at the hotel, he thinks, as he walks up to his room. Then he sits at the window with another glass of port, thinking about his plans for the next few days; smiling at the thought of finding new accomplices, and about how he'll be promoted to a higher rank and start hiring people. It's hard to believe, but it's true, he thinks, raising his glass and knocking back the last few drops. He feels his brain loosening up, as though the alcohol has swept the anger and worry aside, leaving him contented and with a slight pang of excitement. Henry puts down the glass, walks toward the bathroom to pee but collides with the bed, and a jolt of pain sears through his leg, forcing him to take several tiny steps to regain his balance before continuing toward the bathroom door. But then he hears footsteps in the hall outside. He is sure that it's the young waitress, on her way to see him after getting rid of the other guests; and that she's about to knock on the door, slip into his room, and begin unbuttoning her white blouse, right in front of him, in the dim light from the streetlamp outside. Rinnan feels the vibration of the footsteps and puts his ear to the door, listening as they go right past his door and then creak on the floorboards further down the hall. He quickly opens the door to take a look, but it's just a balding fifty-year-old man, about to go into his room.

Yeah, yeah, Henry thinks, as the door clicks shut, and he returns to the bathroom. But now he is both desperate for a piss and horny, and in order to get the job done he has to lean forward on the wooden toilet seat while pushing his erect penis down with his fingers. He stares down at the bathroom floor, as the room sways gently, until he finally hears splashing against the the porcelain. Soon, he manages to return to the bedroom, where he curls up under the quilt, everything slowly rotating, and imagines a huge vortex in the middle of the room, gradually sucking him and his thoughts into a deep sleep.

He wakes up the following morning with a throbbing headache and a tongue that feels like sandpaper. He gets out of bed, looks in the mirror, and washes his face several times, but the pounding continues, like his brain has swollen and is pressing against his skull. *Maybe I drank a bit too much last night,* he thinks, *but I should be allowed to have a bit of fun too, considering how hard I work, and how far*

I've driven to get here. Then he remembers the tube of pills that Flesch gave him before he left; Henry had stopped by the Mission Hotel after a bad night's sleep, and Flesch had commented on how tired he looked.

"Try these, they'll give you a little pep," Flesch said, smiling.

"What kind of pills are they?" Rinnan had asked while rotating the bottle between his fingers.

"Pervitin," replied Flesch, who told Rinnan to remove the cap, tip a few of the pills into his hand, and put one in his mouth. He noticed the effect immediately. They were exactly what he needed.

Henry looks through his suitcase until he finds the small bottle, then puts one of the white pills on his tongue. There's an immediate taste of chemicals, and he leans over the sink to rinse it down with tap water. After showering and eating breakfast, the headache begins to subside, and his strength increases; a power that comes from nowhere. "Thanks!" says Henry to the pill bottle, as he slips it into his trouser pocket. He combs his hair back, adds a little more hair wax, and sweeps his forelock back neatly before checking it in the mirror from both sides. Then he heads to a café known to be frequented by National Party sympathizers, hoping to find some accomplices. He has memorized the address and leaves the hotel in good time, walking the streets of the bombed-out town, where the skeletons of civilization are slowly rising as simple houses and rectangular sheds. The town—which he remembers from previous trips to Steinkjer—was once full of beautiful stone buildings, adorned with towers and bay windows. It's such a shame that they're gone, he thinks, imagining what it would be like if his hometown was bombed like this. Had Levanger been reduced to a pile of smoldering ruins, as Steinkjer had been, he would not have been happy. But they must have had a reason to do it, he thinks. He turns the corner of a new building and sees the café, housed in a simple cabin, with a barbershop at one end. There's no need to use his secret identity here. Rinnan slides the door open and enters the large open room. Inside there are scattered groups of men sitting around drinking coffee, smoking, and reading newspapers. Many of them turn round and look at Henry, who smiles back at them. He orders a drink, takes a seat at one of the tables, and looks around. He listens in on the conversations and chats to some of the men, but they're either unavailable or unsuitable. However, Rinnan does hear that there will be a Christmas party at the café that evening, and the whole town will be present. It is perfect.

So later that evening he's back there again, among a mass of well-dressed men and women, all drinking and smoking and smiling and chatting. He makes a point of asking the men if they might be interested in an assignment, and soon he finds someone happy to talk to him: a blond-haired and blue-eyed man with a shy smile and a somewhat disheveled look about him. His name is Ingvar Aalberg, and says he is *cheering for Germany,* as though they were talking about a football team. Beside Ingvar sits a man glaring at a woman talking to a guy at the bar. His name is Bjarne. They are both available and interested, especially when Rinnan tells them how much money is involved and how simple their mission will be. All they have to do is pretend to be refugees and find someone willing to transport them from Ålesund to the Shetland Islands, then expose the whole network of smugglers and resistance members. Rinnan buys them a round of drinks, they clink their glasses, and the conversation gets louder and rowdier. There are clouds of smoke and random bursts of laughter. A man stumbles and is propped up by the people standing nearby.

"We just need one more thing," says Rinnan, leaning across the table, "and that's someone to act as a messenger. Someone who can go between you and me and report on what's going on. Do you know anyone? Preferably a woman," he says, staring at his glass. He looks up at the men. Bjarne appears to be the brightest and more level-headed of the two. Ingvar would have gone along with absolutely anything; he seemed elated at merely being asked, and responded with a short "no" when Rinnan asked if he had any family. Bjarne is more reserved, but it is Bjarne who says he knows a lady who will help, and he goes off to find her. Soon after he comes back, holding on to the arm of a slightly unprepossessing woman with rugged features and sturdy arms and legs.

Rinnan stands up and reaches out his hand.

"Hi, the name's Rinnan," he says.

"Ragnhild Strøm," she says with a smile. Rinnan asks her to take a seat but can't help feeling disappointed because he had hoped that she might be a little more attractive, and Ragnhild Strøm isn't exactly someone who would have caught his eye. On the other hand, she is a member of the NS and says that she is willing to be a messenger between the two men. They all get drunk, and agree to meet the next day at Ragnhild's house.

The following day they sit round a bottle of liquor that Rinnan has brought, while he instructs them on what they'll be doing. He helps the two men come up with new names, and helps them to practice these new identities, along with their cover story: that they need help to escape from Norway before the Nazis arrest them.

So there's a little role-playing in Ragnhild Strøm's living room before the meeting ends, and a few days later Rinnan drives home again, while Ingvar and Bjarne head to the coast to infiltrate the people-smugglers. They send messages to Rinnan through Ragnhild, who speaks to him on the telephone every day: snippets of information such as the names of the boats being used, the names of the owners, the harbors being used, and the dates on which the boats will sail.

He tells Ingvar and Bjarne to remain undercover, that there's no need to worry, because the operation is about to begin and they'll soon be pulled out. Then he reports everything to Flesch, who is obviously pleased with Henry, and tells him that Operation Seehund II will now begin: fifty armed soldiers will be sent to arrest everyone involved.

Rinnan joins them in one of the trucks and suddenly finds himself in charge of the whole operation. *I can allow myself to feel a tiny bit proud,* thinks Rinnan as they speed through the forest, the soldiers beside him clinging to their seats, swaying from side to side in rhythm with the landscape.

But suddenly one of the trucks gets a puncture, and they come to a crashing halt. Rinnan climbs out, swearing to himself, and walks along the dirt track to tell the soldiers to hurry, that they don't have time for this delay. But it doesn't help.

When they finally arrive at the coast the next day, the refugee boat has already sailed, with Ingvar and Bjarne on board. They're probably terrified of being discovered, thinks Rinnan, staring out at the fjord, as the wind whips up the foam and blows clouds of drizzle across the heaving black waves.

It is typically stormy weather at sea, which could be to their advantage. He calls Ragnhild and she gives him the latest updates from the undercover refugees as well as a list of names of the resistance members involved. Rinnan orders the soldiers to arrest them, and tells them to confiscate the other boats too. He also sends a group of soldiers out to search for the refugee boat, while he stays on land, looking out to sea.

Night goes by. Then a day goes by. And then night returns again before he finally hears that the refugee boat is returning to land because of the storm. Everyone is arrested, and finally the two agents can reveal their identities, break away from the line of refugees, and walk over to the German side. Rinnan gives them both a pat on the back and leads them to a warm shelter. Despite the problems they had come up against, the operation has been a success. Fifty-two people are arrested, twenty-two of them die in captivity. It is January 1942.

The following March, Special Division Lola is established, and Rinnan is told to intensify his efforts to hire more members. And they are also given a headquarters, an apartment at Brattørgata 12B, seized by the Nazis from a man they arrested at the same time as you and David.

×

M for Marie Arentz, who Henry meets for the first time at the home of Ragnhild Strøm, after asking Ragnhild to find a friend to accompany her on a boat trip to Bodø. The two women must pretend to be resistance members and try to enlist new people. He instantly likes the way Marie smiles at him, and they quickly get into conversation. He fills up their glasses and makes her laugh. They all drink together, and he gives them money for cigarettes, discusses their salary, which amounts to a monthly wage for only a few days' work. He tells Marie that she can have a little extra money to buy herself something nice. "Not that you need it!" he adds, winking at her and getting a mischievous smile in return. He thinks of Klara for a moment, then quickly blocks her out of his mind, because why should he feel guilty about Klara when she is so cold and indifferent, when she doesn't even show the tiniest hint of passion, or of wanting to sleep with him because she wants to, she just goes along with it when *he* wants to. So it's her fault if he goes elsewhere, he's entitled to a little bit on the side, he thinks, and he offers to walk Marie home. They are both drunk, and he puts his arm around her waist, and in a dark corner he pulls her body toward him and kisses her. He sees the voracious look in her eyes, and then accompanies her to her bedsit. They both giggle as they climb the stairs, trying to stay quiet. She turns the key and opens the door and he quickly follows her in. Then he pins her to the wall and kisses her again. His hand slides under her clothes, stroking her naked back while she presses herself against him, then she steps back and removes her sweater, twisting the arms inside out. Henry kicks off his shoes and starts unbuttoning his shirt then suddenly feels her hands on his belt, unbuckling it while breathing quickly against his cheek. He slides his hands down to her thighs and pulls up her skirt, then he takes her over to the bed. He looks at her smile, her soft skin, as tender as a first encounter can be.

Anything can happen now, he thinks, while sliding her panties down past her thighs, then he leans over to kiss her stomach, catches the scent of her vagina, and plunges his face into it.

The following morning, Henry leans against a pillow in bed while Marie curls up beside him. He plucks a cigarette from the case, lights up, and inhales deeply. The sun shines through the gaps in the curtains, making the hairs on Marie's arm glitter. They talk, and the conversation skips effortlessly between subjects and places.

Several months later, Marie will escape from the Rinnan gang by signing up to serve abroad. Three years later, they will be together again, and Marie will lie naked in his arms. Only this time she will be dead in the basement of the Gang Monastery with a rope around her neck—and it will be Rinnan who has killed her.

M for Molde, for masque plays and resistance men, such as Bjarne Asp. Bjarne Asp is a fiery opponent of the Nazis. A fearless and intelligent man, who quickly gets himself into the right conversations, at the right cafés. He starts a relationship with a woman named Solveig, who, along with her two brothers, is also an active member of the resistance. Bjarne helps Solveig. They make lists, and attend meetings, and they fuck. And Bjarne tells her enough stories to convince her that he is on her side. They become a couple and start to plan a future together; for when Norway has won the war. They eat, sleep, and travel together.

Six months pass, then one day Bjarne Asp tells Solveig that his name is actually Henry Rinnan; that he runs a secret organization on behalf of the Germans, and that she will have to join him if she wants to remain safe. He tells Solveig that he can prevent her family from being arrested, provided she cooperates; that the Germans are going to win this war, but she can help minimize the Norwegian losses by preventing a British invasion; and that he can at least ensure that her family is unharmed. Solveig agrees. Summer turns to autumn. It is 1943. Special Division Lola expands, and Rinnan gets a new headquarters on the edge of town. A detached house at Jonsvannsveien 46, the Gang Monastery.

They move all their belongings in, and Rinnan has prison cells built in the cellar. In September 1943, Solveig and her eight-year-old daughter also move into the house, where she works as Rinnan's secretary for the rest of the war. She tends the wounds of those being tortured, she makes food for the gang, and allows her daughter to sleep there, despite the screams from below.

M for the musical Jannicke is getting ready to present in the cellar. It is a Saturday night in 1956, and Grete is down there with Jannicke and two of her friends. For several weeks they've been rehearsing after school. Throwing their bags on the floor, saying *hi* to their mother and the maid, and thundering down the stairs, totally unaffected by the musty smell and the cold. It's a place where they can be left to their own devices, where no one complains that their noise is making their mother tired.

They have built a stage where there used to be a bar, and practiced musical numbers and dance routines, while five-year-old Grete stood and watched. Grete has been keen to help, and when she was told she could stand at the door, she ran up the stairs enthusiastically to find some paper and colored pencils and then lie on her tummy, on the cellar's wooden floor, drawing a whole book of tickets.

But when they told their parents about the show, Grete saw a strange look on her mother's face. A forced smile. And she repeated the same question as before: "Is it really necessary to spend so much time in the cellar, in all that stale air and cold?" Jannicke's stock answer had always been that they were wrapped up warm and that it wasn't a problem, and Grete just repeated what her sister said. Their mother had never been able to come up with a better argument.

One evening while Grete lay in bed, she heard her parents in the kitchen. They were talking about the show, and she heard her mother raise her voice and say: "But in the cellar, Gerson! The cellar!"

"Shhh, Ellen," replied Gerson.

"They know nothing about it, of course!" replied her mother. Grete then heard their footsteps move further away, and lifted her head to see the outline of Jannicke's body in the bed beside her. She too was sitting up. Both sisters stared out into the darkness without saying a word. What did Mother mean? They knew nothing about what? Soon the voices quieted in the living room, and Grete heard either her mother or father go to the bathroom, followed by the rush of water in the pipes. And then she must have fallen asleep.

Several days later, the big night has finally arrived and it is time for the première.

The girls have been all over the neighborhood selling tickets. They have carried chairs downstairs and put them out in rows, lit candles, and dressed for the occasion. Everything is ready.

"You can let everyone in now, Grete."

Jannicke smiles to her sister. She is wearing a party dress and high heels. Her lips are painted with red lipstick, her eyelashes are black with mascara, and her face is pale from the powder she borrowed from the maid. Grete nods energetically before turning and running up the stairs. She leaps all the way to the top and listens to the murmur of voices on the other side of the door. Mostly from children. Then she opens it and peers out, right into the faces of the children and parents crammed into the hallway.

"Are you ready?" asks Gerson.

"May I see your tickets?" she replies. Gerson turns and mumbles something to one of the neighbors—she can't hear what it is but it creates a wave of laughter that spreads backward—then he turns back to her and holds out two handmade tickets.

"Thank you," says Grete, casually suppressing her excitement, just as she would have done had she been an adult working the door of the theater in Trondheim. "Please come in and find yourself a seat," she says.

"Are the seats numbered?" asks her father, gently stroking her back and giving her a knowing smile. Grete shakes her head and sees the strained expression on her mother's face. The cellar fills up with neighbors. Grete notices that some of them look around at the walls, as if their noses have suddenly detected a terrible smell.

M for murder, and for the mounting suspicion toward Henry Oliver Rinnan. With the constant reports about the damage he is doing, and the danger he presents, the resistance movement decides that they need Rinnan out of the way. So they make plans to capture him, alive.

One October evening in 1943, just a couple of weeks after they started using the Gang Monastery as their headquarters, Rinnan pulls up outside his family villa in Trondheim, exhausted from the day's workload, his thoughts swirling with new plans and assignments. He steps out of the car but notices that something isn't quite right. There is a strange vehicle parked near the driveway; a car with the engine and lights turned off, but nevertheless he thinks he sees the silhouette of a man behind the wheel. Or are there two men?

Suddenly he is wide awake, on full alert, and reaching for the gun on his belt. As he pulls out the pistol he catches sight of a third man, also armed, coming out from the bushes. His next in charge, Karl Dolmen, rushes out of the car. A tall man, with Aryan hair and blue eyes, always on his watch, always obeying orders.

"Run, Rinnan!" shouts Karl Dolmen, pointing his machine gun at the men and firing.

Rinnan dashes through the gate and hears an exchange of gunfire. He races toward the door, half crouching while holding his pistol up to his chest with both hands. Then he peeps round the corner of the house. There is a scream. An engine starts, followed by the sound of screeching tires, and then the car disappears into the night, while Rinnan sprints along the pavement and into the road. Then he sees Karl coming toward him clutching his stomach. He has been hit. Henry drapes Karl's arm over his shoulder, and while they struggle to the car he looks up and sees Klara standing at the window, partly hidden behind the curtains.

Karl needs immediate medical attention, so explaining all this to Klara will have to wait, but he is already dreading it. He helps Karl into the car and tells the driver to step on it and get them to the hospital. When they arrive, Karl is laid on a stretcher and carried away with a syringe in his arm, while Rinnan waits in the hallway, becoming increasingly angry and refusing to go home until someone tells him that Karl isn't seriously injured. Eventually they tell him that the bullet has missed Karl's vital organs and that he is going to be OK, and so he gets in his car and drives home. He sleeps in the guest room.

Henry lies awake all night, furious that his enemies have stooped so low that they attack him at home! What if one of the shots had gone astray, he thinks, while gnashing his teeth in the dark. What if all the noise had woken his son or daughter? What if they had come to the window and been hit by a bullet and killed? Yes, they're at war of course! But this is different. So no more politeness. No more fucking rules. Anything goes, he thinks, then he orders two gang members to go into the streets and beat up the first person they see as revenge.

As a result, a random passerby is beaten to death on his way home from town that night. Had he gone home later, or chosen a different route, it would have been someone else.

M for mathematics, an entire world that Gerson suddenly realizes he misses one morning while walking to work. He may have put his heart and soul into running the business, and tried moving back to Trondheim to help his mother; and tried to marry a woman from a Jewish family, a family of good standing too—but it just doesn't help. His fulfillment level is null. What does he care about hats and dresses? What does he care about Paris-Vienna and the rich customers who come in needing help, who look at him pleadingly, so hungry for compliments they are willing to swallow any flattering comment thrown their way. He turns the corner of Nordre Street and smiles to someone he knows across the road, something he feels obliged to do, to maintain a good relationship with the regular patrons, so that they will continue to choose Paris-Vienna over their competitors. He has mastered all this very well, he thinks, while once again turning the key in the shop's front door. It's not that he can't succeed in this life, it's just that he gets no pleasure from it. In the short breaks he takes throughout the day, he often finds himself pining for the academic world, for conversations about mathematics, about jazz, literature, and philosophy. He misses the mountaineer-like strain of conquering almost insurmountable problems, and the great sense of clarity that comes from reaching the top and looking out.

All of this lingers in the back of his mind, as he stands there holding the little mirror for his customers to look at themselves, or while searching for their correct size, or talking about the differences in cut, the quality of the fabric, colors, and patterns. Suddenly the telephone rings, and Gerson finds himself talking to an old acquaintance, a friend of the family, and a mathematician, who helped him find work during the war. Now he wants to offer Gerson another job, and not just any old job. He wants him to help develop the Business and Economics Institute, in Oslo. Gerson nods, and says thank you, but has to lower his voice when a customer enters the shop. He says he will think about it, but he already knows that it's impossible, and that he will have to say no. Then, it is finally time to close for the day, and as he accompanies the last customer out the door he feels an unusual heaviness in his movements. He starts walking down the road, aware of what's waiting for him at home, knowing that Ellen is probably tired and withdrawn, as she often is, perhaps lying alone in the upstairs bedroom suffering from another migraine. So he decides to take a detour. He has tried to help, he has really tried to get through to her, for the sake of the girls, but he just can't seem to do it. She is just so helpless, so lacking in initiative and totally unfit for any kind of normal life, he thinks. Suddenly he remembers an incident in the kitchen, shortly after they moved into the house. He had come home from a fishing trip with an old university friend, where he had caught a beautiful large cod, weighing almost two kilos. He had brought it in to Ellen, thinking that she would cook something with it, but she had just stared at him anxiously. She had just wrinkled her nose at the fish, hanging there with blood dripping from its yawning gills. But he was only trying to be nice, hoping she might compliment him and perhaps bake the cod in the oven or make fish soup, since he knew that she loved both. But Ellen simply burst into tears, saying that she had no idea what to do; that she didn't know how to gut or prepare a fish. And she really couldn't, it was true, thinks Gerson, her parents had failed her on that. They had spoiled her, and now the wealth she had relied on in her former life was gone. The factory was gone, the house was gone, the chauffeurs and seamstresses and maids were all gone, and the only thing left was her helplessness, laid bare and unsightly. So Gerson had asked her to go upstairs for a nap. He decided to gut the fish himself and asked the Danish maid to help prepare the dinner.

So, he postpones going home and continues walking down the road, with the voice from the unexpected phone call still echoing in his head. A job in Oslo. Business and economics. The chance to have a career, and to work with what he knows best, something he burns for.

He does a quick calculation: his life, minus Paris-Vienna, minus the customers moaning about their waistlines or breasts being too large or too small, minus the Gang Monastery and everything connected with it, plus math, plus students, plus Oslo.

And, since he is thinking about it, minus Ellen.

N

×　　　×　　　×

N for Nicaea, and the famous church council held there in AD 325, where it was determined that clerks were forbidden from claiming interest on loans. This was later extended to include all Christians, and removed any incentive for lending money, other than to relatives and friends. Foreigners, however, were exempt from the ban, and it was this that gave rise to the idea of the penny-pinching Jew.

N for your numb fingers after gripping the saw or carrying stones, from seven until twelve in the morning, and from lunch until eight in the evening when the insects swarm and swirl in the sunlight between the trees and nature is still at its most vibrant. During winter, the workdays are shorter. Not for your benefit or that of the others being held, but to prevent anyone from using the opportunity to escape under the shelter of darkness.

×

N for Nordstern, or New Trondheim. The new Nordic capital that Hitler was planning on the outskirts of what still is Trondheim, which he had the architect Albert Speer draw plans for. It was supposedly on one of his walks in the Alps that Hitler conceived the idea, on his way to Mooslander Kopf, a mountaintop viewpoint where a small teahouse and a bench were built for him so he could sit down and rest while ruminating over his future plans. From this bench, the landscape unfolded before him and the gray, glacier-scoured mountains plunged into the lake below, an awesome reminder of how small mankind is. He may have occasionally thought of some of the fairytales from his childhood, because according to German folklore there is a mythological giant sleeping beneath the mountains, ready to rise up at Germany's hour of destiny.

It was on one of these trips, with his German shepherd, that Hitler must have deliberated over the problem of the British supply routes operating in the area. He must have thought of how they could be stopped; about strategic places he could build a base. And then the idea of Norway, with its entire coast facing the open sea, came to him. The whole country was occupied, but up in the north he needed a way to restrict and control the shipping in the North Atlantic; a base where German cruisers could set sail from and destroy the British submarines and warships; isolating Britain, so that it truly remained an island, cut off, and unable to supply the resistance men on the continent with courage, ammunition, and machine guns.

Hitler's finger slid over the map, across the strait between Denmark and Norway, to Oslo. Then south along the jagged coastline, round Kristiansand and then northward past Bergen until finally stopping at Trondheim. He glanced over at Russia before sliding his finger across the border into Sweden, as far as Östersund, and then back again.

Trondheim.

Strategically, this was a perfect location for a fleet of U-boats. Here, supplies could be delivered by cargo ships from the continent, and equipment needed for the war on the Eastern Front could be unloaded. If you look at a map of Norway, it becomes extremely narrow in this region, as if a gigantic hand has squeezed the country in the middle. Hitler sent a car to collect Albert Speer, so that they could review the plans together, and asked his assistants to find maps of Trondheim, as detailed as possible. Photographs too.

Then Hitler and Speer redrew the map.

After a few days of intensive work, the first plans were ready. Construction of the new city could begin, a Nordic capital for the Third Reich called Nordstern, with 250,000 inhabitants that would be sent from Germany and architecture that would outshine every other city. A four-lane highway would also be built, connecting Nordstern with Berlin. But first, a tunnel had to be blasted right through the rock, creating an underground base where the German warships and U-boats could dock. From there, German warships would control the entire North Atlantic.

What's left of that U-boat base now houses the Norwegian National Archives. A place where I hope to find Rinnan's notebooks, if they exist; all the records he made of suspicious activity in Trondheim, as he went from café to café. Somewhere in these archives is perhaps proof that you and Marie's brother were arrested because of Rinnan.

As I drive through Trøndelag in my rental car, I call the National Archives to let them know I'm coming, to give them a chance to find and collect the boxes from the vaults. The man on the other end of the line tells me that if Rinnan's notebooks are stored anywhere, they would not be at the National Archives in Trondheim, but in Oslo. Because even though his trial took place in Trondheim, all the documents from the war trials were moved to the main archives in Oslo a few years later, where they are kept today, hidden inside the mountain, a bike ride from where I live.

×

N for November.

N for new members, new proxies, and new headquarters, at a new address.

It is September 1943. Rinnan continues through the entrance hall and enters the living room in the Gang Monastery for the first time, still wearing his shoes, and looks around with a broad smile on his face. It's a great place, he thinks, central yet secluded, and spacious, with views across the fields if anyone ever tries anything. And just a short drive from the house in Trondheim that the Germans have given his family.

He goes over to the window and looks out across the yellowing fruit trees in the garden and blows a cloud of smoke into the air, which fades instantly. Then he turns to the others: Ivar Grande, Karl Dolmen, Kitty and Inga, and Solveig Kleve with her eight-year-old daughter who will also live in the house. They're all young, just like him. They are all excited, just as he is. He shows them where to put the crates they're carrying, then opens one and pulls out a bottle of cognac, bought specially for the occasion. The rest of Trondheim's inhabitants are without cigarettes, without spirits, without cars and gasoline, without jobs—but Rinnan has everything.

"Ivar? Could you go and get some glasses for us?" he asks. Ivar seems to hesitate, perhaps thinking that such menial tasks are beneath his grade and position, but he does as he's told anyway. Inga follows him out of the room, and moments later they're back, gathered around Rinnan in a semicircle, just as he and his siblings had once stood, in the woods, or in the room where they slept. He pours everyone a round, filling glass after glass, and the alcohol fumes waft up from their glasses, so strong their eyes smart, and when all the glasses are full, he raises his own and proposes a toast.

"So, my dear colleagues. Welcome to our new headquarters," he says, bringing the glass to his lips. His mouth tingles and burns from the alcohol, and his head seems to loosen up almost immediately. "Here we'll be able to plan our operations undisturbed. Here we will be able to coordinate our attacks, plan how to infiltrate our opponents and crush them from within."

He immediately sees how excited and lively they all become at his words.

"Together, my friends and colleagues, together we are the Germans' most valuable weapon in Norway! Did you hear what Goebbels said in his speech?! Well, we are the agents he was referring to! We've done such a good job that our reputation has reached the very heart of Germany! And it will only get better! This is our new headquarters, where we will plan our missions . . . and, of course, party!"

The rest of the gang now seem more relaxed, and they raise their glasses. Rinnan takes a few steps toward the fireplace before stopping and turning to look at them again. Then he downs the rest of the cognac in one swallow.

"We are authorized to do whatever we want. We can arrest our opponents, interrogate them, and execute them if necessary. By any means. Just remember how they tried to kill me right outside my own home, while my children slept inside! This is war! And it's a war we're going to win. We're going to crush the resistance, from this house. From here my friends—we are going to write history!" he shouts, while raising his empty glass. Rinnan holds everyone's gaze for a moment, then suddenly hurls the glass into the fireplace. It smashes against the burning logs and showers the brickwork in splintered glass and crackling sparks.

Some of them jump with fright, and some begin to laugh, but they don't fool Rinnan. Now he knows: that they fear him; that they're nervous about what he might do next. That's how he wants it, because that means he can keep controlling them, and it means he knows exactly where he stands with every single one of them. He lights another cigarette and looks around the room as if nothing has happened.

Then he goes downstairs to inspect the cellar.

×

N for names. N for nerves.

N for night and the nagging thoughts that creep up on Ellen Komissar as she lies awake in the darkness of her bedroom in Jonsvannsveien 46. She listens to the sound of Gerson's breathing, trying to figure out if he is sleeping or not, then tries to reach him by whispering.

"Gerson?"

The wallpaper, the bedside tables, and the curtains are all invisible in the pitch-dark. So too are Gerson's eyes, which are open and staring into the darkness, as he lies with his back to her, on the far side of the bed.

"Yes," he answers quietly. A few seconds pass in silence before Ellen opens her mouth again.

"I don't know if I can bear living here any more."

"Ellen . . . I thought we were done with all that?"

"I . . ."

"You *know* I can't leave Jacob here, alone in Trondheim with my mother. Someone has to run the shop . . ."

"Yes, but why do we have to live *here* . . . in this house?"

"Can't you just try a little bit longer? It will get easier."

"You said that before we moved in, but it never does. It keeps getting worse. Everyone I meet asks me what it's like to live here, if I'm afraid of, of . . ."

"Hush, Ellen! You'll wake up Jannicke!"

"But do you know what they did down there, Gerson? Do you *know*?!"

"Yes, of course I do, Ellen, but it was a long time ago!"

"A long time ago?! Today, Jannicke showed me another bullet that she'd found in the cellar. I thought you'd removed them all?"

"I'll take another look, and I'll clean everywhere again. Okay?"

For a few seconds, neither of them says anything, and their thoughts just melt into the dark, but they are like two people fleeing through a dense forest at night, breathless and frightened, push-ing their way through the branches, searching for a way out. Then Gerson finds one.

"You never complained about all the murders that happened at the castle when we went there? Or the wars that happened abroad? It's all in the past! We have to think about the future!"

"I . . ."

"Can't you just try, Ellen?"

"I suppose so . . ."

"Good . . . Now I really have to sleep. Good night, Ellen."

"Good night."

N for nails. One afternoon, in the mid-fifties, the two sisters are climbing the stairs to the rooms in the attic. Behind the closed door in front of them is the room with the arched window, the room they're not allowed to enter because their mother has another migraine and needs to be left in peace, but on their left are two rooms they *can* enter; one is the Candle Club. The secret room that is impossible to enter without crouching down and crawling. This time it is the elder sister leading the way, with a flickering candle in her hand, and who, with a mixture of horror and delight, shows Grete what she has found in there—a little bag, tied up with string, and containing something quite peculiar: a collection of small curved flakes, of something hard and dry. A few seconds pass before Grete realizes what they are: fingernails—and not just the tips either. Whole human nails.

O

× × ×

O for oxen. It is August 1944. Standing in a field just outside Trondheim there is an ox, grazing, with slow, monomaniacal jaw movements and an empty look in its eyes. The sound of voices makes the animal look up from the grass, and it watches as three men and a woman climb over the fence. It is Rinnan, Karl, Ivar, and Inga.

"Oh my God, it's huge," says Inga, glancing quickly at Henry and giggling. Rinnan crouches down slowly, takes a deep breath, scrapes his foot on the ground, and suddenly lets out a loud and convincing: "MOOOOOO!"

Everyone bursts out laughing. The ox swooshes its tail, shakes a fly from its head, and bends down to eat again. Rinnan holds a coil of rope in one hand while tying a slipknot at one end. It is something he has done numerous times when practicing to be a cowboy, and now he really *is* one. The ground is muddy. Ivar steps in cow dung and stands there cursing but Rinnan and Inga can't stop laughing. The ox looks at them again, with its large black eyes, as the lasso throws miss repeatedly. In the end they have to walk right up to the animal and place the lasso over its head before they can finally open the gate and lead the thing out. Karl takes the rope and ties it to the truck's rear bumper, then they climb back in and drive slowly back to the Gang Monastery, forcing the animal to walk behind the car. The ox closes its eyes and pulls its neck sideways but is forced to follow them, its mouth drooling. Finally, once they have parked the truck, near the lower side of the house, right by the barbed-wire fence and the guards, Karl loosens the knot and leads the ox the last few yards.

While Karl holds the rope, Rinnan trudges along beside him pretending to drive. The two German soldiers open the gate for them, looking slightly bemused as he passes them with his imaginary steering wheel in his hands and making engine noises, which seems to delight the two female agents.

"So, why don't we park just here, Karl?" says Rinnan as if this were all perfectly normal, rolling down an imaginary window beside him.

"Excuse me, ladies? Am I allowed to park here?"

One of the agents leans over to him and says: "Of course."

Then she directs them into the garden.

"What sort of car is it?" asks Inga.

"It's a Ford—a Model T-bone," quips Rinnan, and Inga laughs, but her shrill laughter frightens the ox, which suddenly pulls its eleven hundred pounds in the opposite direction.

"And as you can see, it's got quite a lot of horse—I mean . . . ox-power," he says with a grin, and they all laugh, all except Karl, who is leaning right back, gripping the rope with all the strength he can muster.

"Hold tight, Karl," says Rinnan, dropping the chauffeur parody and stepping aside. He pulls his gun from its holster and plays with it in his hand for a moment.

"I feel like there's been a lack of fresh meat here recently. So draw your weapons!"

Everyone does as he says, pointing their pistols and machine guns at the ox, which now sensing the aggression directed toward it tries to move away, but Karl keeps a firm grip. The animal bellows loudly.

"Everybody, on three. One . . . two . . ."

Then there is a barrage of shots, almost simultaneously, like a firing squad. The German soldiers watch the whole thing dumbfounded. The ox lets out a short, roaring sigh before collapsing into a heap on the ground with its large round eyes blinking and its legs scraping the earth as if trying to run. A jet of urine suddenly gushes from behind the animal, splashing up Inga's and Ivar's ankles and forcing them to jump out of the way.

"Well, that's that! Welcome to the slaughterhouse, everyone. Can you get some knives, Karl?"

A few seconds later Karl is back, with a kitchen knife in each hand.

He holds the knives in front of him questioningly, but no one seems keen to take one. Nobody wants to.

"OK. You go first then, Karl," says Rinnan. It is an order, and is accepted as one.

Karl kneels down and presses the tip of the knife against the dry, light-brown hair on the animal's belly, but then he hesitates and looks up at Rinnan with a nervous look in his eyes.

"I've never done this before, I . . . ," he says.

"Come on, Karl! We'd like to start making dinner before Christmas, if that's OK?"

The others laugh nervously. Karl presses the tip of the knife against the dead animal again, then pushes, and blood immediately spurts all over his hand as the blade slides into the flesh. Two flies emerge from the animal's coat, buzzing away from the carcass in the opposite direction. Everyone stands mesmerized as Karl hacks along the animal's belly, which opens up and its intestines bulge out, smooth and otherworldly, in gray and yellow and red.

"There!" says Rinnan, patting Karl on the shoulder and then turning to the others.

"Help yourselves, folks, it's self-service. Carve yourself a piece, as much or as little as you want, take it into the kitchen, and our chefs will take care of the rest."

This turns out to be easier said than done. Nevertheless, they take turns at cutting off chunks of meat, with blood smeared up their arms, over several minutes full of of disgust, excitement, and laughter. Then they carry their plates of meat up to the house, leaving the carcass lying in the garden.

P

×　　×　　×

P for persecution.

P for the patients in the prison infirmary, and the care they initially received. If someone had a cold, for instance, or if their hands were blistered from working in the quarry, or if they had cut their foot in a sawing accident, then their hands or feet would be treated and they would get lozenges for their colds. P for the pitiless way this basic level of care was brought to an end. You heard about Flesch's visit to Falstad and what he said when he found three Jewish prisoners in the infirmary; how he had questioned why on earth the prison was using its resources on sick Jews. "Three bullets, and you will be rid of the problem," he had said.

P for Pervitin, the pills that Rinnan will soon run out of, which means he will have to drop by Flesch's office at the Mission Hotel and ask for more.

"So, they worked, eh?" says Flesch smiling. He reaches for a new metal tube in his desk drawer and hands it over to Rinnan.

Rinnan thanks him, in German, and although he feels like taking a pill immediately, he says "thank you" instead, then whisks himself out the door with all his forthcoming assignments grinding over and over in his head. He stops just outside and pops a pill into his mouth, and a few minutes later it takes effect. He suddenly feels clear-headed and energized. Then he drives home while drumming his fingers on the steering wheel.

P for plan. One afternoon, in the mid-fifties, Ellen comes down the stairs at the Gang Monastery, clutching a five-kroner note in her skirt pocket. She smells meatballs cooking in the oven, hears the sound of potatoes bubbling on the stove, and feels the tension building up within her, because now the moment has come, she is quite sure of it. She had already pictured this scene as she lay resting upstairs, but can't let anyone notice anything. So she slips into the kitchen, smiles to the Danish maid, and tells her how wonderful the cooking smells, then asks if she needs any help, but the maid says it's all fine. Ellen of course knew that the maid would say this, so she leaves the kitchen, checks that the children are busy with something, and walks toward the bathroom. On her way through the hall she puts her hand in her pocket again, and as she passes the maid's coat hanging there, she slips the banknote quickly into its pocket, her heart pounding, before continuing to the bathroom door. She looks around quickly as she opens the door and enters, but nobody has seen her, so she closes the door, blinks hard in front of the mirror, and watches a smile spread across her face. She will have to lose this smile quickly. Ellen turns round and flushes the toilet to make her visit seem convincing, washes her hands, looks in the mirror again, and leaves. She sits with the girls a little and helps them with their homework, aware that she needs to hold back and not appear too keen, because that would look conspicuous.

Soon she hears the front door open in the hall. She hears Gerson shout "Hello?!" and immediately after that he walks into the room. Still she waits.

She waits until the food is served. She waits until everyone has poured gravy over their potatoes and started eating. And then finally she asks Gerson, as though randomly, after he has told them about the day's takings in the shop.

"Speaking of money, Gerson," she says, hesitating a little, seeing that Jannicke looks up from her plate. "Have you taken that five-kroner note I put on the sideboard this morning?"

Gerson looks at her perplexed.

"A five-kroner note?"

"Yes, I put it on the sideboard this morning, I remember quite clearly, because I was going to take it with me into town. But then I went and got ready, and afterward, after you had gone, it wasn't there any more. I just assumed that you needed money for something or other?"

"No. I haven't seen it." Gerson replies, slicing a meatball which is light brown on the inside. The Danish maid has stopped eating and sits there dead silent with her lovely, slender hands and her cute, cute face, beginning to suspect what is about to happen, thinks Ellen, while drying the corners of her mouth with a napkin.

"What about you?" she asks the maid. "Could you have put it away when you arrived, perhaps? Or taken it with you to buy food?"

"No," says the maid, now looking slightly nervous, afraid almost, no doubt because she can sense that an accusation is beginning to form in the air between them.

"No, I see . . . ," says Ellen. "But it can't have just vanished into thin air."

The children eat, and look up. The only sound in the room is the ticking of the grandfather clock, and the chink of knives against porcelain as the girls cut up their food or scoop up gravy.

"Perhaps you've put it somewhere else? Or lost it somewhere?" asks Gerson. "I'm quite sure there's a good explanation."

"You think?" replies Ellen dryly. She skewers one of the meatballs with her fork and holds it up in front of her lips. "It's just that it's not the first time money has gone missing in this house . . . ," she says quietly, as though addressing no one in particular, because now she has to play her cards carefully.

Gerson puts his knife and fork down, a little too hard almost, his frustration showing as they look at each other. Two wills.

"OK," he says. "And what is it you think I should do, Ellen?"

Ellen finishes her mouthful of food, and straightens her shoulders.

"I don't know, I . . . What do you think? Perhaps it's fine that things go missing?"

She looks straight at the maid, who is looking down at the table.

"For God's sake!" says Gerson. "Should I look through her bag then?"

"I don't have a bag," says the maid. "I keep everything in my coat."

"OK. Could I check there, then? If you don't mind?" he asks, while turning to the maid. She nods quietly, perhaps knowing already what is going to happen. Ellen restrains herself from smiling. Gerson's chair scrapes the floor as he pushes it back. Then he goes out into the hallway.

"What is it, Dad?" asks Jannicke.

"Nothing. It's nothing, darling," says Ellen, placing her hand on her daughter's. She feels the soft, soft hand against her own, and notices how the maid is looking at her. She looks up, trying to behave as though nothing is wrong, as if totally unaffected, while the maid stares at her with taut lips.

Gerson walks back into the room with a look of confusion on his face and with the five-kroner note in his hands.

"Is this it?" he asks. Ellen nods.

"Was it in my coat?" asks the maid. Ellen notices the genuine look of surprise on the maid's face, who exchanges several glances with Gerson, who looks back at her, takes a deep breath, then turns to Ellen and gives her a scrutinizing look.

"I didn't put it there," says the maid, rising from her chair. "But that's fine. I cannot stay here," she says. Then she walks away from the table with tears in her eyes. This isn't quite as Ellen had imagined it would play out, she had hoped that Gerson would be a little more convinced, but there is clearly an element of doubt in him. He gives Ellen a cold stare. Then he goes after the maid, and tries to speak with her. But it doesn't help, she packs her things while Ellen and the children finish their dinner, and thirty minutes later she is out of their lives.

P for pogrom, or "погром," which is derived from the Russian verb meaning to crush, or destroy, by any means, no matter how terrible, to eliminate the Jews.

The idea of the Final Solution has evolved over the centuries. Like a plant that has spread its roots in all directions, trying to sprout up into the light, through the clay and gravel and subterranean rock. Until January 20, 1942—the day you were moved from the prison cell in Trondheim to Falstad—when the idea finally emerged round a meeting table at a villa in Wansee, near Berlin. The idea that the only way to solve the Jewish question once and for all was to do what was necessary: to wipe all Jews from the surface of the planet.

To gather all Jews, practicing or not, their spouses and children, and annihilate them.

To gather all of their holy texts, their traditions and recipes, their Torah scrolls and candelabras, and destroy every single bit of it, until the world was no longer polluted and weakened by Judaism.

This idea is like a molecule, a recipe, a building, and its component parts are stories and notions. Like the story of how Jews make sausages from children; the accusation that Jews control the economy; that they are responsible when there's a bad harvest, bad weather, sickness, and plagues. One of the most notorious attempts to smear the world's Jews is a pamphlet called *The Protocols of the Elders of Zion*, which was first published in Russia in 1905. It describes a secret congress in Basel in 1897, which never took place, where Jews from various nations assembled and plotted world domination. The document was fabricated by the Russian tsar's own secret service, and was based on superstition and old propaganda. However, the stories about the pogroms are much older. One of the oldest happened in the decades before the start of our common era, where the Romans attacked the Jewish population of Judea, scattering the Jews to the surrounding areas and beyond. Later, in the year 1096, German and French crusaders attacked the Jewish populations of the cities of Speyer, Worms, and Mainz, killing about two thousand people; and the drownings of Polotsk in 1563, where all who refused to convert to Orthodox Christianity were drowned in the river Dvina.

Between 1881 and 1884, the period in which you grew up, there were over two hundred attacks on Jewish communities throughout the Russian Empire. Long before that, in 1791, Catherine the Great had decided that Russia's Jews must all live within a specific geographic area. The area was called the Pale of Settlement, derived from the Latin word *palus,* a stake, or in broader terms, border; and encompassed much of what is today Lithuania, Belarus, and Ukraine. Its Jewish population lived in small villages called *shtetls,* and had fewer and fewer rights. Your parents lived in one of these villages, a place called Parichi, south of Minsk. Who knows what kind of fear they lived through, in the cramped and filthy streets, between makeshift houses made of stone and planks; their days occupied working in the fields, at the markets, boil-washing their clothes; surrounded by the smell of blazing wood stoves, the whining of dogs, and singing. Fields, dirt, and sweat. I don't. How many hundreds of thousands eventually fled because of the attacks and worsening violence? Some reports put it as high as two million. Moritz Glott went first to Vilnius and was trained at a tobacco factory, before moving to Germany and England to study, before he finally ended up in Norway.

And you? Were you traveling by horse and cart on your journey west? By train? Or on foot?

Gerson wrote the following in one of his few notes about his relatives:

Since we Komissar children grew up without any real contact with our closest, or most distant relatives, it was as though the term "relative" vanished from our lives. Our relationship to our grandparents was unquestionably connected to how our father regularly sent blue airmail letters home to White Russia, written in Yiddish using the Hebrew alphabet, and which ended with a short greeting from us little ones. But then the letters stopped, presumably because of my grandfather's death. He never said a word about his parents' health or living conditions to us. [...]

Our parents' poor level of engagement concerning their own roots formed a part of our own attitude to our previous generations. We totally lost our perspective on our grandparents and what they had actually undertaken. The most likely explanation for this was that the distance from the past we had experienced to the present was simply too great.

What was it you didn't tell your children about? The sudden attacks? How businesses were destroyed by vandals, windows broken, young boys beaten up, and women raped? What did you and the others who fled know about the persecution going on in your homeland, such as the Częstochowa pogrom, where a furious mob attacked shops, killed fourteen Jews, and stoned the Russian soldiers who were deployed to stop the attacks? You must have found life in Oslo and Trondheim peaceful and simple, with friends and family who lived around Grünerløkka and met near the benches at Olaf Rye's, who started businesses and had children, while the situation in the areas you left behind gradually worsened. Perhaps news of this reached the congregations in Oslo's and Trondheim's Jewish communities, and with that the worries too, because from 1903 until 1906 there was what's known as the "second wave" of pogroms in the tsar's Russia, when several thousand people lost their lives trying to protect themselves and their families. How did they defend themselves? With knives, shovels, pitchforks?

This antipathy still exists, almost unnoticed beneath the surface, popping up on rare occasions such as in news articles about the bullying of Jewish children in schools around Europe; or when shots are fired at a synagogue in Oslo, a building my children's great-great-grandparents helped finance the construction of. They had planned its design and helped manage the program, looking after the buying of furniture, the paying of employees, and the heating and maintenance bills. And it was where they celebrated all the Jewish holidays. In both Oslo and Trondheim the different branches of Rikke's family were active in the congregation and the Jewish community, while others withdrew from it and became more assimilated into the Norwegian way of life.

I have occasionally experienced it myself, a sense of discomfort with this identity, despite none of us being religious, because when the children would go to a birthday party they would make their own birthday cards, and my son would nearly always draw a Star of David on the front in colored pencil or felt-tip, without me ever understanding why or where he got it from. It is the same fear that Rikke says she felt during her childhood. It is because, even in a country as peaceful as Norway, you get a sense of what is hiding beneath the surface.

The list of pogroms is long, and is a lesson in pure horror. Such as the Jedwabne pogrom in Poland in 1941, where the Jewish rabbi was forced to lead a parade of around forty congregation members, who were eventually pushed into a barn, murdered, and buried along with fragments of destroyed Lenin monuments. Later the same day, between 250 and 500 people were forced into the same barn, which was then locked and set ablaze. I cannot imagine what it's like to inhale air so hot that it burns your lungs; or what it is like to hold your wife in your arms, or your brother or a child, while the sparks swirl wildly round the room, as the dry grass and wood crackle and spit, and the heat cooks you alive.

There is one other event which many historians consider to be a prelude to the Holocaust: the massacre at Babi Yar, in Kiev, in 1941. Babi Yar, which means "the woman's gorge," refers to a ravine that once marked the perimeter of the kingdom of Kiev, where soldiers who were bored on duty often received visits from their girlfriends.

The massacre took place between the 28th and 29th of September 1941. The Nazis had captured the city ten days earlier, and the commander of *Einsatzgruppe C* had started a rumor that all Jews would be transported by train to the Black Sea, and from there to Palestine. Everyone was then rounded up and led out of the city. A boy called Rubin Stein, who was one of the few survivors, later said that these Jews were stopped at five places along the route, at five different posts.

At the first post they took all our identification papers and threw them onto a fire. At the second post they took all our jewels, gold rings, and gold teeth. At the third post they took furs and bedding, and at the fourth post our suitcases which were thrown onto an enormous pile. At the final post the women and children were separated from the men and teenage boys. This is where I lost sight of my mother.

The ten-year-old boy managed to hide in a large pipe, I don't know what kind, but perhaps it was one of those concrete pipes that diverts streams under the road, like the ones I played in as a child.

According to the report that was sent to Berlin shortly afterward, 33,771 Jewish women, men, boys, and girls were shot and killed, their bodies falling into the ravine. The whole operation took thirty-six hours. Rubin Stein was one of the twenty-nine survivors.

While I'm writing this, it suddenly occurs to me that some of my children's relatives were probably among those killed, because they all came from this area, the tsar's sealed Jewish province. Countless stories cut short.

Q

×   ×   ×

Q for Quisling. As a young man, Vidkun Quisling was continually trying to find his way in life, testing several different paths until he became an enthusiastic supporter of Norway's fascist party, the National Party. Quisling also exaggerated his own importance in the postwar period, making claims about his accomplishments that did no more than highlight his deepest wish, one which exists in so many young men: the burning desire to be someone of importance.

Q for the quiet of the evening when the smell of tobacco smoke rises up from the yard, and the air is filled with chatter and the quacking of ducks flying south for the winter.

R

× × ×

R for Rikke.

"I always knew that something was different at my mother and stepfather's house. Just from the fact that we were as happy decorating a yucca plant in the living room as we were a Christmas tree, and we ate steak on Christmas Eve instead of traditional Christmas food. But Jewish? I've never identified with this term, because it encompasses so much. I have a father from western Norway, a stepfather from the south, and a mother from Oslo. And we've never commemorated any Jewish traditions at home. But I've always been more strongly associated with the Komissar side of the family. There's something about the art and the culture, the food, and the interest in politics and society. These small hints of Jewishness are quite indefinable, like the eight-armed candlestick my grandfather, my grandmother, and Lillemor all had at home. Or the unleavened bread I would get from Aunt Jane. Being

Jewish means acknowledging the fact that I would probably have died had I lived in 1942. A realization that parts of me are undesirable to many people, so undesirable that they are willing to kill to get rid of me. But what am I? I am a Norwegian. Just as my grandmother and grandfather felt they were. I remember once asking my grandfather why he was so unconcerned with being Jewish, to which he replied: 'I am not a Jew, I am a human being.'

"Two events in particular stand out from my childhood, as I remember. The first one is from elementary school, where there was a boy who everyone knew, because he was a Jew. He would often walk home from school with me, perhaps because he knew about my mother's family background. One day three slightly bigger boys came up to us while we were chatting in the street, and they went straight up to him and began pushing the boy around while shouting that word: Jew!

"I remember being scared, and for the first time it struck me that this word could be used as an insult, and that I couldn't let anyone know about my background. The boy they harassed said nothing, even though he must have known. Even though he could have pointed to me and tried to divert their attention to me instead, he just bent down and covered his head with his hands until they got bored and moved on. Then we wandered home in silence while I kicked myself for not stopping them. I should have done something.

"The other event was many years later, when someone I had never seen before was handing out neo-Nazi flyers in the schoolyard. They said something about Jews being exterminated. I remember being shocked and feeling a knot in my stomach. Did this apply to me too? I wasn't sure, but there and then I decided to say something. Because I couldn't remain silent about this for the rest of my life."

R for the roots of the huge pine trees you are sometimes forced to dig up and saw. A task so exhausting that you can barely keep the soup on your spoon afterward because of your trembling, shivering hand.

R for rumors, for rank, and for Rinnan. R for Rørvik.

It is September 7, 1944, and Rinnan is woken early by someone knocking on his bedroom door. His tongue is dry against the roof of his mouth, and he feels the effects of yesterday's drinking pressing against his forehead, but he takes a deep breath and gets up on his elbows. He hears Karl's voice on the other side, asking if he is awake, saying that there's a phone call for him. Rinnan looks at the clock on the bedside table. It is only seven fifteen; something must have happened, he thinks, and he shouts to Karl that he is coming before throwing the quilt aside and placing his feet on the cold floor. There is no one beside him in bed. *I must have slept alone,* he thinks, and he pictures the night before, smiling faces, faces bursting into laughter, liqueur dripping down Inga's chin. He remembers how he stopped her from wiping it off by leaning forward himself and kissing it away, and he could see that she liked it. They had gone down into the basement to get more to drink, and then taken one of the prisoners out of his cell, a young guy, terrified—and he had good reason to be after stupidly refusing to talk—who Karl had forced into a chair, and they had practiced shooting as close to his head as possible, without actually hitting him.

Oh my God, what a noise! It was equally fucking shocking every single time, how the gunfire echoed off the walls; and how the bullet sent splinters flying from the wood panels, before falling into the space in the wall cavity. He remembers coming up with a new game which he called *right/left,* that involved shouting either "right!" or "left!" and the prisoner had to quickly lean right or left to avoid being shot. The look of terror on the guy's face was hilarious. "RIGHT!" Rinnan would shout, and then fire, hitting the back of the chair exactly where he wanted, as the prisoner leaned as far as he possibly could to the right. They'd played a couple of rounds of the game before Rinnan decided he wanted to carry on drinking instead, but when he turned around Inga had gone back upstairs. What time could it have been? Two? Rinnan puts on his shirt and trousers and leans up to the mirror, then pulls the comb from his back pocket and combs his hair back before leaving the bedroom. He walks past the kitchen, where the sink is piled up with dirty plates, and past one of the other gang members resting on the sofa. He gives him a nudge and tells him to go down to the cellar and continue the interrogation. Then he goes looking for Karl, who tells him that Flesch has called and that Rinnan needs to go to the Mission Hotel as soon as possible. As soon as possible? That doesn't sound good. For a moment he worries that he is going to be reprimanded for something, but what could that be?

"I guess we should get going then," says Rinnan, before walking into the kitchen, taking a smoked sausage from the fridge, and pouring himself a glass of milk. Their dog, a German shepherd, hears the sounds from the kitchen and scampers into the room with wide expectant eyes and claws clicking against the hard floor. "Here you go," he says, breaking the sausage in half as the dog wags its tail wildly, oblivious to its thwacking against the door frame. Rinnan holds out the bit of sausage, which the dog chomps straight from his hand, before he strokes the animal's back. He takes a large bite of his own sausage and suddenly feels the pressure in his forehead again. *More fluids*, he thinks, before gulping down the glass of milk. A scream of pain comes from the cellar, which means they must be back at work down there, and that's good. This prisoner needs to start giving them some names, so that they can shut down another branch of the resistance, he thinks, while taking another bite and walking out into the hall where he puts his coat and shoes on. Karl follows him out, and they both jump in the car and drive out the gates, past the armed guards and barbed wire. Whenever he nods at the German soldiers at the gates, he feels a swell of pride about his achievements, because this is all his work. If only they knew. If everyone in Levanger could just see him now, he thinks, while taking the cigarette case from his pocket, tapping a cigarette against the lid, and lighting it. He looks at everyone going to work, with their coat lapels turned up to their ears and their strange little ration books hidden in their inside pockets. But he—he drives around with his own chauffeur, earning ten times the average wage, and can get hold of anything he wants.

They park in front of the Mission Hotel, and the soldiers nod as they open the door for him. Rinnan smiles at the secretary and goes straight to Flesch's office. Two weeks earlier Flesch had ordered him to uncover as many members as possible from the resistance group Milorg, in the Vikna region. In February 1943, Rinnan infiltrated the group under the name of Olof Wisth and had extensive knowledge about the fifty-strong organization, but he hadn't gone to make the arrests himself since he was tired of all the traveling and would rather stay at the Gang Monastery. Instead Rinnan had sent Karl Dolmen, who had done an outstanding job. Karl, with the help of the Germans, had arrested many of the Milorg members, among them Bjørn Holm, who Rinnan already knew was smuggling weapons, along with a certain Reverend Moe.

"During questioning, the prisoner confessed to there being a weapons cache containing five hundred machine guns," Flesch says. "Five hundred! We take this *very* seriously," continues Flesch, before telling Rinnan about the Allies' June invasion of Normandy, and Germany's fear of something similar happening on the west coast of Norway. Rinnan smiles at Flesch while he talks and the interpreter translates, still not quite used to the forced interruptions.

"Your mission, Rinnan, is to go up there as quickly as possible, find these hidden weapons, and confiscate them. The order comes from the *very* highest authority," he says, implying that Hitler himself has ordered the operation.

"And if people won't cooperate, and you don't find anything, you are instructed to shoot two random hostages. That will send the right signal," Flesch concludes.

Rinnan nods, and tells Flesch that he will find the weapons, but he has an uneasy feeling from the moment he walks out the door and drives home to pack his bags; a sense of foreboding that something doesn't add up, because why hasn't he already heard about these weapons? He knows there are some firearms hidden in the Vikna area. But five hundred machine guns? When did they arrive? And why hadn't any of his negative contacts mentioned it, or said anything about the enormous operation that's supposedly being planned?

Buildings and people glide by as he thinks back over all the locations. He pictures all the cellars and faces, trying to imagine what he could have overlooked, on which farm? Which village? Or island?

He drives home, plays with the children a little, and gives Klara a peck on the cheek as he leaves, totally unaffected by the cold atmosphere between them, because he doesn't have any problem attracting women, absolutely not, he thinks. Then he sets off to carry out his mission. He sends a message to two of his operatives in the area that they are to take *Rusken,* one of the confiscated boats, and go by sea, while he will gather the German troops and come by road. He gives them a list of men that are to be arrested and forced to confess. Then he climbs into one of the trucks and sets off. Rinnan doesn't see how this hundred-foot boat sails into the calm waters of the fjord, with the sun streaming down, and the lush green meadows that roll down to the sea. He doesn't see the black boulders that turn speckled gray as his operatives approach, or the bladderwrack, glistening in multiple shades of brown as it swirls back and forth by the shore. Rinnan isn't there in person when they arrest Harald Henrikø, out digging for potatoes when they find him, who simply says farewell to his children and is taken onto the boat. Rinnan doesn't see how Karl and the others then follow the sound of hammering to the neighboring farm, where they find Kyrre Henrikø and his son down by the shore, building a new boathouse, who just have to drop their tools and go with them.

Rinnan only sees the results of the interrogations when he finally arrives in Rørvik in the evening, two days later, along with fifty soldiers from the *Schutzpolizei* and their commander, whose name is Hamm. Rinnan had hoped that everything would be resolved by the time he arrived; that Karl would be there to meet him the moment he stepped from the car, and tell him that the prisoner had cracked under interrogation and they had found all the hidden weapons. But when he sees Karl standing by the harbor, unshaven, with greasy hair and dark rings round his eyes from not sleeping, he immediately realizes that they haven't been able to extract the information they need.

"He's in there, boss," is the only thing Karl says. Rinnan nods and puts his hand on Karl's shoulder. Then, with his boots knocking loudly against the wooden planks, they enter a warehouse they have commandeered, where the prisoner sits in the middle of the room with his hands tied behind his back, his head hanging forward, his mouth half open, and his lips cracked and split.

"He hasn't said a word yet," says Karl.

"Goddammit," says Rinnan, going over to the prisoner and grabbing his face. Spit runs down the man's chin and Rinnan is glad, at least, that he kept his gloves on.

"Hi," says Rinnan, forcing the prisoner's face upward. "You know, just as well as I do, that there are only two ways out of this. Right?"

The man sniffs hard through his nose, and glances around bewilderedly.

"One way involves my men continuing like this, until they pummel the truth out of you—or if that fails they'll just shoot you and throw your corpse into the fjord. That's one way out. You hear me?"

The man nods, and sniffs hard through his nostrils again.

"The other way out, and the easiest option by far, is that you tell us where the weapons are," says Rinnan, suddenly hearing footsteps behind him. He turns round and sees that the German officer has come into the room.

"But I don't . . . know . . . anything," says the prisoner, gasping for breath, on the verge of tears.

"So be it," says Rinnan, letting go of the man's neck. "We'll just have to be a little creative. Go and get Bjørn Holm," he says to Karl, who nods and hurries up the steps, two at a time. It was Bjørn Holm's confession about the weapons cache, during his interrogation at the Mission Hotel, that had led them here; so Rinnan has brought him along as a guide and as a contingency plan. Rinnan lights a cigarette and offers one to the German officer, who says thank you. Then Karl returns, with the prisoner from Trondheim in front of him. Bjørn sees the man in the chair and mumbles "Oh my God" and shakes his head. He has a black eye and his hands tied behind his back.

"Well, look at that, he's wearing eye shadow!" Rinnan mocks. Then he asks one of the gang to tie the prisoner to a chair. He decides upon a method that Flesch taught him: to place an acquaintance of the person being tortured right in front of them, and force them to watch, in the hope that one of them will eventually break down and confess. Karl presses the man down onto the chair.

"I don't know anything!" cries Harald Henrikø desperately. "Dear God, I don't know anything!" he repeats.

"Sure you don't. So why has Bjørn here told us there are five hundred machine guns hidden nearby?" says Rinnan, nodding to the men to continue with the torture.

"I'm sorry!" screams Bjørn and turns to Rinnan: "There *aren't* any weapons! I was forced to confess, but they don't exist!"

"Shut up!" barks Rinnan, who goes over and slaps him round the head, damned if he'll allow Bjørn to give moral support to the guy they're interrogating, there's far too much at stake. He has got to find these fucking weapons, because what will Flesch think if he fails?

He orders the torture to continue. So they get started. Punching. Burning.

Screams, tears, spit, blood.

They beat Henrikø on his arms, on his legs, with clubs and

chains. Then they remove the chair, so he just falls to the floor, and eventually he loses consciousness. Bjørn Holm sits there crying. Rinnan lifts the prisoner's head, but he's out cold. *Fuck!* thinks Rinnan, suddenly realizing that he needs the toilet, and that he is hungry, but it will have to wait. It's such bullshit that they've sent him here—constantly monitored by the German officer watching every single movement—when he could be at back at the Gang Monastery, because the prisoner they're torturing is of course never going to talk. He's done this enough times to know that the man would have said something long before now.

"Carry him out!" says Rinnan. "And get us some food and drink. Then bring the other prisoner, and we'll continue with him."

Shortly after, the other gang members return with a bottle of coffee liqueur, a glass, and the final prisoner, Paul Nygård.

"Put him there and wait," says Rinnan, pointing at the toppled chair. He then pulls the cork from the bottle, pours it into a glass, and knocks it back. The sweet, soft liquid glides down his throat, and a comforting heat spreads through his body.

"I'll be right back," he says, then heads to the toilet. He takes a piss in the tiny little bathroom, while checking his reflection in the mirror. Then he washes his hands and combs his hair once more, sweeping his forelock neatly back. He needs to get some food inside him, anything, he thinks, and then heads straight back to the interrogation.

Paul Nygård screams the moment he sees the knife coming toward him. He screams that he'll talk, that he'll tell them everything.

Karl is totally out of breath now, so focused on the job at hand that he doesn't immediately stop. Hungry for blood, thinks Rinnan, placing a hand on Karl's shoulder to restrain him.

"Good work, Karl!" says Rinnan, patting his friend on the shoulder. "Get yourself something to eat and drink, I'll take over from here," he says, and he sees the relief in Karl's eyes, before turning to look at the desperate prisoner.

"Now then," says Rinnan. "Where are these weapons?" The man breathes heavily, and looks over at Bjørn.

"They're on . . . Gals Island," he says.

"OK," says Rinnan. "Good. And where exactly is Gals Island?"

"It's right . . . out here," says Paul, gasping for breath while staring at the knife.

"Good, then I have no further questions. Let's go!" he says. Rinnan takes the man's arm, forcing him to his feet, and tells everyone to follow him. Harald Henrikø grips the armrests on the chair with his bloody hands and tries to pull himself up, but his legs give way and he collapses onto the floor again. *Great! Now we have to carry him around,* thinks Rinnan, but he notices a wheelbarrow leaning up against the wall and tells Karl to load the cripple into it so they can get going. Then he reports the confession to the officer, while one of the soldiers translates for him, and they walk along the harbor and climb aboard the *Rusken*. The sun is about to rise over the fjord, and the water is as calm as a millpond.

Rinnan takes Paul and Karl up to the bridge, while three soldiers carry the wheelbarrow containing Harald Henrikø on board. The German officer follows Rinnan up, and that's fine, because now he has seen what they are capable of. He has seen that they know how to make people talk, and that they are now very close to finding the weapons cache, which may prevent another Normandy in Norway. This could actually thwart a British invasion and change the course of the war, he thinks, as the boat sails in a gentle curve out of the harbor.

Up on the bridge Rinnan finally gets hold of some coffee and a bread roll. "Now you can show us the way, Paul," he says, patting the man amicably on the shoulder. He sees the fear in Paul's bloodshot eyes, his inflamed skin now covered in cuts and bruises, but had he just told them everything in the first place, he could have avoided all this fuss. *He's lucky to be alive, but the old bastard certainly stuck it out long enough, I was really starting to doubt if there were any weapons,* thinks Rinnan. It takes some guts to absorb that much pain without disclosing the information you're hiding. Then again, none of that helps when you come up against someone that *really* knows what they're doing, he thinks.

"That way," Rinnan says while pointing out to sea. "Gals Island, was it?" says the captain. Rinnan nods, but detects a little reluctance from the captain, but so what, he just needs the guy to steer the boat, and besides, he'll send a few agents to visit the man's family later and find out who he sympathizes with. They head out to sea in the glorious sunshine, it is seven in the morning, and Rinnan is tired; his eyes are sore from the lack of sleep and his movements feel sluggish. He rummages around in his pockets, finds his bottle of pills, and coughs a little, pretending to clear his throat before raising his hand and tossing a few pills in his mouth, swallowing them without water.

He needs it right now, a little pick-me-up, after so much traveling and after interrogating the prisoners all night. A flock of seagulls descend on them, expecting them to haul up a fishing net, but the birds will be disappointed, Rinnan thinks. He asks the captain to point out the island on the map. The area is peppered with hundreds of tiny islands, and Gals Island is no more than a pinprick on the map, so it's a good spot. The Germans would never have found their way to this hideout by themselves, he thinks, imagining the respect Flesch will give him when he tells him the news, or better still: when he has the German soldiers stack the boxes of weapons up in the Mission Hotel.

The pill starts to take effect. Once again his energy returns, his spirits lift, and his thoughts begin to clear. He needs more coffee, so he asks someone to fix some more food and drink for them. Soon the captain points toward an island and says that they have arrived.

"Now then, Paul. Is that it?" asks Rinnan. Paul looks up from the floor and to where Rinnan's finger is pointing. He nods, but blinks several times and his eyes dart around nervously. Rinnan has a bad feeling about this, but decides not to waste his energy on feelings now.

It is a small island, no more than a couple of hundred yards wide, but someone has managed to establish a farm on it, and there is a jetty where they can moor the boat.

"Come then, Paul. Show us the way!" says Rinnan, while one of the soldiers hands him a cup of coffee. Then they step ashore. "Where are they? On the farm?"

"Erm . . . I think so," replies Paul, his eyes still darting all around.

"You *think*? What the fuck do you mean by that?" asks Rinnan.

"I wasn't . . . I wasn't here when they hid them," says Paul.

"But they are here, right?" asks Rinnan.

"Yes, they should be," replies Paul, blinking yet again in quick succession, and Rinnan doesn't like this at all, this shift from being quite certain of the location when he was being interrogated to the vague wording he is using now: *Yes they should be*. But that's how it is, now they just have to scour this wretched island, he thinks, and he orders the soldiers to start searching. First the house and the barn. Then the cellar. There is a family living there, but when asked about the weapons they just look back incredulously, with neither the father nor mother showing any signs of lying. Rinnan warns them both what will happen if it turns out they lied, but even though there are two children in the house the couple swear that they know nothing. They only need to look at how badly beaten Paul is, and at the ten German soldiers carrying machine guns outside, to know that Rinnan isn't joking around.

"They don't know about it," says Paul, blinking rapidly again. "They weren't on the island when the weapons were hidden."

"Oh, is that right? I thought you didn't know where they were?" asks Rinnan.

"I don't know . . . I just heard that the family living here were away, just in case . . . in case they were loyal to the wrong side, or perhaps told someone . . . ," he says. It all seems plausible.

Rinnan takes a sip of his coffee and feels his energy increasing, so much so that he feels capable of anything, he thinks, tightening his hand round the pill bottle. And they stand there waiting in the sun, on this September morning, while the soldiers turn the house upside down. Searching from the cellar to the loft, for hidden trap-doors in the barn, and through the bushes at the back. They look for signs of digging or freshly turned soil, for places where new shoots are coming up, but they find nothing. So Rinnan goes back to the boat, to fetch Karl and the other prisoner, Harald Henrikø, who has to be carried up the steps again by two soldiers and placed in the wheelbarrow. They trundle him over to the farm, while he lies there with his eyes closed, but suddenly he starts crying again.

"Hey!" says Rinnan; he really can't stand any more of this, he just wants this whole operation to be over so he can go home to the Gang Monastery. "Where are the weapons?" he asks, but Harald just weeps, he says that he doesn't know anything, that he has never heard about any weapons, he swears on it. Rinnan takes his pistol from his belt, feeling how nice it sits in his hand, and then points it at Harald's head. He presses the barrel hard against his forehead and stares at the man, with his bloody face and his knotted greasy hair, but it makes no difference. Harald just sobs even louder, and says that he really doesn't know anything, that they have got to believe him, which Rinnan actually does, the guy probably doesn't know shit, he thinks. And that is a problem, because the idea that they may have been tricked begins to resurface, or even worse: it could be that this weapons cache is an imaginary one, a product of torturing a prisoner so desperate to survive, he'll fabricate a story of a secret weapons storage that doesn't exist.

On the other hand, thinks Rinnan, perhaps they really *are* just stubborn bastards; or perhaps there actually *is* a weapons cache, but the resistance has made it totally impossible to find. Perhaps only a limited number of people know where the weapons actually are, because they are so extremely valuable to the British. Rinnan sends the soldiers out to search the whole island.

They search for the weapons the entire morning.

They smoke. They eat. They get the mother in the house to cook food for everyone. They go to the toilet. They wait, and wait, and wait, while the soldiers comb the island back and forth, but they get tired, and reluctant, and eventually lose their enthusiasm. The soldiers continue searching, but only because they have been ordered to.

In the end, they give up without finding any weapons, most likely because there aren't any, thinks Rinnan, closing his eyes. He opens his pill bottle again and pops another pill in his mouth, unconcerned about anyone seeing him because now there's only one plan of action remaining: *And if you don't find anything, you are instructed to shoot two random hostages.*

Those were the orders, and they have to be obeyed, there's no fucking way out of it. Orders are orders. They want a show of force, a deterrent, just as they did with the ten men they executed at Falstad. Someone has to die, as an example of what will happen. *Fuck!* thinks Rinnan, looking at Karl, who walks over to him with an unusually guilt-ridden look on his face.

"Boss . . . I don't think there are any weapons here," Karl says quietly, brushing some grass from his trousers.

"I know, Karl . . . But we still have to carry out our mission," he says. Rinnan walks over to the soldiers, now standing there tired and listless. He tells the officer that his men can withdraw to the boat, the search is over.

A few minutes later they are sailing toward the mainland again while Rinnan scans the landscape with its red barns and farmhouses, knowing that he must select two men from one of them and thinking of how absurd it is that these people are going to die, but don't yet realize it.

There is nothing they can do. The Germans should have let *him* continue his intelligence work instead. Then they could have avoided all this trouble. Obviously, they had extracted a false confession from a man quite prepared to admit he had an army in the cellar and the devil in the loft if they would stop torturing him. So here he is, up to his neck in it, he thinks, as Karl passes him a sandwich, dripping with jam, just as Karl knows he likes it.

"Thanks," Rinnan says, taking a bite. And this breaks the silence enough to give the captain the chance to ask him where they should go. Which is exactly the sign he needed.

"Take us over there," Rinnan says, pointing toward a peaceful-looking farm, with two men working outside. The captain turns the boat to starboard, spraying water up the sides and leaving a foaming wake behind, while below deck the diesel engine chugs quickly like the heart of a little animal. Rinnan sees the two men stop working and turn their attention to the boat as it sails toward the jetty. They appear to be a father and his adult son, both wearing overalls.

The boat draws up beside the jetty, and Rinnan jumps off. The older of the two men goes to shake his hand but quickly lowers it when he sees the German soldiers on board the boat. The younger of the two says something, and looks as if he's about to run away, but his father holds him back.

"Hello there," Rinnan says, as he walks toward the men, followed by Karl with a machine gun slung over his shoulder and the German soldiers behind him.

The man is clearly reluctant to speak, which is something Rinnan has seen many times before, but has no choice but to stand still and wait for all this to be over, as one does with a sudden and unexpected pain.

"What can we do for you?" asks the father.

"Well, there's a man from around here who has confessed to there being a large cache of weapons hidden on one of these farms," says Rinnan, trying to gauge the men's reactions. Hoping that one of them will start looking around nervously or something, but they just look at him blankly.

"Weapons?" repeats the father.

"Yes. Can we take a look inside?" asks Rinnan.

"By all means," says the father.

If the soldiers could only find something now, he'll avoid having to do what he'll soon be forced to do, Rinnan thinks. He tells the soldiers to put the men on the boat and keep an eye on them.

Rinnan knocks on the door and wipes his feet before entering the hall. He peers into the living room where an elderly couple sit; an old man smoking a pipe and his wife knitting.

"Nice and quiet in the sitting room," he says, smiling at them, and the couple smile back. There's no point searching here at all, he thinks, and leaves the house without looking back. He returns to the boat, and with no further hesitation asks the captain to take them to the nearest islet.

Then he collects the prisoners. Karl forces them onto the rocky shore of a small barren skerry, where nothing grows but a few bushes, and nothing goes except seagulls.

Once again Harald has to be carried off the boat, and then all the prisoners are shoved further inland.

"Where are we going?" asks the father, turning to Rinnan.

"We can stop here. Put your hands on your head," says Rinnan, pointing to a small gap in the heather. Then Karl Dolmen and Finn Hoff set up two machine guns and aim them at the men. Karl maintains a front as usual, showing no sign of unease, while Finn, tall as a beanpole, looks agitated; his eyes darting around, he looks at Rinnan panic-stricken, as though trapped and looking for an exit. *Fuck! It just isn't right,* he thinks. They can't just kill these two men, who are completely innocent? Now the son begins to cry, and the father looks like he is about to start too, lowering his arm and holding it against his face, but Karl snaps at him: *"Keep your hands up!"*

And then the old man cracks, tears start rolling down his cheeks, and he starts babbling incoherently to himself.

"Please! Please! We haven't done anything! We're innocent! What is it you want?" he says. "Please! You must be mistaken! We're just farmers! Please don't kill my son!" cries the father with his face now awash with fear and grief and desperation. They just have to get it over with. "What do you want to do, chief?" asks Finn, pointing his machine gun at the men, but with his face turned toward Rinnan.

"Harald!" shouts Rinnan. "Tell us where the weapons are hidden!" But now Harald is crying as well; with mucus pouring from his nostrils and rivers of tears flowing down his battered and bloody face, he says: *"Please God!!! We don't know anything! I don't know anything! Please don't do this!"*

"Are those your final words?" asks Rinnan.

Harald nods, which means there's nothing else to do. *Shit, let's get this tragedy over with as fast as possible,* thinks Rinnan, and he turns to Karl and Finn and nods. The father shouts "No!" but his scream is cut short by the deafening clatter of the two machine guns. The bullets rip through their bodies, and the two men slump to the ground.

"Dear God," whispers Harald, as his head slumps forward. Bjørn just stands there with his eyes screwed up.

Karl walks over to the bodies and rolls them over while Finn stands with his machine gun hanging by his thigh, his head bowed and his forelock hanging over his face.

The son is still breathing, erratically, shaking and blinking while his stomach trembles and blood seeps out from his chest and mouth. He looks pleadingly up at them both and reaches up to Karl for help.

"Ah, for fuck's sake!" says Karl as he points the machine gun once more at the young man's head. Then one final shot echoes across the fjord. Rinnan takes a deep breath, shakes his head, and looks up at the boy now lying silently in the heather. Finn has turned and walked a few yards away, and stands like a solitary line against the sky.

Nobody speaks. A seagull flies overhead and begins to shriek.

"What now, boss?" says Karl.

Rinnan reaches into his coat pocket and touches the pill bottle. He shouldn't take any more, he was warned about taking too many, that it could cause heart failure, but now he really needs something, a drink; he should never have been in this fucking outpost in the first place, he thinks. He asks Karl and Finn to dump the corpses in the fjord, and that marks the end of Operation Seehund II. They pack up and leave as quickly as possible, to avoid giving this sorry affair any more thought; and as soon as they reach the mainland, Rinnan climbs into one of the trucks and returns to Trondheim to submit his report.

More missions are carried out through the autumn. More arrests, more torturing and killing. It never ends.

The Germans start losing on an increasing number of fronts. Russia invades northern Norway.

December comes.

He meets a new girl at a Christmas dinner party. Her name is Gunnlaug Dundas. She is petite, with blue eyes and blonde hair, and seems slightly lost. It turns out that her boyfriend was recently killed by the resistance. Now she needs someone, a safe haven, someone she can be with, who can give her warmth, food, and love. Rinnan can do all these things, and takes an immediate liking to her. She's so young and pure, with the most radiant smile, and a look in her eyes that fills him with a warm glow. They exchange brief comments and glances throughout the meal, while filling their glasses and raising them to their mouths; and tiny sparks fly as they touch hands when passing the bowl of potatoes round, or when he stretches his leg under the table to touch her ankle.

Oh, how wonderful it is!

How wonderful to feel in love again, he thinks, and he can tell immediately that the feeling is mutual; that they will be leaving together; that they will undress one another, and wake up together. Of *course* that's what's going to happen. Normal rules don't apply to him, he has sacrificed so much to be where he is, more than anybody else would have risked, he thinks, and this is his reward; to live by another set of rules, a different kind of freedom, where everything is free-flowing.

×

It is New Year's Eve, 1944, and Rinnan is throwing a party for some of the gang members at home, a short drive from the Gang Monastery. Klara and the children have gone to bed, but the party goes on after midnight, and the rest of them continue drinking in the living room. The table is covered with dirty glasses, and the ashtrays are full of cigarette butts all curled up like tiny animals. Faces glow and laugh in the flickering candlelight, but one person becomes more withdrawn—Finn—who has smiled less and less since the shooting of the two innocent men on the island. Since that day it is as if a dark cloud has descended on him.

Now it is January 1, the first day of the year. Finn empties his glass and pushes himself out of the armchair. He sways about on his feet a little, then brushes his dark hair back and says:

"I think I'll go out and shoot myself."

Rinnan bursts out laughing. "Good luck!" he says, raising his glass for a toast. The others do the same, while Finn squeezes past the sofa with his back hunched. He bumps into the door frame, puts on his boots, and opens the front door.

The party continues, and it's a good while before anyone notices that Finn hasn't returned, but the following day he is found, in an area near where he grew up, with a bullet hole in his temple and a pistol lying in the snow beside him.

This is how 1945 begins.

R for the rain that drums on the roof of the Gang Monastery, rushing down the gutters or trickling down the windowpanes in crooked, unpredictable paths.

It is now April 1945, and the nights and days are like one continuous storm of new orders coming from Flesch, demanding that he carry out more interrogations and more missions. Rinnan drinks, takes pills, takes prisoners, and takes lives. He goes on vacation in March with Gunnlaug, who he calls "Puss"—otherwise the days just blur into one. And now there's no way out. Only this system can reward him with money and power. Only the war can protect him from all those who want him dead.

Then, one afternoon, Rinnan gets a tip that his ex who ran away, Marie Arentz, is back in Norway, after several years in Germany. She and her boyfriend, Bjørn Bjørnebo, who works for a different German intelligence group, are planning to escape across the border to Sweden. They have made contact with someone offering to help them, except these helpers are negative contacts, spying for Rinnan without realizing it themselves. Rinnan thanks the man for the information and tells him to inform the two refugees that they will be picked up later that evening.

He pours himself another glass of coffee liqueur and tells Karl the news.

"Bjørn Bjørnebo. What a funny name as well," he says, referring to the meaning in Norwegian: *Bear Bearhome.*

"Are you going to let them go?" asks Karl, which is a reasonable question because in some cases Rinnan does just that. After consulting with Flesch, he sometimes allows refugees to escape across the border, to send a positive message about the organization and give it some legitimacy. It is a simple calculation, of how many unimportant refugees they can let out versus how many resistance members it allows them to catch.

Rinnan smiles and shakes his head. These two will not be getting away. Not a chance. He takes a sip of his drink, licks the liqueur from his lips, and tells Karl what he intends to do.

Later that night, Marie and Bjørn stand by an unlit road waiting to be collected, when they are suddenly dazzled by headlights as a car pulls up in front of them. Two men sit in the front. Bjørn opens the door for Marie, and after climbing in himself, he sits with a relieved look on his face.

"Thank you so much for being able to get here so quickly," says Bjørn. The driver removes his hat and turns round.

"Hi there. Long time no see," says Rinnan, smiling.

"Henry?" says Marie.

Then Karl turns round in the passenger seat and points his gun at them. It's weird to see her face again; that long hair resting against her skin; those cheeks which he once stroked, lips that he once kissed; and those eyes that once closed with pleasure beneath him. *Now the roles have changed, but that's not my fault,* thinks Rinnan.

"What do you want?" asks Marie.

"I just fancied a little drive," says Rinnan, shifting gears. "But not to Sweden."

"Where then?" asks Bjørn.

"Home to our headquarters," says Rinnan. "And then we'll decide what to do with you two traitors."

R for research, at the National Archives in Oslo. An aging security guard checks my ID card at the main entrance before allowing me to go up the stairs, past the display cases of old books, where I explain what I need to the employee at the archives' front desk. I'm told that all the material on Rinnan has been digitized, and also that the reason I was not admitted before is that there is restricted access to it. Not because of Rinnan, but out of respect for the innocent victims who are mentioned or photographed. The archive contains all the material on him. Everything that still exists, that is, since the officers at the Nazi headquarters in Trondheim attempted to destroy as much evidence as possible in the final days of the war, just as Rinnan did.

There are more than five thousand pages, mostly scanned A4 sheets with typed notes. Rinnan's interrogation notes are among them, along with his outlandish descriptions of his relationship with a Russian agent; how she anesthetized him with chloroform but didn't actually kill him because they were in love with each other. There are also interviews with the prisoners who survived and photographs of some of the corpses. One of them is etched into my mind: it shows a prisoner from the Gang Monastery who was found lying dead in the snow somewhere, his body bent double and tightly bound with rope, as one might tie up a roast chicken or a joint of meat.

I leaf through all the interviews and court transcripts, then come across some folders that are labeled "miscellaneous," and soon find one of Rinnan's notes, one I have already come across in one of his biographies. I continue looking, but I'm unable to find any more of Rinnan's own notes, except the few I already know about. The rest were probably destroyed before the end of the war. In the end, I realize I will never figure out if it really was Rinnan who listened to your conversation and had you arrested. It will remain a mystery.

R for the rigged trial that Rinnan holds at the Gang Monastery. It is the evening of April 19, 1945, and the light from the streetlamp shines in through the living room window, casting long shadows over the two people standing in the middle of the room with their hands tied behind their backs: Marie Arentz and Bjørn Bjørnebo. Rinnan sits behind his writing desk with the other gang members standing on either side. He pours himself a glass of liqueur, licks his lips before taking a sip. Then he clears his throat and turns his attention to the figures standing before him.

"My distinguished guests! The honorable judge Karl Dolmen is presiding, and one of the accused standing over there will be making the defense. So the court is ready!"

He bangs his desk with a school cane brought up from the cellar, smirking at the pathetic slapping noise it makes.

"Not much of a gavel. We'll have to find something better for the judge. Let's see . . ."

Rinnan stands up and walks over to the fireplace and picks up a wooden log. Nobody speaks while he weighs it in his hand before putting it back and shaking his head. Then he looks round the room while everyone follows his gaze, apart from the two defendants, who just stare at the floor in front of them. Suddenly he thinks of something that will work. He walks over to one of the dining chairs and brings it back to Karl.

"Now, your honor, if you could please just loosen one of these judge's gavels for me. They've clearly tried to escape, just as these two have done . . ."

Rinnan scowls theatrically at the two defendants, while several of the other gang members start sniggering.

"This sneaky little judge's gavel here . . . ," he says, while slapping the chair leg against the palm of his hand. "It tried to hide. Not like a bear in its little cave, no. It tried to *pretend* that it is just an innocent chair leg and not a judge's gavel at all!" he says. He sees the effect the words have on the others, and how the joke makes some of them laugh. Then he lowers his voice and places his hand on Karl Dolmen's shoulder.

"But we are not so easily fooled, are we, judge?" Rinnan concludes, before stepping aside to make way.

Karl shakes his head and takes the chair from Rinnan's hands. Then he lays it upside down on the floor, places one foot on the underside of the seat, and bends the chair leg sideways. There is a creak of splintering wood and a metallic squeak of nails being dragged out of their holes.

"There! Yes, your honor! There you have it!" says Rinnan.

Karl slaps the chair leg against his palm a couple of times and looks up.

"Thank you, this will do the job!"

"It's a pleasure to be of assistance, your honor!"

Rinnan walks past Bjørn Bjørnebo and sits back down at his desk. He looks over at Karl and smiles.

"The court is now seated, judge . . . you know, bang the gavel on the table, and so on, and so on."

Karl springs to life and whacks the chair leg three times on the table.

"Yes . . . If the court is seated, then we can begin . . . Can the prosecution start by saying what these two communist turncoats are accused of?"

Rinnan takes a sip of his liqueur, then rises to his feet, scraping his chair as he pushes back.

"Yes, your honor. The two defendants, Marie Arentz and Bjørn Bjørnebo, are charged with treason, mutiny, and attempting to escape."

Karl gives a satisfied nod.

"Good. Thank you! Do the defendants have any objections?"

Marie shakes her head slightly. Bjørn says nothing.

"No objections?" says Rinnan, resting his elbows on the table with his head sunk between his shoulders.

"These are very serious crimes. Do we have evidence to support the claims . . . ? We cannot simply judge people for such grave offenses without some form of evidence . . ."

Karl nods.

"Yes, prosecutor, we need to see some kind of evidence. Do we have it . . . ?"

Rinnan pushes his chair back again and moves in front of his desk.

"Actually we do. We have a witness here in the courtroom, your honor. Can Henry Oliver Rinnan come to the witness stand?"

Inga claps her hands with delight as Rinnan walks over to a small bureau which has been pulled out from the wall, with a vase on top.

"Yes, that's me . . . Yes, thank you . . . Yes . . . ," says Rinnan, from behind the bureau. He looks toward the writing desk, where he had just been playing the role of prosecutor, and nods several times, as though formulating a response to a string of questions. The others laugh.

"Yes. Thank you, prosecutor. I'm happy to share what I know about these two traitors. I first met the accused, Marie Arentz, in 1942, when she was a friend of one of our first members, Ragnhild Strøm. The two of them embarked on an extremely important and successful mission to Bodø, on board the boat MS *King Haa-kon,* where they infiltrated the resistance and exposed several key escape channels to Sweden . . ."

Witness Rinnan then pretends to listen, nodding several times and saying, "Yes, yes, I totally agree," before continuing.

"Yes, Miss Arentz was one of Special Division Lola's leading agents . . . She could have gone a long way, but she went and ran off, as the court has correctly pointed out, and signed up with the Red Cross in Germany, of all things. Had she been smart, she would have stayed there. But instead she returned to Trondheim, where she hooked up with this sorry excuse for a spy here, who goes by the name of . . . let's see . . . what was it again? Wolf Wolfsson, I think it was . . ."

Karl Dolmen's girlfriend, Ingeborg Schevik, laughs out loud, and Gunnlaug also begins to snigger, uncontrollably it seems. Rinnan's eyes meet hers, and he gives her a wry smile, so happy about the whole trial and pleased that she smiles at him, but then he has to return to his role, straighten his back, and say: "No, sorry . . . Bjørn Bjørnebo, from a rival intelligence agency, so useless I haven't even bothered to learn its name."

Rinnan returns to his desk, takes a sip of liqueur, and resumes the role of prosecutor.

"So, Henry Oliver Rinnan. Can you tell us what happened after that, especially regarding why these two are on trial today?"

Rinnan walks back to the witness stand, spreads his hands out on the bureau desk, and addresses Karl Dolmen.

"Yes, your honor. Earlier today one of our negative contacts informed us of a Norwegian couple who were planning to escape, so I made arrangements for their transport to the border. I got hold of a car, drove there, and waited, and soon these two little love-birds arrived, ready to fly across the border. They weren't terribly happy when they saw who sat behind the wheel, I can assure the assembly of that!"

He looks around while everyone's faces light up. Then he walks across the room, right up to Karl, and takes the chair leg from his hands.

"Since is this a case for the Supreme Court, we will be needing several judges, is that correct?"

Karl nods, and Rinnan sees Ingeborg smile and give Gunnlaug a nudge.

"Quite correct," replies Karl, but Rinnan has already walked away, slapping the chair leg against his palm. He looks around the room and sees the spark of expectation in the eyes of the other gang members. Then he goes back behind the desk to continue as prosecutor, facing the empty room where he had just been standing as a witness.

"Outstanding, Mr. Rinnan. Thank you for your short and concise introduction. Do the defendants have any comments regarding these charges?"

Bjørn and Marie shake their heads, but say nothing, and then Rinnan raises his voice and slams the chair leg down onto the table.

"I SAID . . . DO THE DEFENDANTS HAVE ANY COMMENTS REGARDING THE CHARGES?"

Marie and Bjørn jump with fright and look up at Rinnan.

"No," comes the muted reply. First from Marie, and then Bjørn.

"Good. Thank you. Are the defendants aware of the penalty for treason and attempting to escape?"

"No," replies Bjørn.

"No, me neither actually . . . so let's consult our jury here, before the chief justice pronounces his verdict . . ."

They must have known already, while standing there, but it's only now that it really dawns on them. Perhaps Marie had hoped that their earlier relationship would make a difference, that he would spare her somehow, but any hope of that now shatters, and she begins to cry silently. The tears roll down her cheeks and drip onto her dress.

"So! Are there any extenuating circumstances the defense wishes to present to the court?"

Bjørn looks up and shakes his head, in a manner that reveals his insecurity, as though fearing the consequences of saying something wrong.

"None! That's unusual."

Rinnan looks around, and the others in the room smile at him.

"Normally the defense will try and change or soften the verdict as much as possible, but that doesn't seem to be the case here. Defense . . . ?"

Bjørn Bjørnebo shakes his head again.

"Do you have anything to say about this, your honor?"

"Well . . . I can understand that the defense has nothing advantageous to say concerning these offenses," says Karl. "The only nice thing anyone can say about the accused is that Miss Arentz is wearing a pretty dress."

Laughter breaks out around the room and Rinnan beats the chair leg against the writing desk again.

"Exactly. I totally agree. A nice dress, and hiding something nice underneath it, no doubt . . ."

Many of the gang members have now begun clapping their hands, although Rinnan doesn't notice. He just stares directly at the two defendants before him.

"Then the charges stand as they are. What punishment does the court recommend, your honor?" asks Rinnan, handing the chair leg back to Karl again.

Karl looks at Rinnan, he hesitates a little and licks his lips before looking at the two defendants and saying, "I hereby sentence the accused to the strongest penalty allowed: death."

"Great, thank you," says Rinnan. "Please take them down to the cellar."

The words shock Marie to the core, and she turns and runs toward the door, but one of the other gang members catches her and throws her to the floor.

"Nooo!" she screams, kicking her legs, and squirming from side to side.

Bjørn goes over to her, with his hands tied behind him, and just about manages to say "Please don't do this!" before two other gang members throw him to the ground too. Gunnlaug leans against the wall and watches it all while fiddling nervously with her shirt cuffs. She doesn't smile. Not for a long time, in fact, which is fair enough, it's understandable that this is all a bit much for a newcomer like her, then again she should realize that this is all part of the job, a part of what she's paid to do.

"Take the prisoners down!" shouts Rinnan, while winking at Gunnlaug.

And so they are carried out, by their legs and shoulders, a man at each end. Marie flails around, screaming and crying all the way out of the room, all the way to the cellar door and down the stairs. Her screams can be heard from the living room.

"And so, my fellow countrymen, this court is now adjourned!" says Rinnan, walking one last time round the writing desk, strutting out the room and toward the cellar steps. He feels a rush of liqueur and pills that softens his mind and makes his legs feel a little unsteady while leaning against the door frame. Then he turns to the others momentarily and says, "See you all soon, my friends," before descending, step by step, into the basement. The smile disappears on his way down, replaced by a sudden, and unexpected, sadness, because now he knows what he has to do.

R for reconciliation. When I was driving through the county surrounding Trondheim, Rikke called me to say that there was another reason these wartime events had been talked about so rarely within the family. It wasn't simply because of the tough subject, she said, it was something quite different. It was the need to forgive and move on. To realize that what's past is past and can never be changed. Not for the sake of smoothing things over, or to repress or forget. But because the things we *can* change are the way forward. This was the core of Auschwitz survivor Julius Paltiel's work as well. Not to judge, persecute, or blame, but to forgive, and look ahead.

"We live in an era of verbal warfare. Your novel should be a call to look ahead, an opportunity for reconciliation, and forgiveness," Rikke wrote later in a text message.

I detected an element of this in Grete too, during our recent conversations about her mother. A gradual shift from blaming her—for everything she didn't accomplish or didn't do—that has changed slowly, and been replaced by something else: a sense of reconciliation and an understanding that the war had simply broken her mother, destroyed everything she could have been, and could have become. All these discussions, all these scraps and fragments of conversation, have gradually led to at least some reconciliation. The war destroyed the potential of so many people, so many young dreams. Nevertheless, it was from this destruction that my own family emerged.

S

×   ×   ×

S for *Stolperstein*. There are several ways one can try to
reach the inexplicable; ways of coping with events so
incomprehensible and barbaric that our thoughts and
feelings require some form of crutch if we're to even try.
One such device is the ongoing, and ever-growing, *Stolperstein* project. There are currently around sixty-seven
thousand of these brass cobblestones, featuring the
names of the deceased, embedded in pavements in cities
all over Europe. Sixty-seven thousand people who all had
a childhood, personal habits, and music that they liked.
Sixty-seven thousand different people who at one time
fell in love, who dreamt of the future, who became angry,
who laughed and sang.

Sixty-seven thousand struck me as an inconceivably
high number when I heard it for the first time, then it
immediately dawned on me how many are left if this

project is to be fully accomplished. It means that there are almost six million *Stolpersteine* missing. Europe's pavements would be covered in brass if this art project were seen through to the end. It is a dizzying thought, almost impossible to fathom, and I immediately thought of a synagogue in Prague I once visited with Rikke not long after we met. It was a quiet place, where all those who had been killed from this town had their names written in red on the white stone wall, from floor to ceiling, which gave the place a tomb-like atmosphere, while the relentless stream of names just went on, and on, and on, and whispered, wordlessly: *Do not forget me, do not forget me, do not forget me.*

S for the soldiers assigned to work at Falstad, most of them so young, so incapable of fully grasping what they were a part of.

S for the senseless punishment exercise, which can be a number of things, but on this occasion, when *you* are forced to take part, it goes like this: You are lined up and forced to crawl under and over the beds in the cell, squat down on the floor, do a forward roll, and then start the next round as fast as you possibly can, while the soldiers stand along the circuit, lashing out at the prisoners with kicks and punches. A man you know is punched so hard he ends up in the infirmary with a dislocated jaw. You manage to endure it all without any major injury. Just angry, because the maltreatment simply continues until the soldiers get tired and are told they can stop.

S for the silence in the prison cell. S for spit. S for scorn.

S for the sleep which comes in fits and bursts. S for sore muscles. S for the songs that are sung in the workshops to raise everyone's morale. S for the sound of your mother tongue, that enabled you to speak with the Russian and Yugoslav prisoners. S for the sleeping quarters, for the sorrow, and for the sun in the sky, shining over the landscape, oblivious and indifferent to where it is shining, or whose body it is warming, be it that of a prison guard, reclining with his eyes closed, a prisoner forced to crawl around on all fours, or the lucent wings of a butterfly that rests momentarily on the man's back as he lies exhausted in the dirt, before it flies off and disappears over the yellow prison wall.

S for spouse. In one of the few interviews Klara Rinnan gave, she talks about the first time she heard about her husband's infidelity, after someone had seen him leaving a hotel with another woman. Why did she stay married to him? They had three children, he was often away, he was kind to the children when he was home, and last but not least, he earned good money and made sure the family always had what they needed during a time when most people were queueing for rations. She stayed. One day, while walking through Trondheim, Klara saw a young lady walking toward her with their family dog, a German shepherd. As they got nearer, she says the animal recognized her and pulled on its leash to get closer, its tail wagging with excitement. The oblivious lady walking the dog happened to be "Puss," who would be Rinnan's final lover, who became pregnant by him but miscarried in prison, according to Klara.

The two women continued walking right past each other, with Klara trying to avoid too much eye contact with the dog. She just heard the voice of the other woman calling for the German shepherd to come, before pulling on its leash again and disappearing.

S for the screams of terror that come from the cellar at the Gang Monastery. It is April 26, 1945, and it has been about a week since Marie and Bjørn's trial. Now Rinnan comes down the cellar steps after returning from the Mission Hotel, where he told Flesch about the two prisoners and asked him what to do with them.

"Kill them," said Flesch. Quite bluntly. Rinnan had considered asking Flesch about how, or when, but there was no point, he wasn't at all interested, so Rinnan had decided not to bother him any further.

Now the two prisoners are standing with their hands tied behind their backs, with Karl aiming his pistol at them. Marie starts kicking and screaming as soon as she sees Rinnan, who puts his finger to his lips, but it doesn't help. Marie stumbles backward and crashes to the floor, but avoids banging her head. Bjørn tries to go over to her, but Karl grabs him by the shirt and puts the gun to his head. Then Karl turns and looks wide-eyed at Rinnan, ready to receive further orders.

Marie tries wriggling over to the far wall, scraping her bare knees and elbows while sobbing and crying.

"Put him in the empty cell!" shouts Rinnan, and Karl does as he is told, shoving Bjørn forward, forcing him to take dozens of small steps to avoid falling over.

Rinnan walks around the table, where a number of pliers and whips lie, and around one of the wooden barrels. Marie, still lying on the floor, looks up at him and screams, *"Leave me alone! Leave me alone!"* and it's hard to listen to, there's just too much noise, thinks Rinnan, looking around for a solution, and picks up a bottle that has so far not been used, with the magic word *chloroform* written on the label. He twists the cork and pours the fluid onto a nearby cloth.

"Leave me alone! Help! Help me!"

Rinnan starts walking toward Marie, now curled up in the far corner, and she lets out a loud, piercing scream. Rinnan turns round, picks up his gun, and fires it at the wall about a yard away from her.

"Marie!" shouts Bjørn from the cell, but Karl tells him to shut up. Marie cries, but doesn't move.

"Can you please just stop screaming!" says Rinnan as he walks right up to her with the cloth hidden behind his back.

"Just stay totally quiet . . ."

She looks at him in terror, breathing rapidly, and opens her mouth to speak.

Then he produces the cloth, soaked in chloroform, and holds it firmly over her face.

He has watched scenes like this at the movies, where the victim falls unconscious the moment the cloth is held over their face, and the anesthetized person slides calmly and gracefully to the floor, as though lying down in a summer meadow for a nap. That's not what happens here. Marie kicks, and twists, and tenses every muscle she has. Anything to escape.

"*Ah, what the fuck!*" explodes Rinnan, grabbing Marie's shoulder with his available hand and pressing the cloth harder onto her mouth and nose. Marie tries to bite him through the fabric, so he has to cup his hand and press the cloth down even harder. Finally the chloroform takes effect. Rinnan lifts her hand, bends her fingers, feeling how limp her muscles now are from the anesthetic, lifeless, like a dress that has slid from a chair.

Karl comes back into the room, with a stern look on his face.

"Marie!" shouts Bjørn from the cell. Karl goes back out to the cell, bangs his pistol grip against the door, and says, "Shut up!"

Rinnan squats down beside Marie. Her dress has slid up to her waist, revealing her underwear. He walks over to the table and picks up a knife, a fisherman's knife with a birchwood grip and a long, pointed blade. He slides his thumb along its edge and feels how sharp it is, and squats beside Marie again, drawing the knife slowly up to the top of her hips and under the edge of her panties. Then he slips the blade under the cotton and begins to cut through it, careful not to pierce her skin. A couple of tugs on the knife, and the elastic gives way. He takes the loose part and stretches it enough to get the blade under the opposite side, while his arm brushes against her skin and dry pubic hair. One more slit with the knife and her panties are cut on both sides. Rinnan hears Karl approaching, but he doesn't turn round. He just moves the knife up toward her dress, chooses a spot by her waist, and pushes the knife up through the fabric. The only thing remaining then is to grab the two loose pieces of fabric on either side and tear upward.

Marie's chest rises slowly up and down, and her face looks relaxed, peaceful, as it always did on those mornings when they woke up together.

He moves the knife up to her bra and cuts that off too, revealing her breasts, that he had once licked, and sucked, and buried his face between, now spread out with her nipples facing the ceiling.

"What are we going to do with her?" asks Karl.

"Find a rope," says Rinnan, without turning round. He strokes Marie's stomach and cups his hand around one of her breasts.

"Marie! Are you there?" shouts Bjørn from his cell again. Rinnan doesn't respond. He puts the blade to Marie's shoulder and cuts the last two straps holding her dress in place. Then he pulls the garment out, as if it were a paper dress from a magazine, one you might cut out and fold round a paper doll, with small flaps on each side.

Rinnan puts the knife down and moves even closer to Marie. He lifts her up and cradles her lifeless head in his lap. Her eyes are closed. Her hair flows over his trousers. Her lips, slightly parted, are as beautiful and soft as ever. Karl walks over again and sees them both sitting there. He has a rope in his hands and tries to avoid looking at the naked body in front of him.

"Good. Thanks," says Rinnan, without looking up. He strokes Marie's forehead and carefully brushes her hair from her eyes. "Make a nice noose, and hang the rope from the ceiling."

"OK, boss!"

Karl manages to thread the rope through a wooden beam above their heads. Then he ties a noose and holds it up in front of Rinnan, who finally looks up and takes it from him.

"Thank you, Karl," he says as he hangs the rope over Marie's head. He raises the back of her head carefully, to avoid hurting her before tightening the noose round her neck.

"There. You can haul her up now, Karl."

Karl goes over to the rope hanging from the beam and begins

to pull, carefully. Marie's head rises from the floor. Then her upper body, inch by inch, with each pull on the rope from Karl. Her arms flop limply beside her, and at first Rinnan just sits and watches as she floats up from his lap, levitating over the floor, with her arms dangling and head slightly tilted.

"Good, Karl, just a bit more," he says, and again Karl does as he's told, except that now Marie suddenly starts kicking. Rinnan scrambles over and grabs her around her knees, holding her tight, pulling her down to the floor, while Karl pulls on the other end of the rope. He feels the life pulsing through her body. He feels her twist and flinch and writhe in his arms as he presses his face against her thighs, and pulls—pulls down with all his might, until she is hanging there, motionless, rotating slowly from the twisted rope.

Rinnan sits on the floor and looks up at her. It is a strange sight. This naked body, which he once lay beside, now hanging by a rope from the ceiling. He is out of breath after all the struggling, as is Karl. The telephone rings upstairs.

"OK. Now you can let her down again, carefully," says Rinnan. So Karl lets out the rope again, little by little. The rope slides jerkily through the wooden beam in the ceiling, until Marie lies motionless on the floorboards, with a lock of hair in her mouth and her breasts hanging to one side.

"I suppose this will be her funeral, Karl. Can you go and see if we have any flowers up there?" asks Rinnan. Karl goes upstairs, while Rinnan sits beside Marie's body with her head tilted slightly back.

"Hello? Marie?" shouts Bjørn from the cell.

Rinnan strokes Marie's thigh with his finger, and places his hand on her stomach, as he once did when they lay in bed together. He brushes the hair from her face again, to keep the hair out of her eyes.

"Why did you run away, Marie? Why did you do that?"

Just then, Karl comes down again with a vase of flowers taken from the living room.

"Thank you, Karl," says Rinnan quietly, releasing himself from the dead body. Then he removes the flowers and curls Marie's fingers around the stems. He places her hands, still clutching the flowers, between her thighs, partly obscuring her abdomen.

It looks nice. She is lying with her eyes closed and with flowers in her hands, it's the best they can do, Rinnan thinks, before lighting a cigarette and asking Karl to fetch Bjørn, so they can finish him off as well.

"Hello? Marie? Rinnan? What's happening out there?" shouts Bjørn. Karl walks across the room, lifts the key ring from the hook on the wall, and unlocks the padlock to the tiny cell. Then he grabs the prisoner and leads him into the room. Bjørn's movements are fast and erratic, and his eyes dart all over the place. Then he sees the corpse lying in the middle of the room and immediately falls silent. His feet move forward by themselves, and his lips mouth the words No, no, no . . . before he kneels beside Marie, without anyone trying to stop him. Bjørn places his hand on hers, and between the sobbing he says that he wants to die too. He asks them to just get it over with.

"Sure. Let's do just that," says Rinnan. Then he aims the gun barrel at Bjørn's head and pulls the trigger. There's a surprisingly loud bang, and Bjørn's head jerks suddenly, then a pool of blood expands across the floor.

Karl looks over at the other cell, where another prisoner, someone from the resistance, is being held. Then he looks back at Rinnan, who gives him a quick nod. They may as well get rid of him too, to stop him telling anyone about what he has seen.

T

× × ×

T for truth, and for a quote attributed to Rinnan, something he would say to any new prisoner arriving at the Gang Monastery: "Welcome to the only place in Trondheim where the truth is told."

T for torture. T for terror. T for tyrant.

T for the three corpses lying in the cellar. Marie Arentz, Bjørn Bjørnebo, and Dagfinn Frøyland, the resistance member whom they also killed that night since he had witnessed it all. Rinnan makes a phone call upstairs, on his direct line to the Mission Hotel switchboard. He has learned a little German now and wants to show off to the others.

"*Guten Tag*," he says to the man on the other end of the line. "*Drei Kisten, bitte, für Sonderabteilung Lola.*"

They ask him where he wants them delivered, he gives

them the address, and they tell him the delivery will be sent as soon as possible.

"*Vielen dank*," says Rinnan cheerfully, then he hangs up the receiver and takes a sip from his glass. It is a nice liqueur, not too sweet, and it gives a nice warm tingle at the back of the throat. His dog stands up and looks up at him expectantly. Rinnan scratches behind its ears, ruffles its fur, and then goes into the living room. He hears Karl in the bathroom washing his hands, and waits for him to come out.

The other gang members are elsewhere, reading documents, smoking, chatting, or planning new missions. It was a shame about Marie, but she only has herself to blame. It's the price you pay for running off and placing the whole operation in jeopardy, so it's her own fault, he thinks. He looks over at Gunnlaug, standing at the window, also wearing a nice dress, and imagines what he'll do with her later, once these corpses are out of the house. He gives her a smile, although she appears reluctant to smile back. What could it be? he thinks, but then Karl suddenly comes out of the toilet and Rinnan shouts across the room to him. He wants the others to hear him as well.

"I've ordered three coffins for the prisoners downstairs. They'll be arriving any moment," he says.

"OK, boss," says Karl, ready to deal with anything. One needs someone like him, someone prepared to be the hands, when you are the head. Rinnan goes out to the kitchen, still piled high with days-old dirty dishes and overflowing saucepans, but that's fine as long as there's something left to eat, he thinks, looking into a saucepan at the remains of a beef casserole. A dark-brown skin has congealed over it, but it'll be fine after a quick stir, he thinks. He eats a little straight from the saucepan and smiles at Gunnlaug, who enters the room to ask if he wants anything. She walks up to him, seduced just from being allowed near the person in charge, thinks Henry, as he puts his hand around her waist. He hears a car motor outside, several in fact; somebody has arrived. He touches Gunnlaug's slender body just beneath her dress and strokes her back gently, then he asks her to open her mouth, and he feeds her a piece of meat. Her eyes sparkle and he feels her breasts pressing against him, the curve of her back, and a shiver of excitement when his thoughts drift to what they might do later.

In the middle of all this the doorbell rings. *That was quick,* he thinks, bending down to kiss her. He tastes the sauce on her lips and smiles.

"Back to work . . . ," he says, while passing her the saucepan. Then he walks into the hallway, where Karl is just about to open the door.

"It must be the coffins," says Rinnan, leaning against the doorway behind Karl as he opens the door. Outside stand two young German soldiers holding a wooden box made of yellow pine planks. It is not a coffin. Rinnan tenses up, blinks hard, and looks at it. It's a fairly large box, perhaps a meter wide, so it cannot be a coffin. Two more boxes stand behind them, exactly the same.

"*Was ist das?*" asks Rinnan.

"*Drei Kisten,*" replies one of the soldiers, pointing hesitantly at the boxes behind them. Rinnan knows the others are watching him from behind, and turns around to see the nervous smile on Gunnlaug's face. She can see that this is not what he had expected, and the others know it too. Rinnan turns back to the soldiers and is about to ask them if they really are the "*Kisten*" he ordered, but he stops, because they had simply repeated the word he used, the one he had used on the telephone, so it is *his* mistake. Obviously *Kisten,* in German, does not mean "coffin," as it does in Norwegian, it must simply mean "crate." Well, crates will just have to work, thinks Rinnan, because there's no fucking way he's going to admit not knowing the difference and ordering the wrong thing. He won't be putting himself through that embarrassment, he thinks, which means they will just have to make do with what they have, improvise, pretend that the crates were exactly what he expected. Then nobody will dare to question it. Especially now they know what he is capable of.

"*Gut, gut, drei Kisten,*" says Rinnan to the soldiers with a contented smile on his face. *"Vielen dank,"* he says, turning round to the other gang members.

"OK. Karl! Get someone to help you take these crates down into the cellar and put the bodies in them," says Rinnan. He returns to the kitchen to continue eating, hoping to find Gunnlaug. But now she has gone into the living room and is standing there looking the other way. She had spent a whole week alone with him in March, when he finally managed to take a vacation. This sweet young lady; so insecure and easily led.

Yeah, yeah. Naturally she may feel a little uncomfortable about the bodies, he thinks. Perhaps she also found out about his relationship with Marie, now lying dead in the cellar. There's a good chance of it since the prisoners were here all week. Someone would have blabbered to her, and now she is probably worried that she might be next. But of course that's not the case, he thinks, as his feelings for her take hold again, because she is so lovely. So young and innocent and beautiful. It is a long time since he has felt this way about a woman, he thinks, while helping himself to more of the casserole, just the meat, then he looks around to see if there is anything he can have for dessert. A small liqueur maybe. They have some candy too. He pops a cherry drop in his mouth, crunching it between his teeth, then goes into the living room, where Gunnlaug stands with her arms folded, like she doesn't know what to do with her hands, poor thing.

"Here, have a drink," he says, handing her a glass of coffee liqueur. "I'm finished here soon, and then we can go out and do something nice together, OK?" he asks, while raising his glass. The telephone rings and one of the other agents races past him to answer it. Rinnan sips his liqueur, and the warmth of the alcohol spreads through his body and soothes all the tension within him.

Just then Karl comes up from the cellar, red-faced after a lot of struggle. There are beads of sweat on his forehead and a grim, strained look on his face. He doesn't look himself, in fact, he looks nothing like himself.

"They don't fit into the crates, boss," he says nervously, and quietly so that no one else hears. But it makes no difference.

Rinnan puts his hand on his shoulder.

"Excuse me a moment, Puss," he says to Gunnlaug and takes a couple of steps away from her, toward the window. "What did you say, Karl?"

"The bodies . . . there's no room for them in the boxes . . . What are we gonna do?"

"Just squeeze them in, Karl. Whatever it takes. These are the boxes we've been given, and they're what we're going to use. Understand?"

He feels the anger and frustration boiling up within him as he reaches the end of the sentence, because why the fuck is Karl coming up here and demonstrating to absolutely everyone that their leader doesn't know the German word for coffin? Does he not realize how embarrassing it is for him?

"Sure, of course, boss," says Karl, and he turns and walks away, glancing quickly at Gunnlaug before descending the cellar steps again.

Rinnan walks over to Gunnlaug, and they start talking about something else entirely—back to what they are going to do when the war is over, and where they might go on vacation, and little by little she begins to soften up, slowly letting go of the anxiety and moving closer to him again. Then she smiles, and allows him to put his arm around her. She understands full well that he has a demanding job, involving a lot of difficult decisions. A lot of responsibility, he thinks, while stroking the young girl's back.

Then Karl comes up again and taps him on the shoulder. This time with a look of fear in his eyes.

"Sorry to bother you, boss," he says, while taking a few steps back, wanting Rinnan to follow him, which is good thinking on his part, so he doesn't just blurt out more problems in front of his girlfriend.

"What is it?" asks Rinnan.

"I'm sorry, but these crates, they're far too small . . . Even if we bend their knees there's still not enough room . . . What should we do?"

Rinnan feels his last drop of patience run out.

"Look. Either you get these corpses into the boxes, Karl, or I will stuff you into one of them myself. Is that understood? I don't give a shit how you do it, just use your imagination, for fuck's sake!" he hisses.

"Of course. Sorry, boss," says Karl again, but showing no sign of leaving. Presumably because he still has no idea what to do.

"You do know that we have an axe outside?" says Rinnan quietly. Karl nods. Then he turns round and walks out. Gunnlaug has started talking to Ingeborg about something or other, but although Ingeborg laughs, Gunnlaug doesn't seem to be listening to her. Karl walks back into the room with an axe in his hand and glances at Rinnan, as if hoping for a sign to stop, but Rinnan just stares right at him, and Karl goes down to the cellar.

Fifteen minutes go by. Twenty minutes. Then Karl and one of the others come up from the cellar carrying the first box.

"Wonderful, Karl!" shouts Rinnan across the room.

"You can take all the boxes out and then dump them in the fjord," he says.

The living room has now gone totally quiet. Nobody says a word. Everyone is searching for a place to look, something else they can pretend to be doing, or looking at, while the boxes are carried up from the cellar and through the room, with blood dripping from them, and a smell of iron spreading through the living room and the hallway.

Everyone is silent.

"Something bothering you?" asks Henry. "We have a war to fight. Get back to work!" he shouts. He lights a cigarette and asks Ingeborg to open a window. Before long, the three boxes are out.

One of the gang members begins to wash the floor, without being asked, and at long last, night falls.

×

T for Ellen Komissar's turbulent thoughts, as she rushes through Trondheim, staring at the ground, her tongue moving quickly over her lips; faster and faster, while images of Gerson flash through her mind, because now she is certain that he is hiding something. She has felt it ever since the maid quit; that these last few strands of trust between them have snapped; because there was suddenly a colder look in his eyes. He works overtime so often they barely meet, and when he is home he avoids looking at her, and at mealtimes he just sits there engrossed in his newspaper. It's obvious that he is hiding something, Ellen thinks, as she hurries down the street. She pictures herself opening the door of his shop only to find him there with another woman. Or even worse: that Gerson isn't at work at all, as he had told her, and she finds Marie there, who at first doesn't understand what Ellen is talking about because Gerson has led her up the garden path as well. Or perhaps she is in on it too. Perhaps she has some kind of cover story, which involves Gerson being out somewhere picking up stock, while he is in fact at his lover's house, in bed with the young Danish girl of course. *Oh my God,* she thinks, with her heart now pounding in her chest, overwhelmed with anger. She clenches her teeth and starts planning what she will say to him. Perfecting how she will put him in his place; when she forces him to kneel before her and beg for forgiveness. She imagines him saying that he understands her frustration, that they can all move back to Oslo, and she pictures them traveling south again, where the whole family walks through the door of her childhood home. Then she realizes how far-fetched this happy ending of her fantasy actually is. The beginning is more probable, she thinks, as she turns the corner onto the street where the family business lies, now running to get there faster and get some clarification. Then she sees the light from the large windows, and she sees Gerson behind the counter while an elderly woman tries on one of the hats and turns to her husband to ask him for his opinion.

There is no young lady there, and Gerson is busy at work. Ellen stops dead, and is about to turn around when Gerson catches sight of her. At first he looks surprised, his face lights up and it seems like he is about to raise his hand to wave; but then he stops, as though interpreting the accusing look on her face, and she watches his shoulders sink before he turns to the elderly woman with the hat and attempts to smile at her.

Ellen remains where she is. She considers crossing the road to speak to Gerson, but what would she say? Why is she there? To visit him? If that were the case then she wouldn't have snuck up on him like this. She curses herself. *How could I be so stupid,* she thinks, before turning around and walking home in despair.

She puts out flowers and tries to make the house feel homey. She tries to talk with the children, but they are busy with something else and can't understand why she suddenly wants to be so close to them, or why she suddenly wants to cuddle them. They just twist themselves out of her arms and continue playing.

That night, Gerson comes home late from work. He has been drinking, and will not tell Ellen where he has been.

Ellen, who has been waiting for him on the sofa, stands up and smiles at her husband when he appears in the doorway, but he goes straight to the bathroom, and then to bed. He clearly wants to get away from her. The lightness she used to see in his eyes is all gone.

They go to sleep. She reaches out to him in the dark and places her hand on his shoulder, but he mumbles something about being tired, that he just wants to sleep, and turns his back to her.

Ellen closes her eyes tightly. She hears his breathing, regular and calm. She feels the distance between them, and how everything seems to have disintegrated.

A few days later Gerson returns from work early, while the children are out, and he lets it slip that he has been offered a job in Oslo. That he sees no future for the two of them. That he will find an apartment for her, where she can live with the children, and that he wants a divorce.

×

T for trust.

T for time.

T for tipping point.

T for the telephone on Rinnan's desk, ringing on May 7, 1945. Germany is losing on multiple fronts and any hope that their luck might change, after six months of setbacks, is very low. Now the person calling from the Mission Hotel tells him that it is over. Germany has surrendered. The war is over.

My God.

It is over. Everything.

"What is it?" asks Karl, realizing something has happened, but Rinnan cannot reply. All he feels is a numbness spreading through his body. He is almost paralyzed. Perhaps he should kill himself? Just shoot himself down in the cellar? No, he dismisses the thought as soon as it enters his head, because he doesn't need to give up yet, they haven't been caught. Perhaps they can get away somehow, he thinks. Then he hangs up the phone and looks up.

"Wake everyone up! Germany has surrendered, the fools!"

Karl just stares at him. His girlfriend, Ingeborg, has the same grim look on her face.

"Get a move on. We need to burn all the papers, and then get the hell out of here. *Quickly, quickly, quickly!*" he says while slapping his hand against the wall.

Then he finds a bottle of liqueur, knocks back a glass, and starts thinking about what to prioritize, what he absolutely must destroy, while the others stagger round in a daze from room to room, picking things up, putting them down again, and banging on doors to rooms where people are sleeping. He refills his glass, downs it again, and walks toward the filing cabinet, pulling out all the folders of classified documents and shaking the contents onto the floor: papers, plans, lists of agents, lists of negative contacts, and lists of those he has tortured and killed. Then he scrapes all the documents into a pile and throws the whole lot into the fire. Some of the sheets miss, or glide slowly to the floor, but most land in the fireplace, sending a cloud of ash into the air which spreads through the room, forcing him to turn away and hold his breath for a moment before going to find some matches. It'll take forever to light this, he thinks, so he asks Karl to fetch a can of kerosene. Ingeborg helps Rinnan pick up the loose sheets from the floor. Then he soaks the heap of balled-up paper with kerosene, as the smell spreads through the room, and puts a match to it. There's a flash as the kerosene fumes ignite in the air, and a surprisingly loud bang. He starts to laugh, and then thinks about what they need to take with them. Food and drink and cigarettes. All they need to do is reach the Verdal mountains, where there they will be able to cross the Swedish border and make a getaway, vanish, evaporate.

It can be done. He has spent years mapping all these escape routes and really knows the area. They just have to hurry, that's all. He wonders how many cars they have, because they have no time to get any more.

"Listen, everyone! You need to pack weapons, ammunition, and food. We're going to cross the border into Sweden, and we leave in five minutes. Is that clear?"

"Yes," says Karl. Ingeborg too. Gunnlaug leans against the wall, totally worn out, obviously in shock, which is understandable, thinks Rinnan. He goes over to her, but she turns away, saying that she needs to pack. So much for *her* then, the fair-weather whore, and he thought they had something together, well, fuck that.

He has his own stuff to pack anyway, so he finds a bag and fills it with cigarettes, bullets, money. Then he grabs a machine gun, walks through the hallway, and doesn't look back.

He leaves the Gang Monastery for the last time, in the dark, while night hangs over the city.

U

×   ×   ×

U for the unbearable sight of the other prisoners being beaten. A feeling of disgust, merged with an anger you have to suppress if you want to avoid the same treatment. One night you see the Russian prisoners being forced to run in a circle, while the prison guards, wielding broomsticks, beat them so savagely the wood eventually snaps. There is then a short pause in the abuse until someone goes to collect shovels from the workshop instead.

U for understanding. Several years have now passed since the morning when my son and I knelt by your *Stolpersteine* in Trondheim. Several years since I saw the darkness fall across my son's eyes when he asked what had happened to you. Now he is no longer ten, but fourteen; my daughter is no longer six, but ten, soon eleven, and they have of course overheard many of the conversations on this subject over the last few years, without it frightening them the way I thought it might. Not so long ago my son came into the room while I sat working.

"Are you writing about that Rinnan guy?" he asked.

"Yes," I replied. "Have you heard about him?"

"Of course. He was the crazy guy that killed lots of people in the cellar where Grandma grew up, right?"

"Yes, that's him," I said. My son nodded, and then looked at something on his cell phone, but on his way out he turned around and said: "If there's another war, we'll run away to somewhere in the Pacific, right?"

V

×   ×   ×

V for the veins through which your blood is pumped, constant and rhythmic, around the clock. Faster while doing your shift in the workshop, or the quarry, or during your morning drill; slower at night when you are lying still, hour after hour in a deep and dreamless sleep.

V for violence.

V for the Verdal mountains. It is early May, 1945, and the whole gang are packed into several cars, along with the prisoner from the cellar who they have brought with them as a hostage. Rinnan has visited his family, where he gave the confused children a hug, and then drove away, over the mountains, hoping to find an escape route to Sweden.

Ironically enough, however, Rinnan's vehicle suffers a puncture, so they are forced to continue on foot; and although it is May, it is unusually cold and snowy. They walk in single file. Rinnan has his pistol in one hand and a bottle of liqueur in the other. There is a pack of cigarettes stuffed into his coat pocket, except the pocket isn't deep enough, so with each step it feels like they are going to fall out. Gunnlaug is walking right behind him with her head down, pretending to watch the path and not trip over a stone or tread in a snowdrift. What's up with her? Is it just because they're losing this battle? He looks back at the prisoner, Magnus Casperson, trudging along with his head hung low. Fucking mistake they didn't just dump him in the fjord. They really should have gotten rid of him, the man has got a swastika burned into his thigh as evidence of torture, for Christ's sake, but now it's too late, he thinks. On the other hand, he will make a good bargaining chip if they are captured. They just have to make it to Sweden, across the border to safety, which should be plain sailing; and then he and Gunnlaug can settle down in Sweden somewhere, and she can give birth to the child she is carrying, his child, he thinks, while pushing a branch from a pine tree away. They come to a road and suddenly hear the sound of trucks approaching.

He turns and gestures quickly to the others; to run across the road and into the forest on the other side. Then he sprints after them, so fast that the cigarette box falls out of his pocket and slides down a snowdrift. He sees Karl abandon the crate of liquor; the bottles clink loudly as they land in the snow.

"Here, quickly, this way," shouts Rinnan, pointing at a rocky outcrop they can hide behind, and they all run past him, one by one, squeezing themselves up behind the rock. Rinnan then looks back and sees Magnus Casperson turn and run down to the road, waving his arms wildly. Dammit! Now they've lost their hostage, he thinks. To hell with it.

"We have to get out of here!" whispers Rinnan to the others.

"Where to?" asks Karl.

"To Sweden," answers Rinnan. He hears the sound of a truck

stopping nearby, and the sound of doors slamming, and men shouting.

Karl shakes his head and says that it is too far to walk. He suggests they hide in a nearby cabin and wait until things have calmed down. Rinnan screws his eyes up. Things are really starting to fall apart when even his most reliable man won't take his orders, but so be it. Now it's every man for himself, he thinks, and wishes Karl and his girlfriend good luck. Then he tells the others to hurry up if they want to stay alive.

Gunnlaug looks at him, and Rinnan holds his hand out to her and smiles, but she turns away. *I'll deal with this later,* he thinks, and he pats Karl on the shoulder to wish him luck. He waves at the others to come with him, but the steep, rocky terrain, covered in heather, is difficult to walk on. There are potholes everywhere beneath the snow, making it easy to suddenly slip into a crack. The smell of pine needles reminds him of his childhood as he ducks under the branches, feeling the cold snow cascading down the back of his neck and brushing against his legs. He turns around. Their footprints in the snow will be easy to follow. But there's no way of avoiding it, he thinks, rushing ahead. Soon they arrive at a clearing where more of the gang members decide to drop out, and now he can't even be bothered to give orders any more. He just waves them away. It hurts that they don't have more faith in his plan or belief in the person most likely to lead them to safety, which is *him* of course. But he won't stand there and fucking argue with them like some cantankerous little brat; if they want to go off in another direction, then fine, go ahead, good luck, he says. But he can't quite hide his insecurity from Gunnlaug when he asks who's coming with him.

So now there are just six of them, after half the group left, but that suits him, because whoever is pursuing them will follow the others' tracks instead, he thinks. They continue trudging on, in single file, staring downward. Descending into a valley, and across a little road, then climbing again, up a hill overshadowed by huge conifers. Suddenly he hears the clatter of machine guns nearby. Then rifle shots. Then a hand grenade exploding. They all look at each other. Rinnan feels tired, and hungry, and his heart is pounding even harder. There are probably many of them. The shooting stops, and the forest falls silent again. Gunnlaug looks at him dolefully, questioningly; so pretty in her white anorak, even in her wool hat, he thinks, taking a step toward her, wanting so badly to touch her, but then she turns and points at a gap in the trees, and asks if they should go that way.

They keep going, for another fifteen minutes perhaps, and finally they see a little cabin in a clearing. There's no light at the windows and no sign of smoke coming from the chimney. It is perfect, there will probably be food in there as well, he thinks. "We'll stop here and rest," he says. There are no footprints leading to the cabin, just some little round animal tracks from deer that have been foraging nearby.

Rinnan scurries over to one of the windows and peers inside. The place is empty, just as he had thought, so he goes to the door and it's not even locked, they can just go in, he thinks, and he holds the door open to allow the others to enter. Now they just need to find something to eat and drink, he thinks, rushing over to the kitchen. He finds a cupboard full of tinned food and turns to the others with a smile on his face. But suddenly they hear the sound of machine-gun fire again, and the windows explode into the room. They throw themselves to the floor as another volley of gunfire hits, showering them in splintered glass and wood. A bread roll on the table is shot to pieces. Then everything goes quiet. Rinnan peeks up from the floor. Gunnlaug stares hard at him, with contempt almost, before turning her face toward the door.

"RINNAN! WE KNOW YOU ARE IN THERE! COME OUT WITH YOUR HANDS OVER YOUR HEAD!" shouts a man outside.

"DON'T SHOOT!" shouts Rinnan. "I'M COMING OUT!"

He has to negotiate with them, he thinks, pushing himself up while trying to avoid putting his hand on the broken glass. He stands up and walks out the door. There is a man with a machine gun outside, and three more men just behind him. Another man, with an even heavier machine gun, watches from a nearby hill. They won't be able to shoot their way out of this, he thinks. He needs to be smart.

"Hello!" says Rinnan amiably, holding his hands above his head, then lowering them slowly as he steps toward them. "I'd be happy to negotiate about . . . ," he begins, but gets no further, because now the soldier aims his weapon at him and presses the butt against his cheek.

"STOP!" he shouts. "YOU ARE SURROUNDED! DROP YOUR WEAPONS IMMEDIATELY, OR I'LL SHOOT!"

Rinnan looks at him and makes a quick assessment, because it doesn't look like the guy is bluffing. Quite the opposite, in fact: perhaps he actually *wants* to shoot him and is merely looking for an excuse to pull the trigger, thinks Rinnan, taking his pistol slowly out of its holster.

"LIE ON THE GROUND WITH YOUR HANDS IN FRONT! YOU, INSIDE: COME OUT, CALMLY, WITH YOUR HANDS OVER YOUR HEAD. ANYONE HOLDING A WEAPON OR TRYING TO ESCAPE WILL BE SHOT!"

Rinnan feels the cold snow against his cheeks. He turns his head and watches Gunnlaug come out. She looks so exhausted now, so utterly exhausted, but still beautiful, as he feels his hands being yanked behind him and handcuffs being placed around his wrists. It is over. One of the soldiers comes over to him, with his fists clenched and with pure hatred in his eyes. Another soldier stands right behind him.

"Not so tough now, are you!?" says the soldier. Then comes the punch.

V for ventilation hole. Karl Dolmen and his girlfriend chose a different route to Sweden, but were spotted by a patrol of Norwegian soldiers, and after a short chase they hid in a shed on a nearby farm, while a small group of soldiers blocked the road and fired warning shots over the roof. Karl crouched on the floor, licking his lips and weighing his options, while his girlfriend clung tightly to his arm. Their choices were simple. Either they try and escape, or they give themselves up. He could hear the soldiers shouting outside, and he knew that they had machine guns, so it would be hard to escape without taking most of them down and distracting the rest, he thought, while stuffing his hand into his bag. He pulled out a hand grenade, surprised at how heavy it felt. Then he glanced up at the light streaming in from a hole in the wall, high up near the roof.

"What are you doing?" his girlfriend asked while looking down at the grenade.

"Don't worry," whispered Karl before turning toward the door. "OK! WE'RE COMING OUT!" he shouted. Then he stood up, pulled the pin from the hand grenade, and threw it up toward the hole in the wall; but as soon as the grenade left his hand he knew that something was wrong, that his throw wasn't quite as he has planned it. There was a thud, as the grenade hit the wood beside the square hole and bounced back down to them, followed by his girlfriend shouting, "OH MY GOD!" as he leapt forward to catch it in order to sling it back out again, before the grenade exploded right in front of them.

W

×   ×   ×

W for the words we use when we talk about each other, words that not only make up our view of the world, but also create our worlds. It is words that put people in categories and label entire groups cockroaches, words that form conspiracy theories about inferiority and the destruction of the Caucasian race.

Words can make it seem more logical to eliminate the other, by whatever method seems fit. It is how an atrocity becomes not only reality, but a necessity.

W for Wednesday, October 7, 1942.

W for Wehrmacht.

W for Wolfsohn, your wife's maiden name, and the name of one of the Falstad prisoners, David Wolfsohn. He too has a *Stolperstein,* located outside the apartment where he once lived, which later became the Rinnan gang's first headquarters.

W for wine.

W for winter, when the black earth hardens, and the white frost covers the fields and the rooftops; transforming even the spikes on the barbed-wire fence into soft, friendly shapes that could be tiny rabbits, or teddy bears. W for wistfulness, and the sight of a soldier tilting his head back under the lamplight one night, as the snow-flakes melt on his face. W for the washroom where the smuggling of letters and food goes on; messages from the outside world, distributed in the humid, clammy atmosphere of steaming bedsheets and T-shirts. It all feels so soft and friendly against your skin, just as the bedsheets hung outside your childhood home in Parichi once did when you pressed your face against them. You remember the smell, and the gentle coolness of newly washed cotton.

W for the winding road down from the Verdal mountains. It is May 1945, and Rinnan is handcuffed and sitting in a police car, his eyes beaten black and blue, one so swollen he can barely see through it. Now he is on his way back to Trondheim; looking out the window with his uninjured eye; at the houses and the Norwegian flags raised everywhere and, despite everything, he feels a kind of relief—that he has been caught and no longer needs to run. He wonders if he might be able to reach some sort of agreement with the authorities; convince them that he has a lot of information that could be very useful to them if they play their cards right. At least now he'll be able to show them what he can do, he thinks, raising his hand to touch his swollen eye, curious about how it looks. Then he leans his head back on the seat and feels how wonderful it is to finally breathe out. He rests all the way back to the Mission Hotel, which is now back in the hands of the Norwegian authorities. There are no female secretaries sitting there waiting to take orders from him any more. Only Norwegian policemen. Their hatred for him barely hidden. He sees the looks of contempt and schadenfreude beaming from some of them; such as the policeman who takes him into custody, gripping his arm forcefully.

"Well, well, Rinnan. Not so tough now, eh?" he says, as if he has stolen the line from the same film as his colleague, thinks Rinnan, as he is taken away, down the steps he has descended hundreds of times, to the cellar, where he is thrown into a prison cell, almost relieved when the key is turned in the lock. For a minute he was worried the policeman was going to exact his own justice on him, put a bullet in his head right away. Obviously not. He is well taken care of, and later he asks if Odd Sørli can be the one questioning him. Sørli is one of the resistance leaders, and one of the very few people who might understand him, who will know what he is talking about, Rinnan thinks. He knows that Sørli is someone who respects him and what he has done, even though they were on opposing sides.

He soon becomes friends with the cleaning girls, and actually starts to enjoy being down there, talking in detail about what has happened; about all the missions, about all the infiltrations and all the operations involving double agents. He talks about a Russian spy he once had a relationship with; about how they met each other, in secrecy, at hotels or on foreign train journeys; how they would be in bed with each other one minute then forced to fight on opposite sides the next. And it seems like they are taken in by it all. They are all ears, and that's a good thing because he really needs to tell someone about what happened. But his talking is also an attempt to find a way out. If he convinces them that he has inside information on Russian intelligence, he thinks, they might just appreciate that he is worth more to them alive than dead.

Eventually this seems to pay off too, because at Christmas, 1945, the guard bringing him his food leaves his cell door unlocked.

Rinnan waits for a moment. He can feel the excitement building up inside him. Then he steps out of the cell and listens at the next door. There is nobody there. So he turns the handle and peers through the gap. Then he creeps up the stairs, and escapes.

W for the warm spring weather in Sweden, 1945. W for the waves in Ellen's unruly hair; for the woman Gerson falls in love with, who, with her slender fingers, can play piano concertos by heart; who likes to draw and talk about art, just as he does. This upper-class girl who smokes cigarettes from her grandfather's factory, who just smiles and laughs when she cannot master something. W for the wild celebration that breaks out when they hear that the war is over. That the Germans have surrendered. That they can return home again. They go round embracing each other, one by one. Strangers kiss one another, and the spring air is filled with the expectation of a new dawn, a new beginning. Ellen throws her arms around Gerson, and they hold each other, smiling.

"Shall we go home then?" she asks teasingly, standing on tiptoes. Her dark eyes sparkle at him. She's so beautiful, he thinks, as he strokes a curl of hair from her forehead.

"Yes. Now we can go home," he replies, as he suddenly feels her lips pressed against his, and when he opens his eyes, he sees his mother smiling at them.

He grabs a bottle, and the party continues.

X

x   x   x

X for the things that don't work out. For the things that will remain a mystery. X for the X-shaped signs at the railway crossing near Falstad, where the new prisoners are taken off the train and forced to walk the rest of the way. One night, in late September, a new group arrives at midnight. You are asleep, but are woken up by the shouts from soldiers ordering the new inmates to line up in the yard. And then? You get up and peer from the window, even though you are not facing the yard, so you cannot see anything. Then you fall back into a broken sleep, woken now and then by shouts and screams from the yard, but it is none of your concern. In the morning the prisoners are still standing there while you eat breakfast. They have stood there all night, and you feel a pang of guilt for having slept the whole time, as though it would have helped them if you had stayed awake.

Y

×   ×   ×

Y for the drawing of women's genitals, in their most basic and cartoonish form, that you see carved on the toilet door at Falstad. Nature doesn't take breaks. Expectant mothers must give birth alone, even with bombs raining from the sky. Those who have to go to the toilet must rush out and go, even when bullets are flying through the walls. The breathing, the digestion, the hunger, and the desire. Nothing is as it was before; nor does anything stop, not while the blood still flows through your veins, carrying all you need to keep you alive.

Y for year. For 1945, which is almost over, just as the war is now over, and the city is returning to its usual ways. But right now it is Christmas, the first Christmas since the liberation, and people everywhere are at home celebrating with their families. Sitting around tables decked with white cloths. Their faces glowing in the candlelight.

Z

× × ×

Z for zero hour.

There are fewer guards than normal at the Mission Hotel, but when Rinnan comes up the stairs from the cellar and glances quickly at the main entrance he sees at least one guard, chatting to a friend by the front desk.

Luckily he knows his way around after visiting the building so often, because even though he can't leave by the main entrance, he'll find a way out. After all, that must be the point of all this: to enable him to escape. But it can't be too obvious either. They can't allow him to walk straight out the front door when he is the most wanted man in the country, nobody would ever understand that, he thinks, while tiptoeing up to the second floor. People are far too stupid, far too controlled by their emotions, while anyone who knows this game will understand that Rinnan is far more valuable to them as a Norwegian agent, infiltrating the Russians. He would easily outsmart them; and the information he acquired would be crucial for Norway, no doubt about that. Whereas killing him—as an example of victors' justice—what would they gain from that? He hears voices coming from one of the offices, which is a blow because now he's too afraid to sneak along the corridor and escape via the back stairs. Too risky, thinks Rinnan. He peeks into another room, which is empty, so he goes in and closes the door gently behind him.

It is a familiar room, somewhere he often visited when it was an office and the roles were reversed; now it is piled up with boxes. He goes over to the window and carefully opens the latch, squeezing his fingertips between the window and the frame and pulling upward, ever so slowly, so that the wood doesn't creak.

Suddenly the window squeaks loudly as it comes unstuck. He stops and waits. Then the talking in the other room continues, and when it turns to laughter he quickly slides the window up as far as it will go. The cold wind blows in, and a thin layer of snow covers the window ledge. Rinnan pokes his head out quickly and looks down. It is just a quiet side street, and with it being Christmas Eve there's nobody around. *It is a long way down, but I don't really have any choice,* he thinks. He climbs out onto the window ledge and twists himself round, then he slides out feet first; the window frame scraping his hips and waist, and crushing his ribs. His prison uniform gets snagged on a hook, but he tears it free as he feels the snow melting against his stomach. He looks down and hears a car passing below. Then he lets go, falling way too fast, just for a second. His foot hits the ground at a strange angle, and his full body weight comes crashing down on top of it; he throws his arms out and feels his palms slap against the ice as his forehead hits the pavement. Then a burning pain shoots up his leg from his ankle. It's sprained, if not broken, he thinks, looking around. The street is empty. He looks up at the open window. No one there either. Now he must get away, to some place or other. But where? he thinks, limping down the street, cursing his bad landing, because his twisted ankle will surely ruin everything. It will be next to impossible to get out of town alone like this, and that is fucking shitty, because it is Christmas Eve and everyone is busy. He could have stolen a car and driven off, but there's no chance of that now. *Now I need help,* he thinks. He tries to remember if there's anyone living nearby who might let him in and let him hide for a day or two before fleeing the country to get started on his work.

He hobbles down the street and round a corner and remembers a guy living nearby, who might, just might, be willing to help him. *This really has to fucking work!* he thinks, as he knocks and explains the situation; that he is on the run and that he has injured his ankle quite badly. Come in, says the man, you can't stand out there in the cold with a sprained ankle. He offers Rinnan a seat and pours him a shot, while his wife takes off his shoe to take a look at his leg. Rinnan thanks them both, takes a sip of the liquor, and begins to calm down. It has been six months since he last tasted alcohol. The man pours him another glass, and Rinnan asks for his help in finding a hiding place. He is now working as a spy for Norway, he tells them, but that is top secret and it cannot leak out. The man nods, pats him on the shoulder, and fills his glass again. He's going to make some calls, he says, try to arrange transportation and a hiding place.

Rinnan thanks him warmly. They bring him a plate of Christmas dinner and pour him yet another glass of liquor. The pain begins to subside and his spirits lighten. *I'm gonna fucking make this!* he thinks, just as the door opens, and a Norwegian police patrol walks in, armed with machine guns.

Realizing that the man has tricked him, he reaches for his glass and finishes his drink.

"I suppose there won't be time for another one then," he says, before the police take him away.

Rinnan was sent back to prison the same night, and this time the cell door stayed locked. No one ever accepted responsibility for letting him escape. His ankle healed through the winter and spring, but it wasn't until the following winter, in 1946, that the investigation of his case was completed and his trial could begin. By then Rinnan was thirty-one years old, and many of the other gang members were around twenty-five. Photographs of them taken during the trial show them smiling and laughing confidently, as if they really don't care. As the writer and researcher Ann Heberlein writes in *A Little Book on Evil*, we have already justified our actions to ourselves before we carry them out. This is why the action takes place at all, because it has already been deemed right or wrong, something one should or should not do. As soon as the decision is made, the action is already justified. Remorse is then difficult, because it requires one to go back and dare to look at one's motivation and reasoning through a fresh pair of eyes.

One member of the Rinnan gang who went to prison committed suicide by throwing himself from the window of a nursing home, forty years after the war ended. He was more than eighty years old.

It could have been the same man who visited Jannicke at the kiosk at the Majorstua subway station; who talked about his past without actually knowing who Jannicke was. On the other hand, gang member Kitty Grande, in a filmed interview made when she was an elderly woman, says that she felt no remorse; that they did what they felt they had to.

Rinnan winks at one of the other gang members as they take their seats in the courtroom. He seems quite happy about the trial, and enjoying the attention. He chats to the guards, seemingly pleased to have the number 1 pinned to his chest, and brags about murders that he hasn't committed. He lies about his contacts in Russia, and about secret international missions, despite evidence proving he was somewhere else at the time. Nevertheless, some signs of fear and emotion can be detected in the recently found doodles the defendants made on the backs of their number tags during the trial, such as tag 24, which belonged to Harald Grøtte. The entire back of this square card is covered by a pencil sketch of a woman sitting on a bench. There is no indication of who she is; she could be the woman he was involved in mutilating. Two men are drawn standing next to her, and below he has written the words *Death penalty.*

On tag number 11 it says: *This life I was given, was not for living.*

Rinnan's number tag had nothing written or drawn on it; and the only thing he seemed to regret was the execution of the innocent father and son, murdered on the islet in the fjord after their unsuccessful search for weapons. Throughout the long trial, the only time he wavered was when this came up.

On a cold February morning in 1947, Henry Oliver Rinnan gets tied to an execution pole at Kristansten Fortress in Trondheim and shot. His ashes are buried in a secret spot in the cemetery in Levanger, just across the street from where he was born. No funeral and no tombstone. Just the secret burying of his remains, while the rest of the city is sleeping.

Z for the final letter of the alphabet, and for the last day of your life. It is Wednesday, October 7, 1942, early morning, and you are in your cell at Falstad. Your eyes are just opening and you realize that you must have dropped off to sleep in the end, because now the sky has lightened, the other men are climbing down from their bunks, and you hear one of them mumbling something about martial law. You get up from the bed, and two men step aside to let you out. You shake hands with one of them, who introduces himself as Henry Gleditsch, and you suddenly realize that this is Gleditsch the *actor*, and manager of the Trøndelag Theater. You recognize him from the parties you once attended, from Paris-Vienna, and from the theater where you would sometimes bump into him in the foyer when dropping Lillemor off for ballet.

"Henry! What are you doing here?" you ask.

"I know! What can I say?" the theater manager replies, spreading his arms out with a smile on his face as always. "We've got a première today as well, so it's very bad timing, I don't know. Do you think they'll let me out so I can perform?"

He gives you an infectious grin as you ask him what the piece is, and replies that it is *The Wild Duck* by Henrik Ibsen, and tells you they were in the middle of dress rehearsal when the Germans marched onto the stage.

"Why were you arrested?" you ask. But he just shrugs his shoulders and says that he has done one or two things, like refusing to fly the German flag over the theater and then cutting the rope on the flagpole so no one else could do it either.

"But when it comes to our friend here," says the theater manager, placing his hand on the other man's shoulder, "Well. It wasn't such a big surprise that you were arrested, was it?"

"Hans Ekornes," says the other man, offering his hand, while the theater manager takes it upon himself to give a summary of the other man's hazardous life: how he smuggled people and weapons between the Shetland Islands and the coast of Norway, and was responsible for several major resistance operations, until they were infiltrated by the Norwegian double agent Henry Rinnan, who sent two undercover agents posing as refugees and exposed the entire network.

You talk quietly for a few more minutes, but at some point you stop following the conversation and start listening to the voices and footsteps in the corridors and the courtyard outside. There's an unusual level of activity. The others stop and listen too. More men are sitting up in their beds, and then you hear footsteps approaching the door. There's a metallic clank in the lock and the door opens. A young man stands outside, probably no more than nineteen years old, with blue eyes and a face not yet fully developed. He tells you to leave your cells, without saying why or where to, but the timing itself is a bad sign, you think, unless you are being moved elsewhere, to one of the overseas camps maybe. You leave your cells and walk down the stairs. Ten men. Henry Gleditsch, the theater manager, walks in front of you. There's a clattering of feet on the stairs. The air outside is cold and clear.

A solitary birch stands out in the yard. Its branches were naked when you were arrested in January, but sprouted green shoots after a while, and summer came before you were sent north. In the meantime its leaves have yellowed and are now beginning to fall.

You are ordered out of the gate, in the early-morning light, and along the gravel road, in single file, with your hands folded behind your heads. For a moment you consider making a run for it, away from the road and into the pine forest, but there are too many armed soldiers around you.

You probably knew what was coming, because there is no reason for you to be going outside the camp at this time of day, not without saws or shovels. Then you are ordered into the forest. A soldier prods you with the barrel of his gun and tells you to keep walking.

The gravel crunches under the soles of your shoes.

Are you thinking about Gerson and Jacob? About Lillemor? Or Marie? Do you imagine her face smiling at you across the breakfast table as she often did?

Dewdrops sparkle in the grass, the tree trunks are moist, and the soldiers' breath turns to vapor in the cold.

You are led to a small hollow, blindfolded, and your sentence is read out loud. You are to receive the death penalty, to be carried out immediately, with three shots to the heart and two to the head.

And then? It must have all happened at once. First, the shout from the officer. Then the gunshots followed by a surprising, overwhelming pain.

Life is a river. A stream of impulses constantly flowing through everything that lives. And death? Death shuts it all off. The bullets tear into you, and everything explodes in pain, before your muscles give in, like slackened ropes, and you collapse, facedown on the forest floor.

The last thing you feel? A twig scratching your cheek. The last thing you hear? A man shouting: *RELOAD.*

The last thing you see? The faces of your children when they were small. Their soft, round cheeks. Their big round eyes, watchful, open, beautiful. The curls of hair all over their heads. Their hands clutching your finger, and the subtle twitches from their bodies as they fall asleep.

You exhale for the last time through your nostrils. The marshy ground feels cold and wet against your forehead and fingers.

Then your consciousness slips from this world, and your body returns to the cycle of all that is dead; like a broken twig, or the skull of a magpie, or the carcass of a whale lying at the bottom of the sea in the impenetrable dark, while tiny jaws nibble at its flesh.

Two hands grab your wrists, two more grab your ankles, and they lift you up. Your head falls back, eyes wide open, mouth agape. A salty trickle runs from your eye and down to your ear.

Then you are swung back and forth, twice; a motion almost like your first hesitant turn on the rope swing which your neighbor built in a tree near your childhood home in Russia. Forward and back you would swing, the force gripping your stomach, until you finally let go and soar in an arc over the puddle below.

Now it is the soldiers who let go, of your arms and legs, as they drop you into a hole in the ground; a gaping wound in the flesh of the earth. Your body hits the bottom with a thud, and your left arm flops over your face, limp and motionless. Warm urine seeps through the fabric of your trousers and evaporates into the air.

After that?

A short volley of rifle fire. Then silence.

Someone starts crying, pleading for mercy. Then another shot. Silence.

Soil is then thrown over you.

There is a swooshing noise as it slides from the spade. Clumps of earth rain down into the hole in the ground, covering your hands and your face.

Finally the only thing visible is the top of your knee. A little island of wool in an ocean of mud, gradually sinking into the earth until you are totally embedded. Cold. Dark. Silent. Nothing but the patting of the shovel up there on the surface. More shots. Then silence.

A long silence.

The earth freezes and thaws, freezes and thaws, freezes and thaws yet again, and your body slowly disintegrates while above you winter becomes spring.

It is 1945, and the war is coming to an end. For three years now, you have been buried in the marshy soil of Falstad forest, frozen in time, while the warplanes have flown overhead; while the troops have moved here and there, cities have burned to the ground and families have searched for their loved ones among the ruins. The German soldiers have fallen and the tanks have rolled toward Berlin and you have lain silently under the ground, with your arm still folded over your face and your little finger curled up like a sleeping child. Then something happens. I don't know what day it is, but it is spring and had your ears not been crumbling into the soil you would have heard the footsteps above; the spades, digging through the earth, scraping against pebbles and gravel; and then a voice that says *There!* in German, with an urgency suggesting they don't have much time.

Had your skin not lost all its feeling years earlier, you would have felt the hands gripping your ankles and wrists, and lifting you onto the wool blanket. You would have felt them wrap the blanket around you like a cocoon and fasten it with rope to prevent it from opening. And then?

Then you are put on the back of a truck and driven along the narrow country lanes to the sea, where two boats lie waiting at the harbor. You are then lifted into the smaller of the two boats, where you lie, wrapped in blankets and ropes, rocking among the waves.

Oars splash in the water and creak in the oarlocks, and your body lurches forward with each stroke. The air is salty and seagulls screech overhead.

The oars are pulled in. There are voices. Then a splash, and icy cold water begins rushing in, swirling and rising all around you as the boat sinks, inch by inch, into the sea until only the oarlocks are visible on the surface. Then both you and the boat plunge into the darkness.

Past a shoal of herring that dart away. Then deeper still, into the darkness of the abyss, where the light from the surface cannot penetrate.

Then you hit the bottom, disturbing the mud. How deep is it? A hundred yards? More?

How many years will pass before the rope decays and the wool blanket unravels?

Now you are lying on your back. Slowly dissolving into the sand.

Swept back and forth by tides and storms.

More than seventy years pass. The remains of your skeleton are presumably still down there, scattered across the seabed, buried in the cold darkness below. Lines in the silt where your body has been dragged along by the current, just as your name is etched into the *Stolperstein* outside the apartment you once lived in. The pavement with your name, where I once knelt down with Grete, Steinar, Rikke, Lukas, and Olivia.

Dear Hirsch. You were succeeded by a large family. All three of your children survived the war, and all three had children. You have grandchildren, great-grandchildren, and great-great-grandchildren, so many I don't even know the total number. While I am writing these words, two of your great-great-grandchildren are at school. My son has recently had dental braces fitted and is probably leaning over a book or hanging around in the corridor with his friends. My daughter will soon be performing in a new ballet where she will lift herself higher and higher in her new pointe shoes, but right now she is at school too, running around the schoolyard or sliding on her bottom down the slope behind the play area.

A layer of frost covers Oslo.

Life goes on, and I close my eyes, thinking about everything that was set in motion because of that morning beside your *Stolperstein*. And then about all the stories that lie hidden behind each and every one of the others.

We will keep saying their names.

Dear Hirsch.

We will keep saying your name.

Acknowledgments

This novel could not have been written without the help of many others, both dead and living. A special thanks to Rikke, Grete, and Jannicke, for sharing their stories and memories and for countless discussions, thoughts, pictures, and tears. Thanks to my editor Nora Campbell, who can see beyond what is written, and to Hilde Rød-Larsen, who made me send her this manuscript at the most crucial time. Thanks to librarians, scientists, Holocaust survivors, nonfiction writers, and everyone else who have helped me in the process, and to Annette, who sold this novel worldwide before it was even out in Norwegian. I am forever grateful to all of you!

A NOTE ABOUT THE AUTHOR

Born in 1976, Simon Stranger is the author of four previous novels and several books for children, which earned
him a Riksmålsforbundet Prize in 2006. His work has
been translated into more than twenty languages. *Keep
Saying Their Names,* his first to be published in English, was
awarded the highly prestigious Norwegian Booksellers'
Prize in 2018. He lives in Norway.

A NOTE ON THE TYPE

This book was set in Albertina, the best known of the typefaces designed by Chris Brand (b. 1921 in Utrecht, The Netherlands). Issued by The Monotype Corporation in 1965, Albertina was one of the first text fonts made solely for photocomposition. It was first used to catalog the work of Stanley Morison and was exhibited in Brussels at the Albertina Library in 1966.

Typeset by Scribe, Philadelphia, Pennsylvania

Printed and bound by Friesens, Altona, Manitoba

Designed by Anna B. Knighton

STRANGER
2020

1637993